Peter F. Hamilton

MISSPENT YOUTH

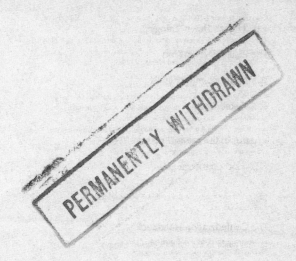

PERMANENTLY WITHDRAWN

PAN BOOKS

First published 2002 by Macmillan

This edition published 2003 by Pan Books
an imprint of Pan Macmillan Ltd
Pan Macmillan, 20 New Wharf Road, London N1 9RR
Basingstoke and Oxford
Associated companies throughout the world
www.panmacmillan.com

ISBN 0 330 48022 7

9 8 7 6 5 4 3 2 1

A CIP catalogue record for this book is available from
the British Library.

Typeset by SetSystems Ltd, Saffron Walden, Essex
Printed and bound in Great Britain by
Mackays of Chatham plc, Chatham, Kent

Acknowledgements

Where do you get your ideas from? The standard question asked of all science fiction writers. Of course we can never tell you. Once we are initiated into the secret society that governs our genre we are sworn to withhold all our tradecraft.

However . . . Where we get our manuscripts criticized, corrected, and knocked into shape is a different matter, one which is fully open to public scrutiny. So in the spirit of transparency, I would like to thank the following people for taking the time and making the effort to read through the first version of this novel, and helping me to smooth down the rough edges.

Kate and Chris, who both disapproved of the same characters. (It must be a chick thing.)

Graham, who wanted to kill off most of the characters.

Peter, who didn't want the characters doing or enjoying *that*, at all.

Colin, who wanted more violence done to the characters.

Ant, who liked the characters the way they were.

And they say focus groups rule the world.

Peter F. Hamilton
Rutland, May 2002

1. MAGIC MEMORIES

There was a particular day which Timothy Baker always remembered whenever he thought back to his childhood. It was the air tattoo at RAF Cottesmore when he'd been six years old. One of the rare events that his parents actually attended together, which to his young mind had made a perfect happy family outing. To start with, at least.

The EuroAir Defence Force had assigned a good number of both combat and transport aircraft to the open day, always eager to show the bolshie English how worthwhile and relevant the unified European squadrons were. It was also well attended by international aerospace companies, as well as senior air staff from over thirty foreign air forces. Elaborate company pavilions lined half of the taxiway, their tiered seating giving patrons and customers an excellent view of the flying exhibition. While the static displays of combat aircraft, transports, tankers, radar cars, and missile batteries stretched along the entire three kilometres of the parking apron.

Over ninety thousand people were expected during the weekend, taxing Rutland's rural transport infrastructure to the limit. By mid-morning on the Saturday Timothy was convinced that most of them had turned up already; he'd never seen so many people in one place before. He walked along between his parents, sometimes managing to hold hands with both of them at once as they roamed around the powerful, lethal hardware. It was a typical late-August day, the incendiary sun glaring down out of a cloudless turquoise sky. The GM tuber grass was still green, if somewhat dry and wiry, after seven straight weeks without rain.

The Baker family walked the entire length of the apron in the morning; Timothy and Jeff, his father, stopped to admire most of the aircraft along the way. Sue, his mother, tagged along gamely as her two enthusiastic boys quizzed the smiling, polite aircrews for facts and squadron stickers. Timothy managed to plead and entreat his way into the cockpits of several helicopters.

They reached the end of the hot concrete apron and began the long walk back, this time through the circus of commercial stalls and mobile shops which had set up camp behind the aircraft. Timothy had spotted several ice-cream vans and doughnut sellers earlier, and was already putting his case for visiting several of them to his tolerant yet unmoved parents.

A middle-aged couple walked past, the squat man glancing at the Bakers longer than was strictly polite.

'Now that,' the man said emphatically, 'is a Viagra kid if ever I saw one.' His voice trailed off into a dirty chuckle when they were several metres away. His wife gave him a sharp nudge.

Timothy twisted round to look at him, but the couple were already vanishing into the crowd. He wasn't quite sure what a Viagra kid was, although he'd heard the phrase a few times now. It was always used in a mocking way.

And he was fairly sure it was something to do with his parents. When he looked up at them for reassurance, his mother was looking straight ahead, her blank smile beaming bright; his father was frowning faintly. Timothy knew his mother was utterly beautiful. When she'd been younger, she had appeared on datasphere adverts, helping to sell perfume and clothes; and her looks hadn't faded – after all she wasn't thirty yet. His father, as he was now uncomfortably aware, was older. Timothy wasn't sure how old exactly, but he had white hair and skin that was wrinkled despite the genoprotein treatments he took every few months.

Jeff caught his son staring up curiously, and smiled. 'Let's go and get you that ice cream.'

'Yes, please!'

Timothy was given a cash card for a hundred Euros, and shot off to the nearest van.

'What's that?' Sue asked suspiciously when he returned with a triple cone dripping sticky brown and yellow blobs onto his hand.

'Double chocolate chip with banana,' Timothy said cheerfully. 'Only fifteen Euros.' He thrust it upwards. 'Want some?'

'No, thank you, dear.'

Timothy couldn't see his mother's eyes behind her wide gold-mirror sunglasses, but he knew from her tone that she was disappointed again. It was always so hard to please her. He licked at the cone, delighted by the weird taste mix.

There was a long row of hangars behind the stalls. Two distinct types, providing a contrast which neatly illustrated the base's history: modern stealth composite bubbles lurking between huge 1950s concrete and corrugated iron structures. The new dark grey hemispheres, looking like lead mushrooms bursting out of the grass, were sealed against curious eyes. They contained the latest European-AerospaceCorporation automated attack fighters, which operated from Cottesmore. In contrast to the secrecy of the hemispheres, the tall rusty panel doors on the older buildings were wide open. Large banners outside advertised the service companies which had taken over the hangars for the weekend. The Bakers went into the first hangar. Few people were inside.

Timothy moved along the company stands. None of them captured his interest. It was all test equipment and maintenance tools. Dull stuff compared to what was outside. Not even the vast array of intricate parts from a dismantled high-speed turbine held his attention for more than a few seconds. Then the stand right at the end made him come to a complete halt.

The company was actually promoting its fuselage-vibration-analysis software, but it was using an 'eternal' tap as part of its advertising. Three slender nylon fishing lines had been tied to the iron rafters of the hangar's gloomy roof high overhead, holding a big old brass tap four metres off the floor. From that, a fat column of water splashed continually into a bowl on a table at the end of the stand. Timothy stared at it in perplexity. The bowl never filled, yet the water splashing into it never stopped. And when he squinted up at the tap he couldn't see any kind of pipe attached. For a moment he thought the tiny nylon lines might be miniature pipes, but there were only three of them, and they were way too small to feed such a big tap. What he was seeing simply wasn't possible. It was like some special effect from a cable show.

'Dad!'

Jeff Baker looked up from the pieces of high-speed turbine he was inspecting.

'Dad, how do they do this? Dad!'

'Do what?'

'This!' Timothy pointed urgently at the tap and its impossible flow of water. 'How, dad, how?'

'Oh, that.' Jeff managed to sound completely uninterested. 'It's magic, son. That's all.'

Timothy pulled an annoyed face. 'No it's not! Do they teleport the water, or something?'

'Teleport!' Jeff shook his head in faint exasperation. 'You watch far too much cable, don't you?'

'No!'

'This is an old hangar; the past is still alive in here. There are lots of pockets of magic left over from olden times, scattered all across the country.' He gestured at the tap. 'And this is one of them. Right, dear?'

Sue raised an eyebrow. 'I think it's lunchtime now.'

Jeff was nonplussed by the reply. 'Guess we'd better eat, then,' he told Timothy. 'What are you having, three puddings?'

'Yeah!'

'No!' Sue said quickly. 'Honestly, you're worse than he is.'

Jeff pulled a face behind her back. Timothy giggled. He couldn't resist one last look at the magic tap as they walked back out into the scorching sunlight.

The Bakers headed for one of the biggest pavilions lining

the taxiway. They weren't on the admission list, but Jeff was insistent with the uniformed steward on the gate. Timothy waited impatiently while a senior company official was summoned from the pavilion; aircraft were taking off from the runway, and the pavilion blocked his view. When he arrived, the official was effusive in his greeting. The company would be greatly honoured to have the Bakers lunch with them, he said, his smile widening eagerly.

Timothy wound up eating with two members of the board in a glassed-off enclosure at the end of the pavilion. Their table gave him a grand view out across the airfield, and if he did miss any of the exciting aircraft flashing past a private TV feed to a pair of three-metre screens allowed him to see the planes twisting and diving at all times. It was great; his mother even let him have more ice cream for pudding, with strawberries.

A lot of visitors stopped by their table, corporate executives from across Europe, all of whom were eagerly introduced to Jeff Baker by the polite ever-smiling board members. Timothy didn't pay much attention to the adults, he was captivated by the sleek flying cruciforms which were the newly declassified AiF-080 USAF pilotless interceptors. The machines were less than half the size of the old Hurricanes flown by the European Silver Sky display team, and a lot more nimble.

Timothy asked to be excused while his parents were enjoying coffee and liqueurs. It was very boring in the dining room, although in truth he couldn't stop thinking about that strange tap. The aircraft were only temporary distractions. He was overwhelmed by the idea that magic could still exist. Such a revelation meant that anything was possible. Anything!

His mother checked that he was wearing his tracker bracelet and let him down from the table. 'You're not to go more than two hundred metres,' she warned as he sped away.

As soon as he was outside, Timothy headed straight for the hangar – it was only a little more than two hundred metres away, after all. Well . . . sort of.

The tap was still there. He stood in front of it, his head cocked to one side as his stare followed the stream of falling water, his brow all furrowed up in puzzlement. It couldn't be real. Yet here it was, happening right in front of him.

'It always looks good, doesn't it?'

Timothy glanced round. One of the saleswomen behind the stall was smiling at him. 'Yes,' he said. Then, suddenly bold, he asked: 'How did you know the magic was here?'

'Magic?' Her smile widened. 'I would have thought a clever boy like you could have worked this out by now.'

'How? I don't know any spells.'

The woman laughed. 'Spells? Well, I don't know about that. We just put a little fountain pump below the bowl, and squirt a jet into the tap. Takes an age to set it up just right.'

Timothy stared resentfully at the treacherous fountain. He couldn't even look at the woman – she must think him the stupidest boy on the planet. Embarrassment gave way to anger and sadness as he slunk away. His father had lied to him. Lied! There wasn't any magic in the world.

There never had been.

2. BEYOND AVARICE

It's difficult for any child growing up to understand that their father is famous. For a start, he is just your father, nothing else, nothing exceptional. Tim was almost ten before he finally grasped that his dad was a little different from everyone else's dad; that people were interested in the old man – what he was doing, what he said, and, most importantly, what he was thinking about. And not just the villagers in Empingham where they lived, but people on a lot of sites in the datasphere. In fact, when Tim, aged nine, loaded 'Jeff Baker' in a findbot, he was rather surprised when it listed two hundred and thirty-eight thousand primary references.

According to the first eight entries (all university libraries) Jeff Baker had designed the molecular structure of solid-state crystal memories, the ultimate electronic storage mechanism. It was the single most important component around which the entire datasphere now revolved. All human information was stored in the one specific type of lattice that his dad had worked out. His dad. The man who wouldn't let him have a puppy, and who was hopeless at playing football with him. His dad! The datasphere had got to be kidding – like magic, Tim told himself sourly.

But the datasphere didn't lie. His dad was truly famous. Not that fame was of much practical use in this case. Fame usually came hand in hand with fabulous wealth. The Bakers were certainly very comfortably off: they lived in a sprawling manor on the edge of the village, with acres and acres of grounds, Tim went to the nearby Oakham School for a private education, and his grandma was well taken care of in her nursing home. But it wasn't an own-your-private-Caribbean-island style of wealth.

It could have been, Tim read with growing dismay. That was the bigger part of Jeff Baker's fame. He could have had a fortune that rivalled Bill Gates or Eleanor Pickard. Memory crystals were universal: without them the entire world would crash to a halt; there would be no information economy, no economy at all, in fact. The tiniest percentage royalty would have given him an income of billions of Euros a year from the uncountable numbers of crystals that were grown to feed the voracious global electronics industry.

Instead, in an act of benevolence and philanthropy which was essentially without parallel, Jeff Baker had refused to patent the crystal structure. Instead, he published it on a Rutnet website, and told anyone who was interested to go right ahead and make it. The Rutnet server crashed for ten days straight due to the millions of attempted hits from across the planet.

Jeff Baker, Tim realized as he read his own family history, didn't have fame so much as respect. A billion datahead nerds regarded his dad as more important than God. Very nice – but what actual use was it? Tim would have much preferred him to be a cable star. At least that way they would have got a constant stream of invitations

9

to glamorous showbiz parties, and he could have mixed with celebrities. That would have done wonders for his kudos at school.

'Is it true?' Tim asked that suppertime. 'Did you invent the datasphere?'

'Not really,' Jeff said, smiling gently. 'But my crystal idea certainly helped it to grow up from being the Internet.'

'Why didn't you make money from it?'

'I did. I've got a whole load of non-executive director-ships. And my consultancy work pays for your schooling, as well as for your mother's clothes. Just.'

Sue Baker narrowed her eyes to give him a cautionary look over the table.

'It said in the sphere that you could have been the richest man in the world,' Tim said.

'Trust me on this, Tim, being the richest man in the world isn't necessarily a good thing.'

'But ... you didn't get anything out of it. I don't understand.'

'I got peace of mind. And I got you.' His smile became one of admiration. 'You're more important than money.'

'Thanks. I just don't think it's fair, that's all,' Tim protested. 'The whole world depends on your idea. You should be rewarded.'

Which was what happened. But not until eight years later.

3. PARTY ON DOWN

As teenage parties went, it was a standard parents' nightmare. Miranda and David Langley had gone away for the weekend, leaving their six-bedroom house in the hands of their eighteen-year-old son, Simon, and his elder brother, Peter, who was back from university for a few days. As soon as the senior Langleys had left, their sons sent an avtxt to all their friends. Those friends avtxted their friends.

Half of Empingham's teenagers descended on the quaint stone house for the evening, their numbers bolstered by contingents from surrounding villages and senior boarders from Oakham School like Zai Reynolds who had managed to get a leave-out from their housemaster.

Tim had been going steady with Zai for four weeks, starting a week after his eighteenth birthday party. He was hopeful that tonight, with all the drink available and the hot, exuberant party atmosphere, they might be able to move along from groping and heavy snogging to real actual sex. Simon's house had enough bedrooms – there were bound to be some unused. So he thought before he arrived.

Even his imagination hadn't projected quite such a

scene. There were people in every room, crammed in so tight that nobody could sit and dancing was near-impossible. Three sound systems were blaring out three different tracks in three different rooms, all of them merging together in the hall and on the landing to make an incoherent wall of sound. Hardly any of the lights were on, leaving the house seriously shadowy. The terracotta-tiled kitchen floor was awash with fluid that was already turning tacky, and it was only half past seven.

Tim and Zai both plunged in. Simon saw them and gave Tim a big hug. He was already drunk. The kiss he gave Zai was overeager; she moved her head aside with an annoyed grimace.

'Your parents will kill you,' Tim shouted above the din.

'No way,' Simon shouted. 'We put anything breakable in the barn this afternoon. The worst they'll find is a couple of strange stains. Pete knows what he's doing. You should hear about the kind of parties he has at uni.'

'Sounds good.' Tim held up the bag full of bottles and cans that he'd brought. 'For your collection.'

'In there.' Simon pointed to the kitchen. His grin widened as his girlfriend pushed her way towards them through the crowd, drinks held high in both hands.

Tim hoped he wasn't staring again. Not that he'd ever been able to help it as far as Annabelle Goddard was concerned. He was used to the savvy upper-middle-class girls who attended Oakham School. Given that most of them were attractive, possessed of the kind of impeccable style and extraordinary self-confidence that only their family money could bestow, he was as accustomed to hanging with delectable girls as best as any eighteen-year-old boy could be. But Annabelle was something else again.

Her face was enchantingly beautiful, fine-boned, with a clear complexion and a few clusters of freckles. To make matters worse she also had an amazing figure, which was the subject of heavy discussion among Tim and his same-gender friends. For the last six weeks, they had all become seriously envious of Simon for managing to date her. Add to that Simon's constant boasts of how much sex the two of them kept having, and his social status was rapidly approaching divinity.

'Hi, Tim,' Annabelle yelled cheerfully. She handed Simon a drink and gave him a forceful kiss.

Tim was sure there were tongues involved. 'Hi,' he said weakly. Annabelle was wearing a shimmering purple miniskirt and a skimpy white T-shirt, thin enough to reveal the outline of her bra underneath.

'Great party, huh?'

'Yeah.' Tim grinned oafishly, hotly aware of the way Zai was looking at him. 'Let's get started,' he said to her.

Zai nodded curtly. 'Yes, let's.'

Tim shoved his way into the kitchen. He knew he'd messed up in front of Zai again. Strange how she was so different to Annabelle: petite and intense, always managing to find fault with him. Whereas Annabelle was so upfront and good-hearted he could never imagine her being angry with anybody. So how was it possible for him to be attracted to complete opposites at the same time?

He made up for his earlier lapse by being overwhelmingly attentive to Zai for the next few hours. After he'd poured her a Bacardi and lemon (heavy on the Bacardi), they danced in the conservatory, swaying about as other couples barged into them. It was hard to see in the dark.

They ran into Martin and Colin when they were taking

13

a break in the dining room. Martin greeted Tim with a straight-arm salute. 'Bonjour, Unionist Comrade. I'm amazed you were allowed out tonight.'

'Why?' Tim asked automatically, and cursed himself for not thinking first.

'I saw the EuroGestapo round at your house the other day. Installing all the State Security machines and Rottweilers, were they?'

'No,' Tim said, with a laboured sigh. He'd been getting a lot of this kind of joshing lately, not all of it good-humoured.

'Must be. It's only, what, a couple of weeks till they uncork your old man, right?'

'Young man,' Colin corrected. His beer bottle waved around as he gestured, foam spilling from the neck.

'About that,' Tim agreed.

'The Commission must be worried. He'll be a valuable piece of property. The Separatists are bound to try something.'

'Shut up, Martin,' Zai said. 'Nobody's going to do anything to Jeff Baker. Don't be so stupid.'

Martin laughed, taking another swig.

Zai pulled Tim away, and they headed back to the kitchen. 'You okay?' she asked.

'Sure. I'm used to it.'

'That's not the point. Martin is such an arsehole.'

Peter Langley's friends from university had brought a load of intubes with them, which they passed around freely. It was a hot synth8, Tim decided as he sucked the atomized vapour down into his lungs. Better than anything he and his friends ever scored from Rutland's seedy replicators; this one had been engineered to slide straight through his lung membranes direct into the blood with zero resistance. A lot of design work must have gone into its constituent molecules. His head buzzed as the music echoed inside his skull; and he felt so light that every movement was effortless. Zai took a deep draw of her own, grinned up at him as it flooded her bloodstream.

They talked to more friends. Danced again. Tried to eat cold pizza slices. Snogged happily. Drank some more. Laughed as Tony stripped off and ran round the garden waving his trousers round his head before falling into the laurel hedge.

Later on – he didn't know what time – Tim hauled himself upstairs. He'd been guzzling beer all evening, and now he badly needed to pee. The downstairs cloakroom was disgusting – bowl clogged with paper, puke all over the floor. Several people were sprawled around the landing, not saying much; two were already asleep. All the bedroom doors were closed. Tim made his way down to the bathroom at the far end of the house. The door was shut. He leaned on the side of it, just able to make out soft chortling and voices that were almost whispers coming from inside.

'Just a sec.'

Tim frowned; he was sure that had been Annabelle's voice.

'Oh, come on.'

Simon's voice, definitely – sly and insistent.

A third person laughed. Tim tried to shake off his lethargy. The laugh had been almost malicious. He didn't know what the heck was going on.

Then Annabelle suddenly went: 'Ta-Raaaa!' Whatever she'd done was greeted by a chorus of raucous cheers. Several people clapped.

Tim knocked on the door. 'Hey, you finished in there yet?' He didn't know what else to say.

Simon barked: 'Oh, fuck off, Tim. I'm taking a crap.' There was a lot of giggling and shuffling round accompanying the sharp sound of zips being done up. The toilet was flushed, which triggered off another round of giggling.

Simon pulled the bolt back and stepped out, grinning inanely. Annabelle was pressed up behind him, her face all flushed, trying hard not to laugh. It was quite obvious she wasn't wearing a bra any more: her breasts were swinging about freely under the thin T-shirt.

As if that wasn't disconcerting enough, Tim *really* didn't know what to do when Peter Langley and his tall blonde girlfriend followed them out. He was suddenly alone in a little cocoon of hot embarrassment, while the four of them stood round him sharing exactly the same superior smile, as if he was some mediocre zoo animal standing there for their amusement.

Simon's hand patted him on the shoulder. 'Finished. You take care in there, Tim.'

The others laughed at him again as his face simply screwed up into more confusion. They made their way down the landing without even looking back at him; it was as if he no longer existed to them.

He went into the bathroom and locked the door. The air inside was thick with the scent of synth8. There was a bra lying on the black and white marble floor next to the hand basin. Tim held it up in front of his face, feeling supremely jealous. The synth8 made his existence so perfectly clear to him. His problem was that he would never be like them, never be so perfectly at ease, never enjoy life so much. Yet that was exactly what he wanted. Right then he would have given anything to have been a part of that devilsome group, to have joined in with hearty abandon, to be their equal. His life completely lacked the kind of Bad Fun that everyone else he knew of was having in abundance.

Tim slung the bra across the bathroom, suddenly furious. He hated everything about himself. Most of all he hated the fact that he was so pathetic that he was helpless to change what he was.

4. MORNING AFTER

That Monday morning, the Rutland Circuit bus dropped Tim off outside Oakham market. A few cars slid along the High Street, smooth and quiet, their power cells venting thin ribbons of snow-white vapour from their rear grilles like some old-style rocket letting off cryogenic gas. Most of the traffic was bicycles and e-trikes, ridden by residents from the sprawling suburban estates who were heading into the town centre for work. A steady line of buses brought commuters in from the outlying villages.

Oakham's centre was a mixture of architectural styles from the mid-nineteenth century up to the late twentieth, by which time the conservationists had finally stymied the developers and planners. It had left the High Street dominated by shop fronts, interspersed with the occasional monolithic stone bank. None of them were particularly relevant to the modern age. The majority of shops had closed as the larger retail groups went on-line, and consumers sourced direct from the manufacturer. Now only small specialist shops and cafés remained, while the rest of the buildings had been converted into offices and service centres wired into the datasphere economy. Even those were beginning to thin out; with the National Cable

Initiative drawing towards completion, companies were adopting decentralized domestic networks for their employees. Several estate-agent *To Let* signs were sticking out discreetly from various façades.

Tim crossed over the road and headed up to the Buttercross. The grandiose old buildings of Oakham School made up two sides of the quaint cobbled square. A horde of boisterous schoolkids was crossing the square, funnelling into the school under its wide iron-arch gateway. Younger ones were dressed in their smart uniforms, while the seniors like Tim wore their own clothes. For all the troubled nature of his relationship with his mother, Tim was grateful for her fashion sense. She always managed to dress him stylishly. Their money helped, of course, but then, everyone at the private school had money; she made sure everything he wore fitted and suited. It helped a lot in keeping him in with his friends.

As he walked through the neat little enclosed garden beside the school's stone chapel, he caught sight of a familiar figure sitting on one of the wooden benches at the far end. Annabelle was turned away from the rush of noisy kids, her head bowed, shoulders slumped.

'What's up?' Tim asked.

Annabelle stirred, brushing her mane of long gold-chestnut hair away from her face. Her eyes were red-rimmed, glistening with moisture. Tim's immediate impulse was to throw his arms around her – anything to help comfort her. A girl as beautiful as Annabelle shouldn't be crying.

'Nothing,' she sniffed, and then smiled. 'Well ... I suppose it's me and Simon. We argued after the party.'

'I'm sorry.'

19

'The two of you are good friends, aren't you?'

'Not particularly. We live in the same village, and we're the same age. That means we hang out. That's all.'

'I don't think I'll be hanging out with him again, myself.'

'Really?' Tim tried hard not to show how elated he was. Annabelle was single again.

'It's just . . . he can take things too far, you know?' she said. Her expression was anxious, needing him to agree.

Tim thought back to when he'd seen Annabelle with Simon at the party, how much she'd *belonged* at the time. 'Completely. You know he and Pete caught hell from their parents afterwards.'

'Yeah.' Annabelle gave a small, vaguely malevolent, grin.

'Look, there's a bunch of us catching the bus back to my house this afternoon after school. We'll probably go for a swim or something. Simon won't be one of them. Why don't you come along? Be a good break for you. Enjoy yourself without him being around.' The indoor pool at his house was one of Tim's biggest social weapons. It didn't quite make him leader of the pack, but along with his father's name it certainly helped make him one of the right people to know.

Annabelle pondered the invitation for a moment. 'Sure. Yeah, okay, I'd like that.'

'Great.' That just left him with inviting everyone else back home. Oh, and telling Zai.

The first lesson that morning was French. Tim hated languages, he was hopeless at them, but it was a compulsory subject at UE level. When the interactive tutorial began he slipped on his PCglasses, pushing the earplugs in and flipping down the tiny wire mic. He murmured quietly into the mic, calling up a fix routine to deal with the French tutorial, convincing the teacher he was hard at work. It left him free to compose avtxts. His finger skated across the keyboard mat, selecting colourful little graphics from the menu file that he began to mix into an invite. He had to keep the audio segments muted – everyone he was sending them to was also in school. The holographic display on his PCglasses flashed replies at him for the remainder of the lesson. Most of the boys who answered had included symbols that gyrated with semi-obscene movements, which nearly made him laugh out loud. When the tutorial ended, he'd collected about a dozen acceptances.

It was a good strategy, he congratulated himself; with so many other people included Annabelle wouldn't feel pressured at all. This was nothing like asking her for a date. Except that by mid-morning he still hadn't decided how he should go about cooling things with Zai. It wasn't something he was accustomed to. Normally girls finished with him; an inevitable conclusion to his relationships, which he greeted with grudging acceptance. But he and Zai were actually getting on pretty well right now. At the end of Saturday's party, loaded on beer and synth8, they'd found a bedroom together. Still no full sex, but it had got remarkably close.

Sunday morning had been spent avtxting long silly messages to each other before she caught the bus to Empingham and had lunch at the Manor with him and his mother. Afternoon had been a lazy time round the swimming pool followed by watching some pre10 movies on the five-metre wallscreen in the lounge.

To be honest, he'd never actually had a girlfriend as

good as Zai before. Everything was chugging along perfectly. His excitement over Annabelle actually agreeing to tag along that afternoon was subdued by his constant feeling of guilt. Zai didn't deserve to be treated like this. He always hated the break-ups, no matter how bad things were at the time. To be given the elbow when things were on the upswing must be terrible. It was the deliberate infliction of pain. He could barely believe he could do such a thing. It was horrid, as if some part of Simon's character was transfusing into him.

Tim sat with Martin and Colin at lunch. The three of them wrapped up discussing their jet-ski project. It was an old machine that they were renovating ready for summer in the hope of having some serious fun with it in the local reservoir.

'So did you forget?'

Zai's voice made Tim blush. He risked looking up to see her standing at the side of his table, holding her lunch tray; her friends Rachel and Sophie were beside her. Too late, Tim remembered he'd sent an avtxt invite to Sophie for this afternoon.

'Forget?' he asked.

'Your little swimming club.'

'Well, I just thought you'd be coming.'

'You asked Annabelle, didn't you?'

Tim glanced round. People were looking at the scene, conversation in the dining hall was drying up. 'What?'

'They haven't split up twenty-four hours and you ask her out. You piece of shit.'

'I haven't—'

'What did you think – having a whole load of people there doesn't make it a date?'

Tim wouldn't have thought it possible for his face to get any hotter, but it did. His skin must have been neon red.

'You didn't even have the courage to break up with me first. Were you going to avtxt me? Is that how you tell people it's over?'

'I was . . . this . . . it's not—'

Zai sneered at him. 'I'd say go screw yourself. Except you can't, can you? Midget dick!' She turned round and walked away. Rachel and Sophie shot him scornful looks and followed after her.

There was a lot of sniggering coming from the surrounding tables. Tim wished she'd just tipped her tray of food over him instead. It would have been less humiliating.

'Wow,' Martin exclaimed. 'Two-timing Tim. I'm impressed.'

'I wasn't . . .' Tim began limply.

Colin gave Tim a hearty slap on his shoulder. 'You are full of surprises. Did you try and get the two of them into bed together?'

'No! Look, I wasn't doing anything wrong. Honest.'

'You sly old sod,' Martin said. 'You just need a better date-organizer program, that's all. Keep them separated better.'

Tim groaned and gave up.

5. AN INSPECTOR CALLS

Sue Baker stood beside the bedroom's tall veranda window, watching the Europol technical security team wandering across the lawns. A gloomy February sky was drizzling solidly, the small droplets as grey and depressing as the clouds from which they came. In their navy-blue rain jackets, the police team seemed almost immune to the conditions. They carried on positioning slender high-technology poles around the edge of the garden, heedless of the mud and water. Another team was doing the same thing in the sloping paddock beyond; two of them with waders were walking along the flooded stream that at present made up one side of the field. She knew there was a third group out there somewhere, sweeping through the woods on the far slope.

They'd arrived earlier that morning in a small fleet of new vehicles that were now parked on the gravel drive at the front of the Manor. That alone told the locals that this was a Europol contingent. Rutland's police only had about six cars to cover the entire county, and most of them were over five years old.

'So what exactly are they doing out there?' she asked.

'Establishing a sensor perimeter,' Lieutenant Krober

said politely. It was the third time he'd explained the team's function today. Sue knew he must think her an idiot, but she'd never understood technical matters. A wonderful irony for the assured, courteous German officer to ponder: that the wife of Jeff Baker couldn't change her own light bulbs without puzzling over the instructions. She was eternally grateful that today's computers were all voice-active – you could just tell them what to do and they got on with it. Back in 2009 when she had started at secondary school all the operating programs still used keyboards and mouse pads; she'd never really got the hang of them. Not that it had mattered: she'd left school behind at fourteen when the modelling agency had signed her up. You didn't need to be a qualified nerd to look hot on the catwalk.

'We do have a security system,' she said. 'A very good one.' From the outside, the Manor certainly looked as if it might have been built in the eighteenth century, but the oldest thing in the house was probably Jeff. It had been designed after the turn of the millennium and incorporated every modern domestic device, as well as being energy-sufficient with its solar-panel roofing and underground heat pumps.

'Yes, ma'am,' Krober said. 'But we are concerned about more than just ordinary burglars. Your husband's treatment will be likely to attract interest from a number of groups, not least the Separatists. Our system will allow us to spot any potential intruders before they get near the house. We can respond more effectively that way.'

'Yes, I'm sure you're very effective.' Sue had already noticed the shoulder holsters the Europol team wore under their tunics. It wasn't the Separatists that bothered her:

they were the almost-legal front for the English Independence Council paramilitaries. And one of the EIC's loudest boasts was how they were far more ruthless than the IRA ever had been. If they ever took an interest . . .

'Three of our officers will remain on duty at the house at all times,' Krober said. 'Our team has taken out rooms at the White Horse on a permanent basis to act as our base station; that puts the majority of us just two minutes away in an emergency. And a female officer will accompany you when you leave home.'

'No.' Sue turned from the veranda door to face Krober. He was a handsome man, with dark brown hair cut in a severe, almost military style. His age was probably late twenties, she thought, certainly no more than thirty. In any other circumstances she would have welcomed his presence at the Manor – flirting with him would have been most enjoyable. He wasn't wearing a wedding ring, she noticed, not that it would have bothered her. 'I don't want that.'

Despite his perfect English, Krober looked as if he hadn't understood. 'The officers have already been given their assignments. They are merely a precaution against any possible incident.'

'I don't want them.' The idea of being followed around twenty-four hours a day was awful. She would forfeit her privacy, her secrets – her life would never be her own again. It wasn't as though Jeff didn't know of her lovers – after all, that had been part of the arrangement – but she did at least keep them quiet and discreet so that they could continue to present the illusion of a stable family life for Tim and the local villagers.

'But they're here,' Krober persisted like a stubborn child.

Sue wanted to call Jeff and complain. This had never been part of their arrangement. But then, his treatment hadn't exactly been part of the arrangement, either. This suffocating police protection was simply the inevitable consequence. If she'd wanted to complain, she should have done so right at the start. This was too far down the line to back out.

'They don't have to start today, surely. Jeff's not due back for ten days yet.'

'That's close enough for the Separatists to start taking an interest,' Lucy Duke said.

Sue hadn't seen her come in. She suspected Krober had called for help as soon as she started being difficult. He was wearing his PCglasses, as was Lucy Duke, though his lenses were clear. 'I can assure you the personal-protection teams are thoroughly professional,' Lucy said smoothly. 'They neither restrict nor judge their client's actions.'

'Thank you for that,' Sue said coldly to the young woman. There was an old joke she remembered – probably classed as politically incorrect or racist or Separatist propaganda these days – about how heaven would be staffed by Europeans with a specific job for each nationality: the British would be the police, the Germans the engineers, the French the cooks, and so on; then you swapped them all round for hell, with the British as cooks, the Germans as police ... Today, Sue thought, you'd have to redefine the British job. Lucy Duke was a Eurohealth Council facilitator on secondment from the Downing Street policy presentation unit. She was dressed in a smart blue and

27

grey Italian business suit, her hair in a neat swept bob, she spoke in a classless accent, and had a file of media contacts as long as a pre10 novel. The British today produced the best spin doctors in the world.

'They're very unobtrusive,' Lucy continued. 'And we wouldn't appoint them if we didn't think they were absolutely necessary. There is only a very small threat of violence, admittedly, but do you really want to take the risk?'

'How long are they going to be with us?'

'Difficult to say.'

Sue took a look around the bedroom. Like all the Manor's rooms, it was large and luxurious. She'd supervised the interior designer herself, remodelling the place twice since she and Jeff had got married. Now it was perfect, representing just how good her life had become. She would hate to leave it, not that Jeff would ever make her, but Tim was past his eighteenth birthday now. That was: Jeff before the treatment, she corrected herself. Her whole damn world was changing, and doing so far too fast.

'Fine, then,' Sue said airily. It was a capitulation, though she couldn't really bring herself to care. Europol and the Duke cow probably knew all about her sex life anyway. 'Wait a minute. If you're giving me a bodyguard, what are you doing about Tim?'

'Naturally we'll provide him with an equal level of coverage. We've already discussed placing arrangements with Oakham School. They've been most accommodating. He's not the only pupil there who needs a watchful eye.'

Sue laughed in Lucy Duke's face. 'Have you spoken to him about all this?'

'We were assuming you would explain this to him, your example should help.'

'You are joking!' Sue kept on laughing. The thought of Tim meekly allowing a Europol officer to trot along behind him was hilarious. 'You don't have children, do you?'

'Not yet,' Lucy said.

'Well, just remember: babies are God's way of persuading parents to have teenagers.'

Krober gave a small smile. 'Do you believe he will be unwilling to cooperate?'

'He might be.'

'Will you tell him that this development is unavoidable, try to make him understand a bodyguard is necessary?'

'No.'

'Excuse me?' Lucy Duke asked.

'I'm not saying a damn thing to him. We're not exactly on the best of terms as it is. You want to guard him, you tell him.'

'But he's your son.'

'Not through choice.' Sue walked out of the bedroom, leaving the astonished spin doctor staring at her back.

The Europol team spent the rest of the day tramping through the Manor and its grounds, bringing mud inside with them. Sue did her best to ignore them by helping Mrs Mayberry, the housekeeper, in the kitchen. Then she took lunch by herself in the conservatory. In the afternoon she had another argument with Lieutenant Krober about placing cameras inside the house. After a heated twenty minutes during which Lucy had to intervene again to cool tempers, they agreed that cameras could cover all the entrances from the outside. After that they'd all wait until Jeff Baker came back before any would be put inside, subject to his approval. Sue conceded that the team could wire the Manor's existing security network into their own secure datasphere port. A command post was set up in the smallest of the five reception rooms downstairs.

Tim arrived back just after five o'clock. Fortunately most of the installation was complete by then. He brought a group of his friends with him, which stalled the inevitable confrontation between him and Lucy Duke. Mrs Mayberry busied herself cooking pizzas for the teenagers as they descended on the swimming pool.

Ever since Jeff had gone for his treatment, fifteen months ago, Sue had slowly relaxed her objections to Tim inviting his dreadful friends round at all hours. The Manor was a huge place for just two people to be living in by themselves, especially two with a history of conflict like her and Tim. For all the qualities she possessed which had convinced Jeff to make his odd marriage proposal, the natural mother's ability to bring up a child was definitely nonexistent. Curiously enough, Jeff's absence had brought about a mild truce between them. There were none of the tantrums and screaming sessions that had so occupied the pair of them during the first half of Tim's teenage years. They hadn't exactly become great pals, but they were certainly civil to each other now.

Besides, it was actually rather nice to have the big place filled with young people, she considered; all their brash laughter and high spirits helped to banish the solemnity that had crept in over the last few months. Not that – as she had made exceptionally clear – she would ever consent to any kind of party like the one that the poor Langleys had been lumbered with. She'd actually grinned, remembering her own teenage years, as Tim and Zai left the house last Saturday evening. If only Tim had known how she used to behave . . .

From the lounge's huge bay windows she could see right into the swimming pool. The building was like an elaborate orangery sprouting from the southern end of the Manor, with tall panes of glass supported by arching white timber frames. The teenagers were running round the edge of the pool, diving and jumping in with excited whoops and yells. The inflatable floating furniture was taking a terrible battering. Plumes of spray would shoot upwards to splash the roof. The spiral slide was in constant use.

Sue had been rather surprised that Zai hadn't been in the group when they'd barged through the front doors. Tim's expression when he'd finally staggered home in the early hours of Sunday morning had provided her with a great deal of amusement. A cat which had not only got the cream but had also managed to gobble down the goldfish as well. Now Zai was nowhere to be seen, and Tim was keeping a civil distance from Annabelle the whole time. Sue had almost laughed at how careful he was being, desperately not showing any favouritism, never singling her out to talk to, making sure she was just one of the lads. He must fancy her rotten. It looked mutual, too.

Sue peered through the bay windows, trying to see how the pair of them were conducting themselves in the pool. Annabelle was amazingly pretty, possessing the kind of figure that any boy would drool over. But then, Sue had caught herself looking hard lately at most of the girls in Tim's group of friends, giving their bodies and complexions a professional assessment as she ran comparisons with herself. She wasn't forty yet, and had certainly managed to keep her own looks and figure despite nine repellent months of pregnancy and then giving birth. Modern genoprotein-based cosmetic treatments were an absolute boon in that respect.

It wasn't just the straight medical pharmaceutical companies which had benefited from the genome-decoding projects of the nineties and noughties. There had been a long period of corporate mergers and buyouts early in the new millennium, as pharmaceutical, biochemical, and cosmetic companies fused into the new-economy giants that they were today. Successful and worthy genetic treatments, originally devised to counter and cure appalling diseases by the use of powerful vectoring technology to deliver improved genes directly to individual cells, had swiftly been adapted to carry genes that made more subtle cellular improvements.

Skin was the first area to come under scrutiny, of course. Restoring its vitality and firmness, and the eradication of wrinkles had been the goal of the cosmetics trade since human prehistory as it attempted to infuse that elusive healthy glow so nonchalantly possessed of adolescents. Now, for the first time, it was actually possible at least to slow down normal epidermal decay with a huge array of new-genes-for-old elixirs that could target particular cells and layers. The market for such products was astonishing – almost as astounding as their cost.

Jeff had always been condescending when she used the dermal genoprotein treatments, and he constantly grumbled about the price of them. He claimed she was far too young to be using the stuff. But not even the genoproteins could actually turn the clock back. So the earlier she started using them, the easier it would be for the treatments to maintain her youthful appearance. Today her skin had the glossy vigour of a twenty-five-year-old's precisely because she had begun using the genoprotein when she was twenty-three. Two years' apparent physical ageing in fifteen chronological years. Oh yes, it was worth the money no matter how much he grouched and cursed.

Treatments for skin and its texture, though, were merely the first of the new products to emerge from the biogenetic laboratories. Men might claim not to care quite so much about their wrinkles and liver spots – though enough of them actually did – but when it came to receding hairlines male vanity knew no bounds nor cost barrier. Follicle genoprotein sales levels were second only to those of skin treatments.

Sue used only the very best of both, along with similar treatments for nails and teeth; and most definitely anti-cellulites, targeting her hips and thighs. To be on the safe side she also used bone and muscle treatments, and a very specific group of genoproteins to prevent her breast tissue from becoming flaccid (the second most popular purchase for women after skin genoprotein). She'd never used the treatment to stimulate breast growth – there was a sus-pected link to cancer blooms, although most women ignored that – one of the reasons she'd never quite made it to supermodel status had been her generous bust size. Not that she had ever considered the reduction treatment, either.

All of her treatments were supervised and administered by a private hospital in Stamford devoted to bodyform courses. As they were combined with a wholesome diet to which she stuck with iron discipline, and a fitness regimen which even impressed the gym staff, her appearance was locked permanently in her early twenties. Despite every miserable day alone, emotional and financial let-downs, arguments with Tim and with Jeff, bad holidays, depressing news reports, her mother's frail condition, and faithless lovers, she could always look at herself in the mirror and be utterly satisfied with what she saw. Not only was she a match for any of the girls currently cavorting round the swimming pool in their skimpy costumes but, thanks to her modelling experience, she had a much better dress sense than the lot of them put together. Men appreciated that.

Tim's friends left around seven, catching the Rutland Circuit bus back to Oakham. He simply grinned and nodded to Annabelle as she and Sophie waved goodbye.

'So what happened to Zai?' Sue asked after the door closed behind them.

'Oh, er, she couldn't make it.'

She tried not to smile: even after eighteen years of being brought up by her and Jeff, he made a bad liar. 'Okay, Tim.'

He gave her a curious look, then shrugged. 'Got some coursework to finish. I'll be upstairs.'

Lucy Duke cleared her throat. Both Tim and Sue turned to look at her as she stood at the bottom of the stairs.

'Hi there, Tim. I'm afraid I need to talk to you about security arrangements,' Lucy said. Her carefully casual attitude made her sound incredibly patronizing.

'What about them?'

Even Sue was impressed by how quickly he could slide from reasonable human being to petulant teenage grouch.

'Well, as you know we've been installing several new systems around the house in anticipation of your father's return. And there are some further requirements we need to implement.'

'Yeah?'

'Yes. You see, it's not just his safety we need to consider. The whole family is included.'

'You mean me?'

'Absolutely. I'm afraid the Separatists aren't particularly pleasant, nor choosy about the people they target.'

Tim slouched and sneered at the same time. 'I know. I subscribe to their newstxt.'

'I see.' Lucy Duke's mouth tightened slightly. 'Tim, this is a little more involved than a few student revolutionary slogans.'

'You got something against students?'

'Not at all. But the people that Lieutenant Krober and his team are concerned about can be a serious problem.'

'Only to foreigners who steal our taxes and oppress us.'

'Tim, we're assigning you a bodyguard.'

'Don't want one.'

'I appreciate this is difficult.' Lucy Duke smiled bravely. 'And it won't be very, um, cool, for this to happen at school, will it? I'm sorry about that, but we wouldn't do it unless we thought it was essential. Your mother's having one as well.'

'So?'

Lucy Duke's humour was fading. 'Tim, these people are evil and violent. You need protection from them. The Europol officers won't interfere with your life.'

'You mean they'll help me score my synth8?'

Sue almost laughed out loud at the appalled expression on the spin doctor's face.

'Do you know how much your father's treatment has cost the government?' Lucy Duke asked curtly.

'I'm not sure. How about: the price of the Prime Minister getting elected President of Europe?'

'That has absolutely nothing to do with this,' the now-furious young woman said.

'Then why are you here?'

'Look. All right. I know you don't want me or any of us here, but we are here and we're staying. And that's because of your father's treatment. Please don't pretend you didn't want him to be treated. Just think of us as the price you have to pay for getting him back.'

'Fine. Move in here with us, then – I don't care. I'm not having a bodyguard.' He slithered past her and took the stairs two at a time.

'You are,' Lucy said firmly. 'They will be with you when you leave the house tomorrow morning.'

Tim might have grunted a reply – it was difficult to tell. He stalked off along the landing. His door slammed shut.

'Told you so,' Sue murmured dryly.

'Oh my God,' Lucy exclaimed. 'I wasn't briefed on this situation. Is he like that all the time?'

'Not at all. Sometimes he can be a real pain in the arse.'

6. THE JET-SKI CONSPIRACY

The jet ski was a twenty-year-old Karuda, sleek silver and purple bodywork wrapped round a powerful marine combustion engine. Quite why his father had ever bought it, Tim never knew. He certainly couldn't remember the machine ever being used. His mother hadn't been able to shed any light on the mystery other than saying: 'Probably a mid-life crisis.'

It had spent most of those two decades stored in a polythene bubble in one of the Manor's many fusty outhouses. Then Tim and his friends had decided to resurrect it for some fun when the warm weather arrived in April. They had carried it over to the stable, which had been converted into a workshop for the gardener, and stripped the protective polythene off. The bodywork had lost its lustre over the intervening years, but the engine had been well oiled before it was cocooned. Now the streamlined machine was clamped on top of a long carpentry bench with a crude wooden frame. Body panels had been removed, exposing the framework, and various dismantled parts were lying around it. The engine was held upright in its own clamp, allowing them to strip it down as best they could.

On the Saturday morning they all gathered round to do a couple of hours' work on it before going out. A big old flat cathode screen was fixed to the plain brick wall behind the bench, displaying the engine's service manual. Tim and Martin were looking at it, trying to match the neat drawings with the oily metal components they were attempting to reassemble on the block.

'I'm surprised they're not in here with you now,' Simon said. He was sitting on a battered old sofa at the other end of the workshop, drinking tea from a mug. 'Then they can make sure we're conforming to Brussels working-practice directives.'

'Piss off,' Tim snapped. Europol had been guarding him for a week now. The first few days had been fun when he'd been eluding the bodyguards. Martin and Colin had helped out quite a bit. He'd sent encrypted avtxts to all his friends, formulating elaborate plans. On the first day he started off walking to the bus stop as usual, then Simon had zoomed by on his e-trike and Tim hopped onto the back. The Europol officer had yelled frantically into the mic on his PCglasses, and the surveillance team's car had pulled out of the White Horse pub's car park within thirty seconds. But Simon drove off down the old Exton road, which Rutland Council had classified as D-status and no longer had a tarmac surface. The Europol car couldn't cope with the narrow limestone-and-moss track, and had to abandon pursuit.

They were waiting stony-faced for him when he walked into his first lesson. Surrounded by laughing friends, Tim just waved impudently. When he got home that evening, Lucy Duke was waiting with a lecture about ingratitude. He listened for a few seconds, then asked her to order a

Chinese takeaway for him. 'You're a public servant, aren't you? So serve.' The contortions on her face as she struggled to keep her temper were hysterical.

On the second day a four-wheel-drive Range Rover-AT was parked conspicuously in front of the pub. It followed the bus closely. Tim waited until they reached Whitwell, then baled out of the bus's rear emergency exit. Colin was waiting by the church with his trail bike. They raced off down the nature-route footpath and through the wood, where the Range Rover couldn't follow.

A Europol captain was sent out from the Nottingham office to give the protection team a dressing down about being outwitted by a teenage boy. The captain and Lucy Duke then spent a fruitless half-hour pleading with Sue Baker. The whole Europol team hated Tim after that, and didn't bother to hide the fact.

Tim hadn't tried to give them the slip for several days, although there were quite a few strategies he hadn't used yet. It was just that actually doing it took such a lot of effort. In any case, Natalie Cherbun had been reassigned from his mother to his day-guard duty: a twenty-five-year-old French officer. Not that Tim liked her, of course, but she was rather easy to look at.

'They're going to be a problem when we take this thing out,' Colin declared as he threaded the new clutch cable through the handlebars.

'No,' Tim said irritably. 'They won't be.'

'The reservoir doesn't allow any sort of powered boat, let alone a jet ski. Your Gestapo mates will never just stand by when we sneak it down to the shoreline. They'll stop us.'

'They're not my mates, and they won't be standing

around. We just wheel it down to Simon's house once we've got it working. You guys take it down to the water while I give the Gestapo the slip again. We know how easy that is.'

'God, Tim, they're just trouble,' Simon said.

Tim clamped his teeth together, and pretended to study the diagram on the big screen for a moment. There had been a lot of verbal tension between him and Simon since the party. 'I can handle them. Can't you?'

'I shouldn't have to handle them, that's the thing.'

Tim turned to face him. Simon was still sprawled on the ramshackle sofa. As usual. He never did much actual work on the jet ski, just hung around while everyone else got their hands dirty. 'You got something else on your mind?'

'Like what?'

'I dunno. Me and Annabelle?' It had been going quite well between them during the last week, despite the clinging presence of Tim's bodyguards. At school, they sat with each other at meals now, and spent a lot of time together in the afternoons. On Thursday she'd come back to the Manor with him, so they could spend the evening studying. Tonight she was coming along with Tim and his friends to Stamford. Most Saturdays – excepting those when there were parties at someone's house – a group of them would tour the town's clubs and then grab a kebab before the last bus home at one-thirty.

'That doesn't bother me in the slightest.' Simon gave Tim a defiant smile. 'I'm on to fresh pastures now.'

'Who?' Martin challenged.

'Rachel, if you must know.'

'Bollocks. She's going out with Nigel.'

'Not any more. She's coming to Stamford with us tonight. And we're going to the summer ball together.'

'Jesus.' Colin looked up from the jet ski's body panel he was working on, trying not to seem worried. 'You've got a date for that already?'

'Durr. It's only the biggest event we've got left at Oakham. And it's only six weeks away. Only total-wanker losers don't have anyone to go with. Haven't you asked Vanessa yet?'

Colin and Tim swapped a mildly apprehensive glance.

'I was going to ask Danielle, actually,' Colin said.

'Buzzt. Wrong answer. Philip's taking her.'

'Shit! You're kidding.'

Always happy to supply bad news, Simon grinned broadly. 'He said he was asking her, he told me. If you're desperate you could always ask Sophie – after all, she's not likely to have a male date, and we're supposed to take a member of the opposite sex. How's that for political incorrectness?'

Tim ignored the jibe about Sophie – it wasn't the first time he'd heard that rumour. He was wondering if it was too early to ask Annabelle if she'd go to the ball with him. It was the senior year's last big event before their final exams. That put a lot of pressure on people to take part, and to do that you had to be a couple. Tim had two friends who'd made pacts with girls almost a year ago to go together; they weren't dating or involved, they were just making sure they got in.

'Maybe I should ask Vanessa,' Colin muttered.

'You're dumping her because she's got tiny tits, aren't you?' Martin said. 'I know you.'

'So? She's still a good laugh. I like her.'

41

'I thought you two were getting on all right,' Tim said.

'We are. It's just I didn't know Danielle was going with someone else.'

'Well, Zai's certainly free these days,' Simon said. 'Try asking her.'

Colin pulled a face. 'I don't think she likes me.'

'She never said that,' Tim assured him.

'And she's certainly got bigger tits than Vanessa,' Martin said.

'Will you pack that in!' Colin said. 'I don't just go for their tits.'

'Course not. There's legs to consider as well.'

'Fuck off. Hey, Tim, have they told you when your dad's out yet?'

'Oh my,' Simon called out. 'Did someone change the subject? It was all done so smoothly I can't tell.'

'Four days,' Tim said. Lucy Duke had told them last night. It was the first time he'd spoken to her for more than thirty seconds, but he was desperate for every detail. The prospect of his father's return left him elated and apprehensive at the same time. 'We've got to take the Eurostar train over to Brussels on Tuesday. There's going to be a big press briefing. The Prime Minister and the President will be there and everything.'

'Bloody hell!' Martin exclaimed. 'You're going to meet them?'

'Suppose so.'

'Well, make sure you tell them what we all think of them.'

7. AUNTIE

Tim had been given the Honda e-trike for his sixteenth birthday. It was powered by a three-cell sealed-circuit regenerator module, which gave it a top speed of eighty kilometres per hour; on a full tank of recombined electrolyte its range was six hundred and fifty kilometres. The Manor's garage, with its solar-panel roof and domestic regenerator module buried under the concrete floor, was capable of supplying enough electricity to keep three big cars running all year round. An e-trike barely registered on the supply monitor. Not that Tim used it much during the winter months; riding in the icy insistent rain was difficult and dangerous. Now that April was here, ending the succession of miserable damp days that comprised England's new wintertime, he was taking it out again.

It took him barely ten minutes to ride over to Manton on the Sunday morning, and that was using the shabby D-class roads linking the villages around the vast reservoir. The Europol team followed a constant hundred metres behind in their Range Rover. Manton was perched on the brow of the slope above Rutland Water's eastern shore; what used to be a small, principally agricultural village had been bolstered over the last four decades by a sprawl of large houses that all looked out over the water. It was primarily a retirement estate, closed off and protected from the rest of the world, built on a solid foundation of wealth, with every domestic and health requirement taken care of.

Tim's Aunt Alison lived there. She'd bought a two-bedroomed bungalow, one of the smallest homes on the estate but with the best view across to the reservoir's peninsula. Tim braked the e-trike beside the wide gates that guarded the entrance to the estate and flashed his identity smart card at the sensor post. They swung open slowly, and he drove in past the sign warning that Livewire Security guarded the estate with an armed-response team. The Range Rover slid in behind him.

Every house along the avenue had an immaculate garden, as if that was a clause of occupancy. This season's daffodils and tulips were in full flower, carpeting the borders between perfectly geometrical GM conifers that came in an astonishing variety of colours. Jet-black hemispherical mower robots grazed slowly on the lawns, the only source of activity while the residents sat round on their patios, warding off the sunlight with big canvas parasols. They were all over fifty, their skin and hair looking as if they belonged to someone twenty years younger. It was their movements, methodical and considered, that gave away their age. That and what Tim regarded as a truly awful dress sense – circa 1950s golfers – which seemed to afflict the whole community.

There was a small BMW parked on Aunt Alison's drive. Tim pulled up behind it, and locked the e-trike. He had his helmet under his arm as he rang the doorbell.

'Tim!' his aunt exclaimed as she swung the door back. Her eyes narrowed as she saw the Europol team in their Range Rover. 'Why didn't you tell me you were coming? Oh!' A palm slapped theatrically against her forehead. 'You did. Didn't you? Come in, darling. Sorry about the mess. Do the police have to come in with you?'

'No,' Tim said firmly.

Aunt Alison was his father's sister, ten years younger than Jeff and, as far as Tim was concerned, a lot more lively. She had the huskiest voice he'd ever heard: a gin-and-forty-cigarettes-a-day voice, his mother called it. Her whole easy-going attitude, her casual old-fashioned dress sense (infinitely superior though it was to that of her neighbours), and complete lack of domesticity, made it plain to Tim that she'd had one hell of a good time when she was younger – and not so younger, as well. He really liked Aunt Alison – they'd always got on well together. Mainly because she always seemed to treat him as an equal. The one time he'd run away from the Manor, aged thirteen and after a particularly bad fight with his mother, this was where he'd instinctively headed.

'Are we going out for lunch?' Alison asked as she led him through the chaos that was her lounge. Every wall was covered in big stainless-steel poster frames, holding blow-ups of the covers of the fantasy books she used to write. Nubile women in brass bikinis (or less) clung to bronzed muscle-bound men as they fought off wyrms and goblin hordes with magic glowing swords; gloomy forests and dark castles tended to feature heavily in the background. The scenes had always inspired Tim when he was younger. He'd even loyally read a couple of Alison's books, though he preferred straight science fiction himself.

'No. I was just coming to see you about dad and next Tuesday.'

'Oh, right.' Alison went out onto the patio. 'You remember Graham, don't you, Tim?'

'Sure.'

Graham Joyce was sitting in one of the sunloungers. He leaned forward and gave Tim a firm handshake. 'Tim, greetings and salutations.' For a man in his eighties he retained a remarkably vigorous air, possessing a gaunt face that genoprotein treatments had never quite managed to soften and a shock of unruly snow-white hair. His voice was like a forceful foghorn.

Tim smiled. 'Hiya.' The old novelist was one of his favourite adults, even more disreputable than Alison if such a thing were possible. Graham had won the last Booker Prize, back in 2012, while the publishing houses were collapsing in tandem with the copyright laws. That didn't make him as famous as Jeff Baker; these days novelists belonged to the same chunk of history as Hollywood and Rock and Roll, but Tim had plenty of respect for Graham. It was more than just the elder statesman thing, he always spoke with such passion that it was impossible to doubt what he said.

'What are you two cooking up?' Tim asked.

'Revolution! Martyrdom!' Graham chuckled, a sound like an aggressive avalanche. 'Going to join us?'

'I'll give it a miss, thanks. I'm seeing my girlfriend later.'

'How is Zai?' Alison asked.

Tim winced. 'Annabelle.'

'God, you're as bad as your father,' Alison said. She settled back into her own sunlounger and picked up a tall glass of gin and tonic. 'I remember what he was like back in the seventies and eighties. Not that the nineties were much better. I had to be very careful about introducing him to my girlfriends in those days. He tried to get most of them into bed.'

Tim was fascinated by this sudden revelation of parental behaviour. 'Really?'

'Pay no heed, Tim,' Graham commanded. 'Alison's so-called history is all feminist revisionism. Your father was a fine bloke. I'll overlook the fact that he annihilated my world and cast all us delicate, sensitive artistic types into eternal purgatory. So who is Annabelle?'

'She's a friend. Lives over in Uppingham. I really like her.'

'Good for you.'

Tim looked round the patio. The wisteria creepers that twined round the awning poles were in full flower. Alison's garden was shaggier than those of her neighbours, but it was just as attractive. And the view across the water as the sun shone on the ripples was fabulous. 'Do you really think you're in purgatory?'

'Come on, you know we were the lucky ones, Tim,' Alison said. 'The only reason I can afford to live in this dreadful ghetto is because I made a mint writing ... what do you call it? Pre10. Yes, pre10 console games.'

'Right.' Tim gave a mildly awkward grin. He'd grown up with every byte in the datasphere being free: that was the natural way of things – instant unlimited access to all files was a fundamental human right. Restriction was the enemy. Evil. Governments restricted information, starving the media and the public of their true behaviour and tyranny, although enough of it leaked out anyway. He'd never really thought of the economic fallout from the macro storage-capability delivered by crystal memories. The concept was simple enough: everything that could be digitized could be stored and distributed across the datasphere, every file could be copied a million – a billion – times over. Once it was released into the public domain, it could never be recalled, providing a universal open-source community.

*

After the turn of the century, as slow phone-line connections were replaced by ultra-high-speed cables into every home, and Jeff Baker's memory crystals took over from sorely limited hard drives and writable CDs, so more and more information was liberated from its original and singular owner. The music industry, always in the forefront of the battle against open access, was the first to crumble. Albums and individual tracks were already available in a dozen different electronic formats, ready to be traded and swapped. Building up total catalogue availability took hardly any time at all.

As ultra-high-definition screens hit the market, so paper books were scanned in or had their e-book versions' encryptions hacked. Films were downloaded as soon as the first rental release appeared – sometimes even before, and on a few celebrated occasions actually prior to their cinema première.

All of these media were provided free from distributed-source networks established by anonymous enthusiasts and fanatics, and even a few dedicated anti-capitalists determined to burn Big Business and stop them making 'excessive profits'. Lawyers and service providers tried to stamp it out. At first they tried very hard. But there was no longer a single source site to quash, no one person to threaten with fines and prison. Information evolution meant that the files were delivered from innumerable computers that simply shared their own specialist-subject architecture software. The Internet had long ago destroyed geography; the datasphere removed traceable identity from the electronic universe – and, with it, responsibility.

Excessive profits took the nosedive that every open-source idealist, Marxist, and crusty wanted. Anybody who'd ever walked into a shop and grumbled about the price of a DVD or a CD finally defeated the rip-off retailer and producer, and started accessing whatever they wanted for free. Record companies, film studios and print publishers saw their income crash dramatically. By 2009 band managers could no longer afford to pay for recording time, session musicians, promotional videos and tours. There was no money coming in from the current blockbusters to invest in the next generation, and certainly no money for art films. Writers could still write their books, but they'd never be paid for them – the datasphere snatched them away the instant the first proof review copy was sent out. New games were hacked and sent flooding through the datasphere like electronic tsunami for everyone to ride and enjoy. Even the BBC and other public-service television companies were hit as their output was channelled directly into the datasphere; nobody bothered to pay their licence fee any more. Why should they?

After 2010, the nature of entertainment changed irrevocably, conforming to the datasphere's dominance. New songs were written and performed by amateurs. Professional writers either wrote scripts for commercial cable television or went back to their day jobs and released their creative work for free; while non-professional writers finally got to expose their rejected manuscripts to the world, which seemed as unappreciative as editors had been. Games were put together by mutual interest teams, more often than not modifying and remixing pre10 originals. Hollywood burned. With the big time over, studios diverted their dwindling resources into cable shows, soaps, and series; they didn't even get syndication and Saturday morning reruns any more, let alone DVD rental fees and sales. Everything was a one-off, released globally and sponsored by commercials and product placement.

It was a heritage Tim had never considered in any detail before. Then, a couple of years back, he'd watched *Dark Sister*, an adaptation of one of Graham's novels. The pre10 film had been spooky and surprisingly suspenseful, and he'd made the error of telling Graham he'd quite liked it. The novelist's response wasn't what he expected. Graham held his hand out and said: 'That'll be five Euros, please.'

'What?' a perplexed Tim asked. He wanted to laugh, but Graham looked fearsomely serious.

'Five Euros – I think that's a reasonable fee, don't you?'

'For what?'

'I wrote the book, I even wrote some of the screenplay. Don't I deserve to be paid for my time and my craft?'

'But it's in the datasphere. It has been for decades.'

'I didn't put it there.'

Tim wasn't sure what to say; he even felt slightly guilty. After all, he'd once complained to Dad about not raking in royalties from crystal memories. But that was different, he told himself: crystal memories were physical, *Dark Sister* was data, pure binary information.

'Fear not, Tim,' Graham said. 'It's an old war now, and we were beaten. Lost causes are the worst kind to fight. I just enjoy a bit of agitation now and then. At my age there's not much fun left in life.'

Tim didn't believe that at all.

*

'Do you want a drink, Tim?' Alison asked.

'No, thanks.' Tim held his helmet up. 'I'm on my e-trike.'

'Good man, Tim,' Graham said. 'Don't touch drink, and don't smoke, either.' He pulled a cigarette out of a packet and lit up.

'Are you coming to Brussels on Tuesday?' Tim asked. 'You haven't answered any of Lucy Duke's txts about it.'

'I certainly haven't. Arrogant little woman. Did you see any of them?'

'Er, no.'

'Someone should teach her to say *please*.'

'Yeah, I know what you mean. So are you coming?'

Alison sighed, and swirled the ice cubes round her glass. 'No, Tim, I'm not. I'm sorry, I don't think I can cope with that damn circus.' She gave him a long glance. 'You do realize it'll be a circus, don't you? The politicians will hijack every news stream to make capital from this.'

'I know.'

'Well, then. Besides, I don't think I'll be much of a priority for my big brother. He'll want to see you more than anything. And your mother.'

'You sure?'

'Yes. I'll watch the news streams from here.'

'Okay. But mum's having a Welcome Home party for him on Saturday evening – she says she'd like you to come to that.'

'I'll be there. I do want to see him, Tim, just not under the spotlight.'

'I understand. I wish I didn't have to do it, either.'

'You're not worried about meeting him again, are you?' Alison asked gently.

'Well. You know. No.'

'Tim. He's going to be delighted to see you. Really. You've handled yourself perfectly these last eighteen months. Anybody would be proud to have you as their son. Hell, I'm proud just to have you as a nephew.'

Tim chewed on his lower lip, hating to show any vulnerability. 'You think?'

'God, yes.'

'I really missed him, you know. I mean, not that we did much together, no football and stuff. He was a bit old for that, even with the genoprotein treatments. But he was always there, you know, he'd listen and try to help. I don't suppose I told him how much I appreciated that. Not very often, anyway.'

'I'd hope not! You're a teenager. You're supposed to spend the entire era in a bad sulk.'

'No way!'

Graham and Alison burst out laughing. Tim blushed, trying not to smile.

Alison patted his knee. 'It'll all work out fine. You'll see.'

8. DREAM ON

It was a warm, hazy summer day with a strange orange-tinted sky – as if twilight had started at lunch. They were on one of the Manor's big lawns, just Timmy and himself. Kicking a football about. Sweaters on the grass marked the goalposts. Timmy was about ten years old, skinny legs sticking out of baggy blue shorts. He ran back and forth, nudging the ball with his toe, swerving round imaginary opponents.

Jeff wanted to run after him. Tackle him. Loose the ball back again. As it should be between father and son. But all he could do was stand in the goal, his joints aching from arthritis, too ancient and wizened to move.

Timmy ran towards him, feet pounding on the ground, the ball bouncing along in front. He took a mighty kick, and the ball sailed past Jeff as his feeble claw hands waved about uselessly in the air.

'Gooooal!' Timmy shrieked. He danced about on the spot, his arms raised high.

Jeff clapped delightedly. 'Well done, son. Jolly well done.'

'Let's play again. Play with me this time, dad, please, I want us to play together.'

'I can't, son.' The tears were rolling down Jeff's cheeks. 'I can't. I'm sorry.'

'Why, dad, why?'

And all Jeff could do was stand there, just as he always did at this moment, hands reaching out while Timmy frowned and sulked. Every time the same. Every time he failed his son.

'Jeff?' It was a female voice, disembodied. 'Jeff, can you hear me?'

Jeff moaned as the Manor and its grounds wavered and darkened. This wasn't part of the dream. Never before, anyway.

'Jeff?'

There was only the darkness of a foggy moonless night. And pain. An all-over sharp prickling that grew and grew, as if his skin was igniting. A thin wail escaped from his mouth. He could barely hear it.

'That's it, Jeff – focus now, please. Focus on me.'

The darkness was fading out, as swirls of bright light emerged from all around. Jeff blinked furiously. He'd been dreaming, so this must be waking, he realized. Damn, it hurt. His skin was still inflamed, and now he could feel a deeper ache in every limb warning him not to move any muscle.

'What?' he gasped feebly.

His one simple word was greeted by a lot of people cheering. Idiots – couldn't they see he needed help?

'Jeff, don't try and move. Just keep calm. You're fine. The suppressants are going to take a while to wear off.'

Soft tissues dabbed at his eyes, soaking up the moisture. The world revolved around him. Unsurprisingly, he was in some kind of hospital room, with a bank of equipment at one side of his bed. Two people dressed in medical smocks were bending over him, instruments in their hands. More people stood at the end of the bed. He frowned, and concentrated on one of them.

'Timmy?' For some reason his gorgeous son was different. Older. His face taut with nervous apprehension.

Memories began to seep into Jeff's sluggish thoughts.

'Hiya, dad.' Tim's voice was choked up with emotion.

'Hello, Jeff,' Sue said politely. She was standing next to Tim.

'Uh ... what happened?' He worried that he'd had some kind of accident.

'Can you tell us?' one of the medical people asked; his voice had a German accent. 'Do you remember the treatment you were scheduled?'

The memories were welling up faster now. *The meetings, endlessly sitting round conference tables with oh-so-serious doctors and geneticists. The agonizing week they gave him to make up his mind, the indecision and fear.* He found some of them frightening. *Back in the public eye again after so long in modest obscurity, reporters from every news stream pounding incessant questions at him. Politicians, hordes of the bastards wanting to be associated with the project. Slick spin doctors.* He wanted to stop remembering, to keep the bright images and sounds sealed away, but the torrent had begun now.

'Jesus wept,' he moaned. His hands were shaking uncontrollably as realization swept him along. Judging from Timmy's age, he must have been out for months, more than a year. That must mean it was over, complete.

'It's okay, dad,' Tim promised anxiously. 'It worked. You're fine. You look great.'

Jeff tried to raise his head. Both the medical staff pressed him down again.

'Mirror,' Jeff said. 'I want a mirror.'

Sue nodded at Tim, who moved closer. He held up a mirror.

*

The Eurohealth Council originally began the research project back in 2023, dispensing grants to universities right across the Continent, and then tying in various corporate laboratories as well. It was exactly the kind of forward-thinking, benefits-the-people endeavour which Europe's ruling political classes were keen to pursue. Officially, the Eurohealth Council called the project 'multilevel synchronous replacement vectoring'. To the news streams it was simply rejuvenation. The concept took genoprotein treatments several stages past organ enhancement and cosmetic improvement. Researchers were aiming for the ability to vector new and complete DNA strands into every component of the human body. It was DNA copied from the patient, then engineered back to the state of late adolescence, before it began losing telomeres and suffering replication errors. Young DNA.

In theory, the next generation of cells reproduced within the body would be those of an adolescent. The patient's entire body would grow progressively younger. But there were billions upon billions of cells in the human body. To produce a new, and perfect, gene for every single one and insert it correctly was immensely difficult – and fabulously expensive. By 2036 when the project leaders announced it had reached fruition and they were ready for their first human subject, the dedicated Eurohealth

Council budget for rejuvenation was larger than that of the European Space Agency. With such generous resources distributed among seventy universities and over nine thousand biomedical subcontractor companies, it was possible for the project to rejuvenate one European citizen every eighteen months.

Before Jeff went into the suspension womb, the Brussels University Medical Centre stopped him from taking the genoprotein treatments which kept his bones reasonably thick and strong, and maintained his smooth skin; they also extracted his ceramic teeth, withdrew his retinal implants, and cancelled the vectors which helped sustain his major organs. This cold turkey process purged his body of the alien biochemicals and aptamers which had kept him fit and active. His true seventy-seven years of age had crept up on him in less than a fortnight. Terrifying in its humbling. He had come to know the wintertime grip of wheezy asthmatic lungs, stiff painful joints, laboured arthritic movements, the degradation of soiled pants and misty vision. He had watched his skin dry and shrivel, his veins protrude, liver spots bloom like invading bacterial cultures; seen virile silver hair fade to grey and fall as dead and desiccated as autumn pine needles, to sully his collar.

Jeff had discovered then exactly how much he hated age. It frightened him badly. The incontinence, the weakness, the frailty – reminding him he was mortal, a reality which a great many of his generation had successfully hidden themselves away from.

He could quite clearly remember the last sight of his wrinkled, decrepit face before he went into the suspension womb. But he had to swim back through decades of compacted and jumbled memories to reach the face he saw now in the mirror, and even that didn't fit perfectly. When he had been twenty, his mouse-brown hair had reached fashionably down to his shoulders. Now he looked at this foreign youth's firm jaw, small pale lips, shocked grey eyes, baby-smooth skin, downy stubble, and a short punky fuzz of hair.

Nonetheless, this face belonged to him.

He was afraid to reach up and paw at the mirror in case its mirage shattered; it seemed fairground trickery. Rejuvenation treatment was a modern alchemy: close your eyes, a long blank second while the wizard waves his staff, open your eyes, and you've been reborn.

Then his personality began to pull together, skittish thoughts calming. This young face, he noted, had slightly thinner cheeks than he recalled himself having fifty-eight years ago. That must be due to diet – the suspension womb would have fed him a perfectly balanced nutrient supply rather than the junk food and bar snacks he'd lived off during his student days.

Jeff Baker grinned at himself, revealing teeth that were perfectly straight and white. He started to laugh, despite the pain.

9. GENES AND CIRCUSES

The European Commission's central briefing theatre was a semicircular chamber with seating for over four hundred people. Like most European government facilities it was grandiose and expensively furnished. Projection and display equipment was state of the art, capable of providing absolute proof that policies and edicts were working well and that tax money was being well spent. It needed to be: the hardened Brussels political press corps still hadn't been tamed into the meek complicity which the EMPs and Commissioners would have preferred.

For once, though, the press corps actually possessed an expectant buzz as they filed into the theatre. This afternoon, in the same place, they would be covering a policy launch initiative to tackle small-town transport-infrastructure decay in the Group3 north-eastern countries. Tomorrow there would be two presentations, one on sustainable energy, and yet another on agriculture. Yesterday Brussels had been dominated by the auditors refusing to sign off the Commission accounts for the fifteenth year in a row. But this was different: this was a human story, this was the official discovery of the fountain of youth.

A long table had been set up on the raised stage, complete with the traditional glasses of water and silver microphones. Behind it, a huge screen was displaying a colourful double helix that writhed and twisted like a tormented serpent. The senior press officer looked across the audience of familiar cynical faces, took a deep breath to calm his chuntering nerves, and announced they were ready to begin. President Jean Brèque walked onto the stage first. The press corps stood up politely. Rob Lacey, the British Prime Minister, was next, producing his standard lopsided smile for the datasphere feed cameras.

Jeff Baker appeared. The theatre was silent for a moment. Then the press broke into thunderous applause. It took a moment, but then the politicians too started clapping. Jeff was slightly taken aback by the response, but recovered to give a quick wave before sitting down. His family followed him in. Sue, of course, looked beautiful; she was dressed stylishly in a ginger-pink silk suit with a high collar. Cameras zoomed in eagerly. Tim didn't quite slouch, but he did give the theatre a sullen glance. He was wearing a vivid higlo Union Jack T-shirt. The British reporters chuckled at that, while the German, French, and Benelux journos scowled disapprovingly.

President Brèque leaned forward to the microphone, smiling broadly. 'Good morning, ladies and gentlemen, and welcome to what I consider one of the most momentous conferences of my tenure. As you can see, Jeff Baker is alive, well, and looking in very good shape. Very young shape, I should say.'

The press applauded again. Jeff gave them a thumbs-up.

'There have been many critics of our rejuvenation

project,' the President continued. 'Both inside our community, and especially abroad. Today, I consider our persistence to be utterly vindicated. Dr Sperber, who heads the project, tells me that Dr Baker has an effective physiological age of a youth in his early twenties. We have been extraordinarily successful. As a result, only Europe is in a position to provide this treatment for its citizens. America with its increasingly isolationist foreign policy and Religious Right cultural dominance is a long way behind us in this field. Our unquestioned leadership here can only be seen as an endorsement of our social inclusiveness: ours is the culture in which the promotion of human life can flourish to its full potential.' He inclined his head graciously. 'But enough of my dull old speechifying. It is my pleasure and privilege to introduce Jeff Baker, father of the datasphere.'

Jeff grinned round, mildly embarrassed, but unable to hide his sense of wonder. In twenty-four hours he'd managed to walk in a reasonable fashion, though his muscles were still woefully weak. But getting used to what he looked like – what he *was*, now – that was difficult, verging on impossible. He was beginning to think the human brain was fundamentally incapable of understanding the transformation.

'Dr Baker, congratulations on your successful treatment, and welcome back,' the *Berlin Stream* news reporter said.

'Thanks.' Jeff knew these were going to be desperately dull and sanitized questions. He'd even been shown them in advance so he could prepare answers; Lucy Duke had sat with him, making suggestions. It didn't particularly bother him; the kind of tough interrogation the old

61

newspaper reporters back home – and thirty years ago – used to dish out had been a hell of an ordeal. He wouldn't be able to face that kind of session right now.

'I know this will appear somewhat trite,' the *Berlin Stream* man went on, 'but could you please tell us how you feel?'

'Easy enough: I feel as if I've been caught up by a miracle. Even when I was going into the suspension womb there was some little part of me that refused to believe this would work. I'm rather glad to be proved wrong. But, trust me, it still takes some getting used to. And, on a personal note, I'd just like to express my public appreciation to Dr Sperber and his team at the university for both their dedication and professionalism.'

'Dr Baker, what will you do first, now your treatment is complete?' the woman from *Monde* asked.

'I'm going to take things easy for a while, build my strength back up – just like the doctors tell me to. I might have new muscles, but they're not used to doing any work right now. Same with my stomach, unfortunately. Before I went into the treatment I made a long list of fabulous meals I was going to eat when I came out. That'll have to wait a few days as well now; I'm on simple stuff to start with, nursery food basically. But most of all I'm just looking forward to being home with my family.' He put one arm round Tim's shoulder, and smiled warmly at Sue. She replied with a fond look. 'This has left me pretty disorientated – I just need to get my feet back on solid ground.'

'Sue, can you tell us how you feel about having your husband back like this?'

'It's hard to describe, really. Like every dream I've ever

had coming true all at once. Now I just want him home where he belongs, and we can have our life back.'

'How about you, Tim?'

'It's good.'

Jeff laughed lightly. 'That's it?' he joshed.

'Well . . .' Tim glanced suspiciously round the theatre. 'He's my dad, you know. Course I want him back. I really missed him badly. And this . . . I just . . . He looks pretty amazing, that's all. It's going to be great.'

This time Jeff gave him a strong hug. Tim turned bright red and managed a limp smile for his father.

'Dr Baker, we're all very impressed with your physical appearance,' the *Line Telegraph* reporter said. 'But it has cost an awful lot of money to give one person something the majority will never have. Do you really think it's justified?'

Jeff kept smiling; he didn't remember this question being on the list. From the corner of his eye, he caught Lucy Duke frowning. 'You're asking the wrong person for an objective opinion, I'm afraid.'

'But rejuvenation is never going to be available to everybody, is it? Don't you think this project is raising false hopes?'

The President leaned forward, giving the reporter an angry glare. 'Absolutely not.'

'If I could answer this,' Jeff said. 'The most obvious parallel is penicillin. When it was first developed during World War Two, there was so little of it to start with that the doctors wouldn't have been able to treat both Churchill and Roosevelt had they needed it at the same time. Today there's so much penicillin and antibiotics that superbug resistance is a real problem for the doctors. Of course, my treatment cost a lot. I'm the first – there is no production line. And I don't suppose it will ever be easy, or get to the point where it's refined down to a simple pill. But thanks to today's pioneers across Europe and the support we give them, it will gradually become more available and cheaper. And I haven't even mentioned the hundreds of spin-off techniques that are benefiting the biogenetics industries. All in all, I'm afraid you asked a bit of a pointless question. People have a right to hope, and this project is certainly justified in giving them that hope.'

There was some scattered applause, led by the President and the Prime Minister.

'Have you met Dr Schrober?' the *Polish Star* asked.

'No,' Jeff said. He was struggling to recall his quick briefing with Lucy Duke. Dr Katerina Schrober was the next rejuvenation subject. She was some kind of molecular biologist, a Nobel laureate. He tried not to smirk at how obligatory the choice was: female and German. So politically correct it was almost a parody. 'But I certainly wish her well. I hope her treatment goes as smoothly as mine.'

The *Lisbon Web* reporter asked: 'How is your mental state, Dr Baker? Do you believe you are up to the job you were given this rejuvenation for?'

'Good question,' Jeff said earnestly. 'I'll be undergoing memory assessment for the next few days. I can certainly remember most of my life, as much as any seventy-eight-year-old can. There will be sections missing, that's inevitable. It's also essential, because I now have another half-century of life to fill those new neurones with. I need the room! As to my intellect and rationality, that seems to be working, although I'll also be undergoing evaluation tests to map my cognitive processes. Once I've settled back in with my family, I'm convinced I'll be able to do the job. Just don't ask me specifics on superconductivity at the moment – I'll need to bring myself up to speed on current research.'

'So you think we should soon have high-temperature superconductors?'

'I think it's a little unfair to ask Dr Baker about deadlines,' Rob Lacey said. 'We all know he was chosen for this because of his unrivalled knowledge and expertise in solid-state physics. The research effort to produce a room-temperature superconductor will be pan-European, much the same as rejuvenation.'

'That's right,' Jeff said. 'It won't be one person that brings about a commercial superconductor; this is about a team effort. I'm not even the team leader, I'll simply be one of a thousand people contributing.'

'A contribution we shall all value, Dr Baker,' the President interjected. 'A room-temperature superconductor will be of enormous advantage to every European, indeed to everyone on this planet. And its effects will be felt immediately. Ecologically and economically, each one of us will benefit. Less power will be lost through transmission cables; it will be possible to build more efficient generators and motors.'

'Better than that,' Jeff said. 'It's a superb way of exploiting geothermal power. Superconductors stay at the same temperature along their whole length. If you put one end of a cable into hot rock, the other end will be able to feed directly into a heat exchanger. There are a thousand and one uses for the stuff. It's another reason why I couldn't turn down the offer of rejuvenation.' His arms spread wide, and he grinned enthusiastically. 'The superconductor project isn't quite as good as getting your youth back, but it certainly registers high up there on the worthiness table. The world needs new energy and new ways of handling that most precious resource. And this is the most promising method of all.'

'High-temperature superconductors have been a goal of the physics community for over fifty years, Dr Baker,' the *New European Scientist* reporter said. 'Don't you think that if it was possible we'd have it by now?'

'Practical rejuvenation has been a goal ever since Crick, Watson and Wilkins discovered the DNA molecule. It took us this long to get it right. And there's a lot of time, effort, and money being channelled into the problem right across the world, not just in Europe. America was doing some superb work on nanonics before I went into treatment; I'm very keen to see where that's leading and how much is applicable to our own effort.'

'I don't know about anyone else,' Rob Lacey said cheerfully. 'But I'm confident that having Dr Baker here on our team will give us in Europe a hell of an advantage. And as Prime Minister I'm proud that it is one of our citizens, a man whose fame is based on his notorious generosity, who will be providing our premier technological project with the impetus it needs for success. We are at the core of Europe, and I hope we can now become its powerhouse.' He looked round contentedly at the reporters, searching out their approval, while somehow managing to avoid the eye of the President whose tight smile was frozen on his face.

10. IN-HOUSE PARTY

The avtxt was clever, with green devil icons performing a mildly obscene cheerleader act, spelling out the words to the invitation. Annabelle had laughed when she received it, sending back a swarm of saucy angels to chant an RSVP. It wasn't quite what she would have chosen to go to, a cocktail party to welcome Jeff Baker home. But Tim had been sure to invite several of their friends, so she wouldn't feel left out. As usual, she thought. Tim was always very careful in his approach, always making sure that everything they went to was on a just-good-friends basis. So careful, in fact, she wouldn't even say they qualified as a couple yet. A small part of her was quite irked by that.

She had to admit, though, the party wasn't as awful as she expected. It was ninety per cent adults, and most of them were over fifty. But the Manor's large reception rooms were wonderfully elegant, and Sue Baker had hired a very upmarket catering team for the event. Waiters and waitresses circulated with glasses of champagne and mounds of delectable canapés on silver trays. The men were mostly in suits, while the women wore expensive dresses. Shame so many of them lacked any sort of elementary fashion sense, Annabelle thought. She'd given a lot of consideration to what she ought to be wearing herself, settling for a simple orange summer dress with quite a short skirt. It earned her a lot of looks from the men, of all ages. There was also the prospect of actually meeting Jeff Baker. The fact that he was Tim's father was something she hadn't quite accustomed herself to yet.

Annabelle had arrived quite early in the evening, calmly tolerating Tim's puppyish enthusiasm. His gaze kept switching between her legs and her chest, with a rest between so that he could blush, hoping she hadn't noticed. At least that aspect of their relationship was predictable: boys around her always acted as if they'd had a lobotomy. He'd introduced her to his aunt Alison, who clearly didn't give a damn about appearance, and was actually a lot of fun. Annabelle chatted to her for a while before the other girls arrived. After that Tim got dragged away by his mother, so she stayed with Rachel, Lorraine, and Danielle; the three of them clustered in a corner, warding off wishful glances from the older men.

'Colin's asked me to the ball,' Danielle gushed. She couldn't keep the smile off her face. 'God, I'm just so much relieved somebody has. Finally! I was worried I'd have to go with Philip.'

'I thought Colin was going with Vanessa,' Rachel said.

'No. Me!'

'Does Vanessa know?' Lorraine murmured.

Annabelle took a sip of her Bacardi and lime to cover the fact she couldn't summon up any zeal for Danielle's success. Tim still hadn't asked her. There was such a thing as playing it too cool, as he was about to find out if he didn't ask pretty damn soon. She listened to Danielle bubbling on about what she was going to wear. The fact that she was going with Colin didn't surprise Annabelle: all Colin's girlfriends tended to follow a pattern, and Danielle with her wasp waist and heavy chest filled it perfectly.

'I've heard Martin and Sophie are going together,' Lorraine said.

'Heavens, you have got to be joking,' Rachel said. 'My God, Sophie is so much a lesbian.'

'She's not,' Annabelle said. Sophie was a good friend of hers and she felt someone should be defending her.

'Really? The last time we came up here for a swim, she was all over me in the changing room. I was scraping off eye tracks for a week after.'

'You're imagining it.'

'It's her imagination I'm worried about.'

The girls all giggled. Annabelle managed a weak smile.

'By the way, hope you don't mind,' Rachel said slyly. 'But Simon's asked me to go.'

'Why should I mind?' Annabelle asked. 'We finished weeks ago.' She tried to think of something to say that would imply strength of character. 'If you want him, have him.' A line she was sure she'd heard on a pre10 movie.

'Oh, I will.'

'Always keep them dangling,' Danielle warned.

'I'll do more than that to him.'

'What are you going to wear?' Lorraine asked.

'Oh, I got my dress weeks ago. Haven't you seen it?'

'No!'

Must be the only one, Annabelle thought sharply; there were porn soaps that had fewer viewers than that dress.

'It's purple satin. Classic strapless from Demoné. With this so much gorgeous lace edging. That's antique, you know. Daddy had a fit when he found out how much it was, but I had to have it. It's just *me*.'

'Wow,' Lorraine breathed.

'I've seen it,' Danielle said brightly. 'It's lovely.'

'Thank you,' Rachel said. 'What about you, Annabelle? Have you bought a dress yet?'

Annabelle finished her Bacardi Breezer in a single long swallow. 'I haven't decided what I'm wearing.' Rachel knew damn well Annabelle hadn't got anyone to go with. That one and Simon were going to be well suited, she decided. 'I'm going to get another drink.' She walked away, her empty glass held casually low, as if she hadn't a care in the world.

God damn Tim for not asking her yet!

*

It must be a sign of true old age to think parties were a pain, to be avoided at all costs. Long before this one started, Jeff had decided there was no way he was going to spend more than an hour pasting on a false smile and saying 'Really, how interesting' to people he didn't like, didn't know, and considered utterly boring. And this was a party in his honour. Age – or grumpiness? he wondered.

However, once it got started he found himself mellowing. For one thing, he could actually enjoy the champagne. Drinking too much in the early evening before he had the regeneration treatment used to mean getting up to pee all bloody night long. No damn genoprotein cure for that! And back then he was sure his taste buds had decayed, while now he found the vintage Veuve Clicquot to be perfectly crisp and light. He'd also got the most awful headaches, which Neurofen could never cushion. Well . . .

he'd just take his chances on the hangover front tomorrow morning.

As ever at these things that Sue organized, Jeff didn't know half the people who were enjoying his own home. Or maybe that was: didn't remember. The two sessions in Brussels he'd undergone to check out his memory retention hadn't been as reassuring as he had expected. About half of his life seemed to have vanished. Old pictures, even videos of himself with other people that they'd shown him to try and stimulate association had done nothing. They really did belong to someone else's life.

Typically, one thing he hadn't lost was Tracy, his first wife. Those painful details still burned hot and bright in his memory. Trust that bloody harpy to cling to him no matter what.

But he'd remembered the one thing that was truly important to him, though. Tim had sat opposite him during the whole Eurostar train trip back to Peterborough. The two of them were nervous and awkward to begin with, as if they were meeting for the first time, but his urgency to find out what his son had been doing for the last eighteen months pushed him past that initial hesitancy. Mutual delight at being in each other's company soon had Tim emerging from his shell. Listening to his son babble on about school grades, and friends, and social events, Jeff could scarcely believe that this young adult was the same gawky lad he'd said goodbye to a year and a half earlier. It was as if he'd expected the world to go into stasis and wait for him. Sue, of course, hadn't changed in any respect, which helped spin out that particular illusion.

The other person he'd been delighted to see was his little sister. Alison had arrived at the Manor for his party, and the two of them had looked at each other for a long emotional moment. Then she parted her lips in a soft indulgent smile as they finally embraced.

'It really is you,' she whispered, sniffing hard and blinking moisture away from her eyes. 'Oh God, Jeff.'

'There, there.' He patted her gently as she cried. 'I'm okay. Everything worked.'

'You're just how I remember. I was at school when you were like this before. You helped me with my homework.'

'I remember.'

She leaned back to study her brother's youthful face. 'We had to write it down in exercise books and on sheets of A4. There were no computers in those days, no dot matrix printers and laser jets. Just pens and calculators.'

'I must have got my Sinclair Spectrum around then. The hours I spent using it! But I don't suppose it was much use for your homework.'

'We always used to do it on the kitchen table.'

'And mum would be fussing round with the ironing, getting supper ready.'

'Waiting for dad to get home.'

'While Ruffles got in the way.'

'Damn stupid dog.' She wiped a hand across her eyes, looking annoyed when she saw the streak of tears on her skin. 'I haven't thought about Ruffles in years.'

'Decades.'

'Yes, decades. And you've got those decades again, haven't you?'

He held her chin in his hand, making her look at him. 'Are you jealous?'

'God, yes! But I'm glad it was you they chose. I mean that, Jeff.'

'Thanks.' He kissed her brow.

'For God's sake,' Alison grunted in mock anger. 'You look so damn good, you're making me self-conscious. I'm going to have to start using those ridiculous cosmetic treatments. I swore I never would.'

'You look great as you are.'

'Oh please! Do you think genoproteins can get me to match up to Sue?'

'No problem.'

'Ha! I'd need two of your treatments before I stood a chance to get equal to her. How is your dear wife taking all this, by the way?'

Jeff grinned at the lack of enthusiasm. Alison had never approved of Sue, though she adored Tim. He waved a hand at the line of waiters hovering with their laden trays. 'In her element.'

Alison grunted, and handed her coat to one of the eager young men. She took a flute of Veuve Clicquot and sniffed at it suspiciously. 'Huh. Gnat's piss lite. Give me a decent gin and tonic every time.'

After that Alan and James arrived, and the three of them greeted each other with childish whoops in the hallway. Alan was seventy-two, a retired aerospace engineer who lived over in Stamford. Taller than Jeff, he didn't spend much of his pension on cosmetic genoproteins, preferring to buy treatments that kept his joints and muscles in shape. By doing so, he was still able to play golf three times a week and keep a nine handicap. It was his only real remaining interest now his old company had quietly dropped him from even token consultancy work. In contrast, James was only sixty-eight, and still working at the finance and asset management company he'd set up nearly forty years before in the first dotcom boom. Unlike most of the companies from that era, his had survived. Not that he put in many hours a week now he was a non-executive director. But his salary allowed him to buy the full range of male cosmetic genoproteins. He'd kept his apparent age in his late forties, with a thick shock of ebony hair, and a skin that was suspiciously permatanned. Unfortunately, not even his treatments could do much about his weight; forty years of expense-account meals had bloated him into a man who waddled rather than walked.

The two of them were among Jeff's closest friends. Out of those that were still alive, Jeff thought sourly. But it was still good to see them.

'Definitely some features I recognize on this appalling teenage youth,' James boomed as his meaty hand enveloped Jeff's. 'Jesus Christ, is it really you?'

'So they tell me,' Jeff said, with a shrug.

'How the hell can you know?' Alan asked. He was giving the young man a strange look. 'I mean, damn, man, where's the evidence?'

'I remember being me.'

'Yeah, but, like, prove it.'

'Give the guy a break,' James protested.

'You can run a DNA fingerprint if you're that worried,' Jeff said.

'I have to concede, it gives the lawyers something to argue about,' James said. 'It's like Tim's found a long-lost older brother. And dear old Jeff wouldn't wear anything like this.' Thick fingers stroked the lapel of Jeff's grey-green jacket. 'New, aren't they?'

'My clothes?' Jeff queried. 'Yes, well, even geniuses can't think of everything.' It was only after he got home that they realized none of his old clothes would fit; until then he'd been wearing loose shirts and trousers supplied by the medical facility. Sue had spent an urgent fifty minutes accessing the menswear departments at Lewis's and Selfridges; then they'd all waited anxiously for the Community Supply Service van to make its afternoon delivery with the first items of his new wardrobe.

'Your wife choose them, then?'

'Yes.'

'Not bad,' Alan said. 'Kind of retro eighties. If you pushed the sleeves up you could be like Tubbs from *Miami Vice*.'

'Crocket,' James corrected immediately. 'Tubbs was the black guy. And you'd need a thinner tie.'

'He's right,' Jeff said, glancing down quizzically at his maroon tie. 'Don Johnson was Crocket.'

James lifted a flute from a passing waiter. 'Ah, Don Johnson. Never better than in *Hot Spot*, his finest hour.'

'Of course it was,' Jeff said. 'Dennis Hopper directed it. And it was *The Hot Spot*.'

'He was much better in *Tin Cup*, playing that golf pro,' Alan said. 'The one up against Kevin Costner in the US Masters.'

'Trust you to think a film about golf was better than one of Dennis Hopper's thrillers. You've obviously forgotten *Hot Spot* had Jennifer Connelly in it. That makes it tops with or without Dennis Hopper.'

'Virginia Madsen was in *The Hot Spot*, too,' Jeff offered. He was starting to relax. Now *this* was a genuine welcome home. They'd barely been in the Manor two minutes, and already they'd fallen back into their usual routine. Sue never had understood the way they talked utter trivia for hours on end. At their age, it was a wonderful substitute for male machismo – who knew the most useless fact of all. 'A major babe in her day, our Virginia.'

'What else did she ever do?' James asked.

'She was in a *Star Trek Voyager* episode, I think,' Jeff said. 'Guest-star appearance.'

'No. It was *Highlander Two*,' Alan said gleefully. 'She was the ecoterrorist.'

'Are you sure?'

'Yeah.'

'God, that was an awful film.'

'Her brother was in *Species Two* – that was even worse.'

'Never watched it. I saw the preview at the cinema once and lost the will to live.'

'Good job Jeff didn't,' James said, laughing at his own joke.

'Oh, tasteful – thanks.'

'Ah.' James brightened suddenly. 'Let's give your memory another little test, shall we?' He started to beckon urgently across the lounge.

Jeff watched with mild interest as an attractive young woman in a little black cocktail dress smiled at James and came over to them. She had the kind of slow walk which drew male attention her way. When she reached them, Jeff noticed the dress wasn't actually that small after all; it was just the way it was cut which made it appear that way to his mind.

'This is Nicole,' James said. 'Nicole, I'm sure you remember Dr Baker.'

'Hi,' she said, with a playful smile. 'Nice to see you again, especially with you looking like this. Congratulations.'

'Thanks. I have to admit my memory hasn't come through this in a perfect state. Did we know each other before?'

James patted Nicole's bare shoulder. 'My granddaughter. She used to come and swim in your pool in the holidays.'

'Oh right!' Jeff suddenly had the image of a ten-year-old kid in a dayglo pink swimming costume running round on the lawn, shrieking and giggling as she chased after a huge inflatable beach ball. That must have been twenty years ago, which put Nicole in her early thirties. Looking at her closely, he suspected some genoprotein treatments: her hair was honey blonde and stylishly cut, while her skin was smooth and healthy, lightly tanned as opposed to her grandfather's oven-roasted tone. 'So what are you doing these days?'

'Helping the family business stay afloat.'

'Taking it over,' James muttered.

'Grandpa!' she chided in mock anger. 'Only the Southern Europe sector. It's still your company.'

'Not really,' he sighed. 'I'm going in less and less. Dempsey doesn't like the way I do things, says I'm too old-fashioned. I depress office morale, and they're frightened of getting sued. Bugger it, when I see something that needs doing, then I bloody well say so. It's called management. But oh no, I've got to be more sensitive to their needs and working environment. Load of Brussels bollocks – that's the attitude that got us into the shit-awful mess we're in today. I say what I think, not what others want me to say.'

'That's not why you're going in less.' Nicole looked straight at Jeff. 'Honestly, we just run a smaller office these days. Everyone works from home on a distributed network. Another five years and we won't even have an office.'

'You've got to have an office,' James complained. 'No matter how networked we get, the human contact is essential at the top level. Money is about trust: our clients have a right to meet us so they can see for themselves what kind of people we are.'

'Yes, grandpa.'

'Oh, bloody hell. This dinosaur needs another drink.'

Jeff shook his head as James wandered off. 'Can't you just give him his gold watch and a pension?'

'James won't retire,' she said. 'The boredom would first drive him crazy, then kill him. Besides, you're a fine one to talk about pensions. I'm curious – what has your personal finance company said about paying you?'

'I'm not sure.'

'If they ever do make this rejuvenation lark cheap enough for the masses, stakeholder investments are going to take a dive. We can't afford to pay out for a hundred years. Funds are designed to last for twenty at the most.'

'Bankers in pain,' Alan said. 'Now there's a happy thought.'

'Uncle Alan, don't be so cruel. We make the world go round.'

'That is one argument against rejuvenation,' Jeff said thoughtfully.

'What?' Nicole asked. 'We can't afford it?'

'No. If you double your lifespan, you double the number of years you have to work. Is it really worth it?'

'Let us know when you find out.' She took a sip from her flute. 'Did you really forget me?'

'Be fair – I haven't seen you for ages.'

'We could remedy that. I don't normally tout for business among family friends. But maybe you should get a professional review of your finances now your circumstances have changed so much.'

'Tell me more,' Jeff said.

*

Sue and her friends Jane, Pamela, and Lynda had taken to calling themselves the Rutland non-working mothers' club. It had started off as a laugh one evening round at Lynda's house, when they'd all been drinking vodka and both of Lynda's young kids had started crying upstairs.

'Oh, leave them to it,' Lynda had grumped. 'They'll cry themselves out eventually.' The nanny was out for the evening, and she was too sloshed to move from her huge armchair.

The name had stuck. And they introduced entry requirements:

Have you left your sick child in bed so you can go and have sex with your lover? If so, how high was the child's temperature?

How much of your Eurosocial child allowance do you spend on sleazy silk underwear that you only wear for your lovers, not your husband?

Have you refused to let the nanny/au pair go out for the night, then left them alone in the house while you seduce their boyfriend?

Have you notched up a speeding fine in your husband's car when you're on your way to see your lover in a hotel?

Sue had an impressively high score for most of them. She enjoyed the company of her fellow club members while she was staying at the Manor. They all shared the same circumstances: young, attractive, married, wealthy, living out in the countryside – bored out of their skulls. Of course, most of her London friends, the set she mixed with while she was staying at the Knightsbridge flat, would have an even higher percentage. But that was metropolitan life for you.

After the welcome-home party had begun, the four of them wound up lurking in the kitchen together. To their exotic tastes, the party was pretty dull, and the kitchen was where they could talk freely. It was also where they could eye up the waiters, all lads in their early twenties from the university in Peterborough. They didn't care what they said in front of the hired staff; shocking them was part of the game.

'I could be named in the divorce papers,' Pamela told the others breathlessly as soon as they'd gathered.

'My God,' Lynda drawled. 'Does Ken know?'

'No. It's only a threat, so far. The bitch's solicitor is just trying it on. Besides, if I don't admit to it, and Johan doesn't, there's bugger-all they can do about it.'

Annabelle followed one of the waiters in, hunting for her fresh drink. Her gaze flicked over the four expensively dressed women, and she hesitated.

'Annabelle,' Sue called. 'Don't be frightened, darling, we don't bite. Girls, this is Annabelle, my son's girlfriend.'

A couple of half-hearted smiles were thrown Annabelle's way.

'But Ken will know, even if they can't stand up in court and say you're the irreconcilable difference,' Jane said.

'So?' Pamela said. 'It's not like he behaves himself. Besides, we've got a pre-nup.'

'Ah, God's little gift to decent women everywhere,'

80

Lynda said; she raised her voice. 'Annabelle, if you ever get hitched, make sure you've got a pre-nup. Take the advice of those who know a thing or two.'

Annabelle gave them a forced smile. One of the waitresses took mercy on her and asked what she wanted.

'I saw you'd brought Patrick along this evening,' Jane said to Sue. She kept one eye on Annabelle. 'Have you introduced him to Jeff yet?'

'No.' Sue knew she should stop her friend from being this much of a bitch in front of the girl, but she'd had vodka shots in her Veuve Clicquot. 'I didn't think it would be appropriate. Why rock the boat now?'

'Are you going to have sex with him?' Lynda asked.

'That's what he's here for.'

'I meant with *Jeff*.'

'Hadn't really thought about it,' Sue said, which wasn't entirely true. In fact, it had been bothering her ever since he'd emerged from that suspension-womb machine. Who would have thought he'd turn out to be so damn good-looking when he was in his twenties? But when she looked at him she just kept seeing an image of the old Jeff. As a contraceptive, it was one hundred per cent effective.

'Lying tart,' Pamela squawked. 'He's fucking gorgeous. I'd shag him.'

'Hands off,' Sue said, a little too curtly.

Pamela chortled. 'So you have been thinking about it. I suppose there's got to be a first time for everything.'

'You could have a honeymoon,' Jane said. 'See if it works out.'

'It's worked for eighteen years the way it is. If it ain't broke, don't try and fix it.'

'He's been fixed, and fixed very well indeed. The best

81

body money can buy. I wonder if they can give men a bigger cock in the suspension womb? They always say there's no real genoprotein treatment for that.'

'Oh, come on Sue,' Lynda implored. 'You've got to try it. This is like the first foot on the moon, or climbing Everest. The first person to have sex with the first rejuvenated man. This is history.'

Sue grinned, shaking her head. 'It's not going to happen.'

The waitress finished filling Annabelle's glass. Annabelle left quickly. The non-working mothers' club regarded her through the closing door.

'How old is she?' Jane asked after a moment.

'Seventeen, I think.'

'Shit. Seventeen years old. Melons growing out of her chest, and no visible arse whatsoever; I mean, forget visible panty lines, she simply doesn't have a bum. Little cow!'

Lynda licked her lips. 'But no money, either. And no style. Did you see that dress? If that's what it was.'

The others smiled.

'Ladies,' Pamela raised her glass. 'A toast.'

'A toast,' they agreed.

'Expensive shopping, older champagne, and younger men.'

The club drank to that.

*

Jeff had dutifully met the two local MEPs, the Westminster MP, and his regional-parliament representatives, as well as a pack of local county councillors and some of the more wealthy members of Sue's social circle, even a few supposed celebrities who lived in the county. It wasn't quite guilt which made him keep going. He simply felt obliged to make sure he got round and said hello to everyone. Certainly, everybody there was very eager to see him. The worst thing wasn't having to feign amusement at the same jokes everyone made about time warps and seventies fashion sense. He'd played the elder statesman at enough corporate and academic functions now to fly on autopilot through the small talk. No, what annoyed him was genuinely not knowing a good half of the people. Sue should have been at his side to introduce him, or whisper names just before he said hello. But she'd vanished along with her demon friends, leaving him to fend for himself. It was her bloody job to help out. It wasn't as if she had anything else to do.

The party had been going for a while when he met Patrick. It was purely by chance: Patrick was leaving the lounge when Jeff came through the door from the other side. Jeff automatically stuck his hand out and bashfully admitted he couldn't recall the other's name.

'How did we know each other?' he asked.

'I'm afraid we didn't,' Patrick admitted.

'Oh?' Jeff didn't quite understand; the man must have been in his late twenties, handsome – if you liked chiselled chins – with thick long hair swept back and highlighted. For some reason he seemed a little perturbed by the meeting, almost as if he wasn't expecting Jeff to be at the party.

'I run the Magpie Gallery over in Uppingham. Your wife and several of her friends are valuable patrons.'

'Ah, social obligation, then?' Jeff said, sympathizing.

'In a way, yes. But it's still a pleasure to meet you. My congratulations. You look splendid.'

'Thanks.'

Patrick nodded politely and moved off.

Jeff gave him a slightly bewildered frown, then saw Alison and gave her a frantic wave.

'How are you doing?' His sister had found herself a gin and tonic. The long cigarette smouldering away in her fingers was earning her disapproving stares from most of the partygoers.

'Badly,' he grunted. 'Is that bloke one of your friends, too? He's an arty type.'

Alison took a drag and squinted where Jeff was pointing. She gave him a strange look. 'No. That's Sue's friend.'

'Yeah. He said.'

'Sue's special friend,' Alison said emphatically.

'Oh.' Jeff just managed to stop himself from doing a double take. He'd never actually met one before. The arrangement was that they didn't come to the Manor. He couldn't understand what Sue was playing at. They were going to have to have a serious talk about obligations tonight.

'Are you okay?' Alison asked.

'What? Oh – yeah. Just a bit tired, that's all.'

'Hmm. You shouldn't be doing stuff like this so soon.'

'Still looking out for me, little sister?'

She grinned up at him. 'Always have done.' Her expression became devious. 'Ah, it looks like Tim's wound up his courage. Now remember, show no disapproval at all; no matter what you think of her.'

'What?'

'I believe your son has someone he wants to introduce you to.' With a last evil wink, she slipped free and disappeared back amid the guests.

Jeff didn't have a clue what she was talking about. Then he caught sight of Tim making his way determinedly across the lounge. There was a girl with him, their hands clasped tightly together. That was when he registered Tim's anxious yet proud expression, and understanding dawned. Little Timmy had a girlfriend. Jeff felt horribly out of his depth. This simply wasn't fair: fathers normally had months of early warning to prepare for this moment. A year and a half earlier, Tim had been a raging knot of hormones and suppressed anger. Your standard teenage nightmare, repellent to anyone but his own kind. Now, by the look of things, he was growing up. For an instant Jeff felt angry at missing out on another part of his son's life.

'Dad, um, I'd like you to meet Annabelle, she's an, um, friend of mine.'

The desperation in his son's voice was almost painful to hear. *Show no disapproval* was running like a mantra through Jeff's head. In a kind of semi-panic he did what he always did, and fell back on the excessive formality he'd learned at his public school. 'I'd be delighted.' He made a small bow. It was only as he straightened up again that he actually realized: Annabelle was utterly gorgeous. His gaze moved slowly up long legs, shown off by the shortish skirt of a flattering rust-coloured dress, and took in a very generous cleavage. When he finally dragged his stare away from her bust he found she had rich brown-gold hair brushing her bare shoulders, and a delicate face – on which there was a quizzical, slightly annoyed expression as she looked closely at him.

Jeff recovered; knowing he would be blushing, he took her hand and kissed her knuckles. 'An absolute pleasure.

85

Tim's kept very quiet about you. I'll have to have a talk with him about that.'

'Thank you, Dr Baker.' Annabelle managed to recover her hand.

'Oh, please: Jeff.'

'Jeff,' she agreed.

'So do you live locally?'

'Yes, in Uppingham. I live there with my father.'

'I see.'

'Mum works in Brussels. But not in the university; she didn't have anything to do with your rejuvenation project. She's one of the environment agency's management directors.' Annabelle wasn't sure why she was talking so much. Probably to try and cover over his weird behaviour. The way he was looking at her was exactly the same way Tim had done when she arrived at the party. It made her realize just how similar they looked; like brothers, with Jeff only a few years older. Which sort of stalled the question she'd been planning to ask Tim, about whether he'd been adopted.

'Sounds like a good job,' Jeff said.

'It is.'

'What subjects are you taking at school?'

'Dad!' Tim said, hotly.

'What? I'm just being polite.'

'Yeah, but school! That droops.'

Jeff turned to Annabelle, spreading his arms wide in appeal. 'All right. So how long have you two been together?'

She smiled before she looked firmly at the floor.

'*Dad!*'

'Sorry, Timmy, I guess I can't be trusted out in public. But look on the good side: I didn't launch into telling Annabelle about how cute you were when you were younger.'

'Was he?' Annabelle asked. It was hard for her not to laugh, Tim was squirming so. In a way Jeff Baker was almost worse than his wife and her friends. A lot more interesting, though.

'Absolutely. When he's not around, I'll dig out some of the old family videos. You can see him running round in his shorts when he was seven.'

'I'll look forward to that.'

Tim groaned in dismay.

'It's a conspiracy, Timmy,' Jeff said. 'The whole world exists simply to make life hell for you.'

'Nice meeting you,' Annabelle said. She squeezed Tim's hand, and they walked away together.

'That was a big mistake,' Tim moaned. He snatched another champagne flute from a passing waiter.

'I expect he needs time to find his feet. This must be very strange for him.' She looked over her shoulder to see Jeff standing alone, holding his flute up as if unsure he should be drinking.

'Yeah, maybe,' Tim said. 'I guess this wasn't the right time to introduce you.'

'Thank you, anyway.' She moved a fraction closer. 'It was nice of you to invite me in the first place.'

Tim's face turned a deeper shade of red. 'Um, about invitations. I don't know if anyone's asked you or anything, or if you've already got someone to go with, but if you haven't, and you'd like to, I wondered if you'd like to go to the ball together. That is, with me. If you were going. I booked some tickets, that's all. And quite a lot of my friends are going.'

'Course I'll go with you.'

'Yeah?' Tim's whole face radiated happiness.

'Yeah.' She poked him in the chest. 'Took you long enough to ask.'

'Sorry. I didn't know if you wanted to.'

'Oh yeah.' Their faces were centimetres apart. 'I wanted to.'

They kissed. Just a teasing toying sort of way, to see how far the other would push it. There was a whoop from across the lounge. Annabelle pulled away, grinning, to see Martin and Colin at their most oafish, making big-time gestures at them. She sneered back at them, and started kissing a delighted Tim again.

*

It wasn't half past nine when Jeff wearily climbed the stairs. Downstairs the party was over, with the catering crew and Mrs Mayberry cleaning up while the Europol team ate the leftover canapés and finished off the open bottles of champagne. Tim and his friends had all gone to catch the bus into Stamford. When Jeff had asked what they were doing, Tim had said: 'Couple of clubs, that's all.' There had been a pause. 'All right?' He sounded as if he wasn't sure he should be asking permission or not.

They had so many boundaries to work out.

'Sure,' Jeff had said. 'Have fun.' He didn't believe the teenagers could possibly possess so much energy. It was all he could do to get to the top of the stairs without pausing for breath.

'I'm going now, Dr Baker.'

That was Lucy Duke. Jeff half turned on the top stair. She was standing in the hallway, buttoning her coat. 'Okay, then.' Jeff hadn't made up his mind about Ms Duke. He imagined it wouldn't be too difficult to dislike someone who tried so hard to be reasonable at all times.

'Have a good weekend, sir. I'll see you on Monday morning. There are several interviews scheduled, mostly foreign press.'

He resisted the impulse to say anything about Continentals being foreign. 'Goodnight.'

'Goodnight. It was an excellent party, by the way.'

The door to Sue's bedroom was open as Jeff walked down the landing. He saw her inside, and rapped lightly on the door frame. They'd had separate bedrooms right from the start, although they were adjacent. She was sitting at the dressing table, touching up her make-up. Her welcome smile turned to genuine concern. 'You look tired.'

'I am.'

'Make sure you get a good sleep tonight. There's nothing on tomorrow. You can rest properly.'

'Right. I met Patrick tonight.'

'Oh, I'm sorry. I didn't think it would matter with so many people about.'

'It doesn't, I suppose.'

'He's waiting for me downstairs now. I'll tell him. He won't come again.'

Jeff suddenly felt lonely. 'Where are you off to?'

'We booked a table at the Black Swan. The food there's lovely; they got a new chef just before Christmas. You'll have to try it.'

'Sure. When do you get back?'

'I don't know, Jeff.' She cocked her head to one side, regarding him carefully. 'Our arrangement hasn't changed, has it?'

'Right.' He turned to leave.

'Hey.' Sue's voice lightened. 'You should worry, now you've got that Nicole after you.'

'Nicole? Oh, James's granddaughter. What do you mean?'

'I saw the two of you together.'

'Yes, she was trying to convince me their company should review my finances.'

Sue arched an eyebrow. 'Is that what they call it these days?'

'What . . .?' A sudden flurry of very disconcerting emotions rustled through Jeff's head. Fright was prominent amid them.

'Come on, Jeff,' Sue said. 'She was all over you.'

'Don't be stupid. She's young enough . . .' He tailed off. Did that phrase actually apply to him now?

'I think you need a long night's sleep. You're going to have to start coming to terms with what you are sooner or later.'

'Jesus Christ!' He hadn't noticed, he really hadn't. Now, all Nicole's mannerisms, the playfulness came flooding back into his mind. She'd been flirting with him.

'Pleasant dreams,' Sue murmured as she left.

Jeff's own bedroom was at the end of the house, with a big veranda looking out over the rear lawns. The wide glass doors were shut, and the curtains closed against the night. His pyjamas were laid out on the big double bed ready for him. He barely got his shoes off before he flopped back on the duvet. Pulling the tie from his neck he said: 'Click.'

The three-metre screen on the wall opposite the bed lit up with the picture of HAL9000's lens in the middle – Jeff had thought that quite droll when he set it up originally.

'Domestic computer on-line.'

'What's on telly tonight?' he asked.

'Do you mean current entertainment feeds?'

'Er, yeah, I suppose so.'

'Do you want English, European, American, or other international?'

'English.' The lens vanished, replaced by a ten-by-fifteen grid of different video images. 'Oh, bloody hell,' Jeff muttered. He'd never kept up with cable shows before the treatment. Now the grid was full of crime soaps, comedy soaps, drama soaps, sci-fi soaps, cowboy soaps, historical soaps, game shows, quiz shows, RealTime life professions with cameras in police cars and fire engines as they raced to their call-outs, a dozen different news streams, and a whole load of sponsored sports. Basically, Saturday-night telly never changed, he mused: it had always been crap, and by the looks of things it always would be. At least when he was younger he could count on a semi-decent film being scheduled. It saved having to think. If he wanted one now, any one at all, he just had to describe it to the domestic computer's search engine. 'Okay, let's go for . . .' He squinted at the grid's title. '*Sunset Marina*.' The images looked less hectic than the others, and one of the actresses was quite young and pretty.

Sunset Marina expanded to fill the big screen. The image was all pastel colours because it was set in a gently lit bedroom. The young actress slipped her dress off, and said how sensual she felt in her new range of silk Pantherlux underwear. Her beau took his trousers down and asked if she liked his Pantherlux briefs. She said yes, but she preferred him out of them. The background music began to thump loudly as they moved together.

'Click! Cancel that.' The grid re-emerged, absorbing the soap. Jeff stared at the multitude of total crap on offer. 'Deary deary me, is this really all my fault? Okay, click, just give me . . . something classic, and easy. I know: *Four Weddings and a Funeral*.'

'What edition?'

'Standard.' It came out almost as a plea.

Jeff sank down into the pillows with a wan smile as Hugh Grant fumbled round for his alarm clock. Even this was crap, but it was reassuringly comfortable to watch.

So Nicole had been interested in him, had she?

11. HERE IS THE NEWS

Monday morning, nine-fifteen was the CNN interview. Lucy Duke spent most of a late breakfast briefing Jeff on technique: how not to smile too much so you don't come across as smug, not to use too many scientific terms, the right clothes to wear (she'd brought along a shirt, tie, and jacket – which caused an argument with Sue), the right humour and jokes to deflect the wrong questions, *verboten* topics. She offered guidance for subjects which were probably beneficial, things that people really wanted to hear. How only Europe had the political ability to pursue such a project. How the Prime Minister had personally supported rejuvenation and pushed for Jeff Baker to receive it against a list of other European worthies. How the booming European economy could easily support such massive projects without being an undue strain on the taxpayer.

'I'm not sure I can talk total bollocks for fifteen minutes solid,' Jeff muttered to Sue as they followed the spin doctor to the conservatory where the camera crew was setting up.

At eleven o'clock it was the *LA Central* news stream session, and at eleven forty-five they went into the garden for the *Nippon Netwide* team. In the afternoon he did the *Warner America, Chicago Mainstream, Washington Tonight,*

Seattle Hiline, and *Toronto National News* streams. *Texas Live* wanted a family interview, which Tim was finally coaxed into performing by Lucy Duke who by the end of the conversation was ready either to hit him or to burst into tears.

On Tuesday it was the turn of South America and several Pacific Rim nations. Wednesday was China and Africa. Jeff had been videoed alone chatting to the interviewer; him and Sue chatting to the interviewer, if the crew was very lucky they got Tim as well. He'd been videoed 'working' in his study; there had been everyday domestic scenes in the kitchen, walking round the garden (the Langleys loaned them Katie, their ridiculously soppy Great Dane, for a more cosy family image), kicking a ball about with Tim, and playing tennis with Sue – his coordination was dreadful. Questions had ranged from the standard 'How do you feel?' to 'What do you think of the situation in Nepal?' and 'Has pizza topping improved over the last seventy years?' to 'Do you approve of the death penalty?'

On Thursday it was back to the European media. By pure coincidence, Rob Lacey paid Jeff a visit on Thursday afternoon to see how he was progressing. The Prime Ministerial convoy of five huge limousines clogged up Empingham's main street, giving local kids a great opportunity to try and dodge the bodyguards to let down the tyres. When they left, they passed by a big home-made banner along the side of the road saying: FREE ENGLAND NOW! The windows on the Prime Minister's limousine darkened even further as it drove past the fluttering fabric.

That evening Jeff sat on the sofa in the main lounge and hopped through the news streams, each of which had advert banners running constantly across the screen. Right from his very first press interview thirty years ago, he'd always hated seeing himself on the telly, but tonight he forced himself. It was the interview with *Berlin Newswatch*, where he'd been sitting outside on one of the patio's oak chairs.

'What did you dream about in the suspension womb?' the interviewer asked. 'You did dream, didn't you?'

'Oh yes,' the Jeff on the patio said. 'Flying was the predominant dream; though it was more like accelerating through the night. It was almost a sense of uncertainty, as if I was racing along beside a clifftop. I knew it was there, but couldn't actually see it.'

'That's most interesting. Now that you're out, how much of your previous life can you remember?'

'Oh, for Christ's sake!' Jeff complained to Sue, who was curled up on the lounge's other sofa. 'My previous life! I've been rejuvenated, not reincarnated. What kind of stupid question is that?'

Up on the screen, Jeff laughed politely and started giving a sincere description of his childhood memories.

'Same as all the other stupid questions we've had this week,' she said. 'Every interviewer is desperately trying to ask something fresh. It's their job.'

'Shame they're so bad at it.'

'Yes, Jeff.'

'Oh . . . to hell with it.' He took a sip of his German beer. It had been good to find he could drink a respectable amount again without suffering a hangover and rushing to pee all night long. 'You know, I haven't done a single minute of real work.'

'I know. Lucy Duke scheduled that for next week.'

'That—' he glanced at the open door '—woman. Jesus, what planet do they import people like that from?'

'Don't know.'

'I could take a good guess,' he muttered sourly. 'Click. Give us the ITN stream, please.'

Berlin Newswatch vanished to be replaced by a picture of a ten-storey office block being consumed by flames. Fire engines were crammed together on the road outside, with hoses squirting powerful jets of foam into the third- and fourth-storey windows. 'The Italian Separatist movement claimed responsibility for the attack on the European Industrial Regulation Council building in Naples,' the announcer said. 'Europol say they received a coded warning five minutes before the detonation, which was not long enough to begin evacuation. The chief of the Europol Naples Bureau said it was a deliberate attempt to inflict maximum casualties. Over two hundred people were caught in the building when the bomb went off. Eighteen were trapped on the upper floors and lost their lives. Medical crews took another fifty-eight people to hospital with burns and smoke-inhalation injuries. President Jean Brèque condemned the attack as outrageous and cowardly, and said that the bombers would be brought to justice. Europol, he said, would be unstinting in their pursuit of terrorists.'

'Christ,' Jeff muttered. 'They should string them up by their balls.'

'Just remember not to say that when you're being interviewed,' Sue warned. 'The EU is officially opposed to the death penalty. It gives the Brussels Parliament another stick to beat the barbaric Americans with.'

'Surely they can make an exception for this?'

'You should have asked Rob Lacey this afternoon. He was keen enough to please you when he was here and the cameras were on.'

Jeff scowled at the devastation on the screen. 'Bastards.'

The next report was of a Customs and Excise raid in Cornwall where the officers had seized a huge load of cannabis which the excited reporter estimated at over eight million Euros. Smugglers had brought it in, avoiding VAT and duty.

'Who uses that any more?' Jeff asked, puzzled. 'I thought everyone dosed up on synth8 from desktop synthesizers.'

'There's still a big medical market,' Sue said. 'Quite a few oldies at mum's care home use spliffs for their arthritis. Even with eighty per cent duty and thirty per cent VAT, it's still a damn sight cheaper than standard painkillers. From a man in the pub, it's even cheaper.'

'Suppose so.' He looked at the big cloth bales being loaded onto a government lorry. The harbour side was swarming with the armed tactical-response team members, excitingly menacing in their black body armour. 'Tim goes clubbing. I remember that whole culture.'

'Don't go there, Jeff.'

'Yeah, right,' he muttered unhappily.

After Cornwall came the European Court of Human Rights where Rebecca Gillespie was suing both the EU Commission and the Catholic Church for violating a number of conventions and thus victimizing her. It was a case that had been going on for eight years, and was followed avidly by the media. Rebecca had been born a duofemale child, her parents both lesbians who had used the Monash treatment to conceive: the ova of one had been fertilized by the genetic material of the other, thanks to a little biochemical encouragement. The treatment, indeed the whole concept, was condemned by the Vatican as an unholy act; and as sperm-free fertilization came under the broad legal definition of human cloning, which the Brussels Parliament was one of the first to make illegal, Rebecca felt somewhat persecuted by both church and state. Her entire adult life had been devoted to fighting judgements that she considered denied her right to exist and which had been handed down on her even before her semi-legal conception in Australia. It was a struggle which had turned her into a minor media celebrity, and produced a great many supporters from across the political spectrum, all of them loud. And once again the Court had deferred judgement on yet another technicality.

Jeff and Sue watched the report in a vaguely embarrassed silence, carefully avoiding looking at each other. But then, Jeff reflected, that was always the way when you'd done something iniquitous a long time ago. Time always dulled the crime to a kind of *If we don't mention it, then it never happened* social gaffe.

Rebecca Gillespie was followed by a feature on the forthcoming NASA sample return mission to Mars. The robot probe was being assembled up at the ageing American space station. Normally Jeff would have watched eagerly as the intricate chunks of astronautic hardware were integrated on the station's satellite-assembly platform. But he couldn't focus on the astronauts in their bulky white suits as they jetted over the structure – his mind was busy with images of Tim scoring batches of dubious chemicals from some pusher in Stamford's clubs. He was only eighteen, for God's sake.

But I was doing it at that age.

Cannabis, though, not weird artificial molecules dreamed up in a university lab and misassembled by dodgy synthesizers. Anybody could handle cannabis. He sighed. *Okay, one or two tabs, as well.* And God alone knew where and how that was cooked up.

As a parent he was out of his depth again. Twice in a week. First girls, now drugs. *What the hell does everyone else do? How do they cope?*

The image on the screen switched from outer space to a small Spanish town, where most of the buildings seemed to have whitewashed walls and red clay-tile roofs. Police crime-scene barriers had cordoned off a long street section, with uniformed, armed Europol officers keeping a few semi-interested members of the public away. At the centre of the cordon, the stone pavement was stained with blood. Forensic team personnel in white overalls were crawling methodically along the road, waving small sensors around.

'There was another so-called Traitor's Pension attack on a retired Englishman on the Costa del Sol last night,' the announcer said. 'First reports from the local police indicate he used to work for the EU Agricultural Directorate. The EIC has already claimed responsibility for the act. This is the fifth in the last three weeks, all of which are believed to have been carried out by the same active EIC cell operating in the area.'

Knowing he didn't want the answer, Jeff asked: 'What's a Traitor's Pension?'

'They knock you down on the ground, then shoot you

up the arse,' Sue explained. 'It doesn't actually kill you, but it ruins your guts. Genoprotein therapy can't repair that kind of damage. The hospitals are getting quite used to the surgical procedure – they've had enough victims to practise on. But you still spend the rest of your life dosed up on painkillers and shitting through a plastic valve.'

'Fuck me.' For the first time, he was grateful for the presence of the Europol bodyguards.

'The EIC wanted to be different and worse than the IRA and their kneecapping,' Sue said. 'I guess they made it. Most of the Separatist paramilitaries use it now.'

The ITN report switched to shots of trim Costa villas almost hidden behind high walls and thick iron gates. Guard dogs barked and slavered, compact cameras were perched on the rooftops, scanning the grounds. 'Sales of security systems have gone up sharply in Marbella and the surrounding area over the last few years,' the announcer said. 'There are a large number of retired EU officials living along the Spanish coast, and all of them are now worried about their safety. A delegation recently protested to the local Europol office about the lack of progress on the case.'

'I remember when they used to call those holiday towns the Costa del Crime,' Jeff said. 'All the big East End villains used to skip out there after they'd held up a security van, or pulled off a heist. The government could never extradite them. I'd like to say this is ironic, but I don't think it's even that.'

ITN went to a studio report covering inflation, with the European Central Bank spokeswoman guaranteeing it was now firmly under control, and would fall below fifteen per cent before the end of summer.

'You're not worried, are you?' Sue asked. 'The EIC hasn't said anything about you. They only target people who worked for the EU.'

'Not worried, exactly, no. But I'm certainly aware it's a possibility. Perhaps I'd better have a word with Tim, tell him not to be quite such a pain to the protection teams.' That and a few other topics.

'Good luck.'

Jeff smiled ruefully. 'I don't think we've had a father to son chat before.'

'Hmm. Well, try not to be too shocked when he explains the facts of life to you.'

12. HARD DAY AT THE OFFICE

Lucy Duke finally called a halt to the media invasion at the end of the week. It meant Jeff could actually get down to some work, one area where the spin doctor didn't intrude. His study was the ground floor of a pentagonal turret-like annexe at the end of the Manor. Curving windows gave him a panoramic view out over the gardens and countryside beyond. His desk sat in the middle, a large and beautiful handmade oak affair with niches for various computer peripherals. He liked to imagine it as the kind of furniture one of the better Bond villains would sit behind as he plotted world domination. The actual neural-hypercube hardware itself was down in the small crypt below the study's parquet floor, along with a massive rack of memory crystals which wasn't even ten per cent full.

He started by requesting a download of all the EU superconductor project files and associated physics papers. Even with his ultra-wideband datasphere connection it took five hours. While that was running he structured some topic filters, in effect designing himself a crash course in modern superconductor theory. As the first sections began to align themselves within his grids he realized it would take months just to bring himself up to date on the general state of the field. Ah well, nobody was demanding instant results.

In the afternoon, he launched into a round of teleconferences, introducing himself to the project's senior team leaders and university administrators. It was almost like the media interviews again: they were far more interested in *Jeff Baker* than they were in any possible contributions he might make; the most they seemed to expect was his association helping with their budget allocation. He could hardly blame them: after all, three-quarters of them hadn't been born when he'd received his physics doctorate.

At five o'clock the computer told him there was an incoming call from Nicole Marchant. It took a moment for him to remember and place the name as James's granddaughter. 'Let it through,' he told the computer.

Two of the screens sank back into their desk niches, leaving the main display directly ahead of him, a tiny camera peeping at him from the top right corner. Nicole was wearing a smart grey business suit, her hair folded up efficiently; the office background was slightly out of focus.

'Hope you don't mind,' she said. 'I hadn't heard from you.'

'Not at all.' His traitor mind kept running Sue's comment. 'Sorry I didn't call. It's been a bit hectic around here.'

'I know, I can't watch a single news stream without you popping up. Incidentally, your tennis needs a lot of work.'

Jeff laughed. 'That wasn't my idea. We were supposed to be showing the viewers my happy home life. I barely know which end of the racquet to hold.'

'I could tell.' She pursed her lips. 'So have you given any thought to my proposition?'

'It sounded very sensible,' he said slowly.

'Would you like to take it further?'

'A proper review would be good.'

'Excellent. We should meet to discuss it fully. Are you free for lunch – say, next Wednesday?'

'Yes.'

'I'll see you at the Warf Inn at Wansford, twelve o'clock. Our company has a permanent account there – they treat us well.'

'I'm sure they do.'

'Until Wednesday, then.'

Jeff smiled cautiously as her image faded. The air in the study was suddenly warm for some reason. *I'm an adult*, he told himself. *There's no reason why I shouldn't be contemplating this kind of thing*. After all, Nicole was young, attractive and single. Wasn't she? 'Oh bugger.' He couldn't remember James mentioning if she had a husband, or partner. And he wasn't about to ask now.

The sound of laughter and shouting made him look up. Tim and his friends were gallivanting about outside again. It was a sunny afternoon, and they'd opened the wide glass doors around the pool building, spilling out onto the grass. Some kind of small strobing ball was being chased. Jeff smiled, glad of the distraction, and it was nice to see the Manor being used and enjoyed. He was almost envious of their youth and energy; it would have been nice to rush out there and join in. Then he laughed at himself. 'Idiot, you are young.' As Nicole plainly thought. That was when he noticed that half the youngsters on the lawn were girls. Annabelle was there, wearing a navy-blue bikini, skin glistening as she bounded about. Shrieking wildly as the ball tumbled towards her.

Jeff didn't want to think how long it had been since he'd had sex. Not that he could remember exactly. Appallingly, it might even have been over a decade. Some now-nameless woman at a science conference who'd been intrigued by who he was; even in his late sixties, notoriety could be alluring. The whole encounter had been pretty wretched. Then, after that . . . well, it was the classic case of diverting his energies into something else, being a good father to his wonderful Timmy.

Annabelle and one of the other girls struggled to grab the ball. Vital teenage bodies gleaming in the husky red-tinged afternoon sunlight as they wrestled together.

'Click! Opaque the windows, please.'

The electrochromic coating on the glass turned smoky brown, blocking the view. Jeff took a moment to himself in the dark, then began to call up the latest theories on organic crystal conductivity.

13. BOY'S-EYE VIEW

Tim wrapped a big towel round his shoulders and sat on one of the sunloungers at the side of the pool. Even though the pool doors had been flung open, it was too early in the year, and the sun too low in the sky, to be lazing around outside yet. Colin and Simon claimed the loungers next to him, leaving Philip and Martin splashing about in the water with the girls.

'She said yes,' Colin announced contentedly.

Tim cracked open a can of lemonade. He would have liked to make it a beer in front of the crew, but he had a lot of study work to do later. 'Who, Danielle?'

'Yep. I just about got the last tickets as well.'

'You always manage to just slide in under the wire,' Simon sniped.

'Well done,' Tim said. 'I heard Philip is taking Vanessa.'

All three of them glanced over to the figures in the pool as the flashing ball zipped between them. Vanessa was standing in the shallow end close to Danielle – the physical difference between the girls was blatant. Simon chortled quietly. If it bothered Colin, he didn't show it. He just kept his slightly smug smile in place.

'I got another avtxt from the Million Citizen Voices,'

Simon said. 'I'm definitely going to go. It'll be a big turnout. They say anyone who's ever wanted a referendum will be supporting, one way or another.'

'I'll be there,' Tim said. The Separatist sites had been highlighting the London summit for a couple of months now. Some big event planned by Brussels on how to best control the introduction of new technology into society. Technocrats denying a democratic debate. 'How about you?'

'I want to,' Colin said.

'Won't your mum let you go?' Simon sneered.

'It's not like that. We're going on holiday. I might not be here.'

'That's okay,' Tim said quickly. 'If you are about, you can come with us.'

'Thanks,' Colin said gratefully.

'So how did Saturday go for you?' Simon asked.

If there was a note of hauteur in his voice, Tim couldn't detect it, and he always listened for it with Simon.

'Bloody amazing, actually. Sex and drugs and rock and roll maxout the whole time.'

'Yeah?' Colin was keen for detail. 'What happened after you guys split?'

'I don't know how many clubs we hit,' Tim said. Saturday night had been essentially their first proper date. To mark it he wanted to do something different from the usual Stamford thing, so he and Annabelle had joined Colin and Danielle and taken the train over to Peterborough. They'd stayed together for a drink at a pub, then split up.

It had been a lot more than amazing for Tim; it was greater than any first date the universe had ever known before. For a start, Annabelle had looked staggeringly sexy, so much so that she was frightening. When she'd opened the door and he'd seen her for the first time that night, he'd almost reverted back to his wretched old self, intimidated and tongue-tied. It was simply impossible for him to have a girlfriend so magnificent. But there she was, dressed in the most in-your-face come-on clothes he'd ever seen.

After the pub they'd hit club after club, seeking out different music each time. It was like Annabelle was determined to sample every era that had ever produced its own sound; from Mersey Beat to acid thrash right up to post10 macromixing. Tim was sucking down intube doses all evening, a neat little synth8 that pushed his usual pathetic self out of sight. With the music ripping into his ears and the alien molecules singing in his blood he could dance properly. Out on the floor he was king of the beat, he had the moves, he had the energy, he took the rhythm and made it his own. They drank litres of water from bottles held high above their heads, laughing as it splashed over them. A tight perfect unit of movement in the middle of a hundred seething bodies.

It was four-thirty when they walked through the sodium glare of the straight civic-plan streets back to the station and caught the train to Uppingham. Arm in arm, leaning happily against each other the whole way. Every word he whispered to her was pure poetry. The looks she gave him in return were those of complete adoration.

That was the moment, with her head resting gently on his shoulder during the train ride home, when they both silently accepted that love had truly bloomed. The knowledge made Tim delirious with joy.

He walked her home, as any gentleman knight would

do for his lady. Uppingham's ancient winding streets were devoid of life in the grey non-light before dawn. And somehow they'd melted into the shadows behind an ancient oak tree. The kiss had gone on and on, while his hands slowly and sensually moved up her body to touch her breasts. Annabelle had snaked her own hands into his trousers, and Tim cried out in ecstasy. They were one. It was heaven.

'So did you get to shag her?' Simon asked.

'Even if I did,' Tim said, 'hell would have to freeze over before I told you.'

'You didn't,' Simon declared. 'Christ, Tim, you ought to have by now. It's been weeks since you started dating. I've only been going out with Rachel for a fortnight, and we spent all of Saturday night in bed together. Jesus, she's hot. I lost count of how many positions we tried.'

The boys turned to look at Rachel who was towelling herself off at the side of the pool. Tim held back his comment about the difference between girls and tarts. Simon and his bullshit bragging and his needle comments truly didn't bother him any more, not after Saturday. The world was too perfect for that now.

'No shit,' Colin said glumly.

For once Tim had the experience of pitying someone else when it came to girls. He was the winner now. At the centre of the inner circle looking out at the envious. It felt superb. 'I did spend the night at Annabelle's house,' he said modestly.

'Yes?' Simon tried not to show how eager he was for information.

'Nothing like that. My e-trike was parked there, and it was gone five o'clock in the morning when we got in. But get this.' He leaned in towards them. 'Her father was still up.'

'What?' Colin was disbelieving. 'You mean like waiting for his daughter to get home?'

'No. Nothing like that. He didn't even notice when we finally rolled up. He was watching the screen, some New Zealand drama soap or something.'

'At five o'clock in the morning!'

'Yeah! I'm not kidding. He was completely wasted.'

Simon dropped his voice, contributing to the prosecution case. 'He's been like that for years, Annabelle said. He was doing the freak routine when I was going out with her. Like he'd make toast and jam, then deep-fry it for lunch.'

'Deep-fry it?' Colin yelped.

'Yeah. Dead on.'

'With jam?'

'Yeah. He thinks it's like super-normal. I reckon he's got an old desktop synthesizer stashed in the house somewhere.'

'The guy's not had a job in years,' Tim said. 'Annabelle told me. He used to be some kind of forensic accountant, which is like the top of the profession. He was on the team investigating one of the Italian sea-solar plants they built outside Venice lagoon, and it all got political, with the Mafia involved and everything. Brussels crashed the report.'

'Unserious.'

'Dead on. He just spends the whole time in front of the screen now.'

'That's why Annabelle's the way she is,' Simon said wisely. He gave Tim a friendly smile.

Tim could relate to that, though the way Simon said it typically made it sound almost insulting. It was the simplicity of Newton's Law: for every reaction there is an equal and opposite reaction. Kids with seriously dippy parents were often the stable type, while kids from perfectly normal homes frequently went wild. Happened at school all the time. *I wonder where I fit into that?*

14. GIRL'S-EYE VIEW

Annabelle squeezed the last drops of water from her hair and started rubbing the damp strands vigorously with her towel. There was always an endless supply of towels in the Manor's changing rooms. It was one of those weird things about the place that she'd managed to get used to very quickly. Actually, the whole way in which the Bakers lived was easy to get used to. Little things like towels, and butter pats. Only the seriously rich had a housekeeper who would cut up their butter ready for them, and arrange it neatly on a silver dish. For every meal, including snacks.

'So spill it for Saturday, then,' Sophie said. She was standing at Annabelle's shoulder, her eyes alight with anticipation.

'Nothing much to tell.'

'Nothing happened – or nothing that you want us to know about?' Rachel shouted out challengingly. Danielle and Lorraine both started giggling. 'I know I wouldn't want too much of my Saturday evenings leaking out.'

'But we all know about them already,' Sophie said. 'You can't get Simon to shut up about what the two of you do with each other.'

Rachel just tossed her head and gave the rest of the

changing room a superior grin. Annabelle experienced a flash of sympathy for the girl. One of the main reasons she'd packed in Simon was his endless bragging to the other boys.

'So how about it?' Sophie persisted.

'It was okay. Okay? A night out in Peterborough, which has got to be better than Stamford or Melton.' Annabelle deliberately turned her back on Sophie and took her bikini halter off, holding the towel modestly across herself as she fished through her pile of clothes for her bra.

'Did you dance the night away?' Sophie enquired in a mock tease.

'Go shrivel. We just toured the clubs, then came home.' Which was short on detail, but encapsulated the evening. It was a shame, really; she'd been looking forward to it for the whole week they'd spent planning, sending each other a hundred avtxts. Then, when the night came around, it hadn't lived up to her expectations. Not that there was much in the world which did right now. All that happened was a trudge around a few clubs, trying to find a DJ who played some decent tracks. Tim had got himself seriously stoned, which she didn't much like. When he was that way he danced like someone was giving him electric shock treatment. He was too close and thudded into her the whole time. In turn, his condition made her dose up more than she normally would.

They'd stumbled home together. Given the state they'd been in, it was a small miracle that they'd actually managed to find the right train. She didn't really blame Tim. He was a nice boy. It was just that everything they did was routine, predictable. He was virtually indistinguishable from all his contemporaries. Which was why she'd gone

113

out with Simon in the first place; at the time he'd seemed more carefree and interesting. Then she'd met his older brother, and found the difference between genuinely cool and simple arrogance.

Annabelle's real problem was the way nothing ever *invigorated* her life. Going out with someone new always kindled the hope that their days would be filled with novel and original events, that she'd be excited and enthusiastic about every moment spent together. Tim didn't quite do that for her. Which was an unfair judgement, because not even Peterborough offered him much scope. The city's clubs were small, except for the Moon Gallery, which had grown up in an old department store; they all lacked glamour. Any gratification she'd experienced that evening was instant, unlasting. Unlike Tim, who'd clearly enjoyed every second, allowing the night to cling to him like an aura for the rest of the week. And school still hampered her – and her home, and both her parents. The only good thing about her age was the way she looked. There were times when she felt like a butterfly trapped by its dead pupa case, looking up at the sky and longing to fly.

Maybe she had transferred too much onto Tim, when really she was going to have to wait until autumn and university before she broke free from all the crappiness caging her life in. She didn't know why that should be. Everyone else in her year seemed to get so much more out of life. Tim was already infatuated, and so very easy to please. His rapture when she'd brought him off behind the oak tree as they stumbled back through Uppingham was her one clear memory of the journey home. What was it about boys that made them so easy? It seemed bloody unreasonable they could never do the same for her, in almost any respect.

'Sounds mediocre,' Sophie said. 'So are you going to dump him?'

Annabelle took her time adjusting her bra before turning to face her friend. The other girls were all waiting for an answer. 'No way. He is so much my boyfriend now.' Not that she was sure she wanted him – though it might turn out to be fun if he just learned to perk up a bit.

15. HIGH FINANCE

The check-up at Peterborough University hospital had gone well. Jeff was shown into the gene-therapy department, where a couple of Norwegian technicians took tiny samples of blood and tissue from him. He also did a few simple physical calibrations, jogging on a treadmill while his heart and lungs and muscles were monitored. The department had a real-time link to the Brussels university, where the rejuvenation team studied the results as they came through. He even spent a couple of mildly awkward minutes chatting with Dr Sperber over a teleconference link

Once he'd been given the all clear he drove his Merc EI8000 out of the city along the A47. Lieutenant Krober sat in the big car's passenger seat, quiet and respectful as always. The rest of the Europol team followed in their dark saloon.

'I wanted to thank you for easing off Tim at the weekend,' Jeff said. Tim had done a lot of pleading about his Saturday evening date, which had put plenty of pressure on Jeff. Negotiating with the Europol officers about clubbing in Peterborough actually made him feel as if he was doing a proper job as a father.

'It was good to avoid conflict with the boy,' Krober said.

'I don't think he saw any of the surveillance team,' Jeff said. 'At least, he never said so to me. And I'm sure he would.' As far as Tim was concerned, he'd been given the whole night off, free and clean from the bodyguards. The actual deal Jeff worked out was slightly different.

'They are most adept at discretion; it is what they are trained for. Neither your son nor Ms Goddard showed any awareness of our officers.'

Krober couldn't have been there himself, Jeff thought. The idea of the eternally formal, emotionless German trying to blend into some Peterborough low-life dive was ludicrous. A brief image of Arnold Schwarzenegger walking into Tech Noir played across Jeff's mind.

Though he hated the subterfuge, Jeff was quietly pleased about the arrangement. Judging by the way Tim had babbled away about the date after he'd got back on Sunday evening he'd had the time of his life. Yet with the Europol team there to watch over him he'd be perfectly safe the whole time. A perfect solution to the parents' eternal problem of how much slack to cut your kids.

So far Jeff had resisted asking Krober for details, like did Tim actually smoke joints, or were he and Annabelle sleeping together. Though he thought he knew the answer to that one, even though Tim swore he'd just stayed over at her house. It made him obscurely proud that his son had a girlfriend that attractive.

Jeff grinned as he turned off the A47 into Wansford. Now dad was hoping for the same kind of lecherous encounter his son was getting.

The cocktail bar in the Warf Inn possessed the kind of

aspirant grandeur which was the province of four-star hotels everywhere. Its hidden lighting was gold-tinged, deepening the hue of the sombre wood panelling. A waiter in a striped waistcoat and snazzy bow tie looked up and smiled from behind the small rosewood counter, then went back to adjusting the multitude of exotic foreign bottles lining the mirrored shelving. Thick, fluffy claret-red carpet absorbed the sound of every footfall as Jeff walked in. He had to wrinkle his nose up against a sneeze; the conditioned air was chilly and clinically lifeless.

Nicole Marchant was waiting for him, sitting by herself at a table in the corner. With her locked-down hairstyle and Chanel business suit, the bar was her perfect milieu.

'I wasn't entirely sure if you'd make it,' she said as he sat down opposite her.

'A no-show was not an option.'

Her gaze slipped over to Krober and two other Europol officers who shuffled round a table on the other side of the bar. The carpet managed to soak up even their noise.

'Are we going to have an audience?' she asked in an arch tone.

'They know this is a private meeting.'

'Our company keeps a suite on the first floor.'

'That sounds perfect.'

She stood up.

Jeff followed her out into the lobby. He was sure it had never been this easy before.

16. TWILIGHT HOUSE

Sue Baker was an only child, and had arrived late into her parents' lives. Her mother was over forty-five when the baby girl was born, her father a great deal older. As such she was loved intensely, spoiled rotten, and guarded with extreme protectiveness. While she was a child she considered such devotion to be wonderful, leading to her developing a personality that the family's politer friends called precocious. Only when she began moving through adolescence did problems with such attention really start to emerge. In any other girl her particular brand of self-centred egotism might have fired a standard teenage rebellion that eventually burned itself out, as is the way of such phases. Unfortunately for Sue, she was born beautiful. 'Standard' never got a look in.

She made her first catwalk appearance at the age of fourteen, to the head-shaking dismay of the *Data Mail* editorial (complete with hyperlinks to pictures of the event) which questioned on behalf of middle England the moral validity of such child-labour exploitation. Money poured in as her career skyrocketed. There were no restraints any more, no governors imposed on her behaviour. Sue was dated by Europe's aristocratic heirs and the sons of nouveau billionaires. Her life was parties, photo shoots, holidays, catwalks, parties, tabloid-fêted romances, global travel, public appearances, parties, her own calendar, weekends on yachts in Monaco harbour, and still more parties. Even her father's death when she was fifteen didn't deter her; if anything, she partied harder to forget the pain. It was a lifestyle that could never last. At best, beauty is fleeting, ephemeral.

Not that Sue had to worry about longevity. The day after her sixteenth birthday party her agency checked her into a private Swiss detox and rehab clinic. That was the first of four such sessions in the next three years, to the horror of her heartbroken mother. Gorgeous she might have been, but there were always prettier, younger girls hot for their shot at the top. For the fashion industry, Sue had stopped being news and was now just bad news. She didn't even have enough money left to cushion her fall. Taxes, managers, agency fees, and her head-on lifestyle with its dangerously large drug habit had consumed that. Her mother had to cash in one of her small pension funds to pay the clinic's final bill; which meant she could no longer afford to live in the cosy country cottage her husband had left her. The *Data Mail* wasn't even interested in paying for an article on a fallen wild child. At nineteen and a half she was washed up; her entire life had been lived and was now finished – she couldn't imagine what to do next. Then she met Jeff Baker, and three weeks later they were married.

Jeff paid for the Mulligan Residential Care Hall in Uppingham where her mother now lived, a private home with round-the-clock nursing and hotel-style facilities. It was part of the marriage arrangement.

Sue went to see her mother at least once a week. It was a level of devotion which she fully acknowledged grew out of the guilt she felt for her wayward teenage years. Nonetheless, she never let a visiting day slip.

Mulligan Hall was on the town's outskirts, its expansive grounds bordering the A47 bypass. It had been built as a hotel thirty years ago, situated so that its residents could benefit from splendid views across the rolling countryside. Since then the town had expanded, surrounding it with an estate of relatively low-cost housing; almost identical yellow-brick boxes with silvered thermoglass windows and shiny black solar-cell roof panels. The golf ball-sized spheres of police District Surveillance Scheme cameras peeped out from the eves, as ubiquitous as twentieth-century TV aerials, providing multiple coverage of the estate's streets. A high brick wall covered in GM thorn-ivy separated the Hall's grounds from those of its neighbours.

Sue's electric Mercedes DX606 coupé slid silently past the open gates. She parked in her usual spot in the shade of a big sycamore tree and walked into the lobby. The young receptionist looked up as she entered. 'I think your mother's in the garden room, Mrs Baker.'

'Thanks.'

'Um.' The girl was colouring. 'The director said to ask if you could see him when you're finished. If you have the time.'

'That's fine,' Sue assured her. It was an unusual request; she couldn't think what the director might want.

As a hotel Mulligan Hall hadn't lasted ten years; bankruptcy arrived in the wake of global fuel-price rises and the increasing dominance of the datasphere. Transport and its related industries were badly hit by the societal, political, and technological changes of the new century. Not that the Hall went unused for long: Europe's badly skewed demographics were giving rise to a vast demand for care facilities as the continent's population aged and the birth rate continued its gradual decline.

In England, care homes run by the local councils were put under greater and greater pressure as the number of residents continued to increase year after year. No matter how much money the government allocated, there was never enough to provide a full service, and carer-staff shortages had been acute for as long as Sue could remember. The European Commission was always issuing performance warnings to the English regional assemblies, reminding them of their statutory obligations – although England's standards were generally higher than other EU member states.

For private care homes things were a little different. Starting with the Thatcher administration, government had been keen to push pension finances into the private sector. As a result, the wealthier section of the population now had the funds to pay for their own care. In that too England was at odds with the rest of the Continent, a running sore ripe for exploitation by the English Separatists. The EU's pension-deficit payment had long ago taken over from the common agricultural policy as the largest budgetary black hole in the Brussels Central Treasury. It was the one financial drain that politicians could never tackle effectively – the overall 'grey' vote in Europe was now approaching fifty per cent. Any attempt to reduce their benefits was politically impossible. Separatist movements could be dismissed as insignificant or as simple terrorist minorities by the Commission, but even they feared the kind of wrath that the pensioners could inflict at the ballot box.

Mulligan Hall was strictly for those who could afford it, for which Sue was profoundly grateful. She couldn't stand the idea of her delicate mother in one of the council homes. Walking down the clean, well-decorated central corridor, she could almost believe the Hall was still a hotel. It was only the functions of the rooms which had altered: the cocktail bar was now a physiotherapy clinic, the snooker room had become a massage and reflexology centre, while the original indoor swimming pool had been greatly extended, providing all sorts of hydrotherapy. Upstairs, the entire third floor was given over to a specialist ward for genoprotein treatments. Best of all, it didn't smell like an old folks' home.

The garden room was a big semicircular lounge with tall glass walls and Victorian-style black and white marble floor tiles. Air-conditioning thrummed away with quiet efficiency, keeping the temperature pleasant despite the thick sunbeams pouring in from across the lawn. Ladies now too old to lunch sipped their afternoon tea as they sat around in the room's cane furniture. Sue's mother, Karen, was curled up in a broad winged chair which faced the lily pond outside. The tea tray on the glass-topped table beside her hadn't been touched.

Sue walked over to her, ignoring the stares and knowing nods from the other residents. She knelt down beside the chair, and touched her mother's arm. 'Hello, mummy.'

Karen's attention wavered from the small screen where she was watching Nicholas Parsons asking the questions on *Sale of the Century*. It was a GoldYear access, a company that rebroadcast seventies, eighties, and nineties programmes in the daily order they were originally shown, even including the day's news. It was a service mainly used by people over fifty to quench their nostalgia. Provider costs were met by a small amount of tweaking from modern image techniques; for ITV programmes the commercials were modified with computer inserts, changing the products the old ads were promoting to contemporary items; while, for the BBC, GoldYear simply used placement inserts.

'Susan, hello.' Karen gave her daughter a slightly puzzled look.

Sue picked the remote off the table and turned the volume down. The way genoprotein treatments had stabilized her looks in her mid-twenties seemed to be a constant source of confusion to the old woman now. Still, at least Karen had recognized her today. The last few years had seen a steady deterioration in her condition. The biomedical companies liked to claim that they'd defeated Alzheimer's Disease with their treatments and therapies. But Karen had contracted a variant which resisted the efforts of standard treatments.

'How are you feeling today, mummy?'

Karen patted at her bare arms. She was wearing a blue cotton flower-pattern dress without any sleeves. 'You know, I think I'm a little cold, dear.'

'Me too. It must be the air-conditioning they've got in here. Shall we go for a walk in the garden? It'll be warmer out there in the sunlight.'

'If you like, dear.' She took a last look at Nicholas Parsons and tried to raise herself out of the chair. Her thin arms trembled as she pushed her way up.

She's only a few years older than Jeff, Sue thought

bitterly. Karen's recent decline hadn't been purely mental; she'd lost a lot of weight, resulting in a turkey neck and long folds of flesh on her arms and legs. Her hair was now pure snow white. Even with the Hall's hairdresser washing and styling it once a week, its thinness could no longer be disguised.

Sue took her mother's arm, and escorted her out through the French windows and onto the brick path circling the garden. The fountain in the lily pond made a loud gurgling sound as the water foamed down the central statue of Venus.

'What a lovely summer it's been,' Karen said.

'Not quite over yet, mummy.'

'No, no, of course not. They do seem to stretch on so these days.'

'I know.' Sue stopped by a bed of luxuriant scarlet rose bushes, their flowers as wide as dinner plates. 'Don't these smell lovely?'

Karen bent over to sniff one. 'My sense of smell isn't what it was, you know, dear. I must be getting old.'

'No, mummy, you're not.'

They moved on.

'When are you going to bring that boy around to see me again?' Karen asked. 'What was his name now? Daniel, was it? I liked him. He has prospects. And you're not getting any younger, my girl, for all you're a pretty thing. You have to start thinking about these things now.'

Sue couldn't help the slight sigh that eased out through her lips. Daniel Roper had been a city executive who had taken her to Italy for a couple of weekends when she'd been seventeen – she couldn't even remember exactly what his job had been now. 'I haven't seen Daniel for a long time, mummy. I'm with Jeff now. You remember Jeff, don't you?' Sue hoped her mother hadn't seen any of the recent media reports on Jeff. God alone knew what kind of reaction that would kindle in her faltering mind. The Hall's domestic computer had been instructed not to allow her to access any current news streams featuring the Baker family.

Karen looked round blankly at the deep turquoise sky. 'Where's Timmy? I always like it when Timmy visits.'

'Tim's at school today, mummy. He couldn't come, but he sends his love.' For whatever reason, Tim never argued with her when she brought him to visit, which happened every six weeks or so. It was as though his grandmother was a sort of neutral territory where their usual domestic war was suspended for the duration. Not that he enjoyed going, Sue never deceived herself about that. But when he talked and listened to Karen he displayed positively human traits of decency and sympathy.

They reached a tall trellis that was swamped by honeysuckle. Karen ran her hand across the long red and gold trumpet flowers. 'Timmy at school? Why, he must be nearly five now. How time flies by.'

'Yes. Doesn't it just.'

Karen gave her a pleasant, expectant smile. 'Are we going home now, dear? It's late. I must get your father's supper ready. You know what he's like if there's nothing for him to eat when he gets home.'

'Just a little while longer,' Sue murmured. It took a lot of discipline not to screw her face up in despair. Over the years she'd surprised herself by how strong she could be when dealing with her mother.

Karen suddenly sucked on her lower lip as her body

made a quick lurch forward. It was as though she'd tripped. Sue gripped her tighter. 'Oh dear,' Karen said brokenly. She looked down at her feet.

Sue followed her gaze. A catheter bag was lying on the brick pavement between her legs.

'They're going to be so cross with me again,' Karen said. She began to wring her hands anxiously.

'Oh Jesus.' Staring at the bag with its leaking tube Sue fought hard to keep her poise. 'How long have you been using those?'

Karen smiled happily. 'Using what, dear?'

*

The director's office was on Mulligan Hall's second floor, looking out over the courtyard at the front. *So he doesn't have to see the residents shuffling round the lawns*, Sue thought grimly. She still hadn't quite recovered from the shock in the garden. A couple of staff had come running when she shouted for help. Her mother was crying softly as they led her back inside. Worst of all, one of the carers had said: 'It's best you don't come with us – it always takes a while to get her settled again after these episodes.'

Sue had stood numbly on the path, watching her utterly bewildered mother being urged inside. Then the director's PA had come out and walked with her up to the office.

Director Fletcher himself sat behind a wide metal desk devoid of any clutter. A single screen had rolled up out of a narrow recess, scrolling a plain-text file at which he kept glancing. To look at, he was in his mid-fifties, though with genoprotein treatments Sue could never quite place people's ages. That's if he was using them. He certainly wasn't taking anything to keep his weight under control, a

127

large man straining the fabric of his dark grey suit and embroidered waistcoat. He still used old-fashioned gold-rimmed glasses – presumably as a badge of authority. His faintly jovial air always put her in mind of some old university don.

'I do apologize once again for any distress the incident may have caused you, Mrs Baker,' Director Fletcher said as soon as his assistant had left.

'It's all right,' she said wearily. 'I suppose I should have expected something like this. I still should have been told, though.'

'The lapse is entirely ours. I have been delaying this meeting for several weeks until your husband was, uh, out. This must be a very stressful time for you.'

'It's been interesting,' Sue said.

'Then I'm afraid I must add to that interest. After consulting with our doctors, I have no alternative but to tell you that regrettably your mother's condition is no longer one which Mulligan Hall can support.'

'What do you mean?'

'We are primarily a residential care home for people who need a modest degree of assistance to maintain a reasonable quality of life. Unfortunately, your mother no longer falls into that category.'

'This place is the best care facility available, that's what you always tell me.'

'For people who remain cognizant, yes. But, as we know, your mother's condition is an unusual one. Our resident doctors have performed a really remarkable job in keeping her deterioration at bay for so long. We have to accept the simple fact, Mrs Baker, that the human body decays no matter what we do.'

'Except for Jeff,' Sue whispered.

'Quite,' the director said. 'As you say, the normal process of decay underwent a phenomenal reversal in your husband's case. However, until that particular treatment is available to the rest of us, we are subject to an entropy which can only be slowed for a while by today's genoprotein treatments. And in the case of your mother, those treatments have reached their limit.'

'What about new ones, different ones? There are thousands of genoproteins available. Money isn't a problem.'

'Mrs Baker, we have complete access to the latest therapies. On occasion we even help some biomedical companies with clinical trials. But even if such things were appropriate in this case, there is nothing more we can do for your mother here. I have to say very clearly to you that the overall prognosis is not good.'

'What, then?' she snapped. 'What is this bloody prognosis of yours? Is she going to die, is that it? Is that what you're saying?' She hated how angry and desperate she sounded, as if confronting him would make all this not so. It made her seem pathetic.

'People suffering from Alzheimer's can live for a considerable time. Providing they have the correct care. Mulligan Hall simply does not have those kinds of facilities. I'm sorry.'

'You're kicking her out? Just like that?'

'Not at all. But you will have to make alternative arrangements over the next few weeks. Your mother is getting to the stage where she requires constant nursing supervision. We're just not set up for a service that intense.'

'Well, where is?'

'I can provide a list of medical centres that we recommend. Several of them are local – one is even run by our parent company. I took the liberty of checking; there are a few places available.'

'Oh God.' Sue put her head in her hands. *I will not cry.* 'How much is all this going to cost?'

'The financial requirement involved is inevitably somewhat higher than the level you're accustomed to here at the Hall. Is that a problem?' he sounded mildly surprised.

'Let me talk this over with my husband. We'll be in touch in a few days.'

'Of course.'

And what the hell was Jeff going to say about this?

17. LINE 'EM UP

It had been years since Jeff had ventured into a pub. A long time ago, before he lived in Empingham, his local had kept his own pewter tankard behind the bar for him. Those were the days when he enthused about real ale and had regular sessions with his friends and colleagues of a Friday night. Twenty years ago now. Probably even longer, if he was honest.

He'd arranged to meet Alan and James in Stamford for a boys' night out, starting off at the Vaults on Broad Street. The whole event was a straight fix of nostalgia, although he wasn't sure for whose benefit. A couple of his Europol team went into the Vaults first for a quick check round, and gave him the okay. When he walked in, James and Alan were waiting with expressions of mild derision.

'Your babysitting squad has approved, then, have they?' James grunted.

'Please,' Jeff said. 'If I get shot, it's your tax money that's wasted. What are you drinking?'

James looked at his pint pot on the table. It was still three-quarters full. 'Bateman's, please.'

'Same here,' Alan said.

Jeff went up to the bar to collect the order. Several

people around the lounge were staring at him. There was an outbreak of heated whispering across the room. The barmaid was very attentive, a blonde girl who couldn't have been twenty. When she smiled at him he tried to avoid looking at the spots on her cheeks.

James had almost finished his first pint by the time Jeff got back to the table. 'Cheers.'

'Cheers.'

'What are you drinking?' Alan asked.

'Lager shandy,' Jeff confessed. 'I've still got to be a bit careful, health-wise.' A polite lie. He simply didn't want to end up like . . . well, James, basically. He'd been down that road once before, thank you very much. Just one last pint and a stop at the all-night burger bar: week after week, year after year. When you were young it didn't matter, your body could handle it. Cumulative effects were so small as to be unnoticeable. It was only in later life that you regretted and cursed all those binges and excesses. This time around he was determined to be more careful, to take care of himself. Nicole had certainly complimented him on the shape he was in. It made him realize he was more frightened by ageing now than ever he had been before.

'I hear you might be coming on board with us,' James said.

'On board?'

'Nicole gave me a full report of what happened.'

Superb self-control prevented Jeff from choking on his beer. 'Oh, that.'

Alan laughed and nudged James. 'See how a young girl can turn his head? He never signed on when you were running the company.'

Jeff gave them a weak smile. There was absolutely no way he was going to be able to tell James about this. It didn't matter that Nicole had made all the moves; sleeping with a friend's granddaughter had got to be pretty close to the top of all time Bad Things. 'She made a good case for you to overhaul my finances. They need looking at properly.' He'd even fixed up a repeat meeting at the hotel for next week.

'Certainly bloody do,' James grunted. 'Brussels keeps changing the rules. Bastards. You've got to stay five steps ahead of them or they'll scoop up your entire salary. We've heard they're going to increase Social Insurance to eighteen per cent of overall income in a couple of years' time. That's on top of income tax. And you've got to be top rated on that, Jeff.'

'It's a pretty frightening figure, yeah.'

'Two years,' Alan mused. 'That puts it conveniently after the Presidential elections.'

'Doesn't matter, nobody votes for the President anyway. Last time it was barely a forty per cent turnout, and most of them were from Luxembourg.'

'None of the candidates would ever mention higher tax anyway, not even if they go negative,' James said. 'That way they all benefit from deniability. Just like Area 56 in *Independence Day*.'

'That was culpable deniability. Randy Quaid told the President about it.'

'Yeah, Quaid was playing Jeff Goldblum's dad.'

'Second time Goldblum was in an alien-invasion film.'

'Remake of *Invasion of the Body Snatchers*,' Alan said promptly. 'Late seventies, with Donald Sutherland and Leonard Nimoy.'

'Tons better than the third version with Gabrielle Anwar.'

'Meg Tilly was in that, wasn't she?'

'No, Jennifer Tilly.'

'Are you sure?'

'Well, *one* of the Tilly sisters was.'

'Got to be an improvement on *Bride of Chucky*, whichever one of them did that.'

'Oh, that was definitely Jennifer.'

Three girls walked in. Jeff doubted if the eldest was more than sixteen. All of them wore incredibly low tops and short skirts. They clustered round the bar, chattering away like a flock of sparrows.

'Jesus,' James muttered. 'Where the hell were they when I was that age?'

'Their parents didn't exist when you were that age,' Alan told him.

The girls all ordered vodka mixers. Jeff couldn't remember what the legal pub age was these days. Was Europe currently being as liberal about booze as it was about drugs (except for that politically incorrect demon, tobacco, of course)?

James stood up and drained the last of his pint. 'My round. Hurry up, chaps.'

'Same again,' Alan said.

'I'll just have a half,' Jeff said.

James gave him a disgruntled look and went off to the bar.

'This'll be my last,' Alan said. 'I can't knock it back like I used to. It doesn't matter how many genoproteins are buzzing round inside me, I'm not as young as I was.'

'Whatever you're comfortable with,' Jeff said.

Alan leaned in across the table. 'I still can't believe that it's really you, that this whole ridiculous procedure worked. I feel like I want to rip it out of you and use it on myself. If it was just a single pill or gadget, then I would. Jesus, Jeff, do you realize what you are?'

'I'm beginning to, I think.'

'Fucking lucky, that's what. The luckiest man that ever walked across the face of the planet. You're young again. You've got your whole life again. Life is always wasted on young people, they don't know what it's about. But not you – you already know. You know what to do to make it count, every bloody minute of it. And you've got Sue to go home to each night as well. Tell me that isn't bloody lucky.'

'Hey, come on, Alan. You're good for another thirty years, and that's just with today's treatments. By the time you're a hundred they'll be giving you that single pill for rejuvenation.'

Alan contemplated the last of his beer. 'Oh bollocks, Jeff. I've got the worst time of my life ahead of me, and our wonderful medical industry will stretch it out and out until I just scream for it to end.'

Jeff wanted to look round to see where the hell James had got to. He needed help here. 'That's crap. Look at me, Alan: I am real. It happened to me, it can happen to you.'

'I'll be dead or demented by the time they start dishing it out to the masses. Oh fuck, Jeff, how did we ever come to this?'

'You haven't come to anything, Alan. You're as active now as you were thirty years ago.'

Alan snorted, his jaw muscles working hard to stop his real anguish from emerging. 'Not active where I want to be. Christ, not for years.'

Jeff muttered *Oh shit* under his breath. Where was James?

'Collecting to support our country's patriots, gentlemen.'

Jeff looked round. There were three men standing beside the table. They were in their late twenties, with close-cropped hair. Jeff could remember the National Front from the first half of his life, their ranks always made up from physically intimidating lads. Somehow they always managed the trick of looking as if violence could explode at any second. These three were almost the same, except one of them was Asian – and Jeff really didn't think the National Front had modified its stance on membership, not even in forty years. Other than that, they were standard beefy lads who obviously took a lot of pride in keeping themselves fit. Gold and scarlet dragon tattoos spiralled round their wrists, the red segments glowing faintly. More tattoos were just visible peeping above their collars. Knuckles and hands were scarred, trophies of a dozen street fights. Each of them wore a Union Jack badge with *Free England* printed across the middle. Seeing that, Jeff finally understood who they were.

'Hope you can contribute,' the one in front said. It wasn't a question. He held out a pouch with several cash cards already in the bottom.

From the corner of his eye, Jeff saw the Europol team rising from their seats. He made a tiny *Be calm* gesture with his hand.

'I'd be happy to,' Jeff said. He fished round in his

pocket for his cash cards, and found one loaded with fifty Euros.

'Jeff!' Alan hissed.

'How's that?' Jeff dropped it into the collection pouch.

The man holding it gave him a careful look. 'Do I know you?'

'Doubt it,' Jeff said. 'I haven't been in this pub for thirty years.'

There was a long moment while the man tried to figure out if Jeff was taking the piss or if he was just drunk.

'Here you go.' Alan dropped another cash card in the pouch.

The man's concentration wavered, moving away from Jeff. 'Thanks, old man. Together we'll bring your country back to how it used to be, don't you worry.' The three of them moved on to the next table where the young girls were sitting giggling.

Jeff breathed out silently, his gaze locked on Alan's. 'Bloody hell.'

James returned to the table. 'Three pints. Jeff, I decided you've got to drink more. What's the matter with you two? You look like—'

Jeff stood up. 'We're leaving.'

'What? I haven't touched this yet.'

'Come on.' He was giving none-too-subtle twists of his head to indicate the three collectors. 'Now. We're eating early tonight.'

James finally glanced at the collection team. 'Oh, right. I've already donated.' He raised his hand and waved at the team. 'Night, boys.'

'Night, James,' the Asian one said. 'You take care of yourself, hear? It's a bad world out there.'

Alan and Jeff exchanged another look. 'Definitely time to leave,' Alan said.

*

As they walked down Broad Street, Jeff slowly became aware of what they looked like together. Alan in his dark green conservative suit with its trousers shiny from too many cleanings and pressings. James, wheezing along in an expensive yellow and green cashmere cardigan with leather buttons. And himself, dressed in loose ochre trousers and black Adol shirt, complemented by a smart leather jacket, all of it chosen by Sue and actually quite stylish, he admitted to himself. Anyone would think he was taking a couple of old uncles out to their twenty-ten reunion club.

People were looking at them that way, too. Youngsters walking about as their own evening kicked off. Boys strutting their stuff in smart clothes, girls huddled together, tottering along on ridiculously tall heels. As they saw Jeff and his friends they dismissed them instantly. Jeff was surprised how much that brush-off hurt. Especially as the youngsters all seemed to be having a good time. Broad Street was full of laughter and giggles, welcoming shouts between groups, music and sharp coloured light spilling out of pubs and club doorways. It was a scene which exerted a strange kind of attraction on Jeff. Everyone was happy, out for a hot night of fun. And they all believed he was not, could not be a part of that. An invisible barrier of exclusion protected the three of them as they walked along in search of the Chinese restaurant where James had booked them a table.

Jeff suddenly wanted to say: 'Come on, lads, let's go hit some of the clubs instead.' And then the three of them would scoot in past the bouncers and party on down until exhaustion and alcohol wiped them out as dawn was rising. Maybe there'd be a few tokes of the wacky baccy as well. It would be *living*, it would be *experiencing*, engaging every sense and emotion a body possessed.

But if he did say it, they wouldn't come and he'd be on his own. So he plodded along dutifully with his old friends and felt obliged to point out that as well as featuring in *The Adventures of Buckaroo Banzai Across the 8th Dimension*, Jeff Goldblum had also starred in *Earth Girls Are Easy*, which was technically an alien-invasion film, so that made it four altogether.

18. LATE HONEYMOON

Jeff got home from the Chinese restaurant just before ten o'clock. The meal had gone pretty much as he'd predicted, and to cap it off the food hadn't been much good.

He hadn't expected Sue to be home, not so early, but her Merc was already in the garage when he parked. She was sitting on the big settee in the lounge, wrapped in an emerald towelling robe, drinking a brandy and eating a bumper box of Thornton's chocolates. *Casablanca* was playing on the big wallscreen, black and white images casting a cool spectral hue across the room.

'You're back early,' he said.

Sue produced an insincere smile. 'Yeah. Didn't much feel like a night out.'

'I know what you mean. I could have done without tonight myself.'

'How are James and Alan?'

Jeff sighed and flopped down onto the settee beside her. 'Oh God, Alan was crying into his beer most of the time. And James was just being James; ranting about Brussels, and taxes, and money and then more money. I've heard it all a million times before.' He wondered what had happened with her and Patrick. A quarrel? It would have had to be something pretty drastic to make Sue binge on chocolate. She was normally inhumanly strict about her diet.

'James has always been just James,' she said. 'I thought that's why you were such good friends with him.'

'Yeah, well, maybe my perspective has shifted a little lately.'

'Hardly surprising.'

'Oh?' He leaned over and plucked a hazelnut swirl from the box.

'You don't have anything in common any more, do you? They're pensioners in every respect. You're a twenty-year-old in every respect but one.'

'Which one?'

'Experience. Apart from that, you've got your whole life to look forward to, that makes you eager and optimistic. That's the opposite of them: they have nothing to look forward to – they hate the way the world is and the way it treats them. You relish change and challenge.'

'I would have thought all that experience makes me cautious, especially about change.'

Sue grinned. 'It means you can avoid the mistakes which Tim and his friends are about to spent the next fifteen years making. You'll enjoy yourself a hell of a lot more this time around.'

'Maybe so.' He munched happily on the chocolate as he looked at her. That small smile, the way one side of her mouth lifted slightly higher than the other, was fascinating. Sue had always been beautiful, staggeringly so when he'd first met her. But it was a notion which had never quite connected for him. It was beauty as abstract: he admired her as he might admire a statue or a painting. For nearly nineteen years he'd held that view. Now, though, sitting beside her on the settee, there were other factors coming into play. How close she was. The musky smell of some perfume or lotion applied to her skin. The way the towelling robe was slightly loose down the front, showing just a hint of her breasts. Legs, long and smooth, curled up comfortably like those of some jungle cat ready to pounce. And that smile . . .

Jeff realized with some surprise he was actually quite turned on by his own wife.

'Definitely so,' Sue said. 'It couldn't be any other way.'

Jeff looked away, partly to cover his slight embarrassment. Then he saw what was playing on the screen. 'Oh my God, that's Ronald Reagan.'

'Who?'

'Ronald Reagan – he's playing Rick.'

Sue frowned at the black and white images. 'So?'

'Humphrey Bogart is Rick. What kind of version are you accessing, a satire?'

'I don't know. The datasphere had quite a few editions listed. I think I chose the as-it-should-be version.'

He laughed. 'Of course – supposedly Reagan auditioned for the part. That find-and-replace morphing technique is very good. I wonder what program they used . . .' He caught himself and grimaced. 'Sorry, I've been talking this kind of complete crap all night. So what did happen to you this evening?'

Sue lowered her head, allowing her thick hair to fall forward and cover her face. 'I went to see mummy this afternoon.'

'Ah. Right. How is she?'

'Not very good.' Her voice had dropped to a whisper.

'Oh, hey.' His arm went out automatically, reaching for her. He stopped with his fingertips a few centimetres away from her arm. After a moment's hesitation he gave her a supportive little squeeze.

Sue looked up, moist eyes regarding him with mild surprise.

'She's a tough old thing,' he said. 'She'll pull through.'

'No, Jeff, she won't. She's getting a lot worse.'

'I'm sorry.' He pulled himself along the settee and put his arm around her shoulder. She was shaking.

'I guess I don't make it any easier for you,' he said. 'Not with me being like this.'

'No. I'm pleased they chose you, of course I am.' Tears started to fall down her cheeks. She smeared them with her knuckles, then gave her hands an angry look, as if they'd betrayed her.

'Is it going to be . . . soon?' Jeff asked.

'No. But . . .'

'What?' he urged gently.

'They can't look after her at the Hall, not any more. She needs a proper nursing home: twenty-four-hour staff, specialist doctors, physical therapists.'

'Well, are there any with places around here?'

'Some, yes.'

'Then no problem. We'll put her into one.'

Sue blinked away her tears, giving him a curious look. 'Do you mean that?'

'Of course I do.'

'Jeff, it'll cost a lot of money.'

'So? We had a deal, remember?'

'I know. But I thought . . . Tim's already eighteen. Not that I ever really lived up to my side of the bargain when

143

it came to being a good mother. And he'll be off to university in a few months anyway. That's it then, isn't it? The end.'

Jeff tightened his hold around her shoulders. 'I thought you were a pretty good mother, actually. It has never been so hard to bring kids up as it is in today's world; there are so many pitfalls waiting for them, so many dark attractions. Yet he's come out of it a good kid. He's no Stepford Child, thank God, but he isn't in jail, or rehab, or therapy, he doesn't hate us too much, and he's worked hard enough at school to make Oxford or Cambridge a near-certainty. I couldn't wish for more. I'm damn proud of him. And you have to take a lot of the credit for that.'

Sue's small smile had returned. 'I never did deserve you, did I?'

'I always thought of it as being the other way round.'

They kissed.

'That was never part of the arrangement,' Sue murmured huskily. Her nose nuzzled his cheek.

Jeff smiled down at her. 'Time to negotiate a new one.'

19. CROWDED BREAKFAST

Tim made it downstairs by nine o'clock on Sunday morning. It hadn't been a particularly late night. They'd all been round at Martin's house, drinking and sending out for pizza. Tim and Annabelle had snuggled up together on the big couch all evening. He had been kind of quietly confident that the two of them would make it to a bedroom at some point during the night. But it hadn't happened. Annabelle went back to Uppingham, taking a bus with Sophie and Vanessa. He'd asked her to come back to the Manor with him. She'd said no, and had kissed him hard to make up for the disappointment. He'd even asked her if she'd like him to escort her back to her house. She'd said no, thanks, and kissed him again.

When they were standing outside the front door, in the dark and out of sight from their friends and the Europol team, he made a last appeal for a quick trip back inside and up to Martin's spare room. Her giggles were loud and playful in his ear, but it was still a 'no' despite the fantastically intimate way she was pressed up against him.

His mood wasn't helped when Simon and Rachel strolled off down the drive together, leaning together and French kissing as they went.

In the morning Tim had a quick shower, and put on a clean sweatshirt before taking the stairs two at a time. When he thought back, last night hadn't been so discouraging after all. He and Annabelle were making a kind of progress towards having full sex. Even that would have been unthinkable two months ago. He heard the voices coming from the kitchen, and barged straight in.

His mother and father were sitting at the long table in the middle of the room. Both of them in towelling robes. There was tea and toast on the table, along with jars of marmalade and honey and jam. The wallscreen was silently playing a news stream.

'Morning,' Tim grunted. He sat down opposite them at the table, and reached for the jug of orange juice.

'Morning, Tim,' his father said.

Tim saw his father's hand move out of his mother's lap where he'd been squeezing her leg. And his voice sounded cheerful. And they were both smiling, leaning close to each other. Two contented people.

Very slowly, Tim's eyes tracked back up to his father's face. A handsome young face, reasonably similar to his own. A young face on a young body. And then there was his mother, gorgeous as always, even with her hair uncombed – which it never was at breakfast. Could they have ... Last night, did they ... Had they actually been ...

'Careful, Tim,' his mother called.

His glass was full, and orange juice was leaking over the rim to flood down his hand. 'Bugger! Sorry.' He stopped pouring, and looked round for a cloth. His face was bright red. He knew that for certain – his skin was surely hot enough to blister.

'Here.' His father pulled a dishcloth off the Aga rail and handed it over.

Tim began dabbing away. 'Thanks.' He concentrated hard on the task. There was *no way* he could glance up. If he did that he'd have to look at their faces. And if they really had . . . *No!*

'So what's the plan for today?' his father asked.

'I've, er, got some, um, friends coming round later.' Tim stood up and dumped the dripping cloth in the washing basket. 'We're moving some stuff.' He sat down again and found the toast.

'Some stuff?'

'Yeah.' At the edge of his vision he could see his father and mother exchange a glance and grin at each other. *God, this is so much embarrassing.*

'What sort of stuff?'

'Er, your old jet ski, actually. We've fixed it up, and we were going to test it round at Simon's. Is that okay?'

'Fine by me.'

Tim slapped some butter on a slice of toast and gulped down his orange juice. 'I should go and get ready. They'll be here soon.' With the toast in his hand he fled out of the kitchen. When he was halfway up the stairs, he was sure he could hear laughter behind him.

20. AWAYDAY

Jeff drove down to London. The Europol team hadn't liked that, nor Lucy Duke; they all wanted him to take the train. But he allowed Lieutenant Krober to come in the car with him while Lucy and the rest of the team followed in their own vehicle.

He didn't do it to be obstinate, he just remembered how much he used to enjoy driving before the nineties when everyone suddenly had three cars and drove like characters out of Wacky Races. Now it was like the early seventies again, except the roads had been in much better condition back then. But with strategic (i.e. punitive) Green fuel taxes and the huge Brussels-funded investment in public transport over the last twenty years, people had reluctantly moved back to the trains and buses. It left long stretches of the A1M motorway where he couldn't see any other vehicles at all. When another car did come into view it was normally a big luxury model like his own; quietly obeying the speed limit. Cameras loaded with profile-capture and number-plate-reading software were perched every kilometre along the road like metallic black vultures, checking his average speed between them, ready to issue an instant fine and an endorsement if he ever went above a hundred and ten kilometres per hour. There were no police patrol cars any more: they belonged exclusively to the past – and to early Burt Reynolds movies.

Despite innumerable restrictions and exorbitant licence costs, lorries were still fairly common; big sixty-tonne juggernauts powered by liquid gas, making the car tremble as they thundered by. Every few kilometres Jeff would pass the burned-out chassis of similar lorries, all of the models dating back about ten years. Fires must have burned fiercely at the time, consuming the surrounding bushes and trees to create little dead zones. These patches of scorched earth had now been reclaimed by keck weed and giant thistles, whose leaves were sallow and misshapen thanks to the bad chemicals which fire-fighting crews had left polluting the soil. With their long rusting metal hulks netted by vines, and every viable component, including the tyres, stripped off, the ruined lorries looked like the aban-doned relics of some mighty Soviet-era transport project.

Jeff avoided making any comment to Krober as he drove past the frequent wrecks. They were all foreign haulers, careless enough to be spotted by their English counterparts or local Separatists. Nobody from the Conti-nent drove through England now. Freight containers were all unloaded at ports and the Eurostar train stations, allowing the final delivery stage to be undertaken by English firms. Or at least English-registered firms.

As soon as he crossed inside the M25 orbital, the car's route computer told him he'd been charged a fifty-Euro fee for a London CityDrive day licence. The traffic picked up when he took the A41 into the West End, with smaller cars and vans closing round him, along with innumerable buses and the city's ubiquitous black taxis. Jeff's route computer kept issuing directions, though he liked to think he could still remember his way through the maze of streets. E-trikes and bicycles tooted angrily at anything with the audacity to be on the same road. Inside the North Circular Road the CityDrive licence fee went up to seventy-five Euros. By the time he got around Hyde Park and arrived at the Knightsbridge flat he was paying a hundred and fifty.

Sue hadn't changed the flat, at least not in the same way that she'd set about the Manor with decorators and interior designers. Half of the furniture was new, and he was sure the kitchen fittings were different. But at least the rooms remained the same shape. He'd bought the entire top floor of a typical five-storey Regency-style town residence that had seen so much refurbishment and development the only original feature remaining was the white façade.

Lucy Duke could barely conceal her jealousy as she looked round the rooms with their high ceilings. When she stepped out onto the tiny roof terrace, the tops of the trees in Hyde Park were just visible.

'This is fabulous,' she said. 'It must be worth a fortune if you sold it now.'

Jeff was peering over the railing at the street below. The traffic was very light, mostly taxis. Their basic design hadn't changed from the last century, although the body-work was now a lightweight carbon-titanium composite and they were all powered by sealed-circuit regenerator modules. The latest ones all had a retro nineteen-thirties look, with chrome spoke wheels and little extendable yellow 'For Hire' signs that flipped out behind the drivers' doors. He thought they looked rather appealing, although the modern holographic adverts on their panelling tended to spoil the effect. 'Thank you,' he said. 'But I didn't buy it to make money. I just wanted somewhere to stay when I'm in town. I've had a lot of bad experiences with hotels over the years. Even if you ever manage to find a good one, they always seem to change management every six months and you're back to square one.'

'I see.'

He masked a smile. The notion must have matched her sense of efficiency.

Back inside he checked to see if the housekeeping service had stocked the big fridge. They'd certainly kept the place clean and tidy. There was fresh linen on the bed, even some yellow roses in the lounge. 'I can provide breakfast for everybody for the next fortnight,' he called out. 'Are you staying here?'

'No,' she said. 'My flat's over in Battersea. It's not far. I'll go home tonight.'

There were three bottles of champagne in the fridge. Jeff pulled one out and read the label. Krug. 'Fine.' He hoped it was Sue's boyfriends who were paying for this stuff rather than his household account.

The surprise of that thought made him frown. *Who gives a fuck, actually?* Everything had changed now between him and Sue, totally for the better. They'd spent the last three days together, and it had been pretty damn good. They knew each other so well there was none of the awkwardness which had cast a shadow over his encounter with Nicole. Sue was also hot, bad, and exciting in bed. So good, in fact, that he'd actually cancelled his next financial review with Nicole.

'If we could review your schedule,' Lucy said.

Jeff put the Krug back on the rack and closed the fridge. 'Sure.'

Lucy had spread her flexscreen over the coffee table in the lounge. Dark blue script was flowing across it as she talked to the management program. Jeff sat on the settee and clasped his hands behind his head as she checked her watch.

'We have three interviews this afternoon, all of them audio,' she said.

'Ah, radio. That makes a change.'

She looked up, slightly flustered. 'Um, yes, I think the companies have direct satellite broadcast capability as well.'

'Of course.'

'These are intended as profile pieces. There will be minimum focus on the superconductor research. If you do say anything on that, try and keep it at pop-science level. The target demographic today is fourteen to twenty-five. They'll only be interested in what it's like coming back to their age again. What soaps you like, a little bit of current affairs, that kind of thing. Oh, and just be careful with Mike Bashley, that's the second interview, he enjoys trying to put one over on his guests. He can be very charming, then he'll slip in questions about which soap starlet you fancy and where you stand on legalizing desktop production of synth8.'

'I'll watch out for it.'

'Good. I've got a car booked to take you round the studios – we're doing it live and physical. That makes everybody concerned think it's an important event.'

'Everybody all of the time,' he muttered.

The script flowed quickly across the spin doctor's flexscreen as she told it to move on. 'We'll be back here for half-past four. That gives you ninety minutes to get ready for tonight. The car will pick you up at six. Even if the traffic's slow, we should be at the Weston Castle hotel by quarter-past.'

'Jolly good.'

'I've got your new dinner jacket.' She pointed to the plastic-wrapped outfit draped over the back of the settee next to her. 'And the shirt is in your suitcase.'

'Yes,' Jeff said hurriedly when she glanced expectantly at him. It was like being back at prep school, being quizzed by his dorm matron about washing behind his ears.

'You'll be on the high table, with the Prime Minister on your left, and the Chair of the joint sciences council on your right. They've both been told that Mrs Baker isn't coming.'

'Right.' He was frustrated that Sue wasn't here, but she needed to sort out her mother's transfer now they'd found a place in a nursing home. The annual pure and industrial science council dinner wasn't exactly Sue's idea of a fun night out, but then, he wasn't looking forward to it himself. At least having her at his side would have made it bearable.

'I've issued copies of your speech to the media already, so please don't stray from the text: it ties in quite neatly with the other two speakers.'

'Right. So no botanist-and-the-butterfly joke, then?'

'No. And we've been invited to an after-dinner party at the Brunel Club; the senior council members and the Prime Minister's deputy chief of staff will be going.'

'Fine.' He wanted to say something like *Why don't you just morph me in for the news streams?* Everything was so predetermined and regulated that there was barely any need for him to be there at all. But Ms Duke lacked any known sense of humour. She'd just give him another tolerant, slightly irritated smile, and carry on with the briefing.

'Any questions?'

'I think it's been organized perfectly,' he said.

'Thank you.' She rolled up her flexscreen and put it into her embossed black leather Yamin shoulder bag. Her watch was checked again. 'Could we access a news stream, please?'

'Sure. Which one?'

'ITN.'

The big wallscreen came alive as he instructed the flat's domestic computer. Red *Live From Downing Street* streamers ran across the top and bottom of the image, almost covering the advertising banners. Lucy sat up straight, staring eagerly at the screen.

Rob Lacey was standing up behind the podium in the press room, wearing a pale blue shirt with a slim red tie. His breast pocket had the circle of gold EU stars stitched across it. The Prime Minister was looking professionally relaxed, grinning at the assembled reporters in his best matey style. 'I believe that my candidacy is the only one able to offer the inclusiveness which our continent so desperately needs. We all know there are alienation problems in every region; if elected I would devote my Presidency to bringing these people back into the family that is a Unified Europe. Only together can we be strong and prosperous.'

He fell silent for a moment. Bedlam erupted among the reporters as they all shouted their questions at him. Was he resigning as Prime Minister to run his Presidential campaign? Would there be negative campaigning? Would he order the Euroarmy into the India–Pakistan security zone to enforce the peace? How was he going to tackle the Russian illegal immigration problem? Would he give the European Space Agency the budget to launch a manned Mars mission ahead of the Americans? Would there be more rejuvenations? What did his wife think about him standing? How would he tackle the radiation leakage from the Ukrainian reactors? How was he going to deal with inflation?

Rob Lacey held up both hands, still smiling benevolently. 'My campaign pledges will be published at one o'clock this afternoon. That statement will set out clearly and unequivocally where I stand on all major items of policy.'

'He's done it,' Lucy Duke whispered. 'He's declared.' She sounded incredulous.

Jeff gave her a sideways glance. She was still staring up at the screen, back held rigid, an expression of unswerving admiration on her face. He'd often wondered what it would take to get her aroused. 'You knew this was going to happen, didn't you?' he asked.

'I was briefed that it was a possibility, yes.'

'Right down to the possible timing.'

Her gaze left the screen as Rob Lacey raised both hands above his head and gave the air a victory punch. His wife had joined him at the podium, clinging adoringly to his side. Jeff's instant impression was of Lady Macbeth encouraging her husband.

'Is that a problem?' Lucy Duke asked.

'If I turn up and sit next to him at the dinner tonight it will appear as though I'm providing a direct endorsement.'

'Not at all. Everybody knows this dinner was arranged weeks ago.'

Jeff indicated the screen. 'Whereas this was purely spontaneous.'

'Tonight is not an endorsement. You will have total public access. If you wanted to denounce Mr Lacey and his policies, this would be your perfect opportunity.'

'He has policies?'

'It was the Prime Minister who pressed very hard for you to be the first to receive rejuvenation. That was his policy.'

'Policy or advantage?'

'If you feel so strongly, you can pull out. We can announce you have a cold.'

'I'm not going to give anybody that big a snub, especially someone who's probably going to be President. All I'm saying is, when you have your early briefings you might have the courtesy to include me in future. Understand?'

She nodded. 'Yes. I'm sorry. It won't happen again.'

'So does he stand a chance?'

'Yes. A very good one. Brèque won't get in again: no serving President has ever been re-elected, not even the good ones, and he's given us bad inflation, increased terrorist attacks, and his foreign policy is a catastrophe. The German Chancellor is suffering badly from his party's cash-for-aircraft scandal. The Italian Prime Minister is damaged goods after that last clash with the Vatican. The only person who could mount a viable challenge is Cherie Beamon.'

'The Environment Commissioner?'

'Yes. She's got a high public profile, and she's Ms Super-

Clean as far as her career is concerned. The media has never been able to dig up anything on her.'

'Jesus Christ, a politician who behaves herself. Maybe she should stand for Pope.'

'Her commitment is actually her major weakness. She's a fanatical Green. The clean-emission legislation she's churned out is hurting companies right across Europe. She's even opposed to the room-temperature supercon-ductor project.'

'That's stupid,' he said automatically. 'Nothing is more environmentally sound than HTS.'

'She thinks anything which can increase energy produc-tion is fundamentally flawed. Our efforts should be focused on reducing consumption.'

'So she won't like me?'

'No. She considered rejuvenation to be a terrible waste of resources.'

'I guess I'll be voting Lacey, then.'

*

There was a huge crowd around the Weston Castle hotel that evening. The police had thrown up a secure zone around the immediate vicinity, complete with barricades. It took Jeff's limousine thirty minutes to get through the crush. Everybody, it seemed, wanted to get in on the act now that Lacey had announced his decision. There were well-wishers and party loyalists with *Lacey For President* banners, though they were in the minority and had been corralled by the police for their own safety. Just about every mainstream and fringe political cause on the planet was represented by a batch of their supporters, determined to make Lacey consider their point of view. They'd come equipped with their own banners, and effigies, and PA systems, and sonic howlers, and spray paint. With the secure zone covered by cameras, a majority of them were wearing Rob Lacey face masks to avoid identification by Europol surveillance. The thin layer of plastic flesh produced a perfect replica of the Prime Minister's features. Even though it moved in unison with the wearer's face, it couldn't produce a wide range of expressions, so most of the demonstrators had chosen a mask with a goofy appearance.

'Christians and lions,' Jeff muttered as some woman's face was squashed against the car's darkened window. She was being held there while two big police officers handcuffed her. Then she slid downwards abruptly, disappearing from sight as a truncheon was whacked across the back of her legs.

'Jesus wept,' Jeff said. It was Third World nation police officers who did that to protesters, not good old English bobbies.

Lucy Duke was looking the other way.

A big loop of road directly in front of the hotel had been kept clear. As they eased onto it, Jeff saw a five-limo convoy complete with police outriders sweep up to the hotel's entrance portico ahead of them. Rob Lacey stepped out of the second limo. The chanting and jeering reached a crescendo. Lacey just smiled and waved at the crowd pressed up against the distant barricade before his security team closed ranks around him. It was the most bizarre sight Jeff had seen in a long while, the genuine article greeting a sea of his own faces. Authorized news-stream camera crews circled round as the hotel manager greeted the Prime Minister warmly and ushered him inside.

By the time Jeff's limo reached the front of the hotel, the protesters had calmed down. Lieutenant Krober was on the portico steps waiting for him. Jeff fiddled nervously with his bow tie and gave the camera crews a tight smile before hurrying up the steps. There was a chorus of whistles from the crowd. He stopped and turned to look at them. Cheers and clapping drifted through the muggy evening air. When he checked with Lucy Duke her face was expressionless. So he did the only thing he could think of, and gave the people behind the barricades an inane double thumbs-up. The volume of the cheering actually went up slightly.

His humour picked up no end. 'Maybe I should run for President,' he said as they walked through the wide entrance into the lobby. Lucy Duke strode on ahead.

The idea behind the joint sciences council was to coordinate all scientific research funded by the government, ensuring that taxEuros were spent sensibly and that there was an end 'product'. In order to obtain a grant, the applicant had to provide a project plan that listed benefits, economic gain, and end-result application. It was the sort of review board that Jeff thoroughly disapproved of: hands-on bureaucratic interference in university and agency programmes always led to pure science being impoverished. In this case it was even worse. The two original councils hadn't been abolished to make way for the new one; instead, the joint council had been created to complement them, producing another tier of bureaucracy – complete with overpaid civil servants – that increased the time it took to process applications.

With true civil-service instinct to protect itself from criticism, the joint sciences council had created the annual project awards to shower praise and continued finance on the most productive ventures conducted under its auspices. In reality, the event was just another rubber-chicken dinner bringing together edgy researchers with bored junior ministers and loafing reporters.

This year, though, the joint-council Chair had got more attention for the awards than she could ever have dreamed of. It resulted in her giving one of the worst after-dinner speeches Jeff had ever winced his way through, with utterly obscure technical references and jokes a ten-year-old wouldn't have bothered telling. It was his turn after that. Decades of experience had made him insist on a short self-deprecating speech that consisted mainly of anecdotes about the pitfalls of recovering from rejuvenation – along with one botanist-and-butterfly joke, which got a big laugh. Then he had to present the five awards for outstanding achievement. After that it was Rob Lacey's job to sum up, which he did with admirable dignity, saying how indebted society was to the unsung heroes of the research teams and giving the inevitable promise of more money for science when he was elected President. The round of applause he won at the end sounded genuine enough.

*

The Brunel Club was, thankfully, a damn sight more lively than the hotel ballroom where the dinner had been held. It had a long curving bar in the lounge, and a darkened dance floor. The DJ was playing an energetic mix of eighties and noughties tracks, and the bar staff boasted about the range of cocktails they could make.

Jeff saw the Chair of the joint council sitting at a table in the corner of the lounge, her head in her hands. Three cut-crystal tumblers were standing on the polished table in front of her and only one of them had any Scotch left in it. Other members of the council were clustered round her, offering heartfelt support. As Brutus had done for Caesar, Jeff thought.

'I'd like to introduce you to the Downing Street deputy chief,' Lucy Duke said. 'If you're up to it.'

'Sure, wheel him on,' Jeff said.

The spin doctor made her way over to the bar. She passed a girl in a glittery dark purple evening gown who smiled coyly at Jeff as she approached.

'Hi,' he said. She was in her late twenties – genuinely so, he thought: there was a kind of enthusiastic air about her, in marked contrast to Sue's sophisticated charm. Her dark hair was cut short to curve around a very pretty freckled face. Now she was standing just in front of him, he couldn't help glancing at her breasts. It was a reflex he found himself committing a lot more recently, along with checking out girls' legs and bums. In fact, just looking at women in general was something he'd been doing more of since the treatment, certainly compared to the decade before. It generated a lot of semi-guilty enjoyment.

'Hi yourself,' she drawled back. 'Good speech, by the way. Liked the joke about the butterfly. Did you really slide off the toilet in the Brussels hospital?'

'Yeah, 'fraid so.'

'I'm Martina. And you're Jeff Baker.'

'That's right. So what do you research?'

'Research?'

'You were at the dinner. The awards are for working scientists.'

'Oh no,' she laughed. 'I'm a production assistant for Thames News. I just lucked out, being here tonight.'

'How is that luck?'

'The start of Lacey's campaign. No offence, but we wouldn't normally give the awards this kind of coverage, not even with you as the guest.'

'No, I don't suppose you would.'

'Do you want to dance?'

He saw Lucy Duke heading back with the determination of a hunter on the scent, the deputy chief in tow. 'Sure.'

21. HOME NOT QUITE ALONE

It had been weeks since Tim tried to give his Europol protection team the slip. Before, he'd always managed to elude them on the roads and paths around Rutland, pulling a fast switch and leaving them behind to shout furiously at him. In other words, they'd always known when he'd escaped. This time, something different was called for.

He and his friends had come up with a variant on the shell game, with people coming in and out of the Manor to visit him all morning. The week before, he'd hacked into the Manor's security cameras so he could alter the feed with stored images. He'd got that idea from several pre10 films about cool heists and bank raids. Not that he was entirely sure it would work, but it was worth a try. And the Manor's security software hadn't detected his tampering. It wasn't quite hacking in the William Gibson league – after all, he already had the access codes – but he was proud of the programs he'd modified.

During the morning Tim had a lot of visitors. All the crew arriving, then leaving, some of them coming back again. There had been a confusing rush of feet pounding up and down the stairs, with lots of car doors being slammed. Vehicles blocking the drive. People wandering round the rooms. Mrs Mayberry getting very annoyed with requests for hot chocolate and biscuits and toast and pizzas at nine o'clock in the morning.

Vanessa, Philip, and Simon stormed out of Tim's room, making as much racket as they could. They were due to leave in the car which Simon had borrowed from his parents. Annabelle was left alone with Tim.

'How are you coping?' she asked.

'Okay.' Tim was looking out of the window, checking the cars and e-trikes on the drive. Martin was just driving in with his borrowed long-base Land Rover.

'Really?'

Tim was twisted up by two conflicting urges. He badly wanted to look at her, today of all days, because she was wearing a very tight black tank top that had *Fondle With Care* printed over her breasts, the sight of which made him feel incredibly randy. Yet there was an instinctive impulse to hold back and avoid talking to her about how he felt because of the turmoil in his mind. He just couldn't understand what was going on with his father.

At least three news-stream society reports had shown the video of Martina Lewis coming out of the Knights-bridge flat at half-past seven in the morning, still wearing her purple evening gown. It wasn't a very clear image: somebody had copied it from one of the street's security cameras. But it did show his father in a bathrobe, standing on the doorstep to kiss her goodbye before she hopped into a taxi. All the reports had given the hyperlink for Ms Lewis's life site, where the latest paragraph she had added said how much fun Jeff Baker was, and how the rejuvenation team had done such a good job – in every department.

Life at the Manor had been pretty much unbearable after that.

'Not bad, I suppose,' Tim said, with a shrug.

'Have they been arguing? I remember my parents arguing a lot when mum got her job in Brussels.'

'A bit. Not exactly arguing. Just cold with each other. Mum was furious, I mean so much angry.' He'd never actually seen Sue so livid before. It was sort of scary, especially when the rest of the Rutland non-working mothers' club rallied round. They'd held several late-night vodka sessions in the lounge, discussing the merits of men. Tim had overheard just part of one conversation and slunk on up to bed, praying they hadn't seen him.

'Well, that's hardly surprising,' Annabelle said. 'He is her husband, and he got caught red-handed.'

'Yeah,' Tim said meekly. He really didn't want to go into his parents' private lives, at least not into what had gone on before with his mother and everything, or rather every*one*. He found it hard to see why she was so bothered about dad having an affair. The publicity, yes, but the actual act . . . 'I don't know why he did it, though. He and mum had been getting on really well since his treatment. I mean *so much* well.'

'Ah,' Annabelle said wisely. 'Well, that Martina looked quite fit, and your dad was away from home.'

'For one night. And mum's a lot better-looking than she is.'

'Way of the world, Tim.'

'It might be, but it's pretty shitty.'

'Your dad's a celebrity, probably the most famous person in Europe right now, if not the world. Certain kinds of women are bound to fling themselves at him.

Would you have said no to Martina if she'd asked you to go to bed with her, if she'd pleaded?'

This time he looked straight at her. 'Right now, yes, I would have. I don't want to go to bed with her or anyone else. Just with you.'

'Thanks, Tim,' Annabelle murmured demurely. She kissed him, which turned into quite a passionate embrace.

'I so much want to go to bed with you,' Tim moaned as if he was in pain.

'I know.'

'Why can't we? I love you. I so much do.'

'You're so sweet.' Her tongue delved down into his throat. She could feel his hands all over her, creeping up her stomach. His desperation was actually quite a turn-on. Being desired and adored so unquestioningly was immensely satisfying. 'Wait.' She moved back from him, nearly laughing at the anguish on his face as she moved away a pace. 'Watch this,' she teased. Her hands went up inside her tank top, moving round to the clip on her bra strap. Then, shrugging out of the shoulder straps, she pulled the bra out from under her top.

Tim's delight at the implied promise of the act was tempered by his amazement at the Houdini bra trick. 'How did you do that?'

'Haven't you ever seen it before?'

'Er, no.'

She moved back up to him, and brushed her lips against his. 'You've been going out with the right kind of girls.'

'You mean, the wrong kind.'

'No. I'm the wrong type.' Grinning dangerously, she pulled the tank top up over her breasts. 'Ta-Raaaa!'

For a moment she thought Tim was going to faint.

'Holy shit,' he whispered. 'They're bloody sensational.'

Annabelle giggled and took hold of his hands, guiding them up so that they cupped her breasts.

They both heard someone pounding along the landing outside.

'Tim!' Martin yelled. 'Hi, Tim, it's me.'

'*Fuck!*' Tim snarled.

Annabelle quickly pulled her tank top back down.

Martin barged in, a wide, happy smile on his face. 'Thought I'd come and see you . . .' which was scripted by the plan. So he wasn't expecting Tim to be staring at him like a pre10 slasher psycho whose next victim has just arrived. 'You okay?' he grunted.

Tim shivered as if he'd been caught in a blast of icy air. 'Sure. Just so great right now, thanks.'

'What did I do?'

'Nothing,' Annabelle said. She ignored the way Martin's eyes bugged as he looked at her obviously bra-less chest. 'Is everything ready?'

Martin closed the door. 'Er, yeah.'

'Great,' Tim grumbled.

'Let's go then,' Annabelle said brightly.

Tim gave her a long, woeful look, then slipped on his PCglasses and instructed his programs to begin the visual substitution. It was Natalie Cherbun who was on duty downstairs, watching the screens, as the camera outside Tim's room began to show yesterday's picture.

All three of them fell silent, listening for any sound that the Europol team had discovered the subversion. 'Here we go,' Tim said after a minute. He opened the French windows and went out onto his narrow balcony. There was a fifteen-foot drop down to the gravel below; Martin's

Land Rover was parked close to the foot of the wall, just out of camera range. Its rear door had been left slightly ajar.

Tim swung a leg over the rail and grabbed hold of the trellis, which supported a thick clematis creeper. He gave Annabelle another longing look. 'Catch you later.'

'I'll be ready for you.'

He started to climb down.

Annabelle shut the French windows.

'Jesus, were you two bonking?' Martin asked eagerly.

Annabelle sneered at him. 'Get a life, you sad little prick.'

He licked his lips. 'Sorry I exist.'

'Go on, clear off, you've got to drive Tim away.'

'Right.' Martin opened the door, and rather too loudly said: 'See ya, Tim.' A nervous wink, and he was gone.

Annabelle sighed, and sat on the bed. She really would have shagged him. It had been the perfect moment, wild and spontaneous. With Tim in that frenzied state, the sex would have been quite something. Her smile slowly returned as she thought about that. She knew full well she could drive him crazy any time she damn well wanted.

Twenty minutes later she went downstairs to the main hall. A couple of the Europol team were sitting in the little lounge they'd taken over, talking quietly. There had been no frantic running round and shouting, no desperate pursuit; they didn't know Tim was gone. She waved casually to Natalie as she went past.

Jeff walked out of his study, carrying a couple of empty tea mugs. 'Hi, Annabelle.' It was like encountering a vision, he thought, something a Catholic saint might witness in the Dark Ages while they were being persecuted – a divine messenger sent by God to inspire them. Except this wasn't quite the Virgin Mary. Annabelle was wearing a gloriously tight tank top that exposed a visual feast of flat midriff. Her denim skirt didn't make it halfway to her knees, while her feet were engulfed by absurdly big grey and black trainers with thick platform soles. White socks were crumpled loosely round her ankles.

She was staring back at him, adopting the kind of slouch that only teenagers could manage. Nothing in the world was relevant or interesting to her.

The way she looked and acted made her so incredibly desirable. He simply wanted her, right there and then. Not only that, he wanted what she was.

'Oh, hi,' she grunted back apathetically.

'Are you coming, or going?'

'Going. Tim's busy revising.'

'That's a shame, I never get to see much of you.' His gaze scanned across her tank top, reading the print. The corner of his mouth lifted to a modest smile. 'I'd love to.'

Annabelle couldn't believe he'd gone and said that. 'I think you've got your hands full at the moment, actually,' she told him, which was wrong because what she meant to say was something like *Fuck off, you should be ashamed.* But then, she conceded, Jeff Baker didn't feel shame. What he and Martina Lewis had got up to made that very clear.

'Not at all,' he said. 'But you could change all that.'

'No, I couldn't.' She walked quickly to the Manor's double doors. Not too fast, that would mean she was flustered. As she emerged into the sunlight, she realized she still hadn't put her bra back on. 'Oh bugger!' she hissed. He must have thought she was putting out signals. Which was so much the opposite reality. *Wasn't it?*

Jeff watched her hurry across the gravel to an e-trike. His hands were shaking. The encounter kept running through his mind like a video file stuck on replay. 'Jesus wept.' He had trouble accepting what he'd just done. Yet his whole body was flying high on guilty joy. It was the most extraordinary sensation. And he'd seen the uncertainty in her eyes.

You can't, he told himself sternly. *You absolutely cannot. Not with her. Anyone else. But not her.*

22. MESSING ABOUT ON THE WATER

There were only a few official access tracks down to the shore of Rutland Water, and they were now all carefully monitored by both wardens and cameras.

The huge reservoir remained a popular fishing spot for anglers. As a consequence, it was an equally popular focus for the anti-angling campaigners. Lone fishermen were a vulnerable and easy target for the hardline activists who raided the shore from time to time. During the summer the Oakham police would be called out two or three times a week to break up fights. Then, two years ago, an elderly angler had drowned after he'd been pushed in. Every protest group denied it had anything to do with it. But his equipment had been smashed and thrown in with him. After that, the Midlands Region Water Agency became seriously concerned about safety and, more importantly, their own legal liability. They began increasing their warden patrols and upgrading surveillance equipment at the car parks and along the tracks.

For anyone who wanted to get down to the water unobserved this heightened security presented a major problem. But Tim and most of his friends had grown up in Rutland. When they were younger they'd cycled round the reservoir year after year, in every season. They knew every centimetre of its shoreline, the surrounding fields, the nearby spinneys with their disused farm tracks, as well as the location of every rusting field gate, no matter how overgrown with hawthorn and sycamore.

Martin took the Egleton turn off the A6003, then stopped the long-base Land Rover beside a field gate. Tim and Simon got out and opened it. They drove through the meadow where grazing sheep paid no attention to them, jouncing down to the Nature Reserve with its neglected copses and dilapidated cycle track. Deep within the mass of brambles and lanky ash trees of the Reserve was a lane that ran straight through, guarded by sagging five-bar gates at each end. Weeks ago, Philip and Martin had cracked the padlocks. Now nobody saw them as they cut through the tangle of trees and emerged to circle round Lax Hill. Martin pulled up ten metres from the edge of the water.

Two of the boys lifted the jet ski out of the back of the badly cramped Land Rover, and carried it down to the shoreline. Tim waited behind, stripping down to his swim shorts and a tatty old mauve sweatshirt.

'You ready?' Simon asked. He was buzzing with excitement. Everyone in the crew shared it. This was their moment. They'd spent the whole long, boring, miserable winter planning this. Now it had come to fruition and the tension was cranked up in their bodies like some hyper synth8 dose.

Tim laced up his trainers. 'Let's go!' They high-fived.

The jet ski was bobbing in the shallows, with Colin and Rachel holding on to it, water coming over their knees. Tim waded out through the scabby mud and managed to wobble his way onto the saddle without capsizing the little machine. Rachel handed him a pair of broad wraparound goggles with gold lenses. Colin checked the choke and throttle, then pressed the starter. The engine kicked in at once, bringing a pack of whoops from the crew standing on the shoreline behind. Tim waited a moment to make sure the engine was running smoothly, then slowly twisted the throttle. The jet ski moved off, its nose riding up as he accelerated out onto the open water. White spray began to curve up from either side, like ragged swans' wings unfurling around him.

Out on the reservoir, small white fishing boats puttered about gently with two or three anglers in each. They were all identical, hired out from the lodge at Normanton, each one running off a single sealed-circuit regenerator module that powered a small impeller. The Midlands Region Water Agency refused to let anything more powerful on the reservoir. As always, a small fleet of them had congregated along the western end of the reservoir, keeping away from the shallows around Lax Hill and the Nature Reserve. Tim sliced through the middle of the genteel flotilla, laughing at the angry shouts and raised fists as his wake slapped at their gunwales. Lines were hurriedly wound in and hands gripped seats as the fishing boats rocked vigorously. He began to test the jet ski's manoeuvrability, turning sharply, making a figure eight around a couple of the boats. One of the anglers threw something in his direction, the angry man's obscene yells carrying over the water. Tim gave him the finger and charged off.

Further eastwards, the sailing club boats were moving sedately along a curving racecourse that took up a quarter of the reservoir's southern segment. Several windsurfers zipped about, all but a couple of daredevils keeping reasonably close to shore. Tim lined up on the nearest buoy that marked out the racecourse. He gunned the throttle up as far as it would go. The jet ski ploughed into the wavelets, skimming from top to top amid huge bursts of spray. He laughed gleefully as the water lashed at his face. The motion picked up, pounding him up and down energetically.

Up ahead, one of the yachts was getting close. Tim curved round on a parallel course, easing back on the throttle before racing ahead of the other craft. The lone yachtsman was screaming curses as the jet ski's wake hit. This had to be the most exhilarating thing since ... well, actually since earlier that morning when Annabelle had shown off her incredible breasts. No day in his life had been so magnificent as this one. His head went back and he opened his mouth wide for a victory yell. Spray went straight down his throat instead, and he coughed, spluttered and laughed like a madman.

The jet ski was approaching a whole cluster of yachts. Tall yellow and scarlet sails were curving gracefully away from the masts as they filled with wind, pushing them along at a civilized pace. They began to move apart, scattering like frightened fish, giving themselves room to manoeuvre should he, the malicious invader choose to steer into their midst. He so chose.

He flung his body weight from side to side, sending the jet ski slaloming about over the choppy grey-blue water. Hulls flashed past, so fast they became simple streaks of colour. Curses and threats flung by the crews mingled with the crash of spray and the howl of the motor. Tim wove an exhilaratingly chaotic course, steering as close as he dared, determined to loop around as many yachts as he could. There were a couple of children on one, under ten, bright yellow woollen hats pulled down tight on their heads. They peered at him nervously as their father checked their lifejacket straps. *Oops!* Not so close to that yacht. But he gave them a friendly wave. All they'd talk about at school for the next week would be how close they'd been to the Anarchy Pirate of Rutland Water – the first of many such legends if Tim and his friends had their way.

A flurry of activity over by the sailing club's slipways resulted in the rescue boat trundling down its ramp. A big inflatable craft with a powerful outboard motor. A puff of blue-grey smoke appeared in the air behind it, and a surge of creamy white foam erupted from its rear.

'Time to go,' Tim informed his antagonistic audience. He performed a neat hundred and eighty degree turn round the prow of a yacht, coming within a couple of metres, and gunned the throttle again.

The rescue boat's engine sounded like the snarl of an angry dragon as it raced towards him. He hadn't realized the damn thing would be so fast. And it was big – its wake was going to cause him difficulties if he ever got trapped broadside. This was going to mean a serious strategy rethink before they launched again.

Tim zoomed past the Old Hall, jutting out on its own spit of land from the Hambledon peninsula, looking like a proud Scottish castle guarding the entrance to some strategic loch. The rescue boat was gaining rapidly as he moved past the building's tall blank windows, the men in its bow leaning forward eagerly in anticipation of catching their impertinent prey. Its wake was already slapping along the limestone blocks of the shore. Anglers and walkers on either side of the Hall had stopped to watch the spectacle.

There was no way Tim was going to get back to the safety of Lax Hill ahead of the rescue boat in a straight race. He altered course slightly, bringing the jet ski round until its nose was aiming for the flotilla of fishing boats again. The rescue boat had to slow drastically in order to manoeuvre through them, reducing its wake and with it the danger of capsizing innocent bystanders. Tim began to S-bend, sweeping close to several of the small white hulls. The raw adrenalin sluicing through his arteries produced another manic laugh. He couldn't believe he was doing this. He couldn't believe he was going to get away with this. It was the ride that was going to make him most equal of all among his friends. He was on the inside now, a hothead daredevil who had Annabelle in his bed. The one they would respect, lionize, and orbit around.

He pulled the jet ski round again, kicking out a plume of spray which splattered against a fishing boat. This was like the slick high-speed chase sequence in some pre10 film. That really old one, *Live and Let Die*, with speedboats surging through the Louisiana swamps while crocodiles snapped at their sterns. If only the whole world could see this chase they'd be able to share in its thrill, and thank him for providing it.

The jet ski broke free of the fishing boats and surged for the shore ahead. He could see his friends already plunging out into the shallows to collect him, while the rescue boat was dropping further and further behind as it negotiated the flotilla.

I did it. Me! I'm the one.

23. CARDINAL PUFF

FOR THE THIRD TIME

'I would like to the drink to the health of Cardinal puff puff for the third and—'

'Wrong!' the rest of them roared exuberantly.

Simon's teeth ground together. 'Oh fuck it, you are unserious!'

'Drink. Drink,' they all whooped.

Simon tried to focus at the Manhattan Island of bottles and tall glasses covering the table. He plucked one at random and guzzled down its contents. Rum and coke trickled down his already wet T-shirt. 'Okay.' The bottle waved round as he tried to put it back down. 'This is is it. I'm doing it right now.' He wiped his lips with the back of his hand, concentrating furiously. He picked the glass up carefully between his thumb and forefinger. 'One finger, see. Okay. Ladies and gentlemen, I would like to health the drink of Cardinal puff—'

'Wrong!'

Simon started giggling, tears of delight running out of his eyes as he slowly slid out of the chair and onto the carpet. Rachel fell on top of him, her shoulders quaking with drunken joy.

Tim thought it was equally hysterical. He tried to throw his arms around Annabelle to share the mirth. They'd been drinking since mid-afternoon after their triumphant return from Rutland Water. Simon's parents were away again, so their conservatory once more hosted the crew's celebration party. Talk had been about the next venture, who would ride the jet ski, what to do about the rescue boat. But all that had come after Tim had told them again and again about his ride.

They listened. For once they listened without interrupting or interjecting sarky comments. He talked about the glory of it all, with Annabelle at his side and a bottle of beer in his hand.

Then more bottles had been brought out. They finished the beer and moved on to spirits.

'It's very simple,' Vanessa said. 'Listen: I want to drink to the health of Cardinal puff . . .' She spluttered off into a laugh.

'No!' Sophie and Natalie chorused.

'You've got to start with: Ladies and gentlemen . . .'

Vanessa tried to drink a Bacardi forfeit while she was still laughing. It sprayed out across her jeans and dribbled down onto the marble floor tiles. She just laughed louder.

Tim, who was now lying across Annabelle's legs, turned round to smile up adoringly at her. 'Come upstairs with me,' he said quietly. 'Please.'

Annabelle shifted her knees, trying to move his weight to a more comfortable position. 'Don't think so, Tim.' There were memories involved with this house's bedrooms that she didn't want to revisit. That was one of the reasons she hadn't really joined in the drinking games. And the more the others poured down their throats, the less attractive it became. She was actually quite cross with Tim for doing it. Either he was so stupid he didn't realize she was willing to carry on where they'd left off this morning, or he put this ridiculous macho bonding ritual before wanting to have sex with her. Either way, he'd let her down. So much.

'Ow, come on,' he slurred.

The others were starting to pay attention. She struggled to her feet, spilling Tim onto the floor. 'I've got a ton of work to revise before Monday,' she said. 'I'll see you.'

Martin and Simon put their arms round each other's shoulders and warbled out a cry of camp derision, which everyone else thought very funny.

A bleary Tim frowned up at her. 'What?'

'Catch you later.'

He tried to get up, but his trainers slipped on a puddle of beer, and he fell back down. For a moment he did nothing as everyone stared silently at him, then he began to snigger.

Annabelle ignored the drunken amusement behind her. Two members of the Europol protection team were waiting with bored patience in the lounge. 'Make sure he gets home all right, won't you,' she said.

'Goodnight,' the Dutch sergeant said; his smile was sympathetic and understanding.

She was just in time to catch the Rutland Circuit bus back to Oakham. At the station it was only a ten-minute wait for the next bus to Uppingham.

Her house was in a twenty-year-old estate that bordered London Road, just behind the grounds of the old local college. The development company had constructed all of them to be energy-efficient and have minimal ecological impact. A squat dark unimaginative box, with silver windows and wind-powered conditioning units whirring away under the eaves like the rustling of dry leaves. As always, she hesitated when she reached the front door.

The Goddard family had moved in when Annabelle was three years old. It had provided a lovely childhood, with both her parents taking care of her. Back then the house had been big and light, filled with laughter and fun. There had been birthday parties with her friends running round everywhere, and magic Christmases with feasts and too much chocolate. During the summer weekends, her parents threw barbecues that would last all afternoon long, with the adults chugging back drink and the children playing together in the pocket-sized garden.

Tonight, when she finally opened the door, the hall lights gave off a meagre glimmer, as if someone had replaced the electric bulbs with candles. The ageing domestic computer with its antique programs was saving power as best it could. Their regenerator module desperately needed new electrolyte gel, and the solar-cell panels on the roof were filthy with algae and moss.

Her father, Roger, was watching the screen in the lounge when she came in. It was an Australian hospital soap sponsored by some health insurance company she'd never heard of. One of the twenty soaps which dominated his life. She never could understand how he could tell them apart, or keep up with the parallel storylines. They all seemed to be written by the same creative-writing program, churning out improbable plots driven by absurd coincidence and long-lost relatives. But he sat there and soaked them up, slumped bonelessly in the deep leather armchair positioned directly opposite the screen. That chair had arrived in its factory packing case on the day the Goddards moved in, as had all the current furniture and carpets. Nothing had changed: the interior had simply grown shabbier with the years.

She went into the kitchen, hoping her father hadn't heard her tiptoeing along the hall. A forlorn hope.

'It's Saturday,' Roger Goddard said. 'I thought you'd be out all night.'

Annabelle was searching through the freezer for some bread to toast. She didn't stop; she'd had nothing to eat all day. 'So I came home – it's not a crime.'

'I know. Are you all right?'

'Just great, thanks.' She found half a loaf and slammed it down on the worktop, separating the frosted slices.

'It's not like you to be back this early, that's all.'

The note of absurd earnestness in his voice infuriated her. As if he had ever shown any real concern. She straightened up, keeping her anger in check, and shoved the bread in the toaster.

Roger looked at the black tank top she was wearing, his lips tightening with disapproval. But he was in one of his trying-to-be-a-father moods, so he never actually said anything. 'Did you have an argument with Tim?'

'No. Dad, just log off, all right? Please. I'm home because I want to be. That's it.'

'I just worry about you. I know you don't think much of me, but you're still my daughter. I care.'

'About what? That I'm home early for once? I thought you'd be glad of that.'

'If I thought it was so you could spend time with me, I would be.'

181

'It's a bit late for that, dad – by about ten years. Okay?'

'I'm sorry. I do my best.'

She wanted to scream at him, let out all her fury in one easy blast of vitriol and accusation. Looking at the shambolic man standing there with his pathetically eager expression held across his face like some kind of shield, the anger shifted to dismay and she felt a sudden wave of exhaustion. There was no way she could ever understand what had happened to him and, through that, to her. Their once-cosy house was degenerating along with the whole estate, where one in three families had no job and kids hung out all day, intimidating anyone on the street. He never did any cleaning or cooking or gardening. The only real money she ever saw was a monthly allowance from her mother, the kind of money which every other girl at school spent in an afternoon. Their only other source of income, the pitiful unemployment benefit her father received, vanished straight into the household account. Every week the domestic computer's finance program would pay off the mortgage and local taxes. Then it would spend a few moments accessing the regional supermarket sites to update itself with their current grocery prices, comparing them with the necessities list she'd loaded in years ago. On Friday the Community Supply Service van would pull up outside and deliver their food for the week, a depressing cluster of supermarket own-brand packages and bargain offers.

There were times when she could remember her childhood, time spent with a man who used to take her out to the parks and play with her. A man who'd tell her stories, and read to her, and watch the children's shows on cable with her. It was difficult to make the connection between that distant figure and the man standing in the kitchen.

In a way she'd got the opposite kind of father to Tim's. Tim always used to complain that Jeff never joined in much when he was a kid.

Jeff Baker.

She pushed that thought away before it had a chance to form.

Roger was still standing, awkward at the silence between them.

'Dad, you know I've applied for university, don't you?'

'I know. I remember, you told me. Just don't do accountancy. You'll wind up like me.' A nervous judder of a laugh.

'That means I'll be leaving at the end of summer. Leaving home.'

His head bowed slowly. 'I know. I'm pleased about that. It's what you need. It'll be good for you.'

'Okay, then.' The slices clunked up out of the toaster, barely brown. She grabbed them.

'So, you're all right, then?' he persisted.

'Dad, yes, I'm fine. I just wanted a night in, that's all. Nothing to worry about.'

24. CELEBRITY STATUS

The barmaid at the Vaults gave Jeff a wide, knowing smile as she pulled three pints for him. He endured it awkwardly, impatient for the glasses to fill. It was like being taunted by schoolyard bullies. Nothing you could say to make her stop, nowhere to go to avoid her gaze.

Once the last drop of beer came out of the pump tap he hurriedly dropped a hundred-Euro cash card on the bar, and fled back to the table with the three full glasses. 'Jesus, does everybody know?'

Alan chuckled as he lifted his glass. ''Fraid so, old boy. There's poetic justice for you.'

'How the hell is this poetic justice?'

'Without your memory crystal there would never have been this God-awful Orwellian twenty-four-hour-a-day, every-street-in-every-town surveillance. We simply couldn't store that much data, not on good old-fashioned videotape. The insurance company would never have put that camera outside your flat. Your little friend could have gone home without anyone ever seeing her. Instead, you came along with your great save-the-world-from-capitalism crusade. These days you can't actually get crime-insurance coverage unless there is a Big Brother camera pointing at your front door. Cheers!' He took a gulp of beer.

'Hey, releasing the memory crystal was never about politics.'

'You changed the world,' James said. 'Now live in it. *We* have to.'

Jeff gave his friend a surprised look. There had been a lot of anger in James's voice. For once the big man wasn't happily slurping down his beer. *Now what have I done?* He'd come to the pub purely so he could get out of the Manor. Life at home was not good right now.

'Could be worse,' Alan mused. 'The world could have turned out like it did in *Blade Runner*.'

James took a long drink. 'That would have been preferable.'

'What the hell is up with you?' Jeff asked.

'Nothing wrong with me. How about you?'

Jeff couldn't figure this out at all. 'I'm fine, thank you.'

'So we gather.'

'You're not seriously upset about me meeting that girl, are you?'

James gave him a moody glare over the rim of his glass. 'I don't know – which one?'

'Come on, you two,' Alan said. He was looking between them with quite a degree of discomfort. 'We're not recreating the end of *The Good, the Bad and the Ugly* here.'

'Good!' Jeff took a long drink, deliberately ignoring James. He knew now. Somehow his old friend had found out about him and Nicole. *And what do you say to that?* The man's granddaughter. Small wonder James was so angry. Jeff suddenly wondered if Nicole had come clean and told James herself because Jeff had kept cancelling their meetings.

'I never could work out which one was supposed to be The Ugly,' Alan said.

'Lee Van Cleef,' James said irritably.

Jeff had always supposed it was Eli Wallach, but kept quiet.

'So what did Lacey have to say for himself at your dinner?' Alan asked.

'Not much. He asked me if I'd say a few words in favour of his campaign.'

'Jesus, what did you tell him?'

'I said I'd think about it. Nobody got back to me about it after the evening, not even Lucy Duke.'

'You're a civil servant,' James said. 'They can't use you, you're supposed to be impartial.'

'I am not a bloody civil servant.'

'Government pays for you, you're a civil servant.'

'That is such a load of crap.'

'Why? We paid for your precious Treatment. And that whole bureaucratic con trick must have added a couple of percentage points to everyone's income tax. Now we're paying you again to work on their next pie in the sky idea. I mean, Jesus H. Christ, top-bracket income tax is going to hit seventy-five per cent next budget. They're already leaking the level so it doesn't come as such a shock. And it gets spent on the likes of you.'

'The high-temperature superconductor is not pie in the sky,' Jeff said with forced politeness. 'It'll be a huge boon for everyone.'

'Except for the established energy suppliers,' James said. 'It will ruin them, and for what purpose?'

Jeff cast a confused glance at Alan, who just shrugged. 'What?'

'We don't need your stupid government project,' James snapped. 'We have enough energy, and if we need more the market will find ways of supplying it.'

'Oh for fuck's sake, we do not have enough energy. How can you say that? You're the same generation as me, you're damn well old enough to remember what we had back in the last century. And now look at us – most of the population can't afford a car any more.'

'They could if you hadn't taxed them out of existence.'

'Me?' Jeff exclaimed. 'What do you mean, me?'

'Well, I don't count you on my side.'

'Oh . . .' Jeff stood up, and gave his old friend a disgusted look. 'Enough. I don't have to put up with this shit.' He made to leave, then turned abruptly, his forefinger wagging accusingly at James. 'And next time, have the courage to come out with what really bothers you.'

25. FEEL THE BURN

Sophie had changed her hairstyle. It had been cut short and dyed an even lighter blonde.

'I like it,' Annabelle told her when they went for their gym session together. It was something she tried to fit in most Sunday evenings. If she couldn't make it then, she rescheduled for sometime during the week. Keeping herself in shape was an interest which had grown steadily over the last few years. The way her figure had developed was a marvellous compensation for a lack of wealth. An advantage over the other girls that she would never relinquish.

Sophie ran her hand through her hair. The front was slightly spiked. 'Yeah?'

'Yes.' It was a kind of cross between butch and cute. 'Suits you.'

'Thanks.'

Annabelle went straight to the bench press and started lifting. Sophie climbed onto the treadmill.

'So what happened after I left?' Annabelle asked. Tim had sent eight avtxts that morning, becoming progressively more frantic. She'd given in and met him for lunch, and had to listen to two hours of mournful apology. Just when she thought he was toughening up, as well.

'We just got totally blasted. I spent the night on one of the settees. God, was I so much hung-over. Not as bad as Colin, though. He looked really ill, like he was dying.'

Annabelle pushed hard, forcing the weights up. She knew Sophie was watching her – there was that odd subconscious awareness of another person's interest scratching round inside her skull. 'What about Tim?'

'Same as the rest of us. His Gestapo babysitting squad took him home.'

Annabelle sat at the upright and wrapped her arms round the hinged front bars, gritting her teeth as she pulled them round. 'I mean was he by himself?'

'Oh yes,' Sophie chuckled. 'After what we got through, nobody was capable of anything, least of all some illicit snogging.'

'Typical.'

'What?'

'I'm not sure if Tim doesn't have a problem, you know. A real one. He gets like that every weekend.'

'We all do.'

'No. Not like that. He goes at it like it's a challenge, either drink or synth8, doesn't matter which. By the end of the night he's always blasted.'

'You know what he's like, always desperate to be one of the pack. Anything we do, he tries to do it that bit harder. Typical male behaviour. Simon's the same. I'd have thought you'd noticed that. They've got a real little contest going there. It's really all about who's got the biggest willy.'

'It's so stupid. What's Tim got to struggle for? He's rich, and he's smart ... well, clever, anyway. Have you seen his grades? He had Oxford and Cambridge offering him scholarships, for Christ's sake. I work my arse off at

189

school, and I can't get those sort of grades. The best I got was an acknowledgement that they'll consider me for a place. Then every Saturday he turns into a total zonehead.'

'That must be frustrating for you.' There was a strong hint of mockery in Sophie's voice.

'It pisses me off, yeah.'

'Is that what last night was all about?'

Annabelle strained harder against the bars. The resistance was set high: not that she wanted gross-out muscles, but the exercise kept her shoulders and arms firm. 'I'd just had enough. It was boring, especially after the reservoir.'

'I suppose you're right. But we needed to celebrate. Did you see we made the East Midlands news stream? Their report lasted about a minute. They even had a video of Tim on the jet ski – someone at the Normanton picnic site had a camera. Not that you could see it was him, fortunately.'

'I caught it this morning.'

'Simon's going next, it was decided – apparently. And guess who after that? Rachel, of course. I would so much like to give that girl a slap.'

'Keep a secret?'

'You bet.'

'I mean *really*.'

'If it's important, yeah.'

'Jeff hit on me yesterday morning.'

'Jeff . . .' Sophie took a moment to make the connection. Her hand slapped the treadmill's off switch. 'You are so much kidding me! Tim's dad, Jeff?'

Annabelle grinned at her friend's reaction; very little managed to shock Sophie. 'Yes.'

'Oh my *God*. That's . . . God. He's just been all over the

news streams with that girl from the awards ceremony. Isn't she enough?'

'Apparently not.'

'Wow, what do they put in that rejuvenation treatment? Neat Viagra? I mean, he's nearly, what, eighty?'

'You've seen how old he looks. Not five years older than Tim.'

'Yeah, but, God. Hitting on you. His son's girlfriend. That's like incest or something. Got to be illegal.'

'Like son, like father.'

'Are you winding me up? How are you so calm?'

'It's not the first time someone's hit on me.'

'No, but not their father.'

'Actually, yes, I think. Mike Haulsey's dad was certainly sneaking looks when he thought I couldn't see.'

Sophie folded her arms, giving Annabelle a strong look. 'So what are you saying: you're a perv magnet?'

'Men always hit on young girls. They have on you. I've seen it.'

'Don't I bloody know it. But they're not like, well . . .'

'Yeah. So far all the eighty-year-olds I've met have looked eighty, even with genoprotein.'

'Does Tim know?'

'God, no. He's insecure enough as it is. That would flip him over the edge.'

'You're really supportive, aren't you? No wonder they all want you as a girlfriend.'

'Don't tell me you think I should tell him?'

'No.' Sophie curled her lips in a half-sneer. 'He's so insecure something like that would flip him right over the edge.'

They shared a sisterly grin.

'Well, then,' Annabelle said.

'So what are you going to do?'

'Don't know – try and stay out of his way, I suppose.'

'I'd scream the house down.'

'What good would that do?'

'It would make sure he wouldn't do it again. Not ever.'

'Yes, but it would hurt other people, too.'

'He needs to be hurt. You're not trying to protect him, are you?'

'No,' Annabelle said sharply.

'Oh my God, you are. I'm right, aren't I?'

'Don't be ridiculous.'

'That's it,' Sophie said, with a delicious gleam in her eye. 'That's why you're sounding me out, to see how I'd react. My God, Annabelle, you're so much atrocious. I don't believe it. You want to shag him.'

'I do not!'

'You just said it. He doesn't look eighty. I mean, he looks barely a couple of years older than Tim. It's actually spooky how similar they are. You want to trade up, don't you?'

'No.' She was trying to laugh, but it was more like a guilty snort.

'Makes sense to me.'

'Stop it.'

'Why not?' Think of the advantages. He's rich, he's famous, he's experienced – which has got to count for something in bed: I bet he knows all sorts of tricks that'll ring your bell. He certainly doesn't have a conscience, so he's not going to plague you afterwards.'

'He's eighty, or something like it. Small detail, but so much valid.'

192

Sophie leaned on the treadmill's rail, licking her lips as she stared down at Annabelle. 'He doesn't look it. How do you judge Jeff Baker's age, anyway? Memory or body? If it's only his body, you've got nothing to worry about. And the age difference obviously doesn't bother him. He must have been sixty-plus when he married Tim's mum. How old was she back then? She only looks about five years older than us now.'

'Are you saying I should?' Annabelle had the uncomfortable recollection of the Rutland non-working mothers' club, and their discussion along similar lines.

'I'm not saying anything. You're the one who has to decide.'

'There is nothing to decide.' Annabelle shoved herself back into the bench, and resumed her lifts. 'Nothing.'

26. END OF A BEAUTIFUL

ARRANGEMENT

It was half-past five in the afternoon when the computer informed Jeff he had an incoming call from Alan. Did he want to receive it?

Jeff sat back in the black leather chair, putting his hands behind his head. He could hear tiny cracking noises as his shoulders stretched. 'Let it through.'

There was an intricate molecular structure playing on the desk's main screen, coiled streamers burning green and tangerine like alien DNA. The arrangement was one of the latest nano filaments produced by Caltech, which he was studying to see how much progress they'd made on bonding alignments. It was replaced by Alan's slightly gaunt features.

'My God, I actually got through,' Alan muttered; it wasn't entirely good-humoured.

'Sorry. I've been getting myself back up to speed on the superconductor project. There're a lot of techniques I need to learn about.'

'Well, I hope Martina Lewis appreciates the effort.'

'Who?'

'The one down at Knightsbridge.'

'Oh, her.' Jeff flinched a smile. 'Yeah, right.'

'Jesus, Jeff. Are you forgetting their names already?'

'Not with everybody so kindly reminding me, no.'

'Ah. How is Sue?'

Jeff pulled a face. 'Unhappy. Is that what you called to ask?'

'No, actually. If she ever allows you out again, James and I were going to meet up on Thursday for a pint. Strictly boys only, you can tell her she has my word on that. You game for it?'

It was the third time Alan had asked him out over the last week. Each time he'd refused. This was going beyond impolite. 'James *wants* me to come along?'

'Well, I did have to use a bit of the old arm-twisting technique. Mind you, he does have a legitimate grouse. She was his granddaughter. Bit off, Jeff.'

'Yeah, yeah. Me seducing her, that sweet little child. How evil of me.'

'He'll behave himself this time. I've made quite sure of that.'

'Right. Ah crap, no, look I've got a whole load of teleconferences with the Americans on Thursday. I really can't make it, sorry.'

Alan stared at the top of the screen, where his return camera was. 'Okay, Jeff,' he said in a level voice. 'When you want to come out with us, you give me a call.'

'Sure. Won't be long. Just got a bit of a backlog on right now.'

Alan's image vanished.

'Bugger it,' Jeff muttered. He'd invested decades in those friendships. It was painful for him to watch antagonism and hurt erode them away. But he simply couldn't stand another miserable night in the pub listening to the same conversation they'd had for the last twenty years being replayed with tiny variants. Not again.

'Click. Give me the local news file copied from last Saturday night, the one with the jet ski.'

The video came up on his screen. A badly focused recording of some lad bounding around on a jet ski, playing havoc with the placid fishing boats on Rutland Water. The rider was wearing some kind of wide reflective glasses, preventing full identification. But there was no way Jeff could fail to recognize those features.

He grinned ruefully at his son. Now he had a second thing to envy Tim for. What he would have given to be a part of that prank. It was truly beautiful. They'd annoyed the hell out of a whole load of adults, harmed no one, and had themselves a huge amount of fun. Just imagining the satisfaction they'd had in pulling it off made him smile longingly. The sheer *panache* of such a stunt was admirable, especially for a bunch of teenagers.

As a genuine father he should have given Tim a stern talking-to. What he actually wanted to do was plead with them to let him join in. Then he could go to the *après* party, drinking heedlessly and content with the company of exuberant friends. Laughter lingering long after midnight, lying around on the lawn as they passed bottles and reefers around, with the stars glittering sweetly above them. Afterwards, sneaking up to a bedroom in whoever's house they were using.

And what must that be like?

The recording of Tim had come to its end, holding with the jet ski caught in mid-bounce between wavelets, spray gushing out from its fuselage. An action shot from some extreme-sports event. Jeff left it on as cold reality sank through him. *I can't.* It was as though his very thoughts were sobbing.

One thing was for certain: he needed to get laid, but good.

He told the Europol team to get ready for an evening in Peterborough. Tim had said there were plenty of clubs there. A girl for the night would be easy enough if Martina Lewis was anything to go by.

*

Sue found him as he was getting dressed ready for a night's clubbing. He'd already chosen loose cream trousers; a geometricist's ideal of a Hawaiian shirt, in black and chrome yellow; grey jacket with a contemporary cut so it didn't meet across the front. Which just left him puzzling over which shoes to wear when she rapped lightly on the door frame and walked into his bedroom.

'Off out?' she asked.

'Yeah, I thought I would.' His voice came over as too defensive.

'I thought we should talk, but it can wait a while.'

'No, that's all right.' He abandoned the shoes and sat on the edge of the bed.

Sue came over and sat beside him. She was very prim and composed, a light mauve cardigan drawn round her white blouse; long ochre skirt. 'It's not working, is it, me being here?'

'I was stupid,' he blurted. 'She was young, and eager, and I was by myself, and it was easy. That sounds so old, I know. But that's the truth of it.'

She gave him a sorrowful little look. 'Maybe that's the way it was that night. But if it hadn't been then, it would have been another night. I think that's what upset me the most. Me of all people, I should have known better.'

'I don't understand.'

'You and I. It was only ever sex. This time round. I mean, were you really expecting us to stay together for another fifty years till death do us part?'

'I don't know. I hadn't really thought about it.'

'I had ... Well, I have now. Let's face it, we barely made it through the last nineteen years, and we only managed that because we didn't spend any time together. All we did was live under the same roof occasionally, which meant we could be polite when we did bump into each other. That's how we survived so long: no emotional entanglement.'

'You're being too negative.'

Her hand rubbed his leg. It was as if she was stroking a pet. 'Did you love me, Jeff, nineteen years ago? Were you smitten and besotted, and ready to lay down your life for me?'

'You know why we got together back then.'

'I do. And I'm not saying it was a bad thing. We both got Tim out of it, even though he's more yours than mine. But it was never meant to last. We would have shaken hands and finished in a civilized fashion; then all this came along and buggered our arrangement to hell.'

'Men and women can never be friends. Good quote.'

'What?'

'It's a line from *When Harry Met Sally*. Billy Crystal, he said men and women can never be just friends – the bloke

198

always wants to sleep with the girl. I think he might be right.'

'You certainly did, didn't you?'

'Yeah,' he sighed. 'Like you said, everything changed.'

'I can't believe I was so stupid. Sex always ruins everything.'

'Hey, it wasn't that bad while it lasted.'

Sue glanced round at the big bed that they'd shared all too briefly. 'All four nights of it.'

'I don't regret it.'

'I do. I kidded myself that it meant something. That it might be the start, not the finish.'

'It still could be. We're grown-ups, we can work round Martina Lewis.'

'And Nicole. And Patrick.'

'We were good together. You know it.'

'In bed, yes. But be honest, Jeff, what else is there? Don't you want someone you can talk to about your work? Someone who'll be sparky and intellectual, and challenge your ideas, and appreciate them? I can't even spell quantum mechanics, Jeff.'

'Don't do that, not ever. Don't sell yourself short.'

'I'm not. That's what makes this the hardest part of all. I was just a shadow of a person when you met me; I had no self-esteem, I couldn't look after myself, I was a complete and utter mess. Well, I've grown up from that silly little girl, Jeff. I've learned how to be a fully fledged modern bitch, which is the only survival trait that counts in this world. I can swim with the sharks now, and they'll be the ones who get scared when I'm in the water. What I cannot be is your trophy wife, not any more. It didn't matter before, when there was no sex. But now there is, and I'm not going to wait loyally at home while you shag everything in a skirt so you can try out your new body. And I know enough about men to know that you won't want me carrying on with my affairs, not if we're properly married. So the way we are today just can't exist. That was my mistake – I fooled myself into believing it could out of pure sentiment. Sex stopped me thinking straight; but then, I never claimed to be that smart now.'

'All right,' he said, though it was a bitter defeat. 'So where do we go from here?'

'The way we always said we would. I kiss you and Tim goodbye, and that contract we signed takes care of me financially.'

'Just like that?'

'Don't go all sullen on me. Let's see if we can prove Billy Crystal wrong. I'd like us to stay in touch; Tim, too, if he'll ever speak to me again.'

'You're his mother.'

'I know.'

He found it hard to believe they were being so casual about an event so enormous. 'So, when will you go?' he asked unsteadily.

'My bags are packed.'

'All of them?'

She smiled at the involuntary high note of surprise in his voice. 'No. Enough clothes for a week or so. I'll collect the rest later, when I've found somewhere to live.'

'Aren't you going to use the flat?'

'I will to start with. But I want somewhere of my own eventually.'

'Ah. Right. Have you got somewhere in mind?'

'I don't know. I've got a lot of friends down in London. Or maybe I'll make a clean break. Cornwall is lovely these days, almost the same climate as the Mediterranean used to have.'

'What about your mother?'

Sue's brittle cheerfulness faltered. 'I don't know. It depends where I end up. I'll have to have her close by, and I don't suppose the location matters to her.'

'Are you sure you don't want to give it one last try?'

'Don't be so gallant. You know this is the only option.'

'So who gets to tell Tim?'

'I suppose we'd better do it together.'

27. FLAKY TRACY AND THE BIG LIE

The biotechnology companies promised such a thing was impossible for the whole of the noughties. Slick, expensively dressed public relations officers ridiculed the crusty Greenpeace protesters on television news and discussion shows. While smooth corporate vice-presidents stood up in front of Westminster's Parliamentary select committees and explained in big technical buzzwords exactly why gene-seepage was not going to happen.

It did. Foreign genes carefully spliced into crops to produce higher yields, or fungal resistance, or immunity to disease, or to harden them against insects, somehow managed to migrate across the species barrier. Most of the new mutations were subtle, not even visible outside of a DNA test. But the ones which the eye, and more importantly the camera, could see, were often spectacular. Cowslips with hand-sized scarlet flowers. Rye grass two metres tall. Nettles with buddleia cone flowers. Honeysuckle with pea pods.

Individual specimens would turn up one year, to be surrounded by camera crews and protesters, and eventually a police cordon. Freaks and one-offs, the company spokesperson would announce, sterile and worthless; only to find next year that a hundred more specimens had germinated. Between 2015 and 2020, if you believed the burgeoning datasphere news streams, the triffids had finally arrived in force. By the time Tim was born, it was old news. Increasingly sophisticated GM sequencing techniques had finally inhibited ninety-nine per cent of gene 'jumps'. Nature had culled the truly invalid mutant varieties, leaving hardy strains that were here to stay.

Of all the mutants rooting down in Europe, elephant keck, as it had been nicknamed, was the most prolific and obvious. Ordinary keck that had picked up a growth gene intended to increase cereal-crop size. It plagued every hedgerow and verge across the continent, with stems burgeoning to between two and three metres high, then sprouting an umbrella of grubby white flowers on spindly stalks; coarse floppy leaves protruded underneath these canopies, a dusky green stained with cabbage purple along the stalks. It cost councils and farmers a fortune to chop them down along the roadsides. Elsewhere, they went unchallenged.

That included the Exton estate, a couple of miles down the road from Empingham. It was a huge domain of arable land, crossed with public and private paths that had been tarmacked for the tractors and other farm machinery. The total absence of ordinary traffic made it a long-term favourite for hikers, dog walkers, and fitness fanatics.

The exercise regimen that the Brussels University Medical Centre had given Jeff assumed a modest climb back up the performance graph to full fitness. Looking at the outline, he wasn't entirely sure what kind of level they envisioned raising him to. Olympic qualification standard, apparently. He hadn't followed any of it with blind devotion, although he'd stuck to their basic requirements. That meant a twice-weekly jog, accompanied by four Europol team members who had no trouble at all keeping up with him (including the female officers).

This morning he'd suggested that Tim join him. After some coaxing the recalcitrant boy gave in and agreed. Jeff was thankful for that; it was a way of spending time with his son without the two of them sitting together at the table in the kitchen and trying to fill the awkward silence with laboured conversation. Tim hadn't taken Sue's departure at all well, dealing with it the only way he knew how: by retreating back into his sulky shell.

There wasn't anything to see on the jog; as soon as they cleared the parkland around Exton village itself the ubiquitous elephant keck rose up on either side of the tarmac, then drooped overhead. It didn't quite form a tunnel, leaving a ragged strip of bright turquoise sky clear directly above.

'How are you coping?' Jeff asked after ten minutes. His wrist-strap monitor showed a heart rate of a hundred and forty-one, and he was barely sweating Not bad, for a seventy-eight-year-old.

'Okay,' Tim wheezed. He was red-faced, breathing heavily.

'Good.' Jeff slowed the pace. 'How's school going?'

'Dad!'

'All right. Shit. Sorry.' He stopped running, and put an arm round Tim's shoulder. There was a moment when he thought the boy would shrug him off. It passed. 'I know this isn't fair. It never is.'

'I can't believe she just left like that.'

'It's not her fault, Tim. You know that. It was me.'

'But . . .'

'Say what you think, son, I'm not going to object. I know every father says this, but I'd like to think we can talk about anything.'

Tim's gaze wandered across the umbrella sprays that were emerging from the top of the elephant keck, thumb-sized flower buds just losing their dark green hue as they prepared to open. The next month was going to be awful for hay-fever sufferers – not that it ever bothered him. 'It doesn't matter.'

'Yes, it does – to me, at least. You were going to say mum's been visiting London for years. Am I right?'

'No, dad, I was going to say mum's slept with more people than you have. I watched them come and go before I even knew what was really happening. It was the day I finally found out what they were when I needed this talk. Okay? And that was about ten years ago.'

'Oh shit. I knew you knew, son, I simply didn't realize how much it bothered you. You never said.'

'What? That my parents had a sham marriage, that it was all a front? Thanks, dad. Are you going to tell me it was for my benefit?'

Jeff took his arm away from Tim's shoulder, and looked unflinchingly into his son's hostile face. 'Okay, look, this is the way it is. Hundred per cent truth. I was old and rich, your mother was young and pretty. It never was a marriage, not in any definition. But we had you because we both wanted to. And that means taking on a lot of responsibility, however politically incorrect that might sound today. So we made the best home life we could for you. Kids get badly hurt if their parents are shouting at each other all day long. We accepted our personal situation for what it was, and made rational choices. Don't believe me if that's what you want, or simply tell me to fuck off and die. But we wanted the best for you. And the way we played it was the only way we could give you a stable time at home. I'm sorry that you saw through us so early, and that I didn't help you then. But can you honestly put your hand on heart and swear we didn't care? Until you've done it, you'll never know how special having a child is. You were our world, Tim, and you still are. Just because Sue's left doesn't mean she's gone and rejected you or anything like that. The one thing that upset her the most was what you'd think about her. Well, I'm asking you not to think anything bad. This split was my fault. Nothing has changed between your mother and I except for physical distance.'

Tim shook his head as if he was getting rid of a persistent wasp. 'You two were getting on. I know you were. You were together. I saw that. I thought, I dunno, things were going to be different.'

'If we bumped up your expectations, then I apologize again. We both agreed that was stupid of us.'

'You didn't give it much of a chance, did you?' Tim said broodily. 'Less than a week.'

'No, I didn't, did I?' Jeff turned away, and started walking. 'I really don't know how to explain that one to you. I don't think there is anything to say.'

Tim caught up with him. The anger had faded a little; now there was just confusion and a fair degree of pain still. 'I just don't get it, dad. She was the first girl you laid eyes on. What did you see in her?'

'I didn't see anything in her. It was just one night.'

'But look at what it did, what happened because of it!'

'I know, Tim! All right. I know. It brought everything

to a head, far too quickly. If I was thinking with my brain instead of my dick then maybe your mum and I would have stretched this out until after you went to university.'

'Oh, so that's what matters: just putting on a front till I'm conveniently out of the way.'

'Anything that would have made this easier for you should have been our priority. We were selfish. But after what I did we didn't have any choices. Look, I know this hurts, but we were never going to stay together.'

'Maybe. I sort of knew that, I suppose. But ... now there's these others, too,' Tim said lamely. 'It's like you're rubbing my face in it.' The first girl had been five days ago, a scant two days after his mother left. He'd come down to breakfast to find her in the kitchen with his father, almost in a repetition of that time he'd found his parents canoodling. She was dressed at least, if you counted her clubbing clothes: a short skirt and lace-up top. One look and he had her branded for ever in his mind as a total bimbo: late twenties, with a hairstyle and make-up that harked back to her teenage years, as if they alone could fool people into seeing her as she had been back then.

Each morning since it had been a different girl. All of them picked up the previous night. All of them spending the night.

'Come on, Tim, you know that's the last thing I'd do,' Jeff told him gently.

There were a lot of things Tim wanted to say. Like: it's so much embarrassing. Couldn't you be discreet like mum was? Or even: how do you do it, pull like that every night? *Because I never can.* All that came out was: 'It's not like you.'

'Not like me,' Jeff repeated in a murmur. Finally they'd come to the end of the wall of elephant keck, stepping out where they had a decent view around. The road dipped steeply away ahead of them to run between a couple of small lakes. They'd both been dug out centuries ago, when the lord of the manor had used them as fish-breeding ponds to supply his own table. Since then, an elaborate stone boathouse had been built on the upper lake, like a miniature castle. It was even called Fort Henry. As follies went, it was quite splendid. 'Come on,' Jeff said. He steered Tim to the side of the road, and they sat on the grassy bank facing the lower lake. The Europol body-guards huddled together on the road, politely out of earshot.

'I'm not like me,' Jeff said eventually. 'Look at me, Tim; physically, I'm your sort of age. You have to know what that means.'

'Yes,' Tim said cautiously.

'Girls, Tim. They're important. In fact, they're a necessity.'

As always, Tim's body betrayed him. He was blushing hot again. 'Um, yeah, suppose so.'

'I know it's been a bit much to absorb all in one week. But when they rejuvenated me they made me very mortal. Weaknesses of the flesh, and all that.'

'I see.'

'You don't sound convinced.'

'I do understand. It's just . . . I don't even remember the names of the first two.'

'Me neither,' Jeff chuckled. It died away as Tim's expression remained blank. 'Ah, now I think I get it. Too many, too quickly – is that right?'

'They're your girlfriends; if that's how you want to treat them, then fine.'

Jeff couldn't help it: he laughed openly at that. 'Girlfriends! Tim, they're one-night stands, okay? We're not talking about replacement wives and mothers here. Don't confuse love with sex, they're very different.'

'I know. It's just that this is all very different for me. I suppose I'll get used to it.' He made it sound as though that would be the hardest thing in the world he could ever do.

'Oh Tim, you haven't gone and put me on a pedestal have you? Not me?'

'You're my dad. We always got on before.'

'We still do, son, and we always will. No matter how awkward it is between us, you can always rely on me, I promise. But please don't make the mistake of thinking I'm some kind of saint. I'm not. Really, I'm batting for the other fella. It's a lot more fun.'

Tim's answering smile was sly. 'No, you're not. You're Jeff Baker. You gave the world memory crystals.'

'Ho shit.' Jeff lay back on the grass. Two swans on the lower lake slid about briskly, leaving almost no wake behind them. A row of cygnets hurried after them, playing among themselves with impish delight. Beyond the lake the landscape of low crumpled valleys rolled away into misty distance, fields fresh with the new green of summer crops. The English countryside as legend told it, as it should be. A vista that made him feel, finally, as if he had come home. With Sue gone, the last of what went before had ended. It was time to start clean. That meant Tim, too; treat the boy as an equal. 'All right, Tim, last shock of the week. If you're up to it. And I'm not joking.'

'How bad?' Tim couldn't tell if he was serious or not.

'Bad. The final skeleton in the closet. You might want to follow your mother and leave after this.'

'It's not ... You didn't kill anyone, did you?' Tim gave the Europol team a quick, guilty glance over his shoulder.

'Oh no. Worse than that. I'm a fraud.'

'No, you're not.'

'Okay, you judge, then.'

'Go on.'

'You know I was married once before?'

'Yeah. You never talked about her, neither did mum. But I caught it when I accessed some of your biographies in the datasphere. They never say much about her. She was called Tracy, wasn't she?'

'She certainly was, dear old Flaky Tracy.'

Tim sniggered. 'Flaky Tracy. What, did she have dandruff?'

'Yeah.' Jeff gave him a conspirator's grin. 'On the inside of her skull.'

Tim laughed.

'Honestly, Tim, I'm not kidding, she was an absolute angel to look at. Small, blonde, utterly adorable, good figure. Maybe not quite as beautiful as your mother, but men looked round when she walked into a room. Know what I mean?'

'Yeah, guess so.'

'Right. But the thing is, you can never believe that anyone who looks so lovely can be anything other than lovely. Especially when it comes to women. I mean, that knowledge is hardwired into a man's genes. Pretty equals nice. Jesus wept, did I ever learn the hard way. I'm not joking, Tim, Flaky Tracy turned out to be the ultimate bitch demon from Hell. The only reason she was sent to roam the Earth was because the Devil got nervous when she was around down below. And that's not me being bitter over the divorce, either. Believe me, thirty-seven years has managed to calm me down quite a lot as far as that one's concerned.'

'She can't have been that bad, surely?'

'Like I said, judge for yourself. We were getting divorced around the time I worked out the molecular structure of the memory crystal. You know what would have happened if I'd patented it, don't you? I, we, you, would have been so bloody rich we could have afforded our own personal space programme. But she would have got half, probably more if that bastard of a solicitor she hired – and slept with – had his say.' Jeff looked at his mildly scandalized son, and smiled broadly. 'So I gave it away. That's it, Tim. I didn't do it as some noble gesture. I wasn't pure in heart. I didn't do it for the betterment of all mankind. I did it because I hated that *cunt* so much you couldn't put it into words. And when she realized what I'd done, that she wasn't going to have more money than an African nation's debt, that solicitor of hers had to hold her down in her chair to stop her attacking me, and he was weeping by that time as well. I can still remember her screaming. Lord, but it was a beautiful sound.' He drew down a long, cleansing breath. 'So you see, I'm not Jeff Baker. I never have been. It was all complete bullshit from start to finish.'

Tim's jaw had opened as he stared at his father. 'But . . . they chose you for rejuvenation because you gave away the memory crystal.'

Jeff quirked his eyebrows. 'Yeah.'

'It cost trillions of Euros.'

211

'Yeah.'

'And you didn't tell them?' Tim tried to laugh, but it came out as a short bark, wavering between outrage and admiration.

'They didn't ask.'

'Oh, my God. Dad!'

'Cheer up, Brian; remember, *Always look on the bright side of life.*' He whistled a few bars of the Monty Python song, smiling contentedly.

Tim started laughing. He couldn't stop, not even when it began to hurt. Jeff put his arms round him and hugged him tight. Tim returned the embrace, bursting with joy to finally know who his father really was. And loving it.

28. EXAM PRESSURE

The finals for PSE (Progressive Secondary Education) courses had started. Over seventy-five per cent of England's eighteen-year-olds were currently fretting their way through them. You couldn't fail if you got a low mark in the finals, that would be tremendously unfair after spending two years doing the coursework, but the exam did make up twenty per cent of the overall course mark, which decided a pupil's grading and therefore which university they went to. Annabelle had done some history mining during her modern social evolution course, and had been horrified to discover that A-levels, which the PSEs had replaced, used to be make-or-break exams. Her finals were nerve-racking enough, she was sure she wouldn't have been able to cope with exams that exerted so much pressure.

All told, she had eight finals to work her way through (Tim had fifteen). It meant she was going to have her PCglasses glued to her head for hours at a time during the two weeks of the finals, revising and running through previous exam questions. She didn't plan on spending much time with her gang of friends in that period, they were too likely to distract her. The jet-ski outing was the last time she got together with all of them. But she couldn't revise the whole time, there had to be periods when she could chill out. That wasn't going to happen at home. Which made the Manor just about perfect, and Tim was ever-eager to make amends for the après-jet-ski party.

The afternoon she went up there they splashed around in the swimming pool for half an hour before dragging a couple of sunloungers out onto the terrace. It was a hot afternoon, with no clouds and no wind; the forecasters were predicting the high would last at least three weeks. Annabelle towelled herself off, then sprayed on factor forty sunblock. She was wearing her navy-blue bikini, which was a shame because she would have preferred an all-over tan, but going topless in front of Tim right now wasn't going to happen – he'd get all the wrong ideas. And the security cameras would have given the Europol team a great peeper's view.

So they lay side by side, with only a small table between the sunloungers. Tim with his head resting on the cushions so he could look at her the whole time. The talk was almost as relaxed as it had been a week ago. Tim was starting to accept his father going out with other girls, though Annabelle wrinkled her nose with distaste when she learned about him going out and crawling round the clubs each night. But it was nice to see Tim returning to some sort of equilibrium. She told him how devastated she'd been when her own mother left.

When it came to the finals, he was cool about them, which sparked not a little envy in her. He apologized, and said he understood about her wanting to get to university and away from her home. They daydreamed together about what it would be like if she got to Oxford or

Cambridge with him. He still hadn't decided which one he'd choose.

The radio they had on in the background, tuned to an eighties music station, began a news report about Rob Lacey's campaign. He was in Spain, speaking at rallies there and trying to make alliances with regional politicians, eager for their endorsement.

'He'll do well out there,' Tim said.

'How come?'

'Spain's always been a good ally to us in Brussels. They usually vote with us to block the central and northern countries.'

'He'll never win.'

'Yes, he will. The Med countries don't have their own candidate. Nobody in France will vote for him, same way as we'd never vote for a Frog. All he has to do is swing the Germans behind him.'

'I can't believe we'll have a President of Europe.'

'Do you think it'll matter?'

'No. Be nice if it did, though. There's so many regulations he needs to liberalize or just abolish.'

'And more he needs to strengthen. The Germans are getting a thousand Russians a day sneaking in over the eastern laser-curtain border. More, if you access the undernet reports.'

'I know,' she sighed. She picked the glass tumbler off the table, only to find it was empty. 'I need more juice.'

'Call Mrs Mayberry,' Tim said.

'Honestly, Tim, you're such a slob.' She climbed to her feet and walked over the lawn to the lounge with its wide-open French windows.

'Get me one, too,' Tim yelled at her.

'One of these coming right up.' Annabelle gave him the finger, and walked into the lounge. It was cooler inside, the air-conditioning murmuring quietly behind slim vents in the skirting board. She pushed her sunglasses up onto her forehead, and blinked while her eyes adjusted to the light.

'You look sensational in that bikini,' Jeff said.

Annabelle just managed not to jump. He was sprawled in one of the deep leather settees, feet up on the armrest, shoes off, a very fat old paperback science fiction book in his hand.

She pursed her lips. 'Thank you. What's your next line? I'd look even better out of it?'

'I wasn't going to say that. If Sue taught me anything about clothes, it was that revealing is always more alluring than revealed. Always leave 'em wanting more.'

'From what I've heard, you're getting more than enough already.'

He gestured, arms wide. 'I wouldn't need more if I had you.'

'Don't start that again.'

'I'm just being honest.'

Annabelle wished her mind would stop running that one insidious phrase *trading up* over and over. Damn that Sophie. 'There's a time and a place for honesty, and this isn't it.'

'Will you let me know where and when it is?'

'It's in your dreams.' She smiled at him with sweet malice and walked on through into the hallway.

*

Tim prodded his sunglasses up as she approached the sunloungers. 'You all right?'

'Fine.'

'I thought you were scowling at me.'

Annabelle stood above his sunlounger, looking down, a glass in each hand. 'No, I wouldn't do that. I'm not unhappy with you.'

Tim managed a slightly nervous smile. 'Good.'

'It's too hot for me out here. I'm going up to your room to cool off.' She put the drinks down on the small table. One eyebrow rose slightly in query. 'Are you coming with me?'

29. TIM IN LOVE

And after all that, all the crap in his life – his mother leaving him, his friends that weren't quite, the constant nervous anxiety of wondering if he'd done and said the right thing to her – the rickety flight that was his life had suddenly levelled out. No, actually, it had done more than that, it had become perfect. His finals were so easy he just sailed through them. The weather was warm and sunny. Dad actually stopped bringing the girls down to breakfast.

And there was Annabelle.

Annabelle, who came round to the Manor most afternoons. They really did spend a couple of hours revising; swimming and sunbathing, too. But each time, they wound up in his room, naked and having sex. There was a whole great long summer holiday coming up ahead of them as well. Over eight long weeks, when neither of them had anything to do. That would mean she could come round every day. Really, how could anything possibly get better?

He began to wonder about after the holiday. She'd probably be going to a different university. At night he made calls, finding out if he could switch from Oxford and Cambridge so they could remain together. He didn't tell her that: it would be his surprise present later on. Just thinking about what she'd do to thank him made him break out in a sweat of excitement.

*

His father seemed happy with the arrangement. Tim kept on saying how happy he was, how wonderful Annabelle was. Jeff would smile, and grip him by the arm, and say: 'That's great, Tim, I'm so pleased. She's a lovely-looking girl.'

He didn't even have a beer. It wasn't just because he'd got to keep a clear head for the finals, he simply wasn't looking for that kind of high any more. Annabelle was satisfied by that. He hadn't realized before how much she disapproved of him getting blasted. Quitting was just another example of how in tune they were now.

'Dad,' he asked one morning. 'How old were you and Tracy when you got married?'

'I was mid-thirties, she was late twenties. Why?'

'Nothing. Mum was twenty, wasn't she?'

'Yeah.' Jeff ordered the kitchen's wallscreen to switch off, and the news stream vanished. 'You thinking of eloping, son?'

Tim shook his head and scooped up another spoonful of cornflakes. 'No.'

'Thank God for that.'

'Dad?'

'Oh shit. Yes?'

'Which university do you think I should go to?'

'Ah. Right. Okay, well, they're both pretty good. I went to Oxford, of course, but I'm not insisting you follow. Have you actually decided what you're taking?'

'General science for my degree. Unless I find something

219

that really grabs me, then I'll switch to that. I'll probably go for a physics doctorate.'

Jeff poured a glass of freshly squeezed orange, giving Tim a smile over the rim. 'Doctorate, eh? That's very focused for you, Tim.'

'Better the qualification, the better the job.'

'I know, but you are only eighteen, you know. I'm just a bit surprised you're thinking along those lines. If you'd like, you can take a gap year, you know. I never did, and I always regretted it.'

'Are you dead-on? I hadn't considered that. I'd have to ask Annabelle what she thought about it.'

'Would you?'

Tim coloured slightly. 'Yeah. If we could do that together, it would be amazing.'

'I'm sure it would. Where would you go?'

'America, Australia, Japan. I don't know. That kind of travel is so bloody expensive.'

'I'm not broke; I could probably pay for a ticket. And once you get there, you can work your way round. I think they still do that kind of visa, certainly in Australia.'

'Really? You'd really pay for that?'

'Sure. I've been taking a peek at your PSE grades. I think you deserve some kind of reward. Especially as you qualify for a scholarship. You've done a hell of a lot of work.'

'Jesus, dad, that's ... Thanks!' He wasn't quite sure how he'd got off the subject of going to university with Annabelle, but this more than compensated.

'How's the planning for the Summer Ball going?' Jeff asked.

'Good, I suppose.'

'That's it? Good? You've got three days left, Tim. Have you hired a dinner jacket? Because I certainly haven't seen a bill for a new one materialize on the household account. How are you travelling down there? Where are you picking Annabelle up from? What flowers have you chosen for her?'

'Oh.' Tim was suddenly crestfallen. Mum usually sorted all that kind of thing. *And I never appreciated it.* 'Dunno.'

'Better get started then, hadn't we?'

*

Annabelle and Tim went with Rachel and Simon, with all of them leaving from the Manor. A beauty therapist from Gazelle's in Oakham turned up at three o'clock to style the girls' hair and apply their make-up.

'We're not leaving till six,' Tim protested when she arrived. The look he got from Annabelle froze any further comment. Sue's old bedroom was taken over for the afternoon. Mrs Mayberry and Lucy Duke were also drafted in to help the girls get ready.

Tim and Simon took a brief quarter of an hour to dress. Tim's dinner jacket had only been delivered by the Community Service Supply van that morning. It had been chosen after several rushed calls with Sue, who had surveyed current suitable evening attire in several London outfitters. In the end she'd gone for a classic style, with a modern cut for his trousers and a slender silk collar on the jacket. Jeff had to tie their bow ties for them. Tim hadn't dared suggest an elastic one to his mother.

The florist arrived at quarter to six, the corsages in a cool storage box on the back of her e-trike. As he waited down in the hall, Tim was beginning to feel the impact of the event with a fluttery stomach and tingling feet. At five past six, Natalie Cherbun appeared at the top of the stairs and coughed. Both boys wheeled round.

Rachel looked superb, her strapless purple satin dress stroking the contours of her figure. Tim never noticed her. Annabelle was dressed in a white evening gown that was so bright it was almost silver: it had a deep plunge back which was countered by a demure neckline blending into a seamless bodice section that was surely sprayed on; the skirt was made up from an array of long panels that slid about fluidly as she walked to reveal momentary glimpses of her legs. Her thick gold-chestnut hair had been swept back and down in a straight glossy mane, with thin strands corkscrewing at either side of her brow.

Tim stood at the foot of the stairs as both girls made their grand entrance. He put his hand out for Annabelle when she was a couple of steps from the bottom, entirely unsurprised to find it was trembling. She took it gently and alighted on the hall's marble tiles.

'You look beautiful,' Tim whispered.

'Thank you.' She brought her lips together for a slight kiss. 'Don't muss me.'

He hadn't even noticed she was wearing make-up it was so subtle, highlighting her strong cheekbones, a mild mascara deepening her eyes. Her scent was the kind of air that gusted off a meadow of summer wild flowers.

'Sorry.' He proffered the corsage, a scarlet rose bordered with tiny saffron freesias. Annabelle curtsied as she took it.

There was a burst of applause around the hall, led by Jeff, with Mrs Mayberry and the Europol team smiling on behind him. The four youngsters were suddenly a knot of happy, flustered grins.

The limousine that had pulled up outside the Manor's portico belonged to the era of movie stars, glam-rock princes and decadent opening nights in London's West End. A stretched white Lincoln with black windows and small orange running lights, a boomerang TV aerial sticking up out of the boot.

Tim saw it and gasped. 'Dad!' He couldn't believe anything like it still existed outside a transport museum.

'My treat,' Jeff said. 'I'm just sorry I couldn't find you a pink Cadillac.'

'It's brilliant!' Rachel squealed. She stood on tiptoe and gave Jeff a kiss. 'Thanks so much.'

'No problem.'

'Yes,' Annabelle said. 'Thank you.' Her lips brushed Jeff's cheek. Their eyes locked for an instant. Then she was pulling Tim down the stairs, both of them laughing gleefully.

'Be good!' Jeff called after them.

The chauffeur held the rear door open, somehow managing to crack open a bottle of champagne at the same time. The kids whooped excitedly as they ducked inside, looking round the extravagant interior. They found the cut-crystal flutes, and held them out for the foaming champagne.

Jeff stood on the top step in the shade of the portico. There was a gentle smile on his lips as he listened to the animated exclamations coming from inside the deliciously ludicrous vehicle. They were cut off abruptly as the chauffeur closed the back door. The Europol team clambered into their own saloon car, slamming the doors shut.

Then the stretch limousine was pulling out of the drive, crunching gravel beneath its whitewalled tyres.

'Didn't little Timmy look grand, just grand,' Mrs Mayberry said. 'And Annabelle's as pretty as a picture. You must be very proud.'

Jeff turned to see the housekeeper clasping her hands together, her face all puckered up as she watched the limousine depart.

'I am, yes.'

30. WILL THE REAL JEFF BAKER
PLEASE STAND UP?

Ten to three in the morning and Jeff had almost gone to sleep. He'd spent the whole evening reviewing data for the superconductor project. Not that he'd had any insights yet; he wasn't expecting any. That would come later, when he had acquired a great more detail and information on the current state of the art. Possibly. That was his thing. Sometimes entire solutions would just rise out of a whole mass of seething raw data, utterly obvious with hindsight. Sometimes the routes to solutions would flare in his mind, little nova-bursts of illumination. Molecules and functions slotting into place to form new solid-state components. Ninety-nine per cent of the time he just slogged along with the rest of the pack, making mistakes and floundering down dead ends. But he did have that elusive ability. His mind could hold aloft the whole problem and look at it from new angles.

Call it genius. Or even intermittent genius. It had worked a few times in his life, though the world at large only knew of the one. The rest were dull stuff, inapplicable outside of esoteric physics laboratories. Although they had cemented his status within the scientific community far more than the showbiz glamour of memory crystals. A status high enough for Brussels to spin their multi-trillion-Euro gamble on his head.

And somehow, throughout the whole ridiculous circus of faith that an entire continent had placed upon him, he didn't feel pressured. Like everyone else, he too believed he might manage to produce results.

A neat trick if you can do it.

As the actress said to the bishop.

The security camera picked up the limousine as it turned back into the drive. Jeff watched it blankly for a moment, his eyes still half registering the scrawl of data on the main display screens. Then he saw the time.

'Oh, bugger it. Click. Save, safe store duplicate, and switch the hell off. We're through for the night.'

'I understand that, Jeff,' HAL 9000's melodiously menacing voice assured him.

The screens blanked out, and began to slide back into their recesses. He stretched elaborately. There were empty cups of tea and his supper plates cluttering one half of the desk. He couldn't be bothered to take them out to the dishwasher.

The limousine braked to a sharp halt before the portico. There was no other motion apart from the Europol team's saloon sliding up the drive. Jeff started to walk down the steps.

The chauffeur's door flew open, and the furious man got out, flinging his cap onto his seat. He stormed off towards the back of the vehicle. The rear door opened before he reached it. Jeff heard the unmistakable sound of someone puking. He rolled his eyes towards the lazy silver stars glittering above. 'Oh Christ,' he muttered.

Tim half-fell out of the limo. He wasn't wearing his jacket any more; his bow tie was askew around his neck, both shirtsleeve cuffs were undone, flapping about. One arm flopped about, patting the gravel. Then he tensed and heaved again.

'Get out of my fucking car!' the chauffeur yelled. He put his hands under Tim's shoulder and started pulling.

'All right,' Jeff said loudly. 'All right, I'll take him from here.'

The chauffeur ignored him, and dropped Tim on the gravel. For one moment Jeff thought he was going to kick the semi-conscious boy. Tim giggled in the gurgling way that only the truly drunk can manage. A sound guaranteed to annoy the sober.

The chauffeur was glaring down, clenching his fists. Jeff stepped in front of him, hands held out to placate the man. 'I've got him.'

'Oh, you've got him have you? Where the hell were you when he was chucking up in the back of my car, man? Huh?'

'I'm sorry, I'll see . . .'

'He threw up in my fucking car. Threw up! That is the most disrespect you can have for me, man. There isn't another car like this left in the country.'

Jeff hardened his voice. 'I said I'm sorry.'

'I've got a fucking passenger booked for tomorrow. What am I going to tell him? Just slide around till you find a clean piece of fucking seat? Is that what I say? That's leather upholstery, man. Real antique leather.'

'Get it cleaned. Bill me. All right.'

'Get it cleaned.' The chauffer waved his arms around. 'Where the fuck am I going to get it cleaned in time for my next passenger? It's gone three o'clock in the fucking morning.'

'Hi, dad.'

'Shut up, Tim. I don't know where you get it cleaned, and I don't care. Just calm down and get the hell out of here. I told you, I will pay.'

Lieutenant Krober was coming down the portico steps. The Europol team from the saloon car were also heading towards the noise.

'Fuck you, man.' The chauffeur looked round at the approaching men. He pointed a rigid forefinger at Jeff, shaking it. 'I got friends, man. Good friends. You fucked with the wrong person tonight, you understand? Friends.'

'You're on an express elevator to hell. Going down. You should get off before it reaches the bottom.'

The chauffeur gawped at him.

Jeff held back a sigh at the reaction. *Doesn't anyone watch the classics any more?* He beckoned to a couple of the Europol team. 'Get him inside, will you, please?' They bent over Tim and hauled him to his feet. The boy groaned, but didn't throw up.

Jeff ducked his head down and looked into the back of the limousine. The smell of vomit was appalling. Annabelle was sitting hunched up on a long sofa bench that ran along one side of the cavernous interior. He was pretty sure she'd been crying. 'Come on,' he said softly, and held a hand out to her. 'Let's get you home, Cinders.'

*

She was silent for most of the drive back to Uppingham. Jeff took her in his Merc, with a thoroughly pissed-off bodyguard squad following behind in their own saloon car.

'He always does it,' she said as they slid along the road through the Chater valley. 'Always.'

'I'm sorry. Really. I wanted you both to have a lovely night.'

'Why?'

'Okay, I guess I deserve that. But seeing you happy makes me feel good.'

'That's pretty weird.' She let her head fall back into the leather seat cover and closed her eyes. The Merc's suspension provided an incredibly smooth ride, almost as if they weren't moving at all. It gave her a strange feeling of isolation. 'I was stupid, you know. Me and Tim. I shouldn't have.'

'You were good for him. In fact, you're probably the best thing that's ever happened to him.'

'But you'd rather I hadn't happened, at least not to him, wouldn't you?'

'You did, though. They can make me young again, they can't put the clock back.'

'It was a reaction. An overreaction. But you know that.'

'Yes, I knew that.'

She smiled into the darkness at her strange little victory. Now all that was left was to wait. Her heart was racing away inside her chest. For someone who was supposed to be calm and in charge that shouldn't be happening.

The Merc drew up outside Annabelle's house. At this time of the morning even the local bad boys had slunk away home. Jeff turned the power off.

'Home, sweet home,' he said.

'No, it's never been that.' Her eyes were still closed. 'Not for a long time, anyway.'

Jeff looked at the delectable teenager in the seat next to him. Weak street-light shimmered through the Merc's windows, showing him her profile in a dry sodium-orange drizzle. He took his time, unrepentant, enjoying the way the gown's bodice clung to her, showing off the shape and size of her breasts. Several skirt panels had slipped down, revealing long stretches of toned thigh muscle.

Seventy-eight years of a good life lived well should have produced an unmatched sophistication and refinement. There ought to have been clever words and wicked lies he could use, rivalling history's great seducers. All Jeff said was: 'I want to fuck you.'

Annabelle opened her eyes, looking round at the familiar street. 'Don't let them see. Not this.'

He found the dial that controlled the opacity of the Merc's windows and turned it up full. The street lights faded away to tiny dim stars. There was just enough light left for him to see her reach round and undo the gown's neck clasp. She pulled the bodice down. His hand clamped down hard on one of her breasts, squeezing to discover the weight, the firmness.

'Sit up,' he told her. When she leaned forward he bent down and used his free hand to turn the chair release. The back hinged down until it was almost horizontal.

There was no real room to move. She couldn't cry out or protest for fear of who else would hear and be drawn to the car. Her skirt panels were clawed aside. His weight pressed her down, shoving her spine into the cushioning of a seat that was now bent awkwardly, making it uncomfortable to the verge of painful. Hands switched between breasts and thighs then back again, always too fierce and desperate. Her feet banged into the dashboard. Fingers curled round her panties and tugged until the cotton ripped.

He manoeuvred himself between her knees, and his heels kicked the windscreen. One of Annabelle's legs was squashed against the door panel, while the other knocked into the steering wheel. It left her thighs just wide enough apart.

There was nothing she could do but lie there while he grunted and thrust into her again and again. It was demeaning and disgraceful. Bodies locked together in cramped darkness; his a deplorable sixty years older than hers. Gown fabric constricting, scrunched too tight against her limbs. Car seat preventing her from moving, escaping. Illicit and depraved. Leather squeaking and sticking, rubbing abrasively against sweating flesh. His strength. The heat. Her boyfriend's father's cock rooting round inside her. Breath panting over her face. All of it receding as her orgasm built, taking over.

In the end she did cry out. It didn't matter who heard, not now. It was a victory cry, pure animal.

He lay on top of her, limp and shaking while she tried to get her breathing back to normal. Then she heard a slight chuckle, and he gingerly raised himself up onto his elbows. His face hung centimetres above hers.

'You okay?' he asked in a frightened little voice.

'Yes.'

'Bloody hell – doing it in a car at my age.'

Annabelle wriggled an arm down between them. Her hand curled round his cock, and moved the way she knew men couldn't resist. 'More,' she whispered. The urgency was like confessing every sin she'd ever committed.

31. REGRETS IN THE AFTERMATH

It was the hangover that would not go away. There was no pain, no thudding headache, no wretched nausea. Those classics had all faded before lunch, with the help of a few Nurofen and a lot of cold water and hot coffee which a hugely unsympathetic Mrs Mayberry had forced down him. No, Tim's burden was a whole lot worse, and due to be carried for a long time.

There wasn't a lot he remembered about last night. The summer ball had started splendidly in a huge marquee with a galaxy of shining silverware laid out on the long tables. A six-piece band playing cheerful pre10 music was sitting beside a raised wooden dance floor. Bar staff handed out large flagons of wine to each couple. An official photographer had taken everyone's picture when they arrived. And the stretch limo had attracted a lot of attention and envy.

Annabelle had stayed close beside him the whole time, as radiant and happy as he'd ever seen her. They greeted their friends and classmates; Vanessa was there, and Lorraine, and Philip, and Martin, and Colin, and Natalie, and Zai, and Sophie (who was there with Martin, which drew more than one comment behind their backs). The whole bunch of them over-eager now the finals were a fading memory. They posed in large groups for the photographer, smiling wide, and with their arms draped around each other. The ball's atmosphere was flush with excitement, although a tingle of melancholia mingled in. This was, after all, the last time they'd all be gathered together. End of an era.

There were drinks and canapés first. Then the formal five-course meal, with wine or beer. Speeches – thankfully short. Then the dancing started, with the bar still serving away enthusiastically.

After that, they'd booked a couple of tables in Low Moonlight in the middle of Oakham, the best club the town could offer. They had more drinks; grazing on pizza. A whole lot of mournful talk about what they were all going to do with their lives. Which of them was going to the Million Citizen Voice protest.

Tim hadn't realized he'd drunk so much. At most a couple of glasses during the meal, surely? Maybe one or two between dances. Social drinking in Low Moonlight.

Obviously not. He couldn't actually remember much about the last half of the ball. And Low Moonlight was a blank, apart from a certainty that he'd been there with the crew. The drive back home had consisted of someone shouting over the intercom.

Then he woke up, and the nightmare began.

'How could you do such a thing?' Mrs Mayberry asked while he was groaning and clamping his hands to his dangerously hot forehead. 'Here.' She slammed a tumbler of water on the kitchen table, several white pills rolling round beside it. The noise was like quarry blasting. Tim thought he might keel over. His hands were shaking badly,

234

his skin icy. 'You don't deserve a nice girl like that, not if that's how you treat her.'

'Please,' Tim croaked. 'Don't.'

'Don't, ha! There isn't a bouquet of flowers big enough in the world to make up for what you did. That poor, poor girl.'

Tim got the first pill into his mouth and managed a single sip of water. His stomach squirmed in rebellion. 'Oh God, what did I do?'

'That ball should have been the happiest night of her life. The pair of you should have danced till dawn. Proper dancing, not that pogo jiving your generation calls dancing. And what do you do? You drink so much your police squad have to carry you to bed, that's what.' Cupboards slammed loudly, and crockery rattled as the housekeeper started to make coffee. He was already dreading the froth roar of the espresso machine.

'Where's Annabelle?'

'As far away from you as possible.'

'Where? Please.'

Mrs Mayberry shot him a slightly softer look. 'At home.'

'I have to call her.' He tried to stand up, but the nausea made him clench his stomach muscles. The shakes started up again.

Mrs Mayberry pointed a wooden spoon at him. 'You get those pills down, young man. And if you upchuck over my floor tiles, it isn't going to be me who cleans them. You understand?'

'Yes,' Tim agreed piteously. He reached for the second pill.

Jeff came into the kitchen and sat down opposite him. 'Morning.'

Tim wondered why he'd actually bothered getting out of bed, in fact why he'd bothered ever waking up. Actually, being born was probably the first big mistake. 'Dad. I'm sorry.'

'I know, son. I've had a few nights like that myself.'

'You have?'

Mrs Mayberry let out a snort of contempt. 'Men.'

Jeff looked at her. 'We'd like some time together, thanks.'

There was a final strident clatter on the workbench surface, and she walked out.

'I didn't mean to,' Tim said. 'It was just . . . everything was going well. I felt so good. Annabelle was happy.'

'Tim, I took her home last night. She wasn't happy. You were throwing up in the limo. It was not nice.'

'Oh God.' He thought he was going to start crying. 'I've got to talk to her.'

'No. Leave it for a while. Believe me, she doesn't want to talk to you right now.'

'But I love her, dad, I really love her. Dead on!' He looked into his father's face, finding a pain which mirrored his own. 'I'm going to call.'

'Tim, don't. That'll only make it worse right now.'

'But I can't leave it!'

'I know. Look, send her flowers, or chocolates, or something. Make sure you send her an avtxt with the most grovelling apology you've ever formatted. Make it very plain that you know you're in the wrong. She's going to be feeling just as upset as you this morning. Give her time, then try and talk. Okay?'

Tim nodded, and bowed his head. 'Yeah. I got it.'

So he did what his father suggested – actually, it made a lot of sense – and ordered a bunch of flowers, and sent an avtxt. Then he called Rachel, who was pretty short with him, but did say she hadn't heard from Annabelle, and Annabelle was too good for him anyway. 'I know,' Tim moaned at the blank screen after she'd switched off.

'God, you so much blew it last night,' Colin said. 'I can't believe how much you knocked back. What were you thinking of?'

'Wasn't everybody else drinking?' Tim asked miserably.

'Yeah, but you always go too far, Tim.'

'Have you heard from Annabelle?'

'Me? Shit, no.'

'Has anybody?'

'I don't know. Doubt it.'

'If you do hear anything . . .'

'I'll call you, mate, no sweat.'

There was no reply to his avtxt. He sent another, longer apology. Then a third. The fourth was a straight-txt begging letter. By five o'clock in the afternoon he couldn't stand it any more, and tried a direct call. The Goddard house's domestic computer informed him he wasn't on the approved caller list and ended the connection.

'Want to come jogging with me?' Jeff asked sympathetically when he found Tim moping about in the lounge. 'It's cooling down a bit outside now.'

'No. I'm going to take my e-trike over to Uppingham.'

'Oh no,' Jeff said. 'No, you don't. There are laws against stalking.'

'Dad! I'm not stalking. I want to see her. I've got to explain.'

237

'I'll make a deal with you. If she hasn't replied to a call by this time tomorrow, I'll drive you over there myself. Okay?'

'Suppose so.'

*

Annabelle allowed his call though the next morning. The screen showed him an image that made him ache. She was wearing a simple red T-shirt with a slightly frayed collar; her hair was pinned back neatly. Only her intimidatingly blank expression gave any hint of how bad things were.

'I'm sorry,' he blurted. 'I'm so much sorry. Really.'

'I know you are, Tim, but that doesn't change what either of us are, does it?'

'Um, no. But it won't happen again.'

'Tim, there isn't going to be an "again" for it to happen in, all right?'

'What?' He thought the connection was glitching. She couldn't have said that.

'Tim, we're over. That's it.'

'No! Look, let me come over, we can talk about this. I'm not going to drink again, all right? I fucked up once, I know that. I won't ever again. I promise, Annabelle, I swear. It'll be different now. God, I hated myself when I woke up. Please. Let's just get together. We can sort this out.'

'I don't want you to come over, Tim. I don't want to talk. It's over. We're over. That's it. That's all there is to it.'

'No.' His fist banged down on the table. 'It was special, Annabelle. I love you.'

'I don't love you, Tim.'

'You did, you really did. I know you did.'

'Don't get sex and love mixed up, Tim. They're very different.'

'Not with us.'

'Yes, with us. Tim, it was good fun, but that was all. Move on. I have.'

'We can move on together. I promise, Annabelle, it'll be so good.'

'What? You're going to tell me we can go to university together? That you'll give up Oxford and Cambridge and come to some second-rate campus to be with me? Face it, Tim, at best we were only going to have a long summer romance.'

'It can be more,' he pleaded.

'Tim, I want you to end this call.'

'No.'

'Tim, you and I are over. Don't make me say bad things. Please. Switch the phone off.'

'Come and talk.'

'You are hurting me by leaving the phone on. Do you want to hurt me?'

'No. Annabelle!'

'Then switch the phone off.'

'Please.'

'Off, Tim.'

Her face hadn't altered; there was no trace of emotion anywhere to be seen. With a last gasp of dismay he pressed the button that ended the call, then collapsed, sobbing.

32. SECOND TIME AROUND

When the Brussels Treasury began to pour its torrent of taxEuros into subsidizing the European train network, England was lucky that most of the lines decommissioned following Dr Beeching's review in the sixties could be revived without too much effort. Nearly all of the old bridges had been knocked down, development projects had spilled across the abandoned stations and marshalling yards, and trees had grown up to clot the embankments out in the countryside. But the cost of resurrecting the old lines was insignificant in comparison to establishing a whole new network. Local trains were able to re-establish their prominence quickly in comparison to other EU countries.

Annabelle had been about five when they reopened Uppingham's station, not that she remembered the ceremony. It wasn't quite in the same place as the old one – the town had grown over the original site – so the new platforms were pushed out towards Bisbrooke. But the last century's embankments had been renovated and reinforced, taking the new electric induction rails along the same route. They meandered along the lush newly forested valley between Glaston and Seaton before linking up with the main regional track that led directly into Stamford.

The modern two-carriage train whisked Annabelle from Uppingham to Stamford in just under fifteen minutes. She walked from the busy little Victorian station to the George Hotel, not five hundred metres away. A couple of the Europol team were sitting round in the wood-panelled lobby. They'd both been in the saloon car after the ball, following her and Jeff back to Uppingham. And now here they were, watching politely as she went up the stairs. She found it embarrassing. *They know what I'm here for, what I'm about to do.* It was as if their watching eyes made her cheap, somehow.

Jeff had booked himself a suite overlooking the long courtyard at the rear of the hotel. In centuries past it had been an enclosure of stables for the coach horses. Now the remnants of Middle England sat under its leafy vines to have their afternoon tea served by waitresses in black uniforms with frilly white aprons.

When the door closed she couldn't bring herself to look at him.

'You came,' he said, sounding surprised and elated at the same time.

'Yes.'

'I wasn't sure you would.'

'I didn't believe you'd ask me.'

He closed the distance with three quick steps, and put his arms round her. 'Believe.'

Annabelle rested her head on his shoulder, nestling dreamily in his embrace. She fitted there perfectly. Belonged there. 'I didn't know if I was another of your one-night stands.'

'No games, not with us. You knew you weren't.'

She smiled. 'We were bad, weren't we?'

'So much. Did you like it?'

She tipped her head back so she could see his face. His lips were raised in a knowing smirk. 'I'm here, aren't I?'

'Yeah.' He slid a hand up to the back of her head, and held her fast so that he could kiss her. She clutched at him, returning the kiss with an intensity that easily matched his. When they broke apart he growled: 'This is going to be good.'

'It better be.'

'There's something I want.'

'What?'

'A treat.'

Just for a moment her bravado faltered. She felt the decades between them again, the things he knew, he'd experienced. Tastes that might incline to the exotic ... 'What sort of treat?'

He picked a long rectangular cardboard box off the bed. It was tied with a wide red silk ribbon. Standing behind her, he pressed one hand against her stomach as he brought the box round in front of her. His tongue licked at the side of her neck. 'Take this into the bathroom, and put it on.'

She took the box and tugged at the bow on top.

'No,' he said. 'In there.' He indicated the open door to the bathroom.

Annabelle gave a casual shrug, and sauntered into the bathroom. Once she'd closed the door, she scrabbled eagerly at the box. In among the folds of thin tissue paper was a white silk negligee. She picked it up by the gossamer shoulder straps and held it high, a slow smile building on her face. It was the sexiest thing she'd ever seen. And she'd accessed enough exclusive store sites to scope-shop their contents to guess what kind of price range it came from.

When she came back out of the bathroom, wearing the negligee – just – the inner blinds had been closed, leaving the room cloaked in a strong diffuse haze of gold sunlight. Jeff was standing by the big four-poster bed without a stitch of clothing on. As her gaze lingered on him, the tip of her tongue emerged to moisten her lips.

Jeff's gaze was equally enthusiastic. 'I am desperate to see you naked.' He stroked her shoulder, fingers tracing the negligee's strap down to her breast. 'And I will. Eventually.'

*

Annabelle flopped back on the bed as he finally rolled off her. Inevitably, and with a tinge of dwindling guilt, she drew comparisons. Tim: skinnier, lighter; puppishly eager as he licked and groped. Then he'd suddenly be pumping away wildly for thirty – maybe forty – seconds before his face contorted in demented joy. His loving, fearful smile, which she had to respond in kind, assuring him it was just as fantastic for her.

And this. Not knowing it could possibly take so long to be stripped out of a garment so tiny, nor that the experience could be so sensual for her as well. Then those relentless, clever hands. He'd laughed delightedly as she'd squirmed and squealed in reaction to each dangerously proficient caress. And all the time his praise and admiration for how magnificent she was rang through her brain, clever words that egged her on.

Trading up? *You better believe it.*

She glanced down at herself, experiencing a sultry pride at how wanton she looked. 'That was me,' she said out loud. 'I did that.'

'You certainly did.' He was lying on his side, skin beaded with sweat. The greed was still hot in his eyes.

'This is a cliché: innocent young girl being taught the facts of life by older man.'

'I wouldn't go so far as to call you innocent.'

Annabelle laughed, stroking her hands and feet across the sheet. 'Not any more. I've never felt so . . . free. I can be as bad as I want, and it doesn't matter. Bad isn't even bad any more, it's just what I enjoy.'

'Damn, you're so much beautiful. And exciting.'

'I excite you?'

'Yes.'

'Martina Lewis was right,' she said. 'They really did rejuvenate every part of you.'

Jeff was flat on his back, staring at the ceiling. 'Yeah, I'm well worth several trillion Euros.'

'Smug pig.' She slapped him playfully, then rolled onto her side to look at him. 'Were you like this before? When you were young, I mean?'

'I dunno. I remember I did get laid quite a lot at university. I was lucky, that was the late seventies, just before AIDS broke out.'

'The seventies,' she said in wonder. 'You have to deep-mine a database to get that far back. It's history, like the World Wars and airships and knights and kings. I know you had CDs back then – did you have computers as well?'

'Other way round, actually. CDs were the eighties. Computers were just starting to get smaller in the seventies. But thanks for making me feel old.'

'You're not old. You just have a lot of memories. That's good.'

'You think so?'

She stroked his chest, fingers tracing the lean lines of muscle. 'Yes,' she murmured. 'When I do think about your age and the difference between us, it's kinky. I like that.'

'There was never anybody like you in the seventies. Maybe that's why I was really chosen for rejuvenation, so I could meet you.'

'We were destined to meet!'

'Yeah.'

She smiled that sultry smile again. 'So what next?'

'Give me a minute, I'll show you.'

'I mean, after today?'

'After today there's tomorrow, and then another tomorrow after that. I've got this suite for a fortnight.'

'I even get turned on by that part of it, though I know that's wrong. This is an illicit affair. Sneaking around behind Tim's back.'

'You know why we have to do that.'

She sobered. 'Yes. He'll never know how much we care about him. That's sad, in a way. I feel quite virtuous protecting him from the truth.'

'He's pretty upset over your bust-up.'

'He'll get over me and find someone else. Look at me, I did.'

'You got a sister he could date?'

'No!'

He grinned at her indignation, then reached for her again.

'Is there anything you really like?' she asked in a half-whisper.

245

'You and another girl.' He wasn't even sure he'd spoken it aloud.

Her sultry expression hardened to a slight frown. 'Bad boy.'

'Failing that, you could turn over.'

'Like this, you mean?' That disgraceful laugh of his told her she'd got that right.

33. AGONY AUNT

The elephant keck was in full bloom, big hemispherical flower clumps swaying in the slightest breeze, sending dead petals to carpet the roads. Councils had a statutory requirement to cut them down, but to do that they needed money; a commodity Rutland County Council was notoriously and historically short of. So the tall invaders were left alone to grow up along the county's D-class roads, blocking the view round every bend.

They didn't make Tim's journey any easier as he rode the e-trike along the strip of dilapidated tarmac ringing the reservoir, weaving about to dodge the potholes. He had to keep the speed low for fear of what was coming the other way. Mostly it was cyclists and other e-trike riders, but once a car purred towards him, well into the middle of the road when it appeared. He was sure it only braked because of the Europol team's Range Rover following him. He was back on probation with the bodyguards following his behaviour at the summer ball; and they had their suspicions about the jet ski, too.

He arrived at the gates to the protected estate and flashed his smart card at the sensor pillar. Aunt Alison was in her little front garden, clipping away determinedly at the straggly rose bushes that were tumbling over the pavement. Her heavy-handed attentions were actually making them look worse. She pushed her straw hat back, and gave him a big welcoming smile. 'Tim! Hello, darling, how are you?'

He endured the wet kiss she gave him as best he could. 'Okay, suppose.'

'Oh dear me – that bad, is it?'

'Maybe.' He frowned. 'Why are you doing gardening?'

Alison gave his shoulder a mock punch. 'A little less of your cheek, young Timothy. I always keep this garden in tip-top shape.'

'No, you don't.'

Alison gave a hearty laugh. 'Got an official letter of complaint from the Residents' Association; they said I was letting down the tone of the estate. I assumed they meant the garden. Do you want to see it?'

'Er, no, thanks.'

'That's my boy – who cares what old people do and say?' She stripped off her thornproof gauntlets. 'Come on through, I've done quite enough vegetable maintenance for today.' Her attention suddenly focused on the Europol team, who were out of the Range Rover, stretching their legs. 'I say, young man, do you think you could possibly help me out?'

Hans Goussfar was unfortunate to be the one closest to Alison. 'In what way, madam?'

Alison waved her clippers at the black dome of the lawnmower robot, which sat inertly in the middle of the front lawn surrounded by grass that was now almost as high as it was. 'It simply stopped the other week. I have no idea what's wrong with the poor thing – I'm utterly dreadful with machinery. Could you possibly take a peek underneath for me?'

'Ah, well . . .'

'Oh, you are such a dear. Thank you. I'll have Timmy bring some tea out to all of you.'

Once the front door was shut, Tim started laughing. 'That was cruel.'

'Pha, about time I got my money's worth out of Brussels, all that bloody tax I pay. It's probably the most useful thing he'll do all year.'

'I doubt he'll be able to fix it. He's a policeman, not an engineer.'

'It just needs the skirt sensors cleaning, the software will reboot once it has all-round coverage again. Oh, and there's a filthy great wad of wet leaves plugging up the engine intake, although they've probably dried solid by now.'

'You do know what's wrong with it!'

Alison winked at him. 'How could I? I'm just a helpless girlie.' She led him through the lounge and out onto her patio. The arch of wisteria creepers had thickened considerably this year, turning the paved area into an emerald cave. Bushes and shrubs in the back garden were climbing skyward as if that was their only escape route. 'Still upset about your mum leaving?'

'Oh, that.'

'I can't believe Jeff announced that on this ridiculous life site of his. You don't brag about separating from your wife. It should be a private thing.'

'Lucy Duke said it was the best way. By being first to break the story we get to pre-empt any media interest and control the angle.'

'Timmy, if she ever gives you advice like that, you will tell her to go take a flying fuck, won't you, dear?'

He grinned sheepishly. 'Yes.'

'You do still talk to your mum, don't you?'

'Oh yes. We're fine, I suppose. But there's something I wanted to talk to you about.'

'That's very flattering, darling. I'll do my best, you know that. Just don't expect miracles, will you?'

Tim sat on the edge of a sunbench, dropping his chin into his hands. 'Me and Annabelle split up.'

'Oh no! She was such a lovely girl, Tim. Oops, sorry.'

'It's all right. She was lovely.'

'Here, have some Pimms.' Alison picked up a big glass jug that was only a third full. The brownish liquid had a lot of fruit slices bobbing round on the surface, along with the remnants of ice cubes. She started to pour some into a highball glass. 'Best summer drink there is. Always cheers me up, especially by the fourth glass.'

'No,' Tim said firmly. He started to tell Aunt Alison what had happened.

When he finished she gave the glass a mildly guilty glance, then took a sip. 'You're a silly old thing, Tim. Don't think there's much more I can tell you. Course, I'm not exactly the one best placed to lecture you on the evils of drink.'

'I wasn't expecting you to. I'm never going to touch any alcohol or synth8 again. I promised myself that.'

'Jolly good.' She started picking up the cigarette packets littering the table, shaking them to find one that had some in it. 'So who's going to be next?'

'Next?'

'Girlfriend, Tim. Annabelle was a damn fine notch on

your bedpost. You can be proud of that. Who's going to be the next?'

'Alison! I just want Annabelle back. I don't want anyone else.'

'The way you told it, Annabelle made it pretty plain you were through.'

'Suppose.'

'That was good psychology on her part, making you end the phone call. I wonder where she learned that?' She found a packet that had a couple of cigarettes left, checked that they were straight nicotine, then lit up.

'How do I get her back, Alison? I don't know what to do. Tell me what to do, what to say.' Tim waved his hand in front of his face, trying to waft the awful smoke away.

'I remember when I was your age.'

'Yes?'

'One boy after another. Dearie me, the reputation I earned myself. Then I had my seventeenth birthday . . . now he was a hell of a present to find in your bed the next morning.'

Tim tried not to smile.

'He was wonderful. Alexander was his name. Tall, blond, handsome, hung like a donkey. Those were the days – that kind don't look at me twice today. Anyway . . . he claimed he was descended from Russian aristocracy. It could have been a family of Russian sanitation engineers for all I cared. I was so in love. I would have followed him anywhere if he'd only asked. He didn't. At least not me. That was my very best friend Siobhan who traipsed along after him for a dirty weekend in Scarborough. Broke my heart.' She blew a long plume of smoke, staring wistfully out over the reservoir.

'Is that why you never married?' Tim asked reverently.

'God, no. You think a prat like that could knock me off the rails? I was too busy enjoying myself when I was younger. Then you reach an age and look round, and all the good ones have been snapped up – so the myth goes. Of course, novelists aren't the easiest creatures to live with, either. I used to have neuroses that could frighten a shrink at twenty paces. Doesn't mean I didn't have long and worthwhile relationships with men, though.'

'Um, yes. Alison, what's this got to do with me and Annabelle?'

Alison shook her head in exasperation. 'Your generation – always want the capitals, never the subtext. You don't learn to read properly, that's the trouble. And don't start telling me you've accessed books. I'm talking about the real thing, good solid paper that you can hold in your hand, and bend the page corners the way you're not supposed to.'

'I wouldn't tell you that.'

'Hmm. The thing is this, Tim: you're eighteen, for ever is about a month at that age. You'll get over her. And move on to the next like the healthy, appallingly randy boy that you are.'

'I don't want to get over her. Why does everybody say that? I want her back.'

'Did you dump Zai?'

Tim was thrown by the abrupt shift. 'Er, yes.'

'She must have felt just like you do now. Except it would have been a lot worse for her. Women get hurt a damn sight more by these things. Not that men ever appreciate that. Oh no, you know and care as much about our feelings as you do about our G-spot.'

252

'I do care.'

'Hmm. So after you'd cast Zai aside because Annabelle had bigger boobs, she was left with her emotions bruised and bleeding, and feeling as low and unwanted as a person can get.'

'I didn't do it like that.'

'But you did leave her. It was your decision. So did she have a date for the ball?'

'Yes.'

'There was never any chance you would get back with her. You were so obsessed by Annabelle you wouldn't even consider it. Zai knew that, so she had no choice. She picked up her life and met someone else. She got over you.'

'Yes.'

'Well, there you are. It's possible. You will survive. Now which of your other friends-who-are-girls do you fancy the most?'

Tim fell back into the sunbench and smiled in dismay. 'I know I'll survive. But I still want Annabelle back.'

'Ah, the lowly servant boy smitten by the unattainable princess. I've written about you so many times.'

'Do I get her in the end, the princess?'

'Unless you've got a magic sword and a flying dragon that does smartarse one-liners, not a snowflake's chance in hell.'

34. GIRLS' TALK

'I'm going home on Friday,' Sophie said. She was on the gym's treadmill again, working at keeping her legs in trim. 'We are going to stay in touch, aren't we? You and me?'

'Of course.' Annabelle made an effort to focus on the present. She gave the small hand-weights she was holding a semi-puzzled look, as if she wasn't sure what she should do with them.

The majority of her year were getting ready to leave. Some had already gone the morning after the ball. It was a poignant time for all of them, saying goodbye to friends that they'd known for six years or more. There was the old Oakhamian avtxt circle, complete with year streaming, to keep up to date with each other; and they all swore blind that they'd turn up at the first reunion dinner in five years' time. Quite a few claimed they'd be supporting the Million Citizen Voices protest. Even so, Annabelle was pretty sure this was the last time she'd ever see most of them.

'Just checking,' Sophie said.

Actually, Annabelle was determined not to let Sophie's friendship go; she'd never made any sort of issue about Annabelle's lack of money, unlike some. 'I will.'

'I got an avtxt from Tim.'

'Yes?'

'Nothing about you. He was inviting me up to the manor for a last barbecue.'

'Oh. Right.'

'Do you mind if I go? Most of the crew will be there.'

'No. That's fine.'

'Okay, that's it!' Sophie got off the treadmill. 'You barely noticed when I mentioned Tim. So what's his name?'

'Who?'

'Whoever he is. Your smile is so much hideously smug. You've got to be getting shagged every night to be this happy.'

Annabelle directed a demure smile at her feet. 'Secret?'

'Even if I shouted it out at the barbecue it wouldn't make any difference. None of us are ever coming back here.'

'I'd rather you didn't do it at the barbecue.' She took a breath. 'I'm having an affair with Jeff.'

Sophie's hands flew to her cheeks. '*What*? My God, you're not.'

'Nearly a week now.'

'Oh my God, you're serious, aren't you? This is for real.'

'Yeah.'

'That's so much . . .' She giggled. 'Evil!'

'We do it every day.'

'Really? What's it like? Tell me, tell me, tell me! Please!'

Annabelle checked round to make sure they really were alone. 'It's like going to bed with my own private porn star.'

'Are you kidding me?' Sophie demanded breathlessly. 'Really, is he really like that?'

'Well, it's not, you know, romantic kissing and candlelit dinners. I'm talking serious, sleazy, steamy, physical stuff. You've no idea how awesome that can be.'

'Annabelle Goddard, you are so much an utter slut.'

Annabelle giggled along with her friend. 'And proud of it. Honestly, it's like I've let go, and now I'm in free fall. I've never been so in charge.'

'You mean, on top.'

'That too. But no, this is like I can finally do what I want with my life. I make the decisions for me now. I haven't got to ask anyone, or do what society expects. It's wonderful, like being high. I've dosed up on myself.'

'It certainly sounds like you're high, all right. So come on, how did it start?'

'Right after the fiasco that was the ball. He took me back home afterwards. We took the long way round.'

'I knew it, he got you on the rebound. He took advantage.'

'No, nothing like that. You remember what you said to me before? Well, you were so much right, Jeff is trading up. You can't go any higher.'

'I can't believe it, an affair with a pensioner.'

'Stop saying that. You've seen him. He's not old. I really . . .'

'Love him?'

'Adore him. And he does me, too.'

'Urgh, excuse me while I vomit. It doesn't matter what he looks like, it's what he is that counts. I mean, where's this leading, Annabelle?'

'For God's sake, we've only been seeing each other a

few days. I'm not asking those sort of questions. I'm just enjoying myself for once. What's so wrong with that? I've never felt like this before. He's right for me here and now, and I don't care what anyone else thinks.'

'Wow there, slow down, I didn't mean that you shouldn't. This is just a shock, that's all.'

'I know.' Annabelle lowered her voice even further. 'Secret. That way you reacted, knowing what people would think if they found out, that just makes it more exciting.'

Sophie put a hand out and touched her fingertips to Annabelle's face, almost as if she was testing to see if her friend was real. 'I never knew you were like this. I admire you for doing your own thing, more than you know.' The hand moved away. 'And I'm really glad you're happy.'

'Thanks. We're going to try and get away together, have a little holiday. Maybe we'll know more about the way it's going to go after that.'

'Nice.' Sophie's lecherous grin returned full force. 'Now tell me more about all the depraved sex.'

35. HAPPY BIRTHDAY TO YOU

It was Annabelle who had to get the door when the bell rang. Roger Goddard was confused by the sound. It was only quarter past eight in the morning, and this wasn't the day when the Community Supply Service van came to restock their house with food. He didn't know what to do about the insistent tone of the bell: it didn't belong in his routine.

She pulled her worn old towelling robe over her equally faded knee-length T-shirt and opened the door, making sure the security chain was engaged. A young man was standing on the step, a safety helmet under his arm, electronic pad in his hand. The e-trike parked behind him had a florist-franchise logo on its cool storage box.

'Ms Goddard?'

'That's me.' She started to smile as soon as she realized what was happening.

'I have two deliveries for you.'

'Oh, that's great. Wait. Two?'

She had to sign twice on the pad before he'd hand the bouquets over. One was big – twenty red roses just starting to open, complimented by long, graceful white orchids. That was from Jeff. The other was even bigger, a wide cone of gold and royal purple paper containing a vast array of flowers, half of which she couldn't name. The little card that came with it said:

> *I never knew losing you could hurt so much.*
> *Please forgive me.*
> *If you can't, have a wonderful birthday anyway.*
>
> *Tim*

Annabelle slumped against the wall at the bottom of the stairs, wincing broadly. 'Oh bugger.' *Get over me, Tim, please.*

'Flowers,' Roger said quizzically. He'd emerged from the lounge to blink in the daylight that streamed in through the front door's frosted glass. 'They're yours, aren't they?'

Annabelle resisted the impulse to roll her eyes. 'Yes, dad. Why don't you go into the kitchen? I'll make us some breakfast.'

Her father looked from her to the flowers, then back to her again. His lower lip started to tremble. Tears welled up in his eyes. 'It's your birthday.'

Oh Christ. 'Yes, dad.'

'I forgot your birthday. My daughter's birthday.'

'It's okay,' she said brightly. 'You can nip out and get me a card later.'

His arms dangled loosely by his side as his head bowed forward. 'I am such a useless fuck-up. How could I forget? That's so horrible of me. Horrible! I'm a horrible person. I don't want to be like this, I really don't.'

'Please, dad, don't.'

'You're eighteen today. You should be having a fabulous

party at a hotel or the town hall. There should be people there, lots of lovely people. And a band playing music. And food; a banquet. And I forgot. I forgot my own daughter's birthday!' His hands came up to slap against his forehead. He did it again and again.

'Dad, don't.' She had to shift the bouquets around to free a hand so she could grab hold of him. 'Stop it, please.'

He twisted his head from side to side. 'I'm so sorry.'

'We'll go out for lunch together, all right? A nice lunch at the Falcon Hotel. Just you and me. How about that?'

'Really? You want to go out with me?'

'Of course I do. You're my dad.'

'I don't deserve you.'

'You'll have to find something to wear. Why don't you go and check your wardrobe?'

'Okay.' His attention switched to the flowers. 'Are they from your boyfriend?'

Her hand curled round Tim's card, crumpling it. 'Yes.'

'Oh Annabelle, you should be out having lunch with him, being happy together. You don't want a meal with me.'

'Yes, I do. I'm seeing . . . him later.' She wasn't sure if she'd actually said *Tim* or *him*.

'You are?' Roger seemed pleased with the idea.

'Yes. We're going out this evening. He's going to take me to a restaurant, then a club. Some of my friends are coming as well. I'm really looking forward to it.'

'Good. That's good. I'm going to go and find something to wear. Something decent, something suitable to take my lovely daughter out to lunch with.'

She held up the bouquets again, aghast by how over

the top Tim's was, then went into the kitchen to find a vase.

*

The champagne cork popped as soon as Annabelle opened the suite door. She gave a little start of surprise, which melted into a smile when she saw Jeff with the foaming magnum in his hands.

'Happy birthday,' he said.

She ran across the room and flung her arms round him, kissing him exuberantly. 'Thank you. The flowers were lovely.'

He kissed her back. 'They were just the warm-up. I've got your real present here. Now sit down and help me pour. Krug is far too expensive to let it spill all over the carpet.'

She plonked herself down on the edge of the bed and held up a pair of saucer glasses for him to fill.

'So, good birthday?'

'Actually, not until I got here, no.'

'Why, what happened? Oh, cheers.'

'Cheers.' She touched the rim of her saucer to his. 'Dad forgot it was my birthday. He was really upset when he realized, so I had to spend most of the morning calming him down. Mum sent me an avtxt greeting. But it was the same as last year's; I think her computer is programmed to send it.'

'Ah, God bless diary programs.'

'And Tim sent me flowers as well. He even used the same site as you did to order them.'

'Ah.' Jeff grimaced. 'Well, we can stay here till late if you'd like.'

'Can we?' She brightened considerably at the prospect. 'Can we really?'

'Sure. I've not got to get back. Neither have you.'

'I so much want to spend the whole night with you.'

'We will. I might even manage better than that. I've got a physics conference in America scheduled in a couple of weeks. Fancy being my assistant?'

'You're joking!'

'No.'

'Oh, my God. America. With you. Oh Jeff, that would be superb.'

'Nothing firm yet, but I think I can swing it.'

She tilted her head up and kissed him again. 'Thank you.'

'Now let's have a look at what we've got here.' He sat on the bed beside her, and pointed to a pair of boxes on the side table. They were both wrapped in dark purple paper, with scarlet ribbons and bows.

Annabelle flashed him a dazzling smile. 'Which one first?'

'That one, I think.'

The first present was another sensual negligee, in gold satin this time. Jeff put his mouth right up to her ear, nuzzling. 'The champagne stains should come out of that quite easily.'

Annabelle went and put it on straight away, knowing how much he liked looking at her when she was dressed like that. In the second box were two sets of black-lace underwear. Then he produced a slim case. Annabelle was almost afraid to open it; she knew it was jewellery of some kind.

A gold necklace chain sat on the black velvet inside the

case. The pendant was an ultramodern-styled platinum triangle, with a diamond on each point. The sight of it stopped her breath. It must have cost a fortune – and he'd spent it on her.

'Oh God, Jeff, it's beautiful.'

'Here, let me.' He picked it up and fastened it round her neck.

The cool metal resting on the skin between her breasts, placed there by her lover, was an incredibly erotic sensation.

'Perfect,' Jeff announced.

Annabelle's eyelids were fluttering, half closed. She smiled warmly at him and took his hand, licking the tip of his thumb. 'I'm going to give you a present this evening, too – one you're going to remember.' Her tongue found his index finger.

His voice was low, warm. 'Oh good, a threesome.'

'Jeff. No.' He always managed to mention the idea at some point during their rendezvous. She'd learned to slide it to one side. 'Tonight there's only me.' She gave him a teasing grin and slowly straddled him until she was sitting in his lap. She tilted her head right back, and slowly tipped her champagne saucer up until the liquid splashed over the front of her neck. It began to foam as it cascaded down her chest, soaking the negligee into transparency. 'And I want another present from you.'

36. THE LAST FAREWELL BARBECUE

Mrs Mayberry had made the burgers using her own special recipe involving lots of fresh herbs, Aberdeen Angus beef, and breadcrumbs. Jeff piled them up on a big plate next to the six-burner gas-fired barbecue. He shouted out to the youngsters on the lawn who were finishing off the rounders match, asking them what sauces they wanted. Mrs Mayberry had provided him with a selection of those as well: chilli, honey and lemon, hot barbecue, and something she called 'sticky smoke'. Jeff used his oversized tongs to dip the burgers into the deep bowls of sauce before dropping them on the grid above the glowing lava rocks. While he was dealing with the first batch the Europol team called in their preferences. Smoke spat and sizzled upward from the meat.

The pork ribs came next, picked out of the sweet and sour marinade. Then it was the sausages, whole ribbons of them. By the time it was all cooking away he hoped the Environment Agency mobile pollution-monitor van wasn't cruising the village for clean-air violations. He was having to stand well back as the acrid scents mixed into a single plume and started to make his eyes water.

'Another beer, uh, Jeff?' Colin asked. He was peering into the big fridge just inside the pool building's door.

'Sounds good – thanks.' He took the can from the smiling youngster. 'What's the score?'

'Ah, we're winning easy. Boys, eighteen. Girls, five so far, and they've only got two bats left.'

Jeff had taken his turn batting earlier. It had been decided he could get on with the cooking when it was the boys' turn to field; one less on the team would even the odds, so the girls claimed.

Lorraine took a mighty swipe at the ball that Tim threw, and knocked it down to the far end of the garden. Philip watched it soar over his head in amazement, and belatedly gave chase. All the girls were running fast between the posts, shouting encouragement to each other. The boys directed a barrage of abuse at the hapless Philip.

'Go, you moron!' Colin yelled.

'We'll still walk it,' Jeff said. He twisted the plastic tab on the top of his can, and gulped down an icy mouthful. It had been a great afternoon. None of the youngsters had minded him joining in when they were splashing around in the pool. That invitation was extended to the croquet game and then the rounders. Jeff hadn't played croquet for twenty years. It was fun remembering all the dirty tricks. Whoever thought croquet was a civilized sport had clearly never played before. It was fun playing rounders, too. And sinking highballs of Pimms.

The afternoon just needed Annabelle to make it perfect. More than anything, he wanted her there, sharing in the exuberance of this lazy sunny day. The youngsters were more her friends than his, after all. But Tim was actually smiling as he lined up to pitch the ball, shaking off the terrible moods that had dominated his days since the summer ball. Balancing the happiness of three people was a profoundly difficult act. Jeff kept wondering how long it would be before he and Annabelle could actually tell Tim about them.

Quite a while, if I know Tim.

The boys won the rounders, eighteen to eight. A raggedy chorus of Queen's 'We Are the Champions' filled the garden.

'Two minutes,' Jeff called.

The youngsters went to find sweatshirts and cardigans now the sun was sinking lower, then grabbed themselves plates and lined up by the barbecue. Jeff was kept busy with the tongs, handing the meat out. There were so many burgers on the grill, he'd completely forgotten which ones had which sauce on them.

Jeff overheard one remark Martin muttered to Tim as the boys sat down together. 'Any bloke who has a whole fridge just for beer is okay by me.' Which made him smile. The Manor had been built with exactly this kind of afternoon in mind; a big lawn and a swimming pool were essentials for Jeff. Although his parents had been comfortably-off professionals, they'd lived in a town house with a very small garden. He'd been envious of all his childhood friends out in the villages with their wide open lawns to run around on.

Not that he'd ever expected to benefit from the Manor – it had always been primarily for Tim. Now, though, twenty years late, he could enjoy it for himself, too; along with all the other things he'd never found time for before. The new car was a good example.

'Is there anything left you'd like to do, Jeff?' Simon asked. 'I mean, this time around? Something you missed out on before?'

The talk had been about coming holidays and their futures after that, what they most wanted to achieve or see.

Jeff shovelled the last couple of burgers onto his own plate, and went over to sit beside Tim. 'Actually, there is one thing I've really wanted to do ever since I was ten years old.'

All the youngsters fell silent, watching him closely.

He shrugged at them. 'Sorry, it's not particularly important, just something I fancy.'

'What?' Tim asked curiously.

'I've always wanted to see the Earth from orbit. Just look down and watch the whole planet roll past underneath me.'

There were a lot of sighs from around the patio. Several of the youngsters nodded sympathetic agreement.

'Comes from an astronaut fixation when I was a kid. That and the fact I grew up in the era of the Apollo programme. I mean, I really did expect to be taking holidays on the moon by the year 2000. All the Sunday newspaper magazines in the early seventies were full of articles about how easy spaceflight would become right after the pioneering part was complete.'

'Were they really saying that?' Vanessa asked. She was sitting on the other side of Tim, peering round him to look at Jeff. It wasn't the first time she and Tim had wound up next to each other that afternoon.

'Oh yes. All of us in those times had a lot of big expectations about how the world was going to turn out.

You know, offhand I can't think of one prediction that ever came true – apart from the datasphere sliding videophones in at us from the side.'

'You can still make it into orbit, though,' Philip said. 'The next generation of spaceplanes are going to use pure scramjets for propulsion. That'll bring the price of spaceflight down to the same as it costs to fly across the Atlantic.'

Jeff laughed. 'Now that's the definition I've been looking for ever since I came out of the suspension womb. I look young, almost as young as you lot; but the real difference between us is cynicism. You don't have any, while I've got a ton of it.'

'I'm cynical,' Philip protested. 'I don't believe a word politicians say.'

'That's not cynicism,' Sophie said. 'That's just common sense.'

Jeff smiled to himself as he tucked into the barbecue. The youngsters chattered avidly around him, losing just about every inhibition when it came to topics and comments. He was pleased about that. Teenage reticence in front of adults was a near absolute. But he'd obviously found a form of acceptance among them. Not, he admitted to himself, that he'd want to hang with them the whole time; their interests and conversation were too shallow for that.

When he thought about it, he wasn't totally sure what kind of group he did want to be with on a permanent social basis. Late twenties, probably, or early thirties. Young enough not to be boring, old enough to have some wisdom.

Now Sue had left, and Tim was on the verge of departing to university, he supposed he ought to make an effort to rebuild a social life. His slightly crazy existence since finishing the treatment had virtually precluded that. It had been a good time, though; not just because of Annabelle. Everything he could physically want, he'd got. Which is what youth should be about: no cares, no responsibilities, enjoying everything you do, and the decades stretching out invitingly ahead of you.

Jeff drank some more beer and ate his burgers, happy that not only was this evening one of the best, but that he could repeat it ad infinitum in the years to come.

*

He took them to see the car after they'd finished their strawberries and cream. It had only been delivered the day before, replacing his old Mercedes saloon. A Jaguar I-type sportster, straight off the new production line at Birmingham; low-slung, two seats, sculpted raw-metal bodywork, broad flex-profile tyres, computer-stabilized suspension, laser proximity sensors, eight recombiner cells delivering power direct to the axle-hub motors, capable of three hundred and twenty kilometres per hour. The sight of it sitting in the garage, yellow light glimmering softly off the blue-metal surface, was enough to draw several gasps of admiration from the eager youngsters. Jeff loved it. Most modern cars were big and sedate, giving the impression of quiet infallible power; while this just looked seriously mean.

'How did you get it?' Colin asked. 'They only started making them this year. I thought there was a two-year waiting list.'

'Being famous has its advantages,' Jeff said. 'Although you will have to put up with me on your spamtxt for the

269

next three months. I did an endorsement deal with Jaguar's PR division.'

They groaned.

'I know,' Jeff said, grinning. 'Sell-out.'

'But worth it,' Simon said. 'Definitely worth it. This is so much dead-on.'

'Can I sit in it?' Rachel asked.

'Of course.' Jeff opened the passenger door for her. She gave him a long thank-you smile as she wriggled past him.

Vanessa stuck her hand up eagerly. 'Me, too.'

'Do we get to ride in it?' Philip asked.

''Fraid not, we've all had too much to drink. And I haven't got a hack for the breath sensor yet.'

'Can I at least sit in the driver's seat?' Colin asked querulously.

'I guess so.' It was the first thing Tim had asked when they went out for a test drive yesterday morning. He'd even let Tim drive the Jag for a couple of miles along the country lanes, where there was no chance of him putting his foot down.

Despite the lack of an open road, the Jag had been a dream to drive. Tyres clung to the crumbling, potholed tarmac as if they were rolling along a newly laid motorway.

Sitting behind the wheel on a sunny morning, U2 cranked up to level twenty on the sound system, gliding through the countryside in a car that would make other men weep, was another of those defining best moments. Jeff's life seemed to be clocking up a lot of them right now.

When he was first young he'd hated the sight of middle-aged men in coupés. They were all posers, with no right to own cars like those. And they all wore the same kind of

270

cap, white canvas with a peak, as if it was some kind of Masonic-uniform requirement. Didn't they realize how sad they looked? He'd always sworn he would never repeat their mistake.

Now here he was, pulling off the whole sports-car scene with considerable class.

Once he'd dropped Tim off he'd zoomed over to Stamford to meet up with the birthday girl in their suite at the George. He couldn't resist driving her home afterwards. Sitting behind the wheel on a warm summer's evening, delectable teenage girlfriend at his side with Bruce Springsteen at level twenty: quality of life had taken a remarkable quantum leap inside a few short hours.

*

After the youngsters had devoted a suitable amount of time to worshipping the Jag, Jeff went back into the study while they settled back around the patio. The call came in a couple of minutes early, just like he knew it would.

'You having a good time?' Annabelle asked. She was in her bedroom at home, a drab box of a room, with ancient burgundy-red curtains already drawn against the night. The single bed she was perched on took up about half of the floor space.

'I just want you to be here,' he said. 'I miss you.'

'I miss you, too.'

'How about you, are you having a good time?'

'Oh yeah.' Her face went all petulant. 'All my friends are round at your place with Tim. And you're there, too. School's finished, I've nowhere else to go. I hate it here, Jeff, I really hate it.'

'I'm sorry. I was there for you this morning, wasn't I?'

'I know. I just want to be with you, Jeff.' Her hand reached out to press against the screen. 'Can't we be together?'

'We can. We will.'

'I'm being selfish. How's the party?'

'Hmm.' Jeff glanced out of the window at the floodlit patio. 'They're getting ready to watch the football match. It's going to be a long evening, I'd guess.'

'Great.'

'This is getting ridiculous, isn't it? I want you here, with me, tonight.'

'I want to be there,' she said mournfully.

'I'm going to go and tell him.'

'No, Jeff.'

'For Christ's sake, the boy's got to learn there's thorns among the roses sometime.'

'Please, Jeff, you're drunk, and randy, and tonight is not the night to tell him.'

'Yeah, maybe.'

'Jeff, promise me you won't.'

'All right, all right.' He waved his arms in a conciliatory motion. 'I'll be good. But you've got to promise me we'll talk about this soon. Creeping around, meeting in hotel rooms is fine and fun for a few days, but I want more of you than that.'

'Really? Do you mean that?'

'Of course I mean that.'

'I'll wait till tomorrow,' she murmured.

'That's the whole point. I don't want to wait.'

*

When Jeff got back out onto the patio he just managed to hold off glaring at Tim. If he had, it would have been noticed. His son had avoided any drink other than water and lemonade all evening; he was the only sober one left. Even so, Jeff must have given away some kind of clue.

As soon as he plonked himself down in the slatted oak chair, Tim leaned over and used a quiet voice to ask: 'Everything okay, dad?'

'Sure.' Jeff slapped his son's knee. 'Sure. I'm fine.'

'Here we go,' Colin yelled.

They'd all pulled their chairs into a semicircle, facing a portable four-metre screen which Tim and Jeff had wheeled out of the pool building earlier. It was showing the Barcelona v. Chelsea European Premier League match, live from Milan.

Vanessa slumped back into her chair. 'This is going to be boring,' she muttered.

The Five Star Sports access-provider logo flashed up over the Milan stadium, Every seat was filled with chanting supporters. Players were running onto the pitch, its grass weirdly bright under the big lighting rigs. A line of ten small grids appeared along the bottom of the screen, providing alternative camera angles: two of them were carried by the captains, mounted on the side of their helmets. The logo faded out to be replaced by Rob Lacey's campaign symbol: a white dove flying out of the circle of gold European stars. A streamer scrolled down one side of the screen, declaring that the match's wideband pan-European access costs were being paid for by the Rob Lacey for President Committee. The advert started in a swirl of music. The main picture and every grid showed shots of Rob Lacey being *involved* with people, talking to groups of children in several European countries, inspecting a modern factory, looking out across the sea from the bridge of a Euronavy destroyer, in shirtsleeves at a Heads of State meeting where he argued his point. 'Rob Lacey,' the announcer said in a magnificently basso voice. 'The man who cares about you.'

The images that had been flipping up to illustrate how magnificent the candidate was suddenly showed Rob Lacey and Jeff walking round the Manor's garden. The Prime Minister was listening with a seriously thoughtful expression on his face as Jeff waved his arms around, chattering enthusiastically.

The youngsters jeered and booed loudly. Jeff stood up with a lazy grin on his face, and gave them a sweeping bow. 'I thank you.'

Up on the screen, Rob Lacey was applauding a modern dance troupe from a German inner-city social regeneration project, half of whom were second-generation immigrants from East Europe and Turkey. The announcer was busy explaining how Rob Lacey would accommodate existing refugees (including registering them for income tax) while being tough on the criminal gangs bringing people over Germany's laser curtain.

Jeff sat down as the advert finished with an appeal for inclusive voting, and any donations possible for the election campaign, ten per cent of which would be given to the charities so ably supported by Mr and Mrs Lacey. He frowned, thinking about the time Lacey had visited the Manor. Hadn't he been talking about pruning the sycamores when they walked round the gardens together?

'At bloody last,' Simon exclaimed. Both football teams

were moving into their positions, with Chelsea taking the kick-off. The ball went zooming in a high trajectory across the pitch, players hurtled towards it. There was a brief clash of bodies and legs, and the ball was spat outwards, towards the Chelsea goalmouth.

'I'm amazed they can even see the damn ball in those helmets,' Jeff mumbled grouchily. 'What happened to the kit they used to wear?'

'You mean, when you were young?' Tim teased.

'Yeah. I mean, a pair of shorts and a team sweater was all they ever used to need. Now look at them.' His elaborate gesture took in the heavily padded and helmeted players scurrying over the pitch. 'They're like bloody American footballers. They can't run, they're carrying so much foam stuffing they just bounce.'

'Got to be like that, Jeff,' Philip said. 'Basic safety.'

'Yeah,' Martin laughed. 'The clubs have got to protect themselves against liability lawyers.'

Jeff took another drink of beer. He knew if he said anything more he'd sound like a reactionary old grandfather. *Everything used to be better in the past.* It wasn't true. The old days were only ever enjoyable from a long way away, and seen through hazy filters. Now was always truly the best time to live in. Now had Annabelle in it, even though she was ten miles away.

*

The noise of shouting and cheers emanating from the patio could just be heard through the study's windows. Barcelona had scored another goal, bringing them back level.

Rachel pulled her bikini back on. 'Can't be long before

275

it's over,' she said. 'I'd better get out there before he notices I've gone.'

'Another five minutes left,' Jeff assured her. 'And there's going to be at least eleven minutes' extra time.'

She struggled into her oversized sweatshirt. 'That's good: he'll remember I was there at the start, and at the finish. Ergo, I must have been there all along.'

'Ergo, eh?'

'Yeah. Not quite a dumb blonde. Disappointed?'

'Not in any way.'

They looked at each other for a long minute.

'Nice knowing you,' Jeff said.

'Yeah, it's been good.' Rachel opened the door, and blew him a kiss before slipping out.

He tugged his T-shirt on before sitting in the big leather office chair behind the desk. His own muted reflection stared back at him out of the dead wall-mounted screen. He shook his head at it. *That was bad of you.* But Rachel was damn attractive. And he missed Annabelle, which meant he was thinking of sex the whole time. It wasn't as if she would ever know.

Two-timing, and got away with it.

The reflection produced a sly smile. If only he could tell the lads about that. But there weren't any lads, not any more. Outside, there was another round of whooping from the patio as the ball struck a goalpost.

'Annabelle was absolutely right about you.'

Jeff spun the chair round. Sophie was standing in the open doorway, wearing her starlight-scarlet one-piece swimsuit, an inscrutable expression on her dainty face.

*

276

For once, Tim didn't have a hangover the morning after he'd had an enjoyable night. He felt incredibly virtuous, having refused every alcoholic drink he'd been offered.

If only Annabelle could have seen me last night.

But that wasn't going to happen, not for a while. He was still more than a little disappointed that she hadn't even acknowledged the flowers he'd sent her on her birthday. Strange thing was, both Vanessa and Sophie had been reticent to discuss her with him last night. Although Vanessa had said he could call her after she got back home to Nottingham tomorrow. He could press her again then, he decided. No way was he giving up on the most wonderful thing ever to happen to him. Just being persistent would make Annabelle realize how much he genuinely loved her.

Tim pulled on the shorts and T-shirt that were laid out ready for him, and made his way downstairs. There were voices coming from the kitchen. When he walked in it was just like a déjà-vu trip back to that morning when he'd found his mother and father together: two people in towelling robes cuddling up together, carefree smiles as they fed each other toast. Suddenly, he really wished it was his mother again; or even any of the other girls his father had brought home after cruising the clubs. But no, he just had to square up to the reality of it being Sophie who was perched on the chair next to his father, cooing and smooching with him.

His legs refused to move, leaving him stranded in the doorway, gawping at the pair of them. Sophie! Sophie was his own age, and a friend. And she'd spent the night upstairs in his father's double bed. The two of them naked and— Tim jammed a halt to that line of thought before any images started to spring up.

277

'Hi, Tim.' Sophie giggled. 'Surprise.'

'Uh. Hi.'

'Morning, Tim,' Jeff said. He seemed slightly abashed, the way Tim always did when he'd been caught out doing something stupid. Not embarrassed, or contrite, not as if he'd done anything wrong. Just ever so slightly disconcerted.

'Dad,' Tim mumbled. He put his head down and went for the cupboard where the cornflakes were kept. There was no way he could look at the two of them together, not without seeing those images in his mind. His discomfort melted away into resentment for what they'd done, for putting him in this horrible position. Resentment at his father for hitting on a friend. And as for Sophie – what the hell did she think she was doing?

I mean, why?

'Something wrong?' Sophie asked.

'Not with me,' Tim growled back at her.

'You're not upset, are you?'

It was the implication he hated her for. That little trace of amusement in her voice that asked: Surely you didn't think you and I would ever happen, did you? As if he was so far beneath her he didn't even register. The elite closing ranks against him again. His own father!

'Is there something I should be upset about?' he asked.

'No. That's the whole point.'

Tim stopped the pretence of searching for breakfast. 'Well, then.' He turned his back on both of them and started to walk out.

'Tim, don't,' Jeff said. There was some genuine worry in his voice, the need to appease. 'I thought we talked about this.'

Tim faced them, exasperation amplifying his surliness. 'No, not *this*, Dad. We did not talk *this* through at all.'

'There was no unspoken agreement, Tim, nothing to say I can't . . .' He broke off, giving Sophie a glance. She pouted back at him.

'And that's the trouble, Dad. You don't think there's anything wrong with this. For God's sake.'

'Well, why don't you tell me where the trouble lies, exactly?' Jeff said, his voice hardening. 'I'd like to know what you think I should and shouldn't be doing.'

'As if you don't know.'

'Excuse me,' Sophie said, her voice icy. 'I am here and present. And if you speak round me again, Tim, I shall give you a slap that'll knock your teeth out.'

Tim's fury withered so quickly he hunched his shoulders in reflex. 'Sorry,' he grumped.

'I went to bed with Jeff because I wanted to. That's it. The end. Live with it.'

Tim nodded contritely, and retreated from the kitchen.

Jeff waited in silence until he heard Tim's feet pounding on the stairs. He let out a low, regretful whistle. 'I think we could have done that better.'

'It was best this way. Trust me. Hard and fast, this way he gets over it quicker. And he doesn't wind up hating himself, either. We take all the blame.'

'I don't want to take the blame, I'm his father.'

'God, you're as bad as him. If you're that sensitive, then last night shouldn't have happened. Not just for Tim's sake, but for Annabelle's, too.'

Jeff's guilt reflex made him look at the door. 'Jesus wept. Why don't you just post it on your life site?'

'Don't look so worried, you're covered. He's never

going to be telling Annabelle. And I don't want to hurt her. She's a friend.'

'Yeah, right.'

'I know. Last night was shabby of me. That's what made it exciting. But it doesn't mean I'm not her friend any more.'

'What she doesn't know can't hurt her, eh? I thought that was my excuse.'

'There is no excuse. That would be self-delusional. It happened because I wanted it, and because you have no self-control.'

Jeff shot her an irked glance. His instinct was to argue, but there was truly nothing to say on his own behalf. He'd known exactly what he was doing when Sophie turned up in the study. This whole situation of being surrounded by eager teenage girls, and all the others in their twenties and thirties, was simply too much to resist. Part of him was ashamed at that, the civilized part, the little voice of conscience whispering that Annabelle was too good a thing to risk. But, always, testosterone drowned that out in the heat of the moment. Always. At least, it did at this age.

Although, to be honest, he couldn't name an age when he hadn't behaved like this. This is what he was. And he was too old now to be ashamed of that.

'I should put you over my knee,' he said.

Sophie crunched down on a slice of toast, chewing it with exaggerated movements. Her eyes glittered with suppressed amusement, fixing on him like some kind of missile radar. 'Promises, promises,' she purred.

*

They went back upstairs to bed. For Jeff, it was almost like a *so there* to Tim. The boy's reaction had left him mildly depressed. If Tim felt like that about him taking a friend to bed, there was no way he was ready for the truth about Annabelle. All the resentment Jeff had felt the previous night bubbled right back up to infect his thoughts again.

Sophie must have picked up on some of it. There was certainly a flash of pique on her face as they began their coupling, as if she knew who he really wanted spreadeagled across the bed in her place.

He was actually quite relieved when she left around mid-morning, although he agreed to keep in touch. As far as he was concerned that was simply politic. Tim was nowhere to be seen, although his Europol protection team was sitting in their small ops room, watching a sports feed from the datasphere.

Jeff went into the study and locked the door with a voice code. His desktop synthesizer was actually housed in a specially designed drawer in the desk's left side. Its lock was voice-coded as well, clicking open smoothly as Jeff spoke to it. To look at it, the unit wasn't much, a cube of grey-white plastic fairly similar in appearance to the last century's laser-jet printers.

When the first models had started to come on the market ten years ago, the editorial commentators of the *Data Mail*, which considered itself to occupy the moral high ground to the right of centre, had denounced them as tools of the drug barons, which would bring degenerate misery into millions of families. The early marques were designed around a couple of programmable molecular sieves which could combine a few base chemicals into an array of drugs. Originally intended to help reduce the stock costs for high-street pharmacies and hospitals, the illegal narcotics trade was eager to exploit their potential. Governments responded with their usual mistrust of their citizenship, and legislated heavily, restricting ownership to legitimate licensed medical concerns. Consequentially a huge and prolific black market for pirated machines flourished in tandem with the lawful industry, gradually forcing back the statutory regulations. Along with that relaxation a multitude of new chemical templates for recreational drugs were released into the datasphere, going under the generic name of synth8.

The complexity and sophistication of the desktop machines advanced swiftly, expanding the range of drugs they could produce. Within ten years, the advanced models incorporated a multitude of programmable sieves, capable of churning out all but the most advanced drugs. The *Data Mail* had been right: it was the age of the ultimate designer drug, although the subsequent predicted crash of civilization showed no sign of occurring. Any student or qualified neurochemist could generate a synth8 template. There were even self-design programs floating around within the datasphere, where you loaded in your required narcotic effect, and they'd give you a template that should do the trick. Whether you used them depended on how keenly you followed the conspiracy tracker sites.

For the biogenetic corporations, desktop synthesizers represented a huge loss of revenue, although supplying phials of high-purity base chemicals certainly went some way towards compensating. What prevented them from suffering the same fate as the publishing, music, and film industries was the sheer range of the new genoprotein and biochemical products, which thanks to their enormous complexity still had to be factory produced.

Seventeen green LEDs glowed on the top of Jeff's unit, showing him the base-chemical phials were all still over thirty per cent full.

'Click, give me the same Viagra dose I used last time.'

'Synthesizing now,' the computer told him.

He'd bought the desktop synthesizer to supply himself with some of the simpler drugs his anti-ageing regimen required. The only time he'd used the machine after he'd returned from his rejuvenation treatment was to churn out some liquid neurofen capsules to take care of Tim's hangovers. But after his second encounter with Annabelle at the George, he'd realized that almost-innocence of hers which he found so desirable had a small price. Sue had kept him aroused all night with her diabolical knowledge. Those were skills which he was slowly and relentlessly teaching Annabelle. But until he'd finished corrupting her, he simply needed a little something extra to keep that initial blissful physical momentum of their sessions going.

The first time he'd come to the study and instructed the computer to find a template for Viagra he'd been astonished by the number of results it had fished out of the datasphere. He should have known, of course, it was now a generic name, along with Aspirin and Caktol. Pharmacists had been refining the principle for decades, gradually eliminating side effects like headaches, loss of balance, constipation, and even tinnitus, until the modern versions could sustain an erection with almost no problem. Even with his programming skills it took five minutes to filter the possible templates down to less than a dozen. After that, he simply took the first one off the list and fed it into the synthesizer. It hadn't disappointed.

The desktop synthesizer pinged discreetly. Three blank turquoise capsules dropped into the little dispenser tray. Jeff put them in his pocket, and locked the unit up again. It was an hour until he was due to meet Annabelle for lunch. After coping with both Rachel and Sophie in the last fifteen hours, he'd probably have to take two of the capsules with his dessert.

37. BIG CITY BLUES

Tim caught the mid-morning express train from Peterborough down to London. He got off at King's Cross station and took the Tube, using the Livingstone Line, to Kensington Gate, which emerged just behind the Royal Albert Hall. From there it was a ten-minute tramp through the streets to the flat, with three of the Europol team walking with him.

When the lift doors opened, Sue was waiting for him in the hallway. She gave him a long hug, resting her head on his shoulder. Tim hugged her back, slightly surprised by the intensity of the greeting. But, he had to admit to himself, it was nice to see his mum again. She represented life from before, when everything was easy and routine.

'You look all right,' she told him as they dumped his single shoulder bag in the largest guest bedroom. There was a touch of admiration in her voice, as if she'd been expecting a hospital case.

'Mum, you haven't been gone a month.'

'I know.' She gave him a quick kiss. 'But it's still nice to see you. Now come along, I've got a taxi booked, we're going to Fortnum and Mason for lunch.'

Natalie Cherbun came in the taxi with them, while the

other two Europol officers were left to catch one of their own. His mother, Tim noticed with some jealousy, no longer had a bodyguard team.

The distinguished old department store on Piccadilly hadn't changed since the last time Tim had visited several years ago – also with his mother. The ground floor was given over entirely to a delicatessen, with long dark wooden shelves stacked with a fantastic array of bottles and packets. It was as if the old store was completely immune to the decay of global transport and all the political instabilities raging across the world. Delicacies from just about every country were stacked neatly in their sections. Tim imagined each brand and variety must have occupied the same part of shelving for decades, as if they'd somehow colonized the place. There was even tea from China available, which had long ago disconnected itself from the datasphere.

His head swivelled round as they walked through, distracted by the smells – first coffee from the big grinding machines behind the counter, then chocolate, then cheese. By the time they reached the far side and walked up the short flight of steps to the raised terrace restaurant overlooking the shop floor, his stomach was growling with hunger.

'So what's happening at home?' Sue asked after they'd ordered their drinks. She hadn't commented on him asking for mineral water, though her raised eyebrow was quite eloquent in itself.

'Nothing much. The usual.'

'Tim, you were desperate to come down here. You might not have said it on the phone, but I am your mother.'

Tim scrunched his lips up, almost forming a sulky pout before he realized what he was doing. 'Well, you know, you and dad separating takes some getting used to. And I did want to see you as well.'

'That's very sweet. How's Annabelle?'

'Dunno.' Tim moved his shoulders in what might have been a shrug.

'Ah.' Sue sipped her champagne thoughtfully. 'I thought that was odd. I haven't heard a word about her out of you since the summer ball. Have you broken up?'

'Yeah.'

'I'm sorry.'

'Everybody says that.'

'Everybody's bound to. You made a good couple.'

'Great.' Tim slumped down petulantly.

'Oh Tim.' Sue reached over and patted his hand. 'It'll be all right eventually. Broken hearts mend. I know that from experience.'

'Who broke your heart?'

'Lots of people. Boys! You're a cruel race.'

'I don't think I broke Annabelle's heart.'

'Of course you did. You're a prime catch. She'll be devastated she was so stupid as to let you go.'

'You think?'

'Absolutely. I know a dozen friends in this town whose daughters would kill to have your datasphere interface number.'

Tim glanced round to see if anyone was listening; not entirely displeased. 'Mum!'

'Well, you are, darling, not just because you're my son, or Jeff's; you're pretty special in your own right. Is that why you're here? To meet new people, get over her?'

'Not really. It's a little tricky with dad at the moment, that's all. I needed a break for a couple of days.'

'Oh God, what's he done now?'

'Nothing really. You remember Sophie?'

'Vaguely. One of your gaggle of friends. Blonde, no chest.'

Tim was momentarily thrown by his mother's description. 'Er, yeah. Well, her and dad . . . you know.'

'Bloody hell! Are you sure?'

Several people at neighbouring tables glanced round.

Tim studied his glass of water. 'Yes.'

'Jesus. That's sailing pretty close to the edge. What did dear Mz Duke say about this?'

'I don't think she knows. It was a bit of a one-night stand. I had a load of people round for an end of term barbecue. It happened that night.'

'It was a pretty awful thing for him to do. And her, come to that. But you're going to have to come to terms with the fact that your father's a celebrity. Worse than that, he's young and rich. It's a combination which does tend to attract girls.'

'I know that! But . . . Sophie.'

'Term's over, Tim, it can't happen again. If I know anything about Jeff, he's probably quite embarrassed about it himself.'

'Right.' Tim picked absently at his bread roll. His father hadn't exactly shown much contrition since that morning. If anything, he'd made Tim feel that he'd somehow been in the wrong by complaining. Tim hated that. Things had just started to ease up at home. He'd thought he was getting on okay with Jeff again. If anything, he'd actually grown to be more comfortable around this new rejuven-

288

ated father than he had been with the slightly distant old man from before the treatment; he felt less inhibited, more able to share and confide. It was as if they had almost become equals. Lost an elderly father, gained a big brother. On top of that he'd come to look forward to his daily phone calls to his mother. They'd begun to chatter away in a fashion they never had while she was at home *being* his mother. Then the summer ball happened, knocking his life out of kilter once again.

'Time, Tim,' Sue said in a near-regretful tone. 'It cures many things. You just need a long dose of it right now.'

'Suppose.'

'So have you decided where you're going, Oxford or Cambridge?'

'Oh yeah, sorry, didn't I tell you? It's Oxford.'

'Good for you.' She picked her menu up. 'Now let's eat. I've got another house to look at this afternoon.'

'Where?'

'Just outside Hounslow. Almost in the countryside, but only a twenty-minute train ride to the centre of town. Want to come along and see it with me?'

'Sure.'

*

The house wasn't anything exceptional, four bedrooms and a reasonable-sized garden – by London standards. Apart from the price, there was nothing appealing about it; and it was underneath Heathrow's flight path. Even with exorbitant aviation fuel prices and two of the airport's terminals now shut, there were still an uncomfortable number of planes landing and taking off.

Tim and Sue had a quick look round. The estate agent

was promptly informed that it wasn't what she wanted. Everybody left unhappy.

When they got back to the flat, Sue told Tim she was going out for the evening. 'Not the sort of dinner party I can take you to, darling – sorry.'

To which he said he didn't mind, he'd stay in and access some soaps or maybe a pre10 movie. She offered to put him in touch with some of her friends who had family around his own age. There was a fabulous club scene in London which they took full advantage of. He turned that down as well. His mood just wasn't connected with that kind of thing right now.

Sue took over an hour to get ready. When she finally came out of her bedroom, she was wearing a backless white and silver dress. 'You look sensational, mum,' Tim told her. He was always staggered by just how beautiful she was, as if she was a different species from all the other mothers he knew.

'Thank you, darling.' She was twisting about, examining herself in the hall's full-length mirror. 'It's not too tarty?'

'You don't do tarty, Mum. It's sheer class. Dead-on.'

She kissed him goodbye, and told him not to wait up.

Tim hadn't asked who her date was for the evening. He'd never asked before. *Why start now?*

Two of the Europol team were left on duty for the night, watching a show in the flat's small second lounge. They'd ordered a takeaway from the local Chinese, asking Tim if he wanted to share. He'd said no; there was a load of food in the fridge that he fancied sampling. The flat was certainly never visited by a Community Supply Service van, its deliveries were all direct from Knightsbridge's exclusive shops and stores who could afford to license their own transport.

Tim settled in the lounge, claiming a nineteen-sixties black globe chair that had cost his mother a fortune in an Islington antique shop. He munched away on smoked-salmon sandwiches, then went on to try wild boar, followed by some weird salami sausage slices. After that he found a packet of sushi, meticulously arranged like some elegant floral display. That got scoffed down quickly, and he began to dip crackers in a little pot of caviar (okay-ish but salty). To finish with he piled some giant GM strawberries in a bowl and scooped Cornish cream all over them.

The lounge screen configured a grid with current shows and the evening's sports matches. There was nothing he fancied watching. He wondered what his mother was doing right now. Probably at some swanky house, enjoying hors d'oeuvres in the drawing room along with all the other guests before taking their places at the dining table. After that some dinner-suited himbo would escort her out and murmur the question: 'My place or yours?'

Stop it!

He hadn't expected to go out with his mother every night, but she might have stayed with him for the first evening. London's theatres and concert halls had enjoyed a huge renaissance after Hollywood burned; live shows were now immensely popular. A comedy would have cheered him up; they could have gone together.

Tim looked from the silent kaleidoscope of tiny images on the screen to the plates and dishes and wrappers scattered all over the floor around the globe chair. That spooky old sense of isolation, the scourge of his life until this year, was returning to depress him.

'Click, real-time call to Annabelle Goddard.'

CALLER CODE REJECTED, the screen printed immediately.

'Oh, fuck it!' *Why won't she talk to me?* He stared at the green script on the screen for a long moment. Everyone kept saying he'd get over her. 'Okay, then. Click, real time call to Vanessa Dowdall.'

The big surround-sound speakers produced the ringing tone, making it seem as if he was in the middle of cathedral bells struck by a rampant robot. After a minute the screen printed: CALL ACCEPTED. AUDIO ONLY.

'Hi, Tim.' Vanessa's voice was raised above a typical pub's background clamour. He could visualize her, sitting at a crowded table with friends, one hand over an ear, the other cupping her mic and mouth.

'Hi, you said to call sometime.'

'Yeah, right, how are you?'

'Fine. I'm down in London.'

'Cool. I'm in Indigo.'

'Where?'

'It's a bar in Nottingham, right in the centre. We're going to hit a few clubs.'

'Sounds good.'

'How about you?'

'I'm waiting for some friends. We're going to take a tour round the West End tonight, see what's happening.'

'So much cool.'

'So shall I give you another call when I get home? Maybe we could meet up.'

'Do that. I'd like it. Hey, drown in fun tonight.'

'You too. Bye.'

'Bye, Tim.'

The screen went blank. 'Who are you trying to fool?' he asked it. From somewhere he found the courage to say: 'Click, real-time call to Goddard house phone, 18 South-brook Crescent, Uppingham, Rutland.' This was it, the last desperate gamble. If he blew it now, they would be over for ever.

The call wasn't rejected by the house's datasphere inter-face. That alone sent his pulse rate up. He waited while the speakers pealed loudly around him. Then they fell silent, and the screen lit up with poor-resolution shadows in a drizzle of emerald sparks. The shadows moved, and he recognized them as Roger Goddard's face. Annabelle's father was frowning heavily. 'Hello?' his deeply puzzled voice queried.

'Hello, Mr Goddard, it's Tim Baker. I wondered if I could talk to Annabelle, please.'

The huge face on the screen displayed a number of strange tics as the question was pondered, changing the frown into an expression of anguish. 'No,' he said quietly. 'No, you can't.'

'Please, if you could just ask her to come to the phone. I just want to talk to her. That's all. Please.'

'I can't, Tim. She's not here. She left this afternoon.'

'She left?'

'Yes. Packed her bag and went. She said it was just for a few days. But I know. This is just the start. I'll be here by myself soon.'

'Where's she gone?'

'She's with her boyfriend, staying at his place.'

'*Her boyfriend?*'

'Yes.'

'Who the fu— Do you know who he is?'

'I'm not sure. I know you used to be. This is somebody else.'

'What's his name? Please, Mr Goddard.'

'I don't know. That's strange. I'm sure she must have told me. But I don't remember.'

'How long has she been seeing him?'

'Quite a while. Was it you she went to the summer ball with, or him?'

'Me. It was *me*.'

'Oh. Well, it was about then.'

'The summer ball? She was seeing him back then?'

'I think so.'

'Oh my God.'

'She was really happy when she left. I couldn't stop her, couldn't say anything. She's so beautiful when she's smiling and excited like that. So full of joy. How could I ask her to stay? All I want is for her to be happy. I can't stand in the way of that. My daughter is so wonderful. And he makes her happy. Shining, she was—'

'Fucking click, fucking end fucking call!'

*

Since the ball. Or even before the ball if her synth-head father was right.

How could she? She knew how much he loved her, how utterly devoted he was. How could she do such a thing? They'd been good together. Everyone said that. A great couple. He made her laugh. They had sex. Lots of sex. Hadn't that meant anything to her? Hadn't he meant anything to her?

Obviously not.

Tim curled up inside the globe chair, frightened he was going to cry. Now she had someone else she would never want him back. And she wasn't merely seeing this new boy, she'd gone to stay with him. Moved in. They'd spend every night in bed, bodies locked together in hot acrobatic lust. The new boy, whoever he was, would never let that opportunity slip by.

The idea produced an actual physical pain in Tim's head. It was so abhorrent. Nobody could love and appreciate Annabelle the way he did. Nobody.

He could finally realize why people did such stupid crazy things when they lost someone they adored. Right there and then he couldn't bear the notion of ever going back to Rutland, where he'd be near her every day, walking through places they'd been together. He could just as easily stay down in London with Mum, spend the summer sampling metropolitan life until university. That idea died as quickly as it was born. Mum had her new life, complete with her men; she was happy.

Maybe he should take that gap year dad had offered him. The other side of the planet was probably the only safe distance to be. Dad would still agree to that. When he started thinking about slinking back to the Manor with his tail between his legs to ask, his mind began conjuring up those images of Sophie's slender body twined round his father's.

The whole world, it seemed, was having a fabulous steamy sex life, except for him.

38. A SNOWFLAKE IN HELL

The summer storm crawled northwards across the hitherto placid azure sky, following some way behind the morning express train from London to Peterborough. Tim changed for the regional train to Stamford, then caught the bus back to Empingham. Thick black clouds were just beginning to fall over the lip of the southern horizon as he walked up the drive to the Manor. The air was heavy with the smell of ozone.

Lieutenant Krober was in the hallway when Tim walked in. 'We didn't expect you back for a few more days,' he said.

To Tim's ears the Europol officer sounded strangely guilty. 'Yeah, well, London didn't work for me.'

'I see.'

'Where's dad?'

'I am not sure.'

'Not sure? You're his bodyguard.'

'He has not gone out. He is in the Manor. Perhaps working.'

Tim frowned at Krober, who was giving Natalie Cherbun a frantic look. He marched into the lounge. Dad wasn't there, but a navy-blue bikini halter was draped over the back of the white leather sofa. Tim stared at it, startled by how familiar it was. The big French windows were open, obviously used that morning. He went out onto the terrace to see if anyone was outside. Behind him he could hear Krober and Cherbun talking in low urgent voices. Nobody was in the garden. The pool was calm and flat, with a single inflatable ball floating in one corner of the deep end.

A girl moaned hoarsely above and behind him. Tim turned slowly to see the veranda doors of his father's bedroom were wide open. He wasn't conscious of climbing up the iron spiral stairs from the terrace. The next thing he knew he was standing on the veranda, shaking in anticipation and fear. The storm's precursor breeze stirred the louvre blinds along the edge of the veranda doors, causing them to sway slightly. There was another cry from inside the bedroom, sharper this time. Tim's whole body had turned numb with a cold dread. Even so, he crept forward until he was standing at the window frame. His face pressed up against the glass, allowing him to peer through the narrow gap between the blinds.

A naked Jeff was lying across the bed. Annabelle was there at his side, on all fours. Her hands were slowly massaging his cock; she grinned down proudly at him, occasionally bending forward to kiss or lick his face. With deliberate slowness she straightened up and pushed her hair back with both hands. Jeff's moan of desperation as he gazed up at her provoked a delighted laugh. Then she slowly straddled him, impaling herself. That delighted grin became a smile of wonder, and her whole body shuddered in pleasure.

Tim appeared to be looking straight into Annabelle's

eyes, though she seemed unable to see anything through her own rapture. So he simply watched with a kind of detached interest as she fucked his father not three metres in front of him. There were little details of the incident which he absorbed calmly. The eager determination lighting her beautiful features as her abdominal muscles flexed sinuously and relentlessly. Sunlight glistening softly off the perspiration that speckled her shoulders. Jeff's easy movements, perfectly synchronized with hers, while an exuberant gloating expression grew over his face.

It was that symmetry which so obviously existed between them that held Tim captive, cowering unseen behind the glass. They had no physical secrets, knowing exactly what to do to inflame the other. Even their cries were delivered in unison, Annabelle's high wail of incredulity mingling with Jeff's animal-glee grunts.

There was never going to be an end to it. They went on and on, relishing the youthful stamina which allowed them to prolong the ecstasy.

The image blurred. Tim blinked, not understanding what was happening. Then he saw big raindrops were splashing against the glass. The storm had arrived from the south, rolling across the sky to shroud the Manor in darkness and thunder. Rain and tears mingled together as they trickled down his cheeks.

39. THE JOY OF KNOWING

'We should go out and make love in the rain,' Annabelle said dreamily. She was lying on her side in the middle of the bed, watching the drops splatter against the windows. There was already a damp patch on the carpet where the veranda doors were open. They'd been so intent on each other that they hadn't even seen the rain washing in, let alone been bothered to go and shut the doors.

'Nice idea,' Jeff said. 'Except that's not rain, it's a bloody deluge.'

She snuggled back into him, enjoying the warmth and touch of his body. 'Next time, then.'

'Yes.' He caressed her hair. 'Next time.'

She glanced over her shoulder as he ran a finger lightly down her flank, tracing the curve of her hip. There was an expression of gentle curiosity on his face, as if he'd never seen her before, never known how it felt to touch her skin. She loved that aspect of him, that he could be as kind as he could be savage, always knowing the right time. 'I spent the night with you,' she murmured in wonder. 'The whole night.' Once they'd gone up to bed, with the lights off and the big house's silence engulfing them, it was as if they were the only two people in the whole universe. She knew that the isolation had brought them closer together than ever before. A union she celebrated by doing everything she could think of to please him sexually.

As always, she could barely believe what she'd allowed him to do to her. But that was always the way with Jeff, each time a little further. Her own curiosity was his greatest ally. If she'd ever had any inhibitions, they'd been discarded that night of the summer ball. Now she became excited just by the way they explored her sexuality: the acts of abandon themselves were almost as pleasurable as the physical climaxes they resulted in. It was as if she was secretly defying the whole world by using her body like this. Sex had become her revenge for the life she'd been forced to live before she met him.

'And you're going to spend tomorrow night here as well,' he said. 'And the night after that.'

She smiled bravely, knowing that she'd have to go home then.

Jeff tightened his grip around her. 'And when Tim comes back, I'm going to tell him that you're here to stay now.'

'Jeff!' There was a small instinct that wanted to say no, that not enough time had passed to cushion the shock. But just seeing how serious he was quashed the urge. 'Do you mean that?'

Jeff lowered his head. 'Dead on.' His tongue moistened one nipple before he started sucking. 'And I'm sober this time, too.'

She ran a hand over his chest, enjoying the supple play of muscle under her palm. 'Thank you.' Then her fingers touched his cock and she peered down in surprise. He was still erect. 'God, you're unbelievable.'

Jeff pulled away from her breast just long enough to chuckle contentedly.

'I mean it,' she said. 'I've been with twenty-year-olds before. They've never managed to stay hard for so long.'

'I'm not twenty.' He switched from one breast to the other.

Despite herself, her body was responding. His head dipped down again. Annabelle moaned as indecent fingers started to massage her. She wondered if he was going to mention a threesome again. The state she was in, she'd probably agree.

There was a firm knock on the door. 'Dr Baker, sir?' It was Lieutenant Krober's voice.

'He's got to be fucking joking,' Jeff grunted.

The knock came again. 'Dr Baker, please, are you there?'

'What do you want?'

'Sir, I believe you should come downstairs, sir.'

'What the hell is happening?'

'Sir, it's downstairs. Please.'

Annabelle pouted teasingly at the irritation on Jeff's face. 'You'd better go.'

'Bloody hell.' He took a deep breath and clambered off her. She started giggling profusely as he tried to tie the belt on his dressing gown. His erection refused to ease. He gave it an exasperated stare, and wound up holding one hand across his front, pressing his cock against his abdomen.

Annabelle squeaked in alarm as he stomped over to the door, just managing to pull the duvet over herself as he opened it. Lieutenant Krober was standing outside. Jeff had never seen the Europol officer so agitated.

'What's the matter? Are we in the middle of some kind of terrorist attack?'

'Sorry, sir.' Krober was taking great care not to look through the bedroom door. 'You should come downstairs.'

'Why?'

'Please. There is a situation there.'

'Oh, for God's sake.' Jeff stomped off down the landing with his hand still firmly covering his groin. His anger chilled rapidly as he started down the stairs. The hallway came into view, and with it the sound of voices arguing heatedly. Tim was there, halfway across the black and white marble tiles. *Tim!* Jeff's heart jumped in shock. His legs refused to move, imprisoning him on the middle of the stairs.

The boy's shirt and trousers were soaking wet, rat-tail strands of hair fringed his forehead. He was attempting to carry a huge cylindrical canvas bag with a strap that kept slipping from his wet shoulder. His other hand was pulling at the extended handle of a big grey suitcase with tiny wheels. Natalie Cherbun was standing in front of him, half-heartedly blocking his progress.

'No, I won't!' Tim yelled as he tried to barge past her. His luggage kept overbalancing, hampering his progress far more than the Europol officer.

At which point Lucy Duke came through the front door. She was out of breath from having run all the way through the village from the White Horse. Water dripped steadily off her black classic-cut raincoat. She started shaking out her umbrella, an act that suddenly halted when she took in the scene before her.

Tim shut up and glared at her. Then Lucy's gaze lifted to Jeff. Tim's body became very still. He slowly turned round. Jeff waited for his son to see him, knowing how a condemned man felt as the gallows loomed through the dawn mist.

The expression of anger and betrayal on his son's face drained away the last of Jeff's strength. 'Look, son—'

Tim sneered at him. He'd never, ever done that before. Raged and sulked, yes. But this was so adult, so contemptuous that Jeff wanted to kneel down and beg forgiveness. Right there and then he would have handed Annabelle back if it was at all possible. An evil thought sprang up: *Why not? She does everything else I tell her to.* Which he rapidly pushed away.

'Now why don't we all take a moment to think what we're all doing?' Lucy Duke said with brittle calm.

'Fuck off, you stupid bitch!' Tim bellowed at her.

'I don't think that's very helpful, now, is it?'

Jeff finally managed to get his legs moving again. He hurried down the last few stairs. 'Tim, just wait up.'

Tim dropped the shoulder bag, and folded his arms across his chest. 'Oh, this should be good. Go on, *dad*, explain to me why it doesn't matter. How we can all live happily ever after.'

'We were going to tell you.' Even before it came out, Jeff knew that was completely the wrong thing to say.

'Really?' Tim said with acid sweetness. 'How were you going to tell me? Would I have to access it on your life site? "Hello, folks, I am now pleased to announce that I am *fucking my son's girlfriend*?"'

Jeff wanted to close his eyes, to cast the whole nightmare back into darkness. The way Tim was standing, his whole body quivering and moisture glinting in his eyes, Jeff couldn't tell if he was going to burst into tears or simply go berserk and charge at him with a chainsaw. Natalie Cherbun was giving him a horrified look. While Lucy Duke had tilted her head back in despair, no doubt calculating what kind of damage-limitation exercise was going to rescue this one. It was the only time Jeff had wanted to consult with her on anything.

Still, he thought, *at least I know the worst of it now, that he saw everything. So that's good.* A desperate laugh threatened to rise up in his throat, one which would tail off into a crazed burble if he ever let it out. 'What Annabelle and I do together is between us,' he said with false dignity. 'We didn't tell you about us because we didn't want to hurt you. Tim, I know this is hard, but she's not your girlfriend. She hasn't been for a while now. We were going to let you get over the break-up, but we were going to tell you.'

'How long?'

'How long, what?'

'How long have you been fucking her, dad?'

'Don't, Tim, you're only hurting yourself.'

'Night of the summer ball, wasn't it?'

Jeff found Tim's keen gaze slicing clean into him. He hadn't thought it possible, but he was actually feeling even more wretched. His shoulders slumped in confession.

'Yeah,' Tim breathed, eager and pleased. 'You really waited, didn't you, dad?' He picked up his shoulder bag, and gave Natalie Cherbun a very determined look. She sighed and stood to one side.

Tim walked across the hall, his big suitcase juddering and squeaking along behind him. Lucy Duke gave him an uncertain look.

'Please,' Tim snarled at her. 'Please do get in my way.'

'Where are you going?' Jeff called.

'What the fuck do you care, *dad*?'

'You haven't even got a coat on. It's pouring down outside. You'll catch cold.'

'I don't get ill.'

The dull certainty of his voice made Jeff draw in a gasp of surprise. *He can't know that . . .* 'Tim, you can't just walk out. This is your home. Don't be so melodramatic.'

Tim opened the front door. Raindrops swirled in, splattering on the marble at his feet. 'That would be melodramatic as opposed to having an illicit affair? Did that make it more exciting for you both, dad? Sneaking round behind my back.' A last contemptuous snort, and he closed the door.

Jeff put his head in his hands. 'Oh, shit.' All he could think of was that he now had to go upstairs and explain to Annabelle. Then there would be a call to Sue. And – oh God – Alison.

Natalie Cherbun coughed discreetly.

'What?' he snapped at her.

She gave his waist a very pointed look. Jeff groaned in frustration, and pulled his robe over to cover his continuing erection.

Natalie Cherbun and Lucy Duke looked at each other. *And what must they be thinking?*

'We should consider how to minimize the media interpretation of this,' Lucy Duke said.

'You can't minimize a total fucking disaster, you—. Not now, all right. We'll do press releases and site revisions later.' He got to the top of the stairs, then turned round. 'Natalie, he probably respects you more than anyone else here right now. Could you go after him and give him a lift, please? Don't stay with him afterwards, just help him get there.'

'Very well,' she nodded shortly, then paused. 'Where?'

'He'll be going to his Aunt Alison. And I know Tim, he'll walk the whole bloody way there even in this rain.'

'I'll get him.'

The bedroom door was closed. Jeff squared his shoulders, and opened it.

40. HOME COMFORTS

'I haven't used this room for ages,' Alison said as she showed Tim into the bungalow's back bedroom. 'It might need a little freshening up.'

Tim looked round, and managed a small smile. The bed was covered in big cardboard boxes full of books, they were stacked three deep. Not that it mattered – there was no way to reach the bed anyway. More boxes and plastic storage bins were littering the floor, along with other stuff, intriguingly shaped items wrapped tightly in newspaper that was yellowed and crumbling. Polythene shopping bags were stuffed full of clothes, or at least with bundles of fabric. When he looked down at his feet, he saw a pair of ancient hiking boots, so old the dark-brown leather had dried out and cracked. It wasn't the kind of footwear he would ever normally associate with Aunt Alison.

'Ah, those,' she said wistfully, following his surprised gaze. 'I've worn those on three continents, you know – other than Europe. Tramped along the Peruvian coast, marched up Ayers Rock, and wandered over the Serengeti. Good times, before the world went the way we know it today.'

'Yeah,' Tim said miserably. 'It's a pretty rotten place now.'

Alison's arm went round his shoulder. 'I was speaking in general terms, not about what happened to you. Now, come on, let's get some space cleared for you.'

They stacked the boxes along one of the walls, making a precariously high half-pyramid. Other containers were taken out to the garage, once Alison had inspected them and reluctantly admitted she might not use them again in the immediate future. The rear wall of the garage wasn't even visible, there was so much junk stored inside already.

When they cleared the bed and she found him a clean duvet cover, they went back into the lounge. The storm had cleared, leaving the sun glinting brightly off the leaves and flowers in the unkempt garden.

Alison settled herself in a deep old armchair and poured a large gin and tonic. Tim was sent to the kitchen to fetch some ice. The freezer was badly frosted up, with just a couple of food packets inside, both of them ready-made meals for one, long past their expiry dates.

'What do you eat?' he asked when he came back with a few ice cubes chinking round in the glass. 'There's hardly anything in there to cook.'

Alison took a long sip, and relaxed even further into the squashed nest of cushions. 'The thing is, Tim, I don't really do cooking. Never was much good at it, not even the microwave stuff. I either pop down to the village pub or get myself a takeaway. You don't mind having those kind of meals, do you?'

'No. That's fine.' Tim was perched on the corner of the settee, staring out across the big reservoir without really seeing it.

'Want to talk about it?'

'No.'

'I think you're supposed to. All of my clever friends say you should rationalize events back to ground zero so you can acknowledge their structural integration within your lifeflow.'

'Alison, that's . . . such a load of crap.'

'I know that.' She grinned at him, and took another sip. 'What they actually mean is, don't bottle things up. They only hurt for longer.'

'There's nothing to talk about. My dad's got my girl-friend. What can you possibly say about that?'

'We could start with how you feel about it.'

'Feel? Alison, she was my girlfriend.'

'I thought it was all over.'

He let his head fall into his hands. 'Yeah, well. It was over because he moved in on her. I found that out today.'

'Are you surprised?'

'Was that a joke?'

'Let me put it this way. If it had been anyone else – anyone other than Jeff – would you be surprised that Annabelle had found herself a new boyfriend?'

'No. Suppose not. She's so beautiful. Why, are you taking his side?'

'No. I think what he's done is despicable. It's not something I'll ever forgive him for, either. But knowing my big brother, I have to say I'm not surprised. And if you can withstand one more observation: I always thought Annabelle was sort of flighty.'

'What do you mean, flighty?'

'Let me put it this way, I don't think the two of you were ever scheduled to get married and live happily ever after. I know she was the prettiest girlfriend you've had so far; and I know this is what I said last time, but you'll find someone else just as nice. No, scratch that, nicer. Let's face it, Tim, it takes two to tango. She's not exactly innocent in all this, now, is she?'

'No.' It came out as a hugely sullen grunt. 'Suppose not.' He really didn't want to examine that part of it: that Annabelle had been just as guilty. But then, that awful image of the two of them locked together still hadn't faded from behind his sight. The way she had taken the lead . . . how uninhibited she'd been . . . her supreme enjoyment.

'You want a drink?' Alison asked.

He was tempted. Just wash her out of his mind, his life, with a huge flush of drink or synth8. The one thing he'd promised himself he would never do again.

Because Annabelle didn't like it.

There were synth8s that would make this a whole load easier to handle. Taking them would be so simple, making his life pleasurable once more. He just had to stop being true to himself.

With every cell in his body screaming to say the opposite, he said: 'No, thanks, Alison, my head's in a big enough mess as it is.'

'Tough it out, eh? Good for you.' She took another big sip of her gin and tonic. 'Have you told your mother yet?'

'No.' He shifted round as if the settee was suddenly crawling with ants. 'I was sort of wondering if you might do that.'

Alison cocked one eyebrow at him. 'How long till you leave for university?'

41. GLOBAL COMMUNICATIONS

'Your sister is calling,' Hal9000's voice said.

'Put her on.'

Alison's face filled the big lounge screen. At the best of times that scale was intimidating. With a scowl on her face she appeared more than a little frightening.

'You stupid, *stupid* shit,' she said. The image vanished.

*

THE OFFICIAL JEFF BAKER LIFE SITE/ NEWS

Following the amicable separation from my wife, I am fortunate to be able to announce that I have found someone new to share my life with. Ms Annabelle Goddard and I have known each other for several weeks, and have grown close during this time. We are now making plans for a long and happy future together.

*

'Call from your wife.'

'Yes.'

'I don't believe even you could do that. You thoughtless bastard. Have you got any idea what you've done to that poor boy?'

'Oh, come on Sue, it was hardly deliberate. You were the one who let him come home early.'

'Jesus wept, don't you dare try and shift the blame on this. I don't care how he found out. You and that juvenile tart should never have happened. Not ever, Jeff! Click, end call.'

*

DATAMAIL LEADER
>hyperlinks<
DataMail/ celebrity site
DataMail/ personal problems site
DataMail/ medical site

Canny old (and we do mean *old!*) Jeff Baker, already the luckiest man on the planet thanks to his rejuvenation, has just had another turn of good fortune. His new girlfriend, the delectably busty Annabelle Goddard, is only eighteen years old, which means there is an astonishing sixty-year age gap between them. This clearly doesn't bother the happy couple, as a close family friend said: 'The two of them are inseparable. She's the best thing that could happen to anyone, let alone Jeff.'

Annabelle (picture >hyperlink<) was a family friend for some time before romance blossomed. The two of them are now living together in Jeff's fabulous country mansion.

When our own medical site's resident doctor, Mike Jones, heard about the development, he offered this advice to the randy pensioner. 'Despite the miracle of rejuvenation, I'd advise Jeff to take things easy. Annabelle's obviously a healthy girl, and will need a lot of physical attention. Even though his treatment has given him a young body, he will need to pace himself in the bedroom.'

Our expert personal-problems analyst Justina
>hyperlink< comments on the development. Is it a
complete mismatch? Can it possibly last? Could they have
found true love?

*

'How did they get that picture of me in my bikini?'

'I've no idea.'

'It was taken here at the Manor, look. That's the terrace behind me.'

'You're right. It must have come from the security camera.'

'Did you let that Duke cow release this?'

'Of course not!'

'It was her. I bet it was her. That bitch.'

*

INTERNATIONAL SUN LEADER
>hyperlinks<
International Sun/ people & politics site
International Sun/ it's your taxmoney site
International Sun/ topless topten site
International Sun/ shirt off for the girls site

Rejuve grandpa bonks schoolgirl
Jeff Baker, the planet's oldest teenager, has scored
with an eighteen-year-old babe (bikini picture
>hyperlink<). The superstud pensioner brazenly
announced on his own life site that he was bedding
the gorgeous Annabelle Goddard. What he didn't
mention was that sensational Bella was just a
schoolgirl when they met (pictured in her uniform

>hyperlink<). The incredible reason why they got together, your International Sun has discovered, was all thanks to Jeff's son, Tim, who was Bella's long-time and devoted boyfriend. Innocent Tim introduced the pair when his old man came back from his fabulously expensive Euro Rejuvenation Treatment. Now the besotted dad's gone and elbowed his pining lad aside so he can grapple with the mega-breasted Bella (bikini picture2 >hyperlink<).

Heartbroken Tim has wound up moving in with his aunty while the couple enjoy nightly romps in the playboy's palatial home where poor Tim grew up. 'I can't stand living there any more,' said the desperate boy, adding: 'They've ruined my life.'

What's more, Bella isn't the first girl the frisky Jeff has bedded since he finished his Treatment. Sad Martina Lewis (picture >hyperlink<) had a very public fling with the insatiable Jeff several weeks ago. 'He was all a girl could dream of between the sheets,' the rejected Martina said yesterday. But she doesn't hold any grudges. 'I wish Bella well. He's a great catch.'

The brainy hunk (picture >hyperlink<) has also featured heavily in Rob Lacey's campaign for the European Presidency. Last night, a spokesperson for the hopeful candidate's office said: 'Jeff Baker is an excellent example of rejuvenation. This latest development only proves how successful the treatment which Prime Minister Lacey endorsed can be.' Asked if Jeff would be taking any further part in the campaign, the spokesperson replied: 'I think he's got his hands full right now.'

The International Sun says: You lucky bastard, Jeff, we're right behind you, mate.

See what big-boobed Bella looks like underneath that tight little bikini she's so fond of cavorting around in. The science boys in our image department have worked through the night to bring you an accurate picture of what Bella's stupendous figure will look like in all its natural glory (Bella's boobs >hyperlink<).

Are you one of the girls Jeff has slept with? If you are and have a story to tell, contact our newsdesk >txtlink<. We pay the best for the best.

*

'Hello, Sophie.'

'Jeff? Hi. Didn't expect to hear from you.'

'Yeah, I figured that. But I've got a favour to ask you.'

'Don't worry, I'm not going to kiss and tell.'

'Oh, right, thanks. That wasn't it, actually.'

'Really?' The tone of Sophie's voice rose to match her scepticism. 'What did you want?'

'I was wondering if you could come and visit for a couple of days. Annabelle's not used to this kind of media interest. She could do with having a good friend around right now.'

'So what are you, then?'

'You know what I mean. A friend other than me that she can talk to, and who'll offer a bit of support.'

'Well . . . Let me think about it, okay?'

'We'd both really appreciate it.'

*

It was the only call in a whole week that Tim roused himself to answer. Even then it was just out of politeness rather than from any real interest.

The scuffed screen in his bedroom showed him Vanessa's heart-shaped face creased with anxiety. She was regarding her own screen's picture with almost maternal concern. 'I should have called earlier,' she said. 'I'm sorry. I wasn't sure if you'd want to speak to anybody. How's it been?'

'Pretty shitty. The residents are furious with Alison for taking me in. There are reporters camped outside the estate gates, and there's already been a couple of fights between them and the security company people.'

'That's awful. They're so much animals. Can't the police do something?'

'They say not. Did you know she was seeing him?'

'No!' She shook her head in regret. 'No, Tim, I didn't. None of us did. Look, I'm majorly sorry it happened, but you're too good for her.'

He knew he should smile at that, but couldn't quite manage it. 'Thanks.'

'I mean it. That's what she's like, Tim. Just a body – there's no character there, no substance. If I'd been dating you, I would never have done that.'

'But we weren't dating.'

'That's just a timing thing. Hey, look, are you still coming to the protest march?'

'Dunno. Hadn't thought about it much.'

'Figures. But you know, you're really due a break. Why don't you come up here to Nottingham for a couple of days before? There's room, and this house has a big walled garden. Nobody would know you're here. We could travel down to meet with the others afterwards.'

It took him a moment to realize what she was saying. How come she'd never given off signals when they were at school? Five years they'd known each other – and nothing. 'That's, er, really kind. I need to check with Alison, and sort out what I can do about the reporters. Call you back in a few days?'

'I'll be here.'

42. MALE FANTASY ISLAND

After a couple of days of dutiful attendance at the Houston physics conference Annabelle and Jeff caught the daily American International flight to Antigua out of Miami. From the capital, St John's, they had to take the resort's transfer boat out to Barbuda itself. The island was one of the most isolated places in the Caribbean. Decades before, it had its own airstrip, but that was when there were enough people taking foreign holidays to make it pay. Now the only way to get there was by boat. A situation that was ideal for the kind of person who really wanted to get away from it all.

Barbuda was little more than a patch of ground, a lot of which was swamp, raised a few metres above the sea. Even before the rising ultraviolet radiation started bleaching tropical vegetation, the island had few farms. The locals still lived much the same life as they always had. They fished, tended their new GM banana trees that had been provided by the UN Tropics Regeneration Office, nurtured small vegetable gardens and harvested natural-growing ganja. Activities which left them almost completely disconnected from the global economy. Their only source of foreign currency came from the exclusive resort that was situated on the island's sole remaining asset: Seven Mile Beach.

Jeff stared at it in mild astonishment as the transfer boat sliced through the clean deep-turquoise water of the Caribbean Sea. It was the kind of landscape he thought couldn't possibly exist in the real world, belonging instead to some mocked-up tourist brochure. The beach really was seven miles long, composed of pristine white sand that gleamed brighter than snow under the dangerous midday sun. Behind it, a thick swathe of GM royal palms and coconut trees marked the boundary between sand and the manky scrub bushes which covered the rest of the island.

As they passed Coco Point at the western end of the shallow cove, the transfer boat began to slide around the big pleasure yachts. Seven of them were anchored offshore, looking like a flotilla of miniature ocean liners. White hulls reflected sunlight across the water, while in complete contrast the long black windows of the upper decks looked like rifts torn into deep space. All of them had swept-back triangular solar fins sprouting from the top deck, looking like bizarre mechanical flower petals.

'Oh wow!' Annabelle exclaimed. She was leaning forward on the transfer boat's rail, a wide smile below her wraparound sunglasses. 'They are fabulous. This whole place is utterly fantastic.' She cuddled into him, her arms going round his shoulders. 'Thank you so much for bringing us here.'

'Hey, this is just as big a kick for me.' He kissed her.

She gave him a beaming smile again, then turned back to the yachts. 'Who do they belong to, do you think?'

'I don't know. I expect we'll see them in the bar tonight. Or maybe the owners don't ever come ashore. I wouldn't.'

He regarded the nearest yacht with low-level envy. A diving platform had been lowered down the stern. Two children were splashing about in the water beside it, overseen by a young man standing on the platform. Up at the bow, a couple of crewmen were washing the superstructure with long brushes.

'Yes, you would.' Annabelle smiled knowingly. 'You'd be bored out of your skull in a week.'

He grinned back at her.

The boat docked at a long wooden jetty that stabbed out from the beach. Looking over the gunwale, the water was so clear it seemed as if they were simply floating on air a couple of metres above the sand. Slender silver and aquamarine fish glided about below them.

The jetty was directly opposite the resort's main building, a white pavilion-style structure that looked as though it had been transplanted from the heart of the British Raj. It contained the reception, restaurant, and bar. Three bellboys in scarlet polo shirts emerged from it and hurried out to the boat to collect the luggage. The resort manager, Mr Sam, greeted his guests at the end of the jetty with a polite bow, and led them along the beach. A long line of wooden chalets was tucked away under the palms, almost invisible amid the shadows and lush foliage. Jeff had booked the one at the end, furthest away from the pavilion building.

As they walked down the beach, sweating from the tremendous heat, they got an impression of their fellow residents. Most of them were American, though they did hear several European languages being spoken. Men lazed around in hammocks, bellies hanging over floral swimming trunks, their eyes hidden away behind PCglasses as they muttered constantly to their interfaces. Their womenfolk were almost without exception in their twenties, uniformly vibrant and attractive. They lay on loungers, tanning themselves under white gauze UV-stopper parasols, or swam through the transparent water. Jeff kept thinking of the background dancers in rock videos. A few older women sported their toyboys, but they were heavily outnumbered.

Annabelle smiled demurely when she saw the other residents, casting a wily look towards Jeff. They held hands, fingers tickling each other.

From the outside, their chalet looked as if it was nothing more than an elaborate version of the local Caribbean huts, with a broad palm-thatch veranda extending round three sides. Inside, its Western heritage was more apparent. The walls and floor were polished hardwood. Air-conditioning hummed efficiently. Big modern settees were lined up on either side of the central table. There was a flat five-metre screen on the wall in the lounge, with a full datasphere interface via the resort's own satellite uplink. The master bedroom had a huge four-poster bed with broad mosquito drapes drawn up to the ceiling in an intricate rosette. Even the guest bedroom had a double bed.

Sophie tested its mattress with one hand, shaking her head in wonder as the bellboy brought in her single case. 'I can't believe this,' she murmured.

Annabelle had gone into the marble-tiled bathroom. A huge spa bath occupied one corner, easily big enough for half a dozen people; while a luxurious massage shower stood opposite, encased by frosted glass. 'Unreal,' she called out.

Jeff thanked Mr Sam, and managed to slip the bellboys some US dollar notes. The three of them were left alone in the lounge, with just the sound of the small waves breaking on the sand. He looked from Annabelle to Sophie. Both of them stared back at him, holding in almost contemptuous laughs.

'Now what?' he asked.

'Are you kidding?' Sophie said as she headed for her bedroom. 'That water is incredible. I'm straight in.'

'Me, too,' Annabelle said. 'Where's my swim stuff?' She started opening cases.

Jeff gave the perfect shoreline another glance through the open doors. The girls were right, it was impossible to resist. He opened the case he thought his own trunks were in.

Getting changed quickly turned into a race. He and Annabelle tugged their travelling clothes off, laughing at each other as sleeves and panties got stuck. Sophie kept shouting, 'No you don't, no you don't,' from the guest bedroom, which made Jeff even more determined to be first out. After Annabelle got her bikini briefs on, she looked round for the halter to see Jeff waving it tauntingly. He threw it up on top of the wardrobe and hurriedly started to pull on his own trunks. 'Sod that,' she said, and simply ran out into the lounge as she was. Sophie wolf-whistled as she dashed past the guest bedroom, then set off in pursuit wearing a tiny white string bikini. The two girls charged out onto the sands, giggling wildly as they sprinted for the water.

Jeff hurried after them as they dived into the shallows. It was a marvellous sight, sexy and uplifting. Annabelle was so happy, so confident, now. Exactly the kind of bloom she'd possessed right up until the day Tim had discovered them *in flagrante*. Slowly, she'd returned to her old self as she'd got over that shock and adjusted to her new world, where she featured heavily in the data-sphere's tabloid streams. Sophie had helped bring back her old spirit, offering reassurance and indignation as required.

The trip to America had been the final comfort. Two days in the relative quiet and calm of Houston, where he'd become the focus of the media again, diverting their attentions away from her. He'd done his part stoically, delivering a couple of standard speeches, and attending papers that were of limited use to the superconductor project. Getting back into the swing of the academic world and its vicious small-minded faction fights with a disingen-uous show of enthusiasm.

Annabelle and Sophie had escaped during the days, taking lengthy trips to the city's malls and landmarks. Jeff, on the other hand, had been trapped in the conven-tion centre, where he'd become uncomfortably aware of people's unspoken attitude towards him. There was never anything said to his face, but their stolen looks kept reminding him of what a drunk Alan had confessed: *If I could rip it out of you, I would.*

So it was his turn to be relieved when they left for Miami, and the surprise present of the holiday he'd booked. And now they were here on Barbuda he couldn't help but keep congratulating himself. He'd been to the Caribbean once before, for his so-called honeymoon with Sue, but the taste, smell, sight, and sound of the sweltering islands was just a faded and fractured memory. This time the imprint was majestic; the islands were a constant bigger, brighter and hotter assault on his everyday senses. He was sure that was partly Annabelle's world-wonder infusing him, allowing him to see everything with the same enthusiasm she did. If that was true, then it was small surprise her cheery nature had returned so strongly in the midst of so much natural grandeur.

Jeff waded into the deliciously warm sea as the girls began a splashing war, fountaining huge jets of water at each other, shrieking with laughter. He joined in with their sport, his arm careening off the surface to fling a plume of spray over both of them. They turned on him in retaliation, the three of them grappling gleefully amid the waves and foam.

43. SPEED KING

Mill Lane was a tiny side road off Tinwell village's main road, its tarmac long since disappeared under the encroachment of weeds and moss. Tim was rocked about gently in the front passenger seat of the Land Rover as Simon cautiously drove down the overgrown track. Rachel kept glaring at him from the second seat every time they bumped together.

'Sorry,' Simon muttered as he twisted the steering wheel about, trying to avoid the potholes lurking below the shaggy grass and mushroom-thistles. The Land Rover lurched on, with the jet ski thumping around noisily in the back.

They reached the end of the Lane, where it split into several private roads belonging to a string of large stone houses that had been built along the banks of the river Welland. Simon parked them close to a small spinney of raggedy hawthorn and elder.

'Give me a hand getting it out?' Tim asked. He wasn't sure if they would. It had been a bad atmosphere right from the start, and not just originating from them. Tim had spent the first week of exile simply hiding in Alison's spare bedroom. Like her, he was quite content surviving off junk-food takeaways. The rest of the time he just lounged about, watching pre10 movies and rock concerts. A couple of times when the estate's residents' committee called round he'd muted the volume so he could listen to the argument Alison had with them on the doorstep. When she came in to talk with him, he simply replied with the words he knew she wanted to hear. He was fortunate that he could claim his withdrawal was all due to the media people encamped outside the gates to the estate. But that was just an excuse, a convenient thing to blame for the way he felt, which was nothing. Not any more. Even those times when he caught reports about Annabelle and his father on one of the news streams it didn't kindle any great emotion. It was like that moment when he'd watched them having sex, numbness stretching on and on.

Eventually he grew restless. That was around the time when Vanessa called, inviting him to stay with her. He ought to accept, he knew that. Do what everyone kept telling him. Get over her – and start again. Except it wasn't just her – it was them.

After all the worry and trauma he'd endured while the Treatment was being performed, the time he'd spent with his father afterwards, all the talking, welcoming him back into his life. This was what happened. This was what his father thought of him: an almost total indifference. Jeff and Annabelle had both done what they wanted, without caring if it was right or wrong, without worrying about the effect it had on anyone else. Between them they'd managed to put him back on the outside again, not understanding how they could live their lives in such a fashion. He wondered if that's what true adult life was: not having to put up with the kind of shit that restricted him the whole time. When he thought about it, he realized he was coming close to envy. They had what it took to make him happy – the forcefulness, the self-certainty.

So he called Simon, and told him to load up the Land Rover. By then the media had gone, and he didn't have the Europol bodyguards any more. Alison was actually happy when he announced he was going out. That made him feel guilty, but not for long. Guilt was one of the things shackling him to his present existence.

Rachel opened the rear of the Land Rover, and all three of them hauled the jet ski out. They had to carry it fifty metres along a muddy bridleway that led through the spinney to get to the river. The Welland's banks were invisible beneath a mass of reeds and nettles. Tim went ahead of the others, breaking through the cloying tangle of vegetation to reach the river itself. Even with the occasional midsummer storm, the water was still shallow. Tim had to push the jet ski out almost to the middle of the river before it floated freely.

Simon backed off to stand at the edge of the reeds, directing a dubious look at him. 'Are you sure you want to do this?'

Tim gave the pair of them a broad grin, and slung a leg over the saddle. 'Absolutely.'

'Well, where are you going to finish?' Rachel asked.

'I'll ride it all the way to The Wash. I figure it'll take a couple of hours.'

'Then what?'

'Take a look around, and come back.'

'Tim . . .'

'What? I'm not even breaking the law; you're allowed to take boats on the Welland. Stop panicking, I'll be fine.'

She glared at Simon, who simply shrugged. 'Just let us know if you need picking up again.'

'Sure thing.' Tim checked the controls, and pressed the starter button. The engine came alive with a steady subdued growl. 'You two get clear,' he called above the noise. 'You know what farmers are like around here.' He eased the throttle round, and the jet ski started to move slowly. When he glanced over his shoulder, Simon was helping Rachel up the bank.

The river and its carpet of weeds meant there was no way he could open the jet ski up full. He had to keep midway between the banks where the water was deepest; and there were some serious oxbow bends just beyond his starting point, which hampered the machine's performance. It was only when he cleared them and saw the bridge carrying the A1 over the river that he was able to accelerate. The jet ski began to kick out a spray as it picked up speed. Wind pushed into his face. That was when his mood started to lift; not long now and he'd reclaim that same exhilaration which he'd enjoyed the last time he took the jet ski out.

He zoomed under the big concrete arches of the bridge. The pump station was ahead on his left, a windowless stone building whose machinery took water out of the Welland to fill Rutland Water. His first real challenge lay just beyond it. A two-section weir had been built across the river, the right-hand side closed by a curving cylinder of metal to divert the water into the left-hand channel. A simple concrete bridge ran over the top. It was very low. Tim crouched down until he was almost flat along the top of the jet ski, then gunned the throttle hard, picking up speed across the wide pool that fronted the concrete barrier. Just before he reached it he cut the engine back, and then he was committed, racing for the very centre where the water was deepest. The river fell away in front of him underneath the bridge, and he was curving over the top, whooping at the top of his voice for the sheer craziness of the manoeuvre. The sound echoed loudly from the base of the bridge which to start with was barely ten centimetres above his head. He plunged downwards with the engine racing, its intake rising out of the powerful flow of water surging cleanly down the weir's sloping face. Then he was in the flat midsection where currents seethed and bubbled around the hull, shaking him about. Finally the jet ski shot out horizontally over the weir's end wall. It fell in a short arc, dipping down. The machine's nose plunged under the surface amid a cauldron of foam, and started to keel over. Tim flung his weight the other way, desperate to keep level. For a horrible instant it was touch and go, but the jet ski slowly righted itself and began to pick up speed again.

Tim laughed wildly at his success, and gave the weir a quick mocking V sign. Past the pump station, the banks had been planted with willows and GM spruce, creating a delightful water avenue with a path along the south side which led right into Stamford's central park. It was just a shame that, after they'd created such an attractive natural-istic landscape, the Midlands Region Water Agency didn't have the money to maintain it properly. Ordinarily, any tree that fell into the river would be cleared away immedi-ately in case it was washed downstream to damage the support piers of the town's historic stone bridge. But in summer, when the waterflow was reduced, the Authority cut back on its inspection patrols, confident there would be little danger.

Tim hadn't even finished steering the jet ski round the mild kink in the river when the sodden trunk of the wind-felled willow just seemed to materialize right in front of him. He yanked frantically at the handlebars, turning violently right. At the same time he twisted the throttle back, killing the engine. It was the proper manoeuvre. But it was too late. There was an almighty crunch as the little composite hull disintegrated on impact. Some giant force wrenched Tim out of the saddle, sending him cartwheeling through the air. His world was completely inverted, putting the sky underneath his feet. The ground descended on him, fast and hard.

44. TROUBLE . . .

Light from a sharp crescent moon illuminated Seven Mile Beach in a gentle silver shimmer which turned the sand a spectral platinum and the palm fronds a ghostly oyster-grey. Out to sea, the yachts were lit up by strings of coloured lights hanging between their solar panels. Overhead, the constellations formed a loose phosphorescent mist, sketching the zodiac across space. Little wavelets sloshed timidly beneath them, providing the only natural movement in the dusky seascape as Jeff walked back to his chalet from the pavilion. He'd taken his sandals off, carrying them on a crooked finger. The soft dry sand, still warm from the brutal afternoon sun, flowed over his toes as he walked.

Both the girls had scampered on ahead as soon as they'd left the restaurant. He could see them as black silhouettes against the lazy silken sea, holding hands as they paddled through the fizzing fringe of surf. They talked quietly together, a conversation occasionally punctuated by one of Sophie's blithe giggles or an exclamation from Annabelle as she pointed at some fresh part of the superb celestial canopy.

He shook his head softly as he absorbed the scene,

labouring to imprint the memory on his mind. This was without doubt the richest world he could ever have wished to be reborn into; every moment of it should be preserved.

A cascade of shooting stars sliced sparkling silver fire-trails across the eastern part of the sky. The girls laughed delightedly at the spectacle. Jeff caught up with them, receiving a kiss first from Annabelle and then from Sophie. He put his arms around both of them, feeling light-headed from the wine they'd had at dinner and the unique aphrodisiac of the night which was to follow. Annabelle leaned in against him, smiling adoringly, and the three of them angled back across the beach, making for their chalet. The veranda light was on to guide them, a warm topaz glimmer under the dark overhang of rustling palm trees.

Jeff's excitement quickened with every step. They'd started to call their chalet the hut at the edge of the world, thanks to the intense feeling of remoteness it generated. With that came a perfect sense of liberation. Nothing here bothered them. In the bar earlier that evening the big wallscreen had been showing a European news stream. In Hamburg, German Separatists had successfully firebombed a twenty-storey office building housing the Euro Trade and Export Bureau; huge flames were shooting horizontally out of smashed windows, so fierce was the inferno raging inside. Commissioner Cherie Beamon had belatedly announced her candidacy for President, allowing media analysts to gleefully demolish her chances with sharp sound-bite summaries condemning her as too late, and too ineffectual. A convoy of three refugee ships attempting to cross the Mediterranean had been intercepted by Euronavy frigates, and was being escorted back to North Africa. Cameras tracked desperate individuals flinging themselves overboard in an attempt to stop the voyage back to the purgatory from which they'd fled. Marines in fast inflatable boats zoomed through the waves, plucking the flailing figures out of the water.

Jeff had sipped his chilled Manhattan as he watched the images with a complete lack of interest. The girls hadn't even looked up as they chatted away with the other residents who'd descended on the bar for pre-dinner cocktails. Immersed in the sanctuary of the resort there was no way any of them could engage with the events being portrayed. It was as if the images had been relayed from a different, distant planet.

The chalet's lounge lights switched on automatically when they came in, casting a faint, cosy coral glow across the polished hardwood. Jeff's PCglasses were on the lounge's table, emitting the small ruby-red laser sparkle that indicated a priority call. There was no way the interface management program would let it through unless it was genuinely urgent. 'Bugger it,' he hissed. When he held the glasses in front of his face he saw the txt icon was from Alison. That was unusual enough to make him hesitate.

Annabelle's nose rubbed against his cheek. 'Leave it,' she murmured. Sophie was standing at her side, an arm draped over her friend's shoulder.

'Just gimme one second,' he pleaded; three Viagra capsules and furious lust were giving him a huge erection.

Annabelle gave Sophie a shrug. 'Okay, then. Night.' The girls giggled as they walked arm in arm into the deep shadows of the master bedroom. They left the door half-open, allowing a sliver of wan light from the lounge to fall across them.

Jeff hooked the mic down in front of his mouth. 'Click, display txt.' Alison's txt message was curt and to the point, telling him Tim had had an accident on the jet ski. The boy had been taken to Peterborough hospital. 'Click, call Alison.' The PCglasses' standard management display expanded across the lens. On the other side of the crawling neon-glow script the girls gave each other a coquettish kiss.

'Jeff?' Alison said. 'Thank Christ you called.'

'What the hell happened?'

'I don't know. He was riding that damn jet ski on the Welland. I didn't even know he was doing it – he told me he'd gone out to see friends. I didn't know, Jeff.' Her voice sounded anguished.

'Okay, it's all right, just tell me what happened.'

'Nobody knows, really. There was some sort of crash. A couple of fishermen found him on the side of the river and called an ambulance. They took him to Peterborough's casualty department.'

Sophie whispered fervently in Annabelle's ear, her eyes looking back tauntingly at Jeff. Annabelle stared at her friend for a long moment before nodding a reserved agreement to whatever had been suggested. The girls disappeared into the en suite bathroom together.

'How is he?' Jeff asked. 'What sort of injuries are there?'

'There was a lot of bruising and grazing, that kind of thing. He's twisted his ankle badly and dislocated a shoulder.'

Jeff stopped trying to peer into the en suite bathroom. 'Alison! How is he *now*?'

'I think he'll be all right. He was unconscious when they brought him in. But he was awake just before I got here. They've put him under again for the night; they said that was the best thing. He was in mild shock. They thought he might have been concussed, as well.'

Jeff let out a long breath that fright had gathered inside him. 'So he's going to be okay, then?'

'You know doctors, they won't commit themselves to anything. The hospital was more interested in what kind of insurance rating he had.'

'Typical.'

'When can you get here?

Annabelle was first out of the en suite bathroom, dressed in a backless, black silk negligee that made her look little more than an enchanting ghost in the bedroom's deep gloaming. Sophie emerged behind her, completely naked. She gave Jeff a fleeting exultant glance as she followed Annabelle towards the four-poster bed.

'Jeff?' Alison demanded.

Jeff moved slightly to keep the two silhouettes in sight. The half-open door blocked his view. 'Do I need to be there? It sounds like he just took a few knocks, nothing too serious.'

'Has all that heat in Texas fried your brain? You're his father, you should be here. And this is the perfect opportunity for the pair of you to patch things up.'

'Probably, yeah. But a couple of days either way won't make that much difference. And getting an early flight out of here is going to be tough. Look, I'll call you tomorrow and find out how he's getting on, okay? Maybe you can persuade him to accept a call from me.'

'That's not good enough, Jeff, and you know it.'

'I'll call you tomorrow.' With calm, precise movements, he took his PCglasses off and folded them up before setting them back down on the table. He put his palm flat on the bedroom door, pushing it open.

A blissed-out Sophie was making love to Annabelle. Jeff never took his eyes off the pair of them as he unhurriedly removed all his clothes. He moved over to the four-poster, and the girls widened their embrace to welcome him.

45. BACK HOME

The hospital had issued Tim with crutches, his case nurse ordering him to keep his weight off his sprained ankle for at least a week. His cuts and grazes were sealed away to heal behind artificial skin. An electronic monitor bracelet gripped his wrist, its sensors linked to the hospital in real time through the datasphere. 'Only for another twenty-four hours,' the doctor told him. 'We just want to be certain you're on the mend.' Tim nodded meekly; his head still felt woozy from the drugs they'd used to make him sleep.

He limped out to the taxi with Alison, wincing as he eased himself into the back seat. She sat beside him, watching him with attentive concern.

'I'm all right,' he insisted.

She smiled tightly, and nodded.

The physical pain was negligible compared to the hot embarrassment he was feeling. 'Thanks,' he said sheepishly.

'What for?'

'Taking me back. I was a bit of a prat.'

Alison lit a cigarette, ignoring the glare the driver gave her in the mirror. She waved the smoke away from Tim. 'Actually, no – you were a big prat. Don't ever do anything like that again, do you hear? I'm too old to be getting these kind of shocks.'

'Sorry. I didn't mean to.'

'I should bloody well hope not.'

'Did dad call again?'

'Yes.'

'What did he say?'

'Not much. He was upset you didn't want to talk to him.'

'Huh!' Tim turned to stare at the passing landscape through the taxi's window.

'Tim, he does love you. More than I do, even. And all this has at least made me realize just how much you really do mean to me. You're making him suffer badly by not taking a call.'

'Good. Maybe he'll know what it's like.'

'It's not the same, Tim. What he and Annabelle did was pretty awful, I know. But you're his son, and you were injured, rushed to hospital. He's desperate with worry.'

'Not desperate enough to come back.'

'That's not fair, either. It's difficult, not like when he and I were young, and there were dozens of transatlantic flights every day.'

'Maybe.' He sank back deeper into the seat, scowling as his shoulder protested. He simply wasn't used to pain or illness of any kind: whenever bugs got passed round at school he always seemed immune to them. 'Was he really concerned?'

'Very much, yes. Look, you don't have to say much, just stick your tongue out at him and make a farting sound if that's what you want. Show him you're alive and kicking.

338

It would mean an awful lot to me, you know. I hate this whole business.'

Despite himself, a tiny smile played around Tim's mouth. 'How loud a farting sound?'

'That's my boy.'

*

The reporters were thankfully still absent from the entrance to the Manton estate. By some miracle, news that he'd had an accident hadn't yet leaked from the hospital. They drove past the estate's regimented houses where disapproving residents watched the taxi from their patio chairs. When they reached Alison's bungalow they couldn't park in the drive. A van and a pick-up truck were already occupying it. The van belonged to a commercial house-cleaning company, while the pick-up had the name of a landscape gardener printed down the side. Behind them Sue's Merc coupé had drawn up beside the pavement. Tim blinked at it as he lumbered out of the taxi. He shot Alison an astonished look. She merely shrugged gamely.

The back of the pick-up was already full of hedge trimmings, branches pruned from trees and shrubs, and half a dozen black polythene bags bulging with cuttings and weeds. Three men were working hard on the front garden, cutting the privet bushes back into shape and spreading mulch over the freshly weeded borders. Tim hadn't ever known the bushes were topiary. A big mower robot was trundling across the lawn, shaving the ragged grass down to a golf-course neatness and scarifying the abundant moss.

Tim was just about to ask what was going on when his mother came out of the front door. Without a word she put her arms round him and hugged him tight. Tim didn't protest at what the embrace was doing to his poorly shoulder.

'I love you,' she whispered. 'Don't you ever do anything like that again.'

It looked like that was shaping up as the theme of the day. He tried to give her a reassuring smile when she let go, but it faltered when he saw the tears glinting in her eyes. She wiped them away quickly.

'I'm sorry,' he told her earnestly. 'That wasn't me. Really. That was somebody else, somebody stupid. He's gone. Honestly.'

'Thank you.' She kissed his brow, then straightened up. 'Come on, let's get you inside.'

Tim was sure he must have been away for a month. The cleaning crew had magicked a complete transformation of the bungalow's interior. Carpets were still slightly damp, and smelling faintly of chemicals, but revealing colours he'd never seen before. Wooden furniture had been polished to a smooth sheen, while painted surfaces had brightened by several shades. Windows were now fully transparent. His bed was made up with freshly pressed linen which he recognized from the Manor. 'Mrs Mayberry brought it over,' Sue said. The wardrobe was full of his clothes, all neatly laundered. Two plastic boxes were crammed with other essentials from his room: crystals loaded with software and games, PCglasses, his personal datasphere interface module, peripherals, books, badminton racket and shuttle-cocks, along with a whole load of other junk.

'Thanks, Mum.'

*

340

Sue and Alison had obviously established some weird kind of truce. They were civil to each other the whole time. Tim sat in the lounge, studying the newly manicured back garden while Sue made tea in the kitchen. He'd checked that out earlier, too: the freezer was full of new food packets, almost all of which were his favourite meals.

'Who's taking care of all this?' he asked, waving an arm vaguely towards the clean flagstones of the patio.

'Your father is,' Sue said firmly. 'He'll see the invoices on the household account when he gets home. If he's got a problem with that he can complain to me.'

'Oh.' Tim took a drink of his tea.

'He can't just sling you out and expect you to cope like some sort of charity case. Whether he likes it or not, he has responsibilities.'

Tim considered that quietly. The concept of responsibility wasn't one he'd connected with Jeff recently, nor with Annabelle. But it did seem a more adult trait than the heedless exuberance they practised. *Or racing a jet ski down a river.* 'I've still got my allowance.'

'Which he'll have to review. It was fine for when you were living at home, but now you're heading off for university that'll need revising upwards.'

Which was a prospect that Tim savoured.

'Are you going to talk to him?' Alison asked.

'Suppose so.'

Alison told her domestic computer to connect them. Tim sat back in the settee, grateful to have his mother beside him, as the big wall-mounted screen lit up. His father must have been waiting for the call; when the image came up it showed him sitting expectantly in a lounge with wooden floors and walls. The room didn't look very Texan to Tim.

Jeff leaned forward in his cane chair, giving the screen an intent stare. 'Tim. You don't look too bad, son.'

'I'm all right.'

'I haven't slept all night from worry.'

'It's just some cuts and stuff.' He lifted his leg up to show the camera the thick layer of artificial skin wrapping his swollen ankle. 'And this.'

'What did the doctors say?'

'Nothing much – they're monitoring me.'

'Good. That's good.'

Tim wondered if Jeff was feeling as discomfited as he did; he certainly looked very self-conscious. There were a whole load of things he wanted to say, maybe even shout at him again. But not with his mum and Alison in the same room.

'Uh, Annabelle says hello, and she hopes you're all right.'

'Really?' Out of the corner of his eye, Tim could see his mother's expression hardening.

'Tim, I'll be back in a few days,' Jeff hurried on. 'I'd be truly grateful if I could come over and talk to you. I know I can't put right what's happened, but please don't shut me out. You mean the world to me. After what happened on the jet ski I know that more than ever. I was really frightened for you. So if all you want to do is shout at me and tell me how vile I've been, then feel free. If that's the price of seeing you again, I'm more than happy to pay it.'

Tim hung his head, unable to look at the camera lens. Blokes just didn't talk all this emotional stuff, it was embarrassing. 'I'll be around for a while before I go to Oxford. If you want.'

'I do, Tim. I want that very much. And thank you for giving me the chance. I love you, son.'

'Yeah. Well. Okay. I'll maybe see you when you get back, then.'

Jeff's understanding smile lingered a while after the rest of the image vanished from the screen. Tim shook his head gravely, not quite sure who had been forgiving whom.

'You did well,' Sue assured him. 'He knows he's the one who has to grovel.'

'I don't think I really want that. I just . . . I want everything to have not happened.'

'There's a lot of things in my life I feel the same about,' Alison said as she lit another cigarette. 'You've just got to face them down and—'

'Move on,' Tim said. 'Yeah, I think I've got that message now.'

*

He waited until later that evening, after his mother had left and when he was alone in his room, before calling Vanessa.

'My God,' she squealed. 'Are you all right? Rachel called me and told me what happened. What were you thinking of?'

'I wasn't, really. That was the problem. I was . . . I don't know, angry with the world, I suppose.'

'Does it hurt?'

'Only when I laugh.'

Her smile of admiration was wide and sincere. Tim had never noticed how big her smile actually was before, on a face that was so compact and dainty it was almost overwhelming.

'You still staying with your aunt?'

'Till I go to Oxford, yeah.'

He hadn't known how easy she was to chat to, either. They talked away for over half an hour, their conversation butterflying through subjects. It was strange, he didn't try and impress her or be smart or cool. There wasn't a lot of point, she knew him too well for that. Yet she still kept talking and joking with him. In the end he simply said: 'My ankle should be all right again in a few days. Is that invitation to come and stay still open?'

'Course it is.'

46. FIRST CONTACT

Annabelle and Jeff said goodbye to Sophie at Heathrow while they waited for their baggage to be brought to them. Jeff wasn't quite sure how to handle it. Exactly what do you say to someone who has just spent ten days making your greatest sexual fantasy real? She wasn't a one-night stand, a no-regrets and it-was-fun peck on the cheek and a fond wave. And yet, for all the physical intimacy they'd enjoyed, she wasn't a lover in the way Annabelle was. Holiday romance, then? Deep in his heart he knew what they'd been to each other could never last. He'd be a fool to try and carry it on now they were back in the drab familiarity of home. The whole time on Barbuda had been a magnificent one-off.

So he looked directly into her eyes and said a profound 'Thank you,' before giving her a strong kiss.

She seemed to accept that, understanding as he did.

Annabelle hugged her intently, trying hard not to sniffle as they kissed. 'Call me when you get home.'

Sophie promised she would. Then they came out of the customs hall where Lieutenant Krober and the rest of the Europol team were waiting for them. The officers closed in protectively around their two charges. The last he saw of Sophie was her waving manically as the escalator took her down to the airport's Tube station.

Little was said between the two of them during the drive back to the Manor. When they finally got home Lucy Duke was waiting with a whole file of engagements and interviews she'd fixed up.

'I've organized your conference panels and speaking-fixtures schedule for the Euro Socio-Industrial summit conference,' she said enthusiastically. 'But we'll have to start damage limitation before any new public appearances. That's going to mean a big positive charm offensive. The media have been giving you an easy time of it while you were away.' She flicked a half-guilty glance towards Annabelle. 'But we have to remind them what a great human being you are; that the money spent on your Treatment hasn't been wasted. I believe we can use your personal life to our advantage. Having a ... younger partner can be used to emphasize how young you are in real terms. There's been a lot of discussion on how to actually measure your age now. We should push hard for adopting physical appearance as the only acceptable scale. You're as young as you look.'

Jeff gave her his best irritating grin. 'I thought a man was only as young as the woman he feels.'

'This isn't funny,' Lucy Duke retorted. 'You stand to lose a great deal of sympathy over this if it isn't played exactly right.'

'Yeah, yeah. Right now my only priority is trying to convince my son that I'm not a total shit of a human being. If I can do that I'll take a look at that schedule of yours.'

*

Annabelle almost laughed aloud at the way they got ready for bed that evening. Travelling and jet lag had left her weary without actually making her sleepy. So after supper they got undressed and folded their clothes neatly, slipped into dressing gowns and brushed their teeth. She felt as though they'd been married for fifty years. They lay on top of the bed, side by side, while the big wallscreen buzzed away with news-stream images she wasn't watching.

In the resort's chalet Jeff and Sophie would have stripped her naked by now, making her writhe in exquisite frenzy between their shameless bodies.

'I was only here for a few days before,' she said. 'But it feels like home already.'

Jeff squeezed her shoulder. 'It *is* your home.'

'Do you mean that?'

'I do.'

She rolled onto her side, and put her arm around him. 'Thank you. I don't want to go back to my dad's house. Not now. Not after everything.'

'I don't want you to go back to Uppingham, either. I told you that before Tim found us. I still mean it.'

'I think I'm a little scared of that. I've never had a boyfriend who lasted more than a couple of months before. Now here I am with you, in your house. I feel like I should be doing something, but I don't know what. There's nothing more I can give you physically.'

'There's more to us than sex.'

'Is there?' She tightened her grip, seeking reassurance.

'Yes. Not that I'm knocking the sex.'

'Good.'

'We fit together. We both knew that the first time we saw each other. There are no secrets, and we've never played games. We can talk, we make each other laugh, we make each other happy, we excite each other. Trust me, that's so much more than most relationships have.'

'Is that enough? Will that make it last?'

'For a hundred years, no. But I've started relationships with a lot less going for them.'

'What about the rest of it, the other stuff?'

'What other stuff?'

'For a start, I don't have any money.'

'I have more than enough.'

'I need an education. I can't be a kept sex kitten for those ninety-nine years. We'd both wind up hating each other. In any case, that kind of arrangement is so demeaning for the girl.'

He smiled down at her, stroking her hair lazily. 'Details. That's all. We'll sit down tomorrow and work out what you want to do, and how you can make it happen, and what compromises we have to make for each other.'

'You don't mind that?'

'You having a life? God, no. I'd mind if you didn't. Part of what makes you so special is the way you see the whole world as a personal challenge. I know how much you want to get out there and make it sit up and take notice. I want that to happen just as much as you do. And it will.'

She moved round until she was lying on top of him, her head resting against his neck, eyes closed. 'I love you, Jeff,' she whispered. 'I love you so much.'

*

The next morning Jeff woke up with a mild headache. He put it down to the flight back from Miami: even now, after all the health scares and regulations, aircraft still had awful

348

cabin air. And getting up with a headache was always a rotten way to start the morning – it invariably meant the rest of the day would go badly. After he took a couple of synthesized neurofens he drove the Jag over to Manton. A Livewire Security car was parked by the housing estate's gates, with a couple of staff sitting in the front, giving a hard stare to anyone who drew up outside. He gave them a friendly wave, which they ignored, as he showed his identity smart card at the sensor post.

Alison greeted him at the door. Her thick straw hair was awry, coffee stains pimpled the green cardigan she wore, and the last centimetre of her cigarette oozed out a strand of smoke as she put her arm around him for a sisterly kiss.

'Expecting someone important?' he asked cheerfully.

'Don't.' Her throaty voice was even deeper than usual. 'I've just had your wife here, remember? I felt like I should be wearing my Sunday best the whole time.'

'I know she was here,' he said grimly, looking round the spruced-up hall. 'I saw the invoices this morning.'

'That's the very least you should be paying for.'

'I know.'

She shut the door. 'You look very fit and tanned.'

'Thanks. Is Tim up?'

'He's in the lounge. And you be careful what you say.'

'Yes!'

'I can't believe you did that to him.'

'Alison. Please.'

'All right, I'll go and do domestic things in the kitchen like a good girl. There's probably some water drops spilt on the counter. I'd hate to be shot for not wiping them up quickly enough.'

Jeff was in half a mind to ask her to stay with him. Walking into the lounge required the same kind of courage as telling the doctor to get on with a surgical procedure.

Despite Sue's clean-up operation, the pictures on the lounge wall hadn't changed. Jeff smiled at the warrior maidens in their brass bikinis. He even remembered one of them, a model he'd managed to meet, thanks to the cover artist. That must have been fifty years ago. *What must she look like now?*

Tim was lying on one of the patio's sunloungers, wearing just a pair of navy-blue shorts. His body was slightly dappled by tiny sunbeams which had broken through the shade of the neatly trimmed remnants of wisteria. The lighting made the marquetry patches of artificial skin very prominent, a strange grey-white colour against the boy's natural skin. His crutches were propped up beside him.

'Hello, son.'

'Dad.' Tim pushed his PCglasses up onto his forehead.

Jeff sat down on the edge of the sunlounger opposite, almost toppling it over. 'Shit.' He sat back properly. 'Great start.'

'You're very brown. Didn't you wear sunblock in Texas?'

'Yes, I put sunblock on. How are you?' He indicated the medical coverings.

'Not so bad. They itch a bit.'

'You need to learn to steer better.'

'Yeah. I'm sorry about the jet ski.'

'Don't even bother thinking about it. All I care is that you're on the mend. I never used the stupid thing anyway.

In any case, it's me who's in the wrong. We both know that.'

Just when he finally thought he was coming to terms with it all, Tim could feel the tears welling up behind his eyes. It was difficult to make his throat work properly: the muscles seemed to be tightening up. 'She was my girlfriend, dad.'

'Oh, shit. I don't know what to say, son. Sorry is so pathetic.'

'You knew I loved her. You knew that.'

'We were really trying to stop you from finding out about us. We'd have kept it quiet until you'd got over her. You know there's no way I'd have wanted you to be hurt like this. You do know that, don't you?'

The amount of desperation in his father's voice was making Tim squirm inside. But he was resolved not to give in, not to take the easy route. Staying resolute was being adult, and true to himself. 'Dad, there's a big difference between me not knowing and the two of you getting involved. Trying to spare my feelings doesn't cut it, you know.'

'Yeah.' The time Jeff had spent on Barbuda was shrinking to a wistful memory now, along with the accompanying delight. He was worried that Tim would ask him to do something to prove his contrition, which was a selfish thought. He almost wished there really was some act of penance to perform which would close this down. 'Um, look, do you want to go and see a shrink about all this? I'll come with you.'

'Oh thanks, dad,' Tim snorted. 'Now I'm a nutcase on top of everything else.'

'No, you're not. I just wondered if that would help you come to terms with what's happened.'

'Ah, that's what this is about. I've got to be the one who adjusts. It's me who has to accept this with a smile.'

'You think I can go through life knowing my son hates me?'

'Then you shouldn't have done it, should you?'

Jeff was badly tempted. All it would take was one sentence. *It wasn't just me, you've no idea what Annabelle is really like.* But it was the one thing he couldn't say; Tim would reject him completely. He could still remember the feeling of hopelessness permeating his own life before he met Sue, believing, despite memory crystals and the accolades he'd earned, that he'd wasted his life. The day Tim had been born was the happiest he'd ever known. The memory of that joy far outshone any physical satisfaction of getting Annabelle in bed. It was a strange way to learn that as a parent his love was truly unconditional and everlasting. 'I never deserved a son like you,' he said forlornly. 'Just promise me you won't screw up like me.'

'Why did you screw up, dad? You keep saying how much I meant to you. How much you love me. Why? If all that's true, why did you do it?'

'Because I'm stupid. Because I made a mistake. Because my dick was doing all my thinking. I knew all along I shouldn't be doing it. I just couldn't stop.' He took a steadying breath. 'Tim, I don't know how old I am. You just can't know what that's like. I've got this mind that maps out everything sensibly and rationally. While my body is saying to hell with it, do what you want to and do it now because that's what you are, and you'll never get another chance. Except this is my second chance. Jesus, everything is so fucked up.'

'If you put it like that, maybe a shrink's not such a bad idea after all.'

Jeff grinned bleakly. 'I hate those bastards. They're so *smug*.'

'I didn't really want to go to one.'

They looked at each other. Before today, Jeff knew, they would have shared an identical smile. Now Tim was just studying him, looking for any glimpse of the man from before the rejuvenation treatment. The decent man, who really wouldn't have done this to his son.

'Is she . . .' Tim turned away, looking out across the water. 'Is she at the Manor?'

'Annabelle has moved in with me, yes.'

'Thought so. Do you love her?'

'Yes, Tim.'

'Yeah. You'd have to, really. It would have been easy for you to leave her with all this going on.'

'Well, I haven't.' Jeff almost put his hand out to touch Tim reassuringly; the boy suddenly seemed so lonely. But physical contact would probably have been a mistake at this point. One stage at a time. 'I'm not going to leave you, either.'

'Right.'

'I know your mother's been and straightened out the whole bungalow for you, but is there anything else you need?'

'Oh.' Tim glanced round the patio, almost as if he was confused by the question. 'No, don't think so.'

'Well, if you do think of anything, just call me. I'll bring it straight over.'

'Okay. Thanks.'

Jeff stood up. *Don't ask, tell, don't give him a chance to refuse.* 'I'll be back to see you again tomorrow anyway.' He held his breath to see if Tim would object, or just tell him to his face not to come. But there was no response. 'I love you, son.' He certainly didn't expect a reply to that. Not for a long, long time. But if you love someone enough it's hard for them not to love you back. That was the hope he clung to as he left.

47. OPPOSITES

Jeff did go back the next day, and the day after, and the day after that. Sitting with Tim on the patio, wondering how in hell to keep the conversation going was exhausting, emotionally draining work. But trying to regain the boy's trust after such a monstrous violation was never going to be quick and easy. Jeff knew that, but was determined to put in the time. Decades, if necessary.

'Ten out of ten for effort,' Sue said dryly during one of her calls.

'Has he said anything to you?'

'Just that you keep visiting. I'm impressed.'

'This isn't a game,' he told her crossly. 'He's my son.'

'Yes, really *yours*; I know that better than anyone else on this planet. You know, this is so ironic.'

'How?'

'Before your Treatment, you were the one he loved the most. I was just an ogre. Now, Tim and I are a lot closer. While you two . . .'

'Yeah, it's a real hoot.'

'When are you coming down to London?'

'Right after the weekend. Don't worry, we're staying at the conference centre. We don't need the flat.'

'I think I've found a house. I should be out of here in a couple of weeks.'

'That's good. Somewhere nice?'

'Just off Holland Park.'

His expression grew phlegmatic. 'Sounds expensive.'

'When was I ever anything else?'

'Do you want to meet up for lunch while I'm in town? Just the two of us.' He knew there was no way she would ever sit at the same table as Annabelle without spending the whole time sniping.

'Sure.' A troubled frown touched her forehead for an instant. 'Jeff, you will be careful while you're down here, won't you?'

'I wasn't planning on anything too wild. Why?'

'There are a lot of protesters here to picket your summit. My taxi driver had to take a big detour to avoid a march yesterday, and the silly thing doesn't even start until next week.'

'Don't worry. Our hotel is part of the centre itself. We're inside the security zone. Krober was quite insistent about that. It'll be perfectly safe.'

*

On the Saturday morning at breakfast Jeff called Alison's house as usual to check she and Tim were up before he went over. It was Alison who answered. 'Looks like you've got the weekend off,' she told him.

'What do you mean?'

'I mean he was out of here first thing this morning. For someone who's been moping about, all thanks to you, he made a remarkable recovery yesterday afternoon once you'd left.'

'Where's he gone?'

'Nottingham, apparently. Some friend lives in a village just outside.'

'What friend?'

'Someone called Vanessa. You know her?'

'Tim's gone to stay with Vanessa?'

Across the kitchen table, Annabelle shot him a surprised look. Her lips parted in a sunlight smile, and she gave him a thumbs-up.

'Yes,' Alison drawled. 'He said it was just for the weekend.'

'I don't care if it's only for an hour. That's fantastic news, Alison.'

'Happy to oblige. Now you two relax for a couple of days before the summit.'

'Will do.'

Annabelle's smile had become impish. 'Well, when did that start?'

'I've no idea.' Jeff shivered as he rubbed his hands against his upper arms, feeling the goose bumps under his fingers. 'Can we turn the air-conditioning down? It's freezing in here.'

'Sure.' She thumbed the remote. 'I suppose they'll go down to London together.'

He gave her a perplexed glance. It was as though he'd missed a chunk of conversation somewhere. 'Why are they going down to London?'

'To join the anti-technocrat Million Citizen Voices. We all agreed to do it months ago.'

'You're kidding! You mean Tim is going to be outside the summit, protesting with all the other hippies, while I'm inside presenting a paper?'

Annabelle examined her toast. 'Yes.'

'Well, thanks, everyone, for telling me. Jesus wept!'

'I thought you knew.'

'No, I did not bloody know. God damn it, how is this going to help? We're going to be right back on opposite sides again. All that bloody effort I've made . . .'

'No.' She reached out and put a reassuring hand on his arm. 'Kids always have different politics to their parents.'

'Hardly.'

'Mostly. And anyway, Tim's known you've been going to the summit ever since Lucy Duke fixed it up. That was weeks ago. If he was resentful about that, he would have said. I don't think it's an issue, I really don't.'

Jeff could feel another headache starting behind his temples. He rubbed his palm irritably along his forehead. 'Maybe. I don't know. I ought to check with Alison, see if he said anything to her.' He picked up his PCglasses. Annabelle held his wrist.

'No,' she said. 'Let it happen. Don't make an issue out of this.'

He hesitated for a long moment. 'Okay. All right. But if there's any trouble down there, I want him safe back here in Rutland.'

48. LIFE GOES ON

The start of Tim's break found him more relaxed than he'd ever been while staying with Alison. He was looking forward to seeing Vanessa – for several reasons – and the last of his artificial skin had been taken off, leaving only mild tingles where his injuries used to be.

Vanessa was waiting for him when he got off the train at Nottingham's elaborate brick-built station, and drove him out to the village where her family lived. She'd borrowed her mother's Ford ZA-7, a twenty-year-old, two-seater urban car powered by polymer batteries. 'It looks like a plastic rickshaw,' Tim exclaimed delightedly as he walked a circle round the well-maintained antique.

'Shut up or I'll make you walk alongside.'

'Are you sure you could keep up?'

Her home was a lovely old rectory house, with stone walls besieged by climbing roses and evergreen clematis creepers. There was no air-conditioning like Tim was accustomed to: the thickness of the stone, over a metre, helped keep it cool inside throughout the long hot summer months. She showed him his room. 'Right next to mine,' she said, pointing at the next door along the landing. They looked at each other for a moment before smiling. Nothing was said, but Tim's ill-defined hopes suddenly skyrocketed. This was nothing like the usual frantic game of chase they'd all played together for the last three or four years at school. What the two of them had begun now was a lot more casual and cool than that. He liked it. There was no pressure.

A large garden at the back of the rectory was bounded by a three-metre-high stone wall, whose individual blocks were slowly being consumed by moss and lichens. They protected a traditional layout of flower borders and a small lavender bed. Hordes of butterflies danced erratically through the air between the purple flower stems, hounded by Vanessa's two young sisters. Both of them waved and said a cheery hello to Tim.

'Nobody's going to see in through these,' Vanessa said as they walked round the walls.

'You wouldn't believe what the reporters did in Manton,' Tim told her. 'They were tramping through crop fields and everything to try and get a view of Alison's bungalow. Someone said a couple with ultra-zoom lenses were set up at Hambleton. That's kilometres away.'

'I hate the media. They debase everybody.'

A tall GM evergreen beech hedge marked the end of the broad lawn. Vanessa led Tim through the wrought-iron gates in the middle. A broad orchard lay beyond it, also enclosed by the beech hedge. To one side of the gate was a small outdoor swimming pool, with a tiny whitewashed Spanish-style building behind it for changing and showering. Opposite that was a line of wooden stables running out from the end of a big old stone barn.

'Do you ride?' she asked.

'Haven't for ages.'

'We can try going for a hack tomorrow if you like.'

'Yeah, why not?' Tim was looking longingly at the pool. He hadn't realized how much he'd missed swimming.

'There's trunks inside,' she told him sympathetically.

He tried not to make his stare too blatant as they splashed about together. That was probably the most difficult part of the day; in her small chrome-yellow bikini Vanessa was quite something. It was hard not to leave eye tracks all over her.

'Like old times,' she said eventually. After a while they'd stopped swimming and now just lay about on big inflatable chairs, drifting randomly round the pool as the mild late-afternoon breeze pushed them along.

'Yeah,' Tim agreed. He was wearing wraparound sunglasses, so she couldn't see him looking at her now.

'Do you still miss her?'

'I don't really think about her, to be honest.'

'Good.' Vanessa was at the far end of the pool, her head tipped back with her eyes closed as the big chair started to twirl round. 'Boys always think they like bad girls best. You think they're more exciting. And she was bad – the rest of us all knew it.'

'You never said.'

'Would you have listened, or even believed?'

'No.'

'I hope she didn't hurt you too much.'

'It doesn't get much worse, though it wasn't just her.'

'I know. I'd just die if my dad ever hit on one of my friends, never mind the pair of them actually going to bed. Urrgh! That is so much the worst thing in the world.'

Tim grinned, amazed at how easy it was to talk about what had happened – he never could with Alison. One hand trailed lightly in the water, a tiny push for the inflatable chair, moving the two of them closer. 'I'm really glad you asked me here. It feels good to be away from dad. He's so desperate to try and make up. Every day I have to listen to him going on about regrets and how being young again makes things difficult for him, that he hasn't got a perspective back on his life and who he should be. It almost makes me feel guilty for getting pissed off with him for what he did.'

'So how do you feel about that?'

'Now? Not much, I suppose. It was a real bastard when it happened. I hated them so bad I could have killed them. And I still resent the hell out of the pair of them for screwing up my life like this. But . . . everyone was right – which I really hate, too. If Annabelle could do that to me, then she wasn't worth getting worked up over in the first place.'

'Sounds like you've got perfectly healthy reactions, if you ask me.'

'I've just calmed down, I guess. Time always quietens emotions. That doesn't mean I've forgiven him, though.'

'Will you ever?'

'I don't know. It would be kind of weird. Besides, that would be like admitting they were right to do it. I can never do that.'

'Then why are you talking to him?'

Tim shrugged, which just produced a squeaking sound between his skin and the plastic chair. 'I don't know. He's my dad. Can you ever really hate your parents?'

Her chair touched his. She smiled and put a hand out across his backrest, holding them together. 'Any other good reasons for coming here?'

'Maybe a few.' He leaned over. She giggled as the chairs started to dip down in unison. Then they were kissing, and the angle of contact was increasing rapidly. They fell into the pool together, both of them laughing as they surfaced. He put his arms around her for a more insistent kiss. Vanessa clung to him, he felt one leg curling round the small of his back as she climbed up against him. Thankfully they were in the shallow end, so he could keep his feet on the bottom.

'Vanessa!'

They broke apart to see Margret, her youngest sister, shouting at them from the edge of the pool. 'Vanessa, there's a fight in London, a big one. It's on all the news streams.'

'A fight?'

'One of the marches. People are throwing things and everything. It's horrible.'

They made their way back to the house and occupied the big old leather chesterfield sofa in the lounge. The screen on the wall was showing one of the pre-protest marches. Over two thousand people were moving along Whitehall, intent on handing in a petition to Downing Street calling for the summit to be cancelled. But the police weren't letting anyone near the solid metal security gates sealing off the Prime Minister's residence. There was a lot of pushing and shoving, cans and plastic cartons hurled by the demonstrators were raining down on the police. Several fist fights had broken out.

'That was stupid of the police,' Tim said. 'If they'd just let them hand in the petition there wouldn't have been any trouble.'

Vanessa frowned, searching the faces of the crowd. The

news stream was showing images from cameras within the main body of the march. There was a great deal of anger and frustration building up. 'I'm not so sure. They look like they're out for trouble, no matter what.'

'You still want to go down on Monday?'

'Yes. Brussels won't listen to us otherwise; we have to show them just how strongly we feel about them. This is our only option.'

They carried on watching the news all afternoon, seeing the police block off Parliament Square with big metal and concrete barricades. The marchers began to spill back into Trafalgar Square. Shop windows were broken. Police vehicles raced in from side streets.

*

In the evening, Vanessa put some frozen pizzas in the microwave. They sat around on the old chesterfield, eating slices and swigging beer straight from the bottle as the news continued relentlessly. Sometime after ten o'clock an overturned police Land Rover was burning furiously outside the National Gallery. Vanessa had curled up against Tim, with his arms holding her protectively. She stirred, finally repelled by the images on the screen, and turned to kiss him. They made their way upstairs.

In bed together, their lovemaking was more for comfort's sake than for passion. A physical action whose excitement and pleasure managed to obscure the grim outside world with all its pain and tragedy. For a while, at least.

49. . . . ALWAYS COMES . . .

Jeff recalled the blithe comment about personal safety he'd made to Sue as soon as he arrived in London. With all private cars banned from passing through the security cordon around the summit, he had to take the train down from Peterborough to King's Cross. As soon as they stepped off the carriage they were greeted by a raucous barrage of sound. Protesters were thronging the end of the platform, letting off horns and pressure whistles. Fresh columns of Million Citizen Voices participants arriving on the train greeted the welcome with cheers and began chanting obscenities at the line of riot-uniformed police who were struggling to keep the station concourse open for the other passengers. Jeff wondered gloomily if Tim and his new girl had been on the same train.

Lieutenant Krober took one look at the situation and hurried Jeff and Annabelle out of a side exit onto York Way. He called ahead for their car on his secure encrypted link. The big black saloon drew up beside them as they emerged from the gloomy Victorian brick edifice and into the bright sunlight. There were dozens of shops along the other side of the road from the station, groovy franchises which Jeff had never heard of, all boarded up and closed to stave off looting by the protesters. A dozen police vans were parked along the kerb. Apart from the pigeons, nothing moved along the length of the canyon-like street. Lucy Duke glanced down towards the front of the station, where the protesters were contained behind a high wire-mesh fence. 'I didn't realize there would be so many of them,' she muttered nervously.

The summit was being held in a massive ten-year-old convention complex, the Marshall Centre, that had been built on the site of the old London City Airport. It occupied the entire wharf between the Albert and King George Docks; a collection of auditoriums, conference theatres, restaurants, cafés, bars, and hotels enclosed by a single structure, with a fifty-storey octagonal tower soaring up out of the centre. Protesters had swamped the University of East London, whose modern eco-sympathetic buildings ran along the northern side of the Albert Dock in the broad, sweeping curves of concrete that belonged to the kind of future that the 1930s had believed in. The university campus ran parallel to the conference complex, allowing the protesters to gaze across the grubby waters of the ancient dock itself at the sheer façade of black carbon girders and goldmirror glass.

At the west end of the dock, the police had kept the Connaught Bridge open to officially sanctioned traffic. As they drove over, it was clear to Jeff that the police were only just managing to hold the protesters off the road. He wondered if they were all wearing Rob Lacey masks again, but he was too far away to see clearly. Somehow he doubted it: this wasn't nearly as relaxed as the last protest, the one outside the Weston Castle hotel. Stones, bottles, and chunks of wood were being thrown over the police lines to litter the tarmac on the slip roads at the big raised roundabout. The chanting and taunts carried a strong current of menace. There was nothing good-natured about this crowd: they were committed and serious.

The Euro Socio-Industrial summit was intended to provide a forum for discussion between academics, corporate researchers and legislators. As with most government-organized summits the intention was a noble one. With so much new technology emerging so rapidly, especially in automation and cybernetics, the effect and upheaval on people's lives were becoming progressively larger. If, however, the Brussels Parliament and the European Commissioners knew what was going to be released into the market, they could predict the effect it might have on employment levels and social patterns. That way, once trends could be anticipated, then legislation could be drawn up to smooth the introduction. Of course, the reverse was also true: desirable trends could, possibly, be induced by new innovations and developments, of which a high-temperature superconductor was the prime example. Legislative and financial incentives could therefore be formulated to encourage and facilitate such advancement. Every scientific discipline was involved and invited, from microbiological waste-processing to optronic computing, genoprotein therapy to reusable packaging.

To a broad spectrum of Europe's minority ideologists, cause activists, and the dispossessed underclass, it was a monstrous technocrat attempt at social engineering. Who decided what was a desirable trait and trend? Where was the slightest hint of democratic input? Where, every Separatist movement demanded to know, was consideration for national integrity and sovereign culture?

The summit had managed to provoke a phenomenal amount of antagonism over the preceding months. The coalition of protest groups formed to counter it talked of mobilizing a Million Citizen Voices to have their say. By the time the delegates were arriving to register, police put the numbers massing outside the Marshall Centre at close to twenty thousand. Thousands more were assembling at every mainline railway station across London with the intention of marching on the Centre. They'd arrived from right across Europe, most of them earnest but peaceable.

In line with their extraordinarily wide common-security brief, Europol had been monitoring encrypted-data traffic between the coalition's more extreme groups for the last six months. It had issued warnings to the Internal Security Commissioner's Bureau and the English Home Office concerning the strong possibility of riots and civil disturbances being orchestrated by known radicals and anarchists. As with any major event, the protest had snowballed far beyond the original concept of its instigators. When the first groups started to announce their intention to picket the venue, and an equally strident Commission declared it would not be intimidated by such non-inclusive, violence-orientated parties, the media had quickly realized this was going to be one of the biggest civil demonstrations in years, if not of the decade. The malign publicity helped attract even more people.

It was a strange atmosphere crackling through the Marshall Centre when Jeff registered at the main desk and collected his bulging summit-information pack. People were scurrying about with a slightly defiant air, greeting friends and colleagues a little too effusively. The determination to carry on naturally in the face of adversity was reminiscent of a wartime mentality. It wasn't far from the truth. The huge arboretum/reception area faced the Albert Dock. Delegates could look out directly at their adversaries milling round the sealed-off university campus buildings and see the laser-lit banners shining at them, most format-ted with obscene slogans and caricatures. Hundreds of national flags were being waved; Jeff hadn't seen so many Union Jacks clustered together since the last Last Night of the Proms the year the BBC went bankrupt. Nothing was audible – the thick glass shielded those inside from the sound – but despite that the collective voice of hatred directed towards them could still be sensed. The officials from Brussels were wearily familiar with the odium directed towards them and managed to ignore it; while the science complement were altogether more jittery.

Jeff kept a strong hold on Annabelle who had been uncharacteristically quiet since they got off the train. 'Let's go and find our hotel room,' he said once he was clutching his pack.

They had to take several consecutive pedwalks along the central concourse before they reached the foot of the octagonal tower which housed the hotel. Their room was on the thirty-third floor, facing north-west, which gave them a superb view out over the city. Annabelle pressed herself to the window, looking down on the Albert Dock and the protesters on the other side. 'There's so many of them,' she said mournfully.

Jeff came over to stand cautiously behind her; he'd never been particularly comfortable with heights. The long drop down to the muddy water below seemed to be weakening his calf muscles. When he looked over her shoulder he could see the protesters had also taken over

Beckton Park behind the university campus. Its grass had been churned away by the foot traffic of several thousand campers wandering round the random zigzag avenues formed by a small town of tents and makeshift shacks that had erupted out of the dusty earth. Bonfires burned in some of the wider spaces, attracting large congregations. Jeff couldn't imagine why; he was thankful the hotel had air-conditioning – the afternoon summer sun was so powerful.

'I wonder if Tim's down there,' he muttered. He didn't like to think of Tim being jostled about in the middle of that crush. There were just too many people. Things could get very bad very quickly.

'Couldn't we just go home?' Annabelle asked. 'There's going to be a riot, I know there is. It'll be like the Bonn Finance summit again. Lots of people are going to get hurt.'

'We'll be quite safe in the Centre. Those police boys down there know what they're doing – they've had a lot of experience dealing with crowds like this.'

'I thought you didn't approve of the European Parliament and the Commission.'

'Of course I don't. It's a bureaucratic nightmare that either needs total reform or abolishing altogether. The protesters are quite right, it's completely anti-democratic. But that doesn't give them the right to intimidate people into adopting their agenda.'

Annabelle gave the protesters a sad moue. 'This is the only way people have left to object today. The Commission doesn't allow any democratic opposition, not to their core policies. Only pan-European parties can stand for the

Brussels Parliament, and they're never going to allow us a referendum.'

'Are you a Separatist?' he asked in surprise.

'Isn't everyone?'

'I don't know. Are they?'

'Everyone at school is. Europe is so oppressive. We haven't got any of the freedoms your generation had.'

'Oh.' Jeff had always viewed the Separatist movement with very ambivalent feelings. For anyone like him who'd lived in England during the seventies and eighties when the IRA mainland bombing campaign was at its worst, Separatist methods had too many resonances to make him entirely comfortable with their goals. Besides, he considered their views simplistic. National economies and industries had become heavily integrated; any kind of political and financial break-up would trigger continent-wide problems. *But then, what cost freedom?*

Youth, with its high idealism quotient, considered almost any price worth paying. From his unique double viewpoint, looking out over Europe from two distinct generations, he could see both sides' arguments and how valid they were to their supporters. He just wished he knew who was right.

His hands began a gentle massage on her shoulders. 'Don't worry, something has to give way eventually. Europe can't carry on like this.'

'I'm just frightened it will all end in some kind of civil war.'

'That's what federalization was supposed to make impossible.'

A big movement of people on the other side of the

371

water caught his attention. The front rank of protesters at the head of the roundabout's southern slip road were surging forwards, pressuring the police barricades. Smoke bombs were hurled over the heads of the officers. Thick plumes of scarlet smoke gushed out across the tarmac. Then white smoke appeared amid the protesters. The crowd's cohesion broke, turning them back into individuals, all desperately running away from the barricades, pushing and shoving their way back down the slip road.

Tear gas, Jeff realized. And the summit hadn't even started yet.

'I think I'm going to stay here today,' Annabelle said. 'I don't want to try and travel through that.'

'Good.' Jeff put his arms round her to offer some comfort, and steered her away from the window. 'Your visits to the agencies can wait for another day or so. We can stay on in London after the summit so you can see them then.'

Annabelle had received over fifteen thousand avtxt messages in the couple of weeks following her exposure in the tabloid news streams. Some wished her well, some congratulated her and Jeff, a great many asked for money, still more asked her to join their sect/religion/commune/political party/charity. An unpleasant percentage contained some kind of threat (which Krober forwarded to Europol's Domestic Analysis Division for cross-referencing and tracking). Some were funny, and some were from cranks; teenage (and older) boys wanted high-resolution pictures of her, preferably in a bikini or less; proposals of marriage were common. In among the deluge were several genuine offers of work and contracts from modelling agencies, keen to exploit her looks and public profile. The kind of money they were promising was unreal.

Jeff had turned to Sue for advice about which ones to consider seriously. 'Talk about life going in cycles,' she'd said snidely. But once she'd stopped laughing at him she told him which of the agencies had reasonable reputations. They'd arranged for a couple of interviews and a studio session, which Annabelle would carry out while he was busy at the summit.

The pack Jeff had been given at the reception desk contained several dozen invitations to parties sponsored by various companies, universities, and government bureaux. Then there were extra forums supported by news streams. The brochure was over a hundred pages thick. 'And totally pointless,' he grunted as he thumbed through it, glossy pictures of industrial machinery and smiling community groups which made the whole thing resemble some kind of share-flotation prospectus. The loose sheaf of invitations fluttered down across the bed. 'You could spend the entire time eating and drinking at all these parties without ever getting to a session.'

'How many are we going to?' she asked.

'Why, want to start showing off some of those new clothes?'

'Don't start that again. I don't want to let you down at these functions, that's all. I had to have something decent to wear.'

'Nobody's even going to notice me when you start wearing those so-called dresses.'

She struck a pose. 'Jealous?'

His PCglasses pinged and began emitting a red laser

flash; he stuck his tongue out at her as he picked the unit off the bed. The call was from Alison. 'Click, accept,' he told the glasses.

'Are you two all right?' Alison asked hurriedly.

'Sure. We just got to the hotel. Why?'

'Graham just called me. He was at Euston station when it was evacuated.'

'Evacuated?'

'Access a news stream, Jeff. There was a clash between the police and the anti-technocrat alliance. The ticket office is on fire. Graham said he saw the police shooting some kind of tear-gas rounds inside the station. Some of the younger alliance members had to carry him out.'

'What the hell is Graham doing there in the first place? He's in his eighties.'

'Age doesn't stop you from taking part in the democratic process, not if it's important enough.'

'Is he okay?'

'I think so. That modern tear gas is nasty stuff. It's got chemical marker dye mixed in – God knows what that does to your lungs. But he said he was going to get cleaned up, then join the main protest outside the Marshall Centre.'

Jeff clamped a hand over his forehead; he couldn't believe what she was saying. 'Listen, Alison, if you've got any influence over him at all, get him to go home. Please. It's really not pretty down here.'

'I'll tell him, but I don't suppose it'll do much good. You know what he's like.'

'Yeah.'

Jeff gave his PCglasses a long look. 'I'm going to call Tim,' he said.

50. TALKING ABOUT A REVOLUTION

Tim was surprised by the reception at King's Cross. As soon as he and Vanessa got off the train the police marshalled them along the platform, a busy line of people all treading on each other's heels. It was the start of the pushing which he was going to have to endure most of the day.

'Are you with this lot?' a policeman shouted at him as they got to the end of the platform. The man's voice was muffled by his helmet filters; he was jabbing a gauntlet towards the yelling, chanting protesters packed into the concourse.

Vanessa pulled herself tighter against Tim, her face anxious as she took in the huge mass of bodies.

'No,' Tim yelled back. 'We're here to visit some friends.'

'Did you ever pick the wrong day,' the policeman said. 'Get out through there. This lot are all going to Docklands. You don't want any part of that.'

The two closest protesters screamed obscene abuse at him. Tim shoved his way through the throng towards the side exit that the policeman had indicated, keeping a close hold on Vanessa. They finally made it outside to the deserted taxi rank. Tim took a deep breath. Vanessa was shaking.

'I didn't think it was going to be like that,' she said in a small voice. There was no traffic on the Euston Road, the crowds outside King's Cross and St Pancras had spilled over the tarmac as they waited for their march to Docklands to begin. Stewards had long since given up trying to shepherd them along their designated route. Every arriving train seemed to bring hundreds more.

Tim put his PCglasses on and called Colin.

'Where the hell are you?' Colin asked.

'Just got in. Where are you?'

'Halfway to Docklands, I think. Simon and Rachel are here. We're in the middle of a march. Nobody knows what's happening. There aren't any stewards. We're just following along.'

'Can you get out? We should meet up.'

'Yeah, right. Hang on, my GPS says we're in Whitechapel. We'll try and get across to Bethnal Green tube station. Can you get there?'

'I think so.' Tim's PCglasses showed him a London street map. 'We'll walk up to the Angel and catch a Tube. It might take a while.'

He was right. They had to take a long detour to Islington High Street where the Tube station was. Traffic had backed up into a solid gridlock to make way for the various marches. Everywhere they went, tempers were fragile.

The Tube trains were crammed with unhappy passengers. As always, the only air below ground was hot and stale. They had to switch lines twice – Bank station was closed because of security precautions in the City – waiting a long time for each connection on platforms that became dangerously crowded. This part of the network was nothing like the efficient, modern section in the central zone which Tim normally used when he came down to the city.

An hour and a half after arriving at King's Cross they finally met up with their friends outside Bethnal Green station. Tim was relieved to see them. Somehow he found comfort in numbers.

'What now?' Colin asked.

'I guess we walk,' Simon said.

Tim and Vanessa exchanged a look. 'You still want to do this?' Tim asked.

'Sure.' Simon gestured round. The road they were on seemed normal enough, with open shops, pedestrians, and plenty of bus traffic. 'This is history, you know. There's never been a protest this big before. We have to be part of it.'

'I'm not going with any more marchers,' Rachel said firmly. 'Half of them were looking for trouble.'

'No problem,' Simon said. His PCglasses were throwing up a map. 'We'll just head east, then cut down when we're north of Docklands.'

The five of them started off, with a visible lack of enthusiasm, along Roman Road. Tim could hear emergency-vehicle sirens in the distance – the sound was near-constant in London on this day.

'Hey, Tim,' Colin asked. 'Is your dad still taking part?'

'Yeah,' Tim said glumly.

*

By two o'clock they'd reached East Ham, and were heading down towards Beckton. They'd all been accessing the news streams, seeing the protest based around the university campus grow and grow. Any eagerness they might have felt originally had all but vanished.

Participants in the Million Citizen Voices were all around them on the street, everybody striding out to join the main protest. They weren't quite what Tim and his friends were expecting. It was as if they were caught up with a bunch of football supporters straight out of the tabloid news streams, the ones that featured tribes and organized violence. For a start, most of them were carrying bottles or cans from which they were swigging heavily. Ordinary pedestrians were thinning out rapidly, intimidated off the streets. Shops were bringing down their metal roller blinds.

'Where have they all come from?' Vanessa asked. There was a nervous edge to her voice which she was trying to disguise. The shouting voices around them were mostly foreign, with German and Spanish in the majority.

'Same places as the delegates, I guess,' Colin said.

Rachel was staying close to Simon. 'I wonder why they're here,' she muttered disapprovingly.

'Come on,' Tim said generously. 'Everybody's here for the same thing.'

'You reckon?' Simon said.

Over on the other side of the street an Asian woman with a scruffy tartan-print shopping trolley was trying to avoid a group of drunk young men who had their arms around each other, chanting and jiving as they hurried along the pavement. One of the trolley wheels got stuck in a cracked slab, and the woman struggled to free it. The next second she was sprawling on the tarmac, and the men were screaming and jeering in Italian as they jostled on past.

Tim rushed over to help, the others following right behind him. When he reached the woman he was horrified at the way she cowered from him. 'I'm helping you,' he protested. At the back of his mind he realized that nobody else had hurried to lend a hand. The protesters surged past, either ignoring the teenagers or sneering.

Oranges and tins of beans had spilled out of the woman's trolley to roll along the gutter. Rachel and Colin scampered after them, picking them up. Tim took one of her arms, and Simon the other. They gingerly lifted the woman to her feet. 'Thank you, dear,' she said uncertainly. Blood was oozing from a graze on her wrist and she dabbed a handkerchief at it.

'You should go home,' Vanessa said.

'I was trying to,' the woman said. She was close to tears. 'Thirty years I've lived here. Nothing like this has ever happened before. Not even on Cup Final day.'

'It probably won't happen again,' Tim said. 'I don't think I'll be bothering to support them next time round.'

'Support who?'

Rachel was stuffing battered tins back into the woman's trolley. 'The Million Citizen Voices, down at Docklands. It's a big political rally.'

'Oh, I don't pay attention to any of that stuff,' the woman said. 'Politicians, they're all as bad as each other.'

They walked with her for another dozen metres or so, until she headed off down a little side street. She gave them a half-hearted wave as she left, still not sure if they weren't hooligans like all the others. Almost everybody on the street now was a protester. All the shops were shut.

'Come on,' Simon said. 'Let's go with the flow.' It sounded like the last thing he wanted to be doing.

Tim's PCglasses threw up an incoming-call icon. It was Jeff.

'Hi, dad.'

'Tim, where are you?'

'Uh ... just outside Brampton Park. We should be there in twenty minutes or so.'

'Son, please, don't. It's getting nasty outside.'

'So?'

'I don't want you to be part of it.'

'We're not going to accomplish anything by sitting at home doing nothing.'

'Believe me, your side is achieving quite a lot without you.'

Tim came to a halt in the middle of the pavement, and put his hands on his hips. 'That's so typical of you to patronize me like that.'

'I am not patronizing you. I'm concerned about you, actually. Very concerned.'

'Look, I don't want to walk into any kind of trouble. But this is all we've got left to us. You people just won't listen.' Shouts broke out up ahead. Tim peered through the graphic icons to see a fight break out between two men – nothing like the pushing and shoving when people lost their tempers at school. These guys were trying to kill each other. Fists flew, and booted feet kicked. A bottle smashed, glass flying in wild arcs. Then they were wrapped together, rolling over and over along the road as they mauled each other like a pair of dogs. Blood began to soak their clothes. He could see one biting at the other's ear, jerking his head back to try and rip it off. A gang of men formed a circle round them, cheering them on and pouring beer over them.

'Don't include me in this,' Jeff's voice said in his ear, a sound now so remote it could have come from New Zealand.

'You're there, aren't you? You're going to decide our future for us.' The brutal fight was over. One of the men climbed to his feet, swaying badly. Blood was pouring down his face. He aimed a kick at the head of his unconscious rival. It connected with a sickening *crack*. Tim spun away. Vanessa's hand was covering her mouth. She'd turned pale, on the verge of being sick. Tim hurriedly put his arm protectively round her shoulder.

'I'm presenting a physics paper, for Christ's sake. There's only thirty people in the world who really understand the maths involved.'

'Then you don't need to be there, do you? You're just helping Brussels.'

There was such a long pause before Jeff answered that Tim wasn't sure if the connection had failed. The gang of fight spectators was breaking up, leaving the loser's body sprawled on the road, soaked in blood and beer. Eventually his father said: 'I'm not helping Brussels, Tim. I had no idea this summit had become such a symbol, nor that it meant so much to you. You know damn well I don't want to make things worse between us.'

'Then leave.'

'What?'

'I'll do you a deal. I won't go, I won't take another step forward if you leave; today, now.'

'I can't do that.'

'Then look down. I'll be there, waving at you. Click, cancel call.'

'You did the right thing,' Colin said. He kept glancing

at the motionless fight victim. 'We can't show any weakness.'

'Yeah, I know. It's just . . .' Tim gave Vanessa a quick squeeze; she was shivering as she pressed up against him. 'He did sound worried.'

51. FREE SPEECH

Rob Lacey arrived at the Marshall Centre by EuroAir Defence Force helicopter at five o'clock that afternoon. He was due to make the key welcoming speech at the opening ceremony. When he alighted, the numbers of the anti-technocrat alliance laying siege to the Centre had grown to alarming levels. The first eight columns of marchers had wound their way through central London, from main-line and Tube stations, to bolster the mass of protesters just after two o'clock. By four o'clock the police squads on the security cordon enforcement duty were having trouble holding the line at the end of the Connaught Bridge roundabout. The senior district officer gave the order to fall back and form a new line on the middle of the bridge itself. The concrete dual carriageway was narrow enough for his officers to hold indefinitely.

With estimates of the protesters' numbers now nudging the fifty thousand mark, the Metropolitan Police Chief ordered the remaining eleven marches currently converging on Docklands to halt and disperse. Police on escort duty weren't prepared to enforce that kind of order, even if they'd had enough officers to implement it successfully. When they reluctantly tried to stop the marchers, scuffles

broke out, quickly evolving into fights. Most of the marchers were able to break through and rampage along their
route. Shop windows were smashed. Looting distracted
large gangs who then set about beating up camera crews
and local bystanders. Police retreated quickly from a barrage of missiles. Parked vehicles were overturned and set
on fire. The lines of conflict began to snake their way
across the city, converging on Docklands.

News of the attempted restrictions against the marchers
flashed through the protesters already swarming through
the university campus, and they began to get angry. Smoke
bombs were fired from home-made launchers, arching out
over the calm dark water. The entire length of the Albert
Dock was soon smothered in a haze of red smog. Real
fireworks were let off, big rockets angled low to burst
against the Marshall Centre's sturdy glass cliff-face wall.
None actually penetrated, but the vividly colourful explo-
sions writhing against the reinforced windows frightened
the hell out of the delegates inside.

Wavelike surges among the agitated crowds sent people
tumbling over the side of the dock to splash into the water
where they started frantically yelling for help. Inflatable
dinghies were quickly lowered, although the small crews
ignored those thrashing about in distress and eagerly
paddled their way towards the Centre. Fast police launches
raced in from the Thames to intercept them.

That was when Rob Lacey's helicopter emerged from
the haze over the hot city to settle on the Marshall Centre's
rooftop landing pad, just above the layers of red smoke.
The protesters knew exactly who it was carrying. Lacey's
arrival was the final act of provocation. What until then

had been a perilously wild demonstration detonated into a full-blown riot.

London became the principal topic on all the primary European news streams, and a majority of the big internationals. For Jeff and Annabelle, sitting up in their hotel room, it didn't matter which company they called up from the datasphere, every grid on every news stream had a different camera shot of the same event. Helicopters hovered over the Royal Albert Docks, showing choking strands of smoke and tear gas mingling before flowing like mercury around the roads and buildings on either side of the water. Every now and then Jeff would sneak over to the window and get a different perspective on the same scene, almost as if he didn't believe the camera coverage. It was very strange having such a thing unfolding a few hundred metres away, yet remain totally insulated from it. Half the time he imagined he actually did catch sight of Tim down there amid the chaos.

The marches, which had turned to chaos and violence, were covered by camera crews on the tops of buildings, who focused on the people rampaging along the streets below. Balaclava-clad anarchists flung Molotovs into buildings, creating avenues of fire down the city's broader thoroughfares. Billowing columns of black smoke began to rise above the rooftops, marking the firebombers' progress. On-the-ground reporters tried to follow the fire engines, but the police were dangerously overstretched and unable to guarantee the safety of the emergency crews. Fires were left to burn unchecked in several areas as the engines waited impotently in side roads hundreds of metres back from the roaring flames.

Blurred, shaky camera shots from inside the packs of marchers showed canisters of tear gas twirling through the air towards them, bouncing and spinning off the roads and pavements. Equally erratic views from behind police lines showed a deluge of stones and lumps of wood smashing down onto riot shields.

'My God,' Annabelle murmured. 'It's like watching the fall of Ancient Rome.'

'Not quite that bad,' Jeff said. He wished he could sound more convincing.

An aerial shot of Trafalgar Square showed streams of people pouring into it from streets to its west and north before merging together to flood along the Strand. The camera zoomed in to reveal a gang of men armed with scaffolding poles attacking one of the fountains. Hundreds more stood around watching and cheering. Then a group waving Union Jack flags approached the fountain. A violent fight started. The water in the fountain's pool swiftly turned red.

'They're turning on each other,' she said.

'There's a lot of different groups down there. They don't all share the same views.'

Annabelle was flinching as the screen displayed the violence in high-resolution detail. 'It's awful.'

Jeff ordered the screen to go back to a news studio. The anchorwoman was busy receiving updates from police and government sources. Prime Minister Lacey had left the Marshall Centre after barely ten minutes; his presence had been deemed counterproductive by his security team. The police guarding the summit area exclusion zone absolutely refuted the allegation that they were in danger of losing control of the docks to the protesters.

'Ah,' Jeff murmured. They'd both seen the helicopter take off a few minutes earlier and wondered what was happening.

An official estimate of the number of protesters in London was ninety thousand, although the reporters were hinting it was actually closer to quarter of a million. Other, more localized trouble spots were flaring as people realized there were no police left on the beat to enforce law and order. The Metropolitan Police Chief had officially requested reinforcements from Europol. Even with the express Eurostar link from Paris and Brussels direct into King's Cross, it would take the new troops several hours to arrive, and then they would have to deploy. Full order would be restored by the next morning, the Chief promised.

'Ye gods, they must mean the Europol Riot-Suppression Force,' Jeff said in dismay. 'They've never been deployed in England before. People aren't going to like that.' He glanced anxiously towards the window.

An unconfirmed report from Downing Street suggested that when the scale of the protest was assessed last week the Metropolitan Police Chief had asked for Europol reserves to be moved to standby positions in England. He'd been turned down by Brussels on Central Treasury orders.

The marchers whom the police had wanted to halt earlier were now arriving, moving through Canning Town and East Ham to swell the ranks of the existing protesters on the university campus. Lines of fires, blazing like beacons, marked their erratic progress out of central London. Halls of residence and faculty buildings had also been broken into, with large-scale looting now in progress.

Up on the Connaught Bridge, the police line was holding, though it was almost invisible to cameras beneath a pall of smoke and tear gas. Dark military-style vehicles with water cannon were rumoured to be moving along roads in Beckton, Silvertown, and North Woolwich, though the camera crews seemed unable to track them down.

'That does it,' Jeff said. 'I'm calling Tim again. He's got to leave.'

'Do you think he will?'

'I don't know, but I can't just stand back and do nothing.' Despite the physical pandemonium raging round the Marshall Centre, the datasphere interface with Jeff's hotel room was perfect. The call went through immediately. There was a lot of noise and background shouting coming through the link; Jeff automatically raised his voice. 'Tim, are you all right?'

'Yeah, I guess so.'

Jeff frowned – the boy sounded terribly weary. 'Where are you?'

'Up on the big road behind the university. It's not so bad here. Rachel got a dose of the gas the bastards are shooting at us. We had to take her away from the front line. Some people gave us water to wash her eyes out. She's not so bad now. We're taking a breather before we go back.'

The front line! Oh, Jesus. 'Tim, listen to me. The police have called the Europol Riot-Suppression Force in. You have to leave.'

'No.'

'Tim, you've won, okay? They've cancelled all of tonight's events; and tomorrow morning's are "under review". One of the organizers told me the government was considering announcing that the summit is off. They were hoping that would make the protesters pack up and go home, but I think it's too late for that now. You have to get out.'

'Are you leaving?'

'Not for a while. They won't let us out.'

'Then I'm staying.'

'You can't, not because of me. Tim, I don't contribute anything to this. I'm a physicist – I'm just one of the dancing bears, for God's sake.'

'No, you're not, dad; you're a lot more than that. You're the proof that Brussels works. They justify themselves through you.'

Jeff heard himself groan out loud. This went way beyond standard parental concern. He just knew there was going to be major trouble when the RSF arrived. Tim could very well get hurt, badly hurt, because he was young and stupid and full of hope. And he was going to stay to make his point. Something like the RSF wasn't part of the equation that Tim and his friends considered, because they weren't real and bad things didn't happen to good people, and anyway this was all an exciting game. *Eurocrats in their grey suits will listen if we shout loud enough, and the world will become a better place because of it.* Jeff realized he was seriously going to have to do something, make some gesture. Tim really was stubborn enough to stay outside because he was inside. And Jeff just couldn't allow his son to come to any harm. He was surprised by how strong that determination was, like some kind of tectonic force moving him irresistibly. *Just like risking so much for Annabelle.*

'All right, Tim, I'll leave.'

'What?'

'Jeff!' Annabelle hissed. 'You can't.'

He held up a finger, pleading for silence. 'I'll leave. But you have to promise to leave with me.'

'Do you mean that?'

'Yes. Do you?'

'Er, guess so. How are you going to get out?'

'Leave that to me. Can you make your way up to the Connaught roundabout?'

'Yes.'

'I'll see you there.' He ended the call.

'How do you think you're going to get to him?' Annabelle asked. 'Jeff, this is crazy, it's a war zone out there.'

He shivered and glanced down out of the window, rubbing his hands against the cold generated by the room's air-conditioning. The police and protesters on the bridge were taking a break. There were about thirty metres between them; the smoke and tear gas had cleared, with the occasional stone or bottle still being thrown. 'Not all the time. I'll just wait for a pause.'

'What about me?'

The accusation in her voice was crippling. He circled his arms round her. 'I want you to stay here. It's safe.'

'No. I want to be with you.'

'Annabelle, I couldn't live with myself if both you and Tim get hurt.'

'I'm not staying here by myself, it's too scary. What if that mob breaks in?'

'Natalie and the others will stay with you; they can hardly go out onto the streets. You'll be safe.'

'Please, Jeff, don't do this. Don't leave me.'

'I have to go, you know I do. It's not because I want to

prove anything to Tim. It's because I really do care for him, and I cannot allow him to be hurt. And he will be. The RSF will come storming in and crack as many heads as they can. It'll be like Bonn and Paris and Copenhagen all over again, but much bigger. I have to go. I'm sorry, but I have to.'

'Then I'm coming with you.' She gave him a glare. 'What, you think you can lock me in?'

He shook his head, and gave her a gentle kiss. 'No. But look, if it gets really dangerous . . .'

'Then I'm running right back to the bodyguards. I'm not that brave.'

52. COMMITMENT

Lucy Duke was waiting in the lobby when the lift doors opened. Krober must have called ahead to warn her when they were all on their way down.

'What do you think you're doing?' she asked.

'Leaving.' Jeff hopped onto the pedwalk, with Annabelle at his side.

Lucy and the two bodyguards followed him on. 'You're crazy. Nobody's allowed out.'

'It's a free coun— oh, no, it isn't any more, is it?' He smiled ingratiatingly at her.

'Why are you doing this? Where are you going?'

'To collect my son. He's out there with the others, and your lot have just called in the storm troopers.'

For once Lucy's composure cracked at the mention of Tim, and she grimaced in annoyance. 'All right, look, let me see what I can do. There are undercover officers out there, they can take him to safety.'

'Don't you get it? It has to be me. I'm the real reason he's out there.'

'Suppose someone recognizes you?'

'With the way you've handled my profile, I'd be amazed if there's anyone left out there who doesn't.'

'You can't leave. You can't. That's giving in to them, whatever personal reasons you might have. This is what you are, this summit, the superconductor project.'

Jeff turned and gave her a sad little smile. 'But it's not what I want to be.'

*

The camera crews covering the confrontation on the Connaught Bridge found them almost at once. A little knot of disturbance behind the police line, slowly moving forward towards the front rank, where officers were crouched down behind their shields. Lenses zoomed in to see Jeff pushing past the furious officers; Annabelle had her arms round his waist, almost as if she was being towed along behind. In unison, a dozen news anchors yelped: 'That's Jeff Baker.'

Jeff had to force himself along, every centimetre of the way. It was like being trapped inside a perpetual rugby scrum. Every time he shoved another policeman to one side he was screamed at.

'Where the fuck do you think you're going?'

'Piss off, dickhead.'

Awkwardly held batons thumped painfully into his sides. He kept banging his head against the wide helmet collars as officers turned to see what was happening.

'Fucking moron, what are you doing?'

The air was heavy with the stench of burnt rubber, it was mixed with a stronger, more acidic, gas. He practically gagged each time he took a breath. His eyes were already smarting, big tears making everything smeary. Something landed on the helmet of the police officer next to him. The man swore as the plastic bottle shattered, drenching him in warm urine. 'Little shits – I'm gonna kill me one later.'

Jeff used a sleeve to wipe the disgusting fluid that had splashed onto his face. The edge of a riot shield smacked across his shin. He held in the squawk of pain, trying to tough it out for Annabelle's sake. He could feel her arms shaking badly as she clung on to him.

Abruptly there was no more resistance. He'd reached the front row. Police were crouched before him, holding their overlapping shields firm against the tarmac like an ancient army of pikemen. In front of the scuffed and stained plastic was about twenty metres of road, empty apart from the litter of missiles. Then there were the protesters. An ever-moving row of youths with their heads covered in balaclavas or makeshift scarves. They taunted and chanted as they ran a few paces forward in challenge before scuttling back to be absorbed by the mass. There was always someone in the act of flinging an object at the police, sending it in a high arc over the resolute barrier of shields.

It wouldn't be long until another full-on clash, Jeff knew. The distance between the two sides was already closing.

'Now,' he called out to Annabelle. He stepped over the crouched policemen, shoving the shields aside like some kind of jammed door.

'Hey, what the fuck—'

The fingers of a big gauntlet closed around Jeff's shoulder. He snapped his head round and stared directly into the goggles of a large policeman who'd grabbed him, seeing the confusion in the other's eyes. 'Take your hand off me, sonny boy,' he growled. The fingers lost their grip.

Jeff stepped out through the gap in the shields. It was one of those moments where a single rational thought would have sent him racing back behind the police line, desperate for sanctuary. Instead, he just made sure Annabelle got clear all right, then he started to walk, striding along as if this was the most normal thing in the world.

It was only when he'd covered half the distance that he realized what he was actually doing, and muttered: 'Oh shit, oh shit.' The youths ahead were the kind he'd spent most of his adult life trying to avoid. Hard-faced and cruel, brought up on some terrifying lawless sink estate, they'd stab him for a single Euro. Meeting one was every middle-class boy's nightmare.

'Jeff?' Annabelle called.

'Nothing, it's okay.'

Someone up ahead pointed. 'Oi, it's Jeff Baker.' The name rumbled along the crowd like a small roll of thunder.

Jeff directed a modest shrug towards them. Quite a few people were staring at him now. He was closing the gap quickly now, not giving them any time to react, keeping them off balance. The strategy seemed to work: he could see a lot of puzzled frowns above the bright triangles of cloth they wore over their lower faces.

Just before he reached the first of them, he turned round. With a broad grin, he raised a single stiff finger to the massed ranks of the now-silent riot police.

Cheers and whoops of delight rolled out from the protesters; several of them started clapping. Someone flung their arms round Jeff in greeting. More hands slapped him on the back. Annabelle was kissed several times. Dozens of people crowded round, wanting to say hello, to welcome him, to say thank you. 'We knew you were all right, Jeff.' 'You're one of us, mate.' 'This'll show the bastards.'

They made their way slowly through the protesters, an

osmotic process gradually filtering them away from the front line and along the bridge. It was like some campaign rally: he had to shake hands with everyone they passed, to smile and say how much their cause meant to him. He'd never realized the bridge was so long.

Angry shouting broke out behind him. The distinctive dull *thud* of tear gas canisters being fired reverberated through the late-afternoon sky. Jeff and Annabelle both flinched, ducking down. Nobody was paying attention to them any more; the conflict had resumed.

'Come on.' Jeff took her hand and they jogged away from the disturbance. With the other hand he fumbled his PCglasses on, and called Tim.

'You did it,' Tim cried down the link. 'You really did it.'

Jeff dodged aside from a team of ten or so men with intent faces hurrying towards the skirmish; they looked like military types to him. 'Of course I did it. Now, where are you?'

They managed to find each other by shouting locations and directions in a farcical manner. Jeff would have laughed at how bizarre it was, not a hundred metres apart and having to go: 'Where? How far? Which way?' Except it was all too tragic for real humour.

Tim, Vanessa, Colin, Simon and Rachel were all sheltering at the top of the roundabout's slip road. Looking at them, Jeff remembered that last barbecue at the Manor when they'd all fooled around in the pool and on the lawns. Happy youngsters keen for what the future might hold. It was as if a decade had passed. Tim's hair was greasy, plastered down on his skull. Misty green dye had settled on his clothes in long streaks, staining his neck and fingers, a long smear covered his nose where he'd wiped a hand. His eyes were dark and looked very tired. Even his PCglasses were bent.

He managed a forlorn little smile when Jeff and Annabelle emerged through the running throng. Jeff gave him a quick hug. 'You look like shit.'

'Thanks.' Tim was reluctant to let go; he held up his PCglasses. 'We watched it, all of us. Every news stream showed you walking across. I couldn't believe it.'

'You've got balls of steel, Jeff,' Simon said, grinning with admiration. 'I would never have done that.'

Jeff didn't take his eyes off Tim. 'I had to.'

'You really came. I . . . I don't know what to say, dad.' He peered round Jeff's shoulder. 'You too, Annabelle. Thanks.'

'Hi yourself, Tim.' She sounded as if she was about to burst into tears. Jeff put his arm round her, stroking her in concern.

'So, are you going to live up to your side of the deal?' Jeff asked.

'Yeah,' Tim said weakly. 'None of this is what I expected.'

'Life never is, son.'

'Dad?'

'Yeah?'

'Thank you.'

53. AN EVENING IN

Sue buzzed the outside lock as soon as she saw them on the porch's CCTV monitor. She was waiting in the vestibule when the lift arrived. Jeff was first out. She gave him a quick smile, then looked anxiously behind him. Tim was standing there, looking exhausted. His clothes were filthy and messed up, covered with broad smears of green dye. She flung her arms round him and squeezed tight.

'I'm okay,' he said. 'We're all okay now.'

Sue nodded welcome to the other youngsters. The three girls looked wrecked. The boys weren't much better. 'Come on in,' she said.

Vanessa, Rachel and Annabelle claimed the master bedroom with its en suite bathroom. Sue gave them a pile of her casual clothes, and found them some more soap and shampoo, though she doubted if they would be any good against the dye. The boys had taken over the biggest guest bedroom and were soon heard larking about as they got ready to shower. She called to Tim through the door, telling him which wardrobe had his old clothes, and that he was to share them out. As she walked away she heard Colin and Simon joshing him about being told what to do by his mum. A secretive grin lifted her lips; it actually felt good looking after them all, as if she'd become some kind of earth mother.

She found Jeff in the kitchen, swigging down a bottle of premium-strength lager.

'That was quite something you did this afternoon,' she said.

He handed her a second bottle. She expertly snapped the top off against the edge of one of the granite worktops, then smiled, wishing Tim had seen her do that.

'Second scare he's given me in a month,' Jeff said.

'First one you've given me in quite a while. I watched you on the news streams.'

'Has the government put its spin on that yet?'

'I think they're a little busy blaming Brussels for the riot right now.'

'Never mind, I'm sure they'll get round to it.'

'Everybody saw you, there's not much they can change in people's minds. And when they find out you did that because you were concerned about your son . . . You really could run for President, you know.'

'What a ghastly thought.'

'And Annabelle went with you. I'm going to have to revise my opinion about that one.'

Jeff took a big swig. 'Go easy on her tonight, she's had a hard time.'

'I wasn't planning on being a bitch, Jeff.'

'I'm glad you were here.'

Sue raised her bottle in salute. 'Me, too.'

'Right then. Let's get supper sorted – I'm starving. You have got proper food here, haven't you, not just that delicatessen crap?'

Sue stuck her tongue out at him, and opened the

freezer. Jeff chuckled appreciatively as they pulled the packets out.

Once the youngsters were all washed and dressed in clean dry clothes, they sat round the kitchen table and wolfed down sausages and eggs and potato fritters and spaghetti and garlic bread. 'Nursery food,' Tim called it contentedly. 'Thanks, mum.'

Listening to all the banter and mild teasing going on around the table was almost like old times to Jeff. With one exception. Annabelle never left his side, and he could return the affection she showed him in front of Tim and Sue without any hesitation.

The big screen in the lounge was switched to a news stream, and everyone settled in chairs or sprawled over cushions to watch. Jeff sat on the settee with Annabelle curled up beside him. She was nice and warm against his side. He was feeling the cold again, though the others all claimed the lounge was hot.

By eight-thirty the first squads of the Europol RSF had arrived from Paris, though none had yet been seen emerging from the trains. Cameras showed protesters retreating from the streets around King's Cross. Rob Lacey appeared in Ten Downing Street's Rose Garden for a live press statement, claiming that the nihilists wrecking the streets of our great capital would be brought to justice, no matter how long it took.

'They always say that,' Simon exclaimed. 'Any sort of big crime gets committed, and politicians say exactly the same line every time. They never do it, though.'

By nine o'clock the Metropolitan Police had managed to escort fire engines to most of the blazes that were burning outside the Docklands area. There was coverage of the infernos raging through dozens of buildings, sending flames twisting high into the night sky. News streams competed against each other with dramatic shots of fire crews sending huge jets of foaming water through broken windows and over crumbled masonry, trying to stop the conflagration's spread. Some of the more hysterical reporters were talking about the Second Fire of London, a concept the authorities were eager to quash. Cameras lingered on the sombre black ruins of buildings already burned out.

There was no official curfew, although Scotland Yard kept stressing that law-abiding citizens should not go outside.

The Brussels Parliament went into emergency session to debate the civil situation. Furious English MEPs rose to condemn foreign agitators for wrecking the capital, claiming it amounted to an invasion force. Continental MEPs protested at the use of such provocative, near-racist terms. Shouts and counter-shouts grew louder; objects were thrown across the chamber. The Speaker called a recess so that tempers could calm.

At half past ten, over three and a half thousand RSF officers had arrived at King's Cross, along with their vehicles and equipment. They began to deploy through the city under the overall command of the Metropolitan Police Chief in tandem with Europol's senior Commander. Downing Street and the Home Office made the joint nature of the command structure quite clear from the start, promising their full support for whatever actions were necessary to bring the troublemakers to justice.

The RSF began to establish an isolation cordon around the outside of the University of East London campus. Big water-cannon vehicles led the way down streets, high-pressure hoses washing away anyone who stood in front of them. Protesters were slammed to the ground as the water hit them, then pummelled over and over by the jets to lie semi-conscious on the side of the road where RSF officers picked them up and flung them into the prisoner-containment carriers that were following behind the water cannons.

Just after midnight, Rachel and Vanessa announced they'd had enough, and went off to bed; tired by their strange, fatiguing day and depressed by the relentless bad news on the screen. Half an hour later Sue said she'd also seen enough. Jeff agreed, and said goodnight to the boys who were camping out in the lounge.

He and Annabelle used the smaller of the guest bedrooms. It only had a narrow bed, but they made love with the same kind of desperation as that first time in the car. Both of them were needy, demanding reassurance and physical comfort from the other. For once he didn't bother with the Viagra; his body was as eager as hers.

They clung together afterwards, trembling in relief, thankful that they had each other. Both accepting in their own way that the day had brought them closer. The small screen on the wall played on silently, casting a wan grey-blue light across their bodies until Jeff finally drew the duvet over them.

In the early hours they saw eight thousand RSF troops, Europe's total contingent, had now surrounded the University of East London and Beckton Park. The entire campus was ablaze, its elegant circular halls of residence burning like giant brick braziers, aspirational faculty

402

buildings haloed by flame as curving roofs buckled and subsided.

The RSF advanced, taking a more Continental approach to law enforcement than the exhausted Metropolitan Police whom they had replaced. Plastic baton rounds were fired directly at protesters, with ranges down to a near-lethal two metres. Any protester unlucky enough to fall or stumble as the RSF closed in would be surrounded by black-clad officers wielding whip-like truncheons that pounded away until the body stopped moving. English civil-rights activists were demanding the arrest of the RSF commanders who authorized such illegal brutality. Snatch squads dragged bleeding, screaming protesters into prisoner-containment carriers. Vivid flames from burning buildings and wrecked cars competed with blue and red emergency-vehicle strobes to illuminate the shocking scenes in macabre flares of light.

Out of the bedlam in some nameless street in Beckton, the first gunshots of the conflict were heard. A chorus of screams followed. People surged in terror and panic, not knowing which way to flee. The air was thick with missiles and the stench of burning plastic. Two RSF officers lay prone on the pavement. Twenty cameras zoomed in for a close-up, showing the pools of blood slowly expanding across the tarmac. Enraged RSF troops charged into the nearest group of protesters. Lenses backed by light-amplification circuitry followed their long steel-webbed truncheons as they rose and fell, striking at unprotected flesh with the fury of enraged hornets.

In another part of town, more shots were fired. Protesters and RSF lines clashed again and again.

'They have to give us a referendum now,' Annabelle said. 'Look what's happening because they don't care about us.'

Jeff turned to look at her face; the faint light from the screen revealed only placid features. 'That's not Brussels bureaucrats out there burning the streets.'

'They're the cause, ultimately. I hate them. Why can't they leave us alone? Why can't we make our own decisions? None of those rioters would be allowed in the country if we were in charge of ourselves again.'

'Funny thing. They all hate Brussels as much as we do.'

'Then they should go and burn Brussels down, not London.'

'I expect they will. Eventually,' Jeff said.

*

Dawn revealed numerous bodies lying in the street: RSF officers given traitors' pensions, civilians battered to death. Their ignominy was the same in the wan light. Over a hundred burnt-out buildings sent up thin streamers of rancid smoke as firemen waded through their sodden interiors to begin safe securement procedures. Special courts were convened to process and charge everyone the RSF had arrested. Politicians flocked into early-morning news studios, all of them managing to condemn the way Europol had behaved, pointing out how little difference there was between them and the foreign marauders. First cost estimates of the damage to the city were in the range of ten billion Euros. Both the Mayor and the Prime Minister demanded that the Central Treasury paid for it all – after all, most of the damage had been caused by Continental citizens. President Jean Brèque promised to consider any such request sympathetically. Such vagueness was eagerly seized upon by his opponents as further evidence of his administration's laxity.

Over forty thousand protesters were still camped out amid the ruins of the university campus. They were surrounded by seven thousand RSF troops, who waited patiently for them to surrender, their orders simply to starve them out of the smouldering desolation which they had created. It took another three days until the last diehard activists were hauled away in prisoner-containment carriers. The political blame throwing went on for a great deal longer.

54. ALIEN HOME GROUND

When Tim looked round the front of the Manor he was almost surprised that nothing had changed. So many other aspects of his life had altered it seemed unreasonable that the façade and gardens remained the same. It was another standard high-season afternoon, a roasting sun turning the air so thick that it soaked up any sounds.

He pushed the e-trike's parking legs down onto the gravel and took his helmet off. The Jag was sitting outside the garage. One of the younger boys from the village had just washed it, and was now rubbing down the gleaming bodywork with a chamois-leather cloth. Tim gave him a hurried wave before pulling his sunglasses on.

The front doors were open. He went into the hall where the air-conditioning was losing its fight against the encroaching heat. Natalie Cherbun was in the little side room watching the monitor screens. She gave him a small, authentic smile. 'Hello, Tim.'

'Hi. You're all okay, then?'

'I wasn't out on the streets, no. I had the easy duty in the hotel. Especially after your father left.'

'Ah. Right. Good.' He found it tough to look her in the eye, especially as he was so conscious of the dye stains still marking his neck. It was a week since the last of the protesters had been picked up. A week in which every English news stream and current-affairs show had been filled with vitriolic demands that the disgrace which was Europol should be disbanded at the very least, and President Brèque thrown into jail along with the force's senior officers. While the foreign animals who'd run amok should be tried in England by English judges; there was even talk of bringing back the jury system. Agreeing with such claims was easy when they were on screen, but when facing a Europol officer in the flesh it was a mite more difficult. 'I'll, er, go through, then.'

'Good luck.'

Annabelle was sunbathing out on the terrace. Tim approached her slowly, still a little unsure how to behave towards her. She was lying on one of the sunloungers under a floppy ultraviolet-filter parasol. Topless, of course, offering her body up to the muted sun. He'd never seen her such a dark shade before. Naturally, Annabelle's skin didn't merely go brown: her tan gave her a wondrously healthy golden hue.

Someone was sitting on the sunlounger beside her. Another girl, the two of them chattering away and laughing.

Tim almost backed away. Then Annabelle saw him and let out a happy cry. 'Tim!' She bounded up off the sunlounger, her smile wide and welcoming. Just the way he always remembered. Her arms had come up to reach for him before she caught herself, lowering them in an awkward jerk. 'How are you?'

'I'm okay. Suppose.'

Her expression settled into something close to serious. 'It's nice to see you again.'

'Yeah, same.'

'I'm glad you're here and cool about it,' she said. 'Last week changed a lot of things for all of us, didn't it?'

'Yeah.'

'So? Friends again?'

'Sure.' Tim gave her a lame smile. It was all he ever could do with Annabelle, just get washed along in her wake trying desperately to keep his head above water. Her hair was different now, he noticed; she'd had it straightened, although it looked very naturalistic. She'd lost a few kilos as well, which made her body look even fitter than before – if such a thing were possible. The overall effect was to keep her appearance girlish, but with a touch of sophistication she'd previously lacked.

He couldn't recall exactly who'd said it was better to have loved and lost than never to have loved at all, but they'd clearly never stood in front of a near-naked Annabelle remembering what it had been like . . .

Annabelle darted forward and kissed him before he had time to react, or dodge. There was just the hint of a tease to her smile. 'I want you to meet someone,' she said, beckoning the other girl. 'This is Sandrine.'

'Hi, Tim,' Sandrine said. 'Pleased to meet you. I've heard all about you.' She giggled wildly.

At first Tim thought she was drunk: her voice was childlike, and the way she looked at him was so spaced out she could have been a groupie to his rock star. She was three or four years older than him and Annabelle, and quite beautiful. Raven-black hair licked round a long oval face with perfect expressive green eyes. She was slimmer than Annabelle, but just as tall, although never skinny. He could see that. A tight black leather T-shirt thinner than cotton was moulded to her torso; there was a broad strip of abdomen visible between that and a micro skirt, with a couple of gold waist-chains looped round her waist chinking softly at every movement. Clusters of bracelets skittered about on her bare arms. Tim held back a frown: who wore leather in weather like this? But it belonged to what she was, some über-trendy city girl with an even worse attitude than Rachel's.

Sandrine planted a big kiss on Tim's cheek. He squirmed, not wanting to shove her away, but really . . .

Her hands clapped together. 'Oh, he's so cute.'

Panic froze Tim's smile in place. 'Thanks. You, er, look sensational.'

'I do? Wheeee!' Her whistle could have split stone.

Annabelle was grinning at his discomfort. 'Sandrine's from the agency. She's my chaperone when I go on assignments.'

'Right,' Tim said. It opened up a whole file of questions which he simply refused to ask.

'Fibber! I'm more than that to her, Tim. I do make-up, and I'm developing my talent as a stylist. I want to get behind the camera as well. I'm going to show the whole industry I'm more than just eye candy.'

'That's nice.'

'Oh, you're so desperately eatable. What's your star sign?'

'I've no idea.'

'Let me guess, I'm good at this.' Her hand slapped against her forehead as she squeezed her eyes shut. 'I'm getting it. You have a strong aura.'

Tim gave Annabelle an accusing look. She winked back.

'You're a Virgo,' Sandrine announced. 'You have to be.'

'Dead on. You got me.'

'I knew it! Yes! I'm an Aries, and I was born in the afternoon.'

'Excellent.'

'Isn't it just. So, are you doing anything tonight? We could double date with Jeff and Annabelle if you wanted. The club scene in Peterborough isn't bad. They showed me round last night.'

'I don't think we want to do that,' Annabelle told her kindly.

'Ow.' Sandrine frowned. 'You're so like Jeff, too. It would be such fun.'

'Another time,' Tim said. He hated people like her, never respecting anyone else, always an embarrassment in public – and in private.

'Back in a sec,' Annabelle told Sandrine. She inclined her head, and Tim walked with her out onto the lawn.

'She's from an agency,' Tim said thoughtfully. 'I heard you were doing some modelling.'

'Yes. I couldn't really turn that kind of money down. I've already done one shoot for Harice. Docini have booked me for next week. And I've got a catwalk gig coming up, too. It's fantastic.'

'Congratulations.'

'I'm not going to live off him, Tim. I'm not like that.'

'What's going to happen when you go to university?' He knew he was being unnecessarily cruel now, and he simply didn't care. Or maybe it was just a test, to see if they could talk. 'Are you going to commute back here at the weekends?'

Annabelle looked out across the garden. 'I'm not going

to university. Not away to one, anyway. I've already signed up for an Open-line University course. That way I can hold on to everything I want to in my life. I can work, I can study, and I can be with Jeff.'

'I don't believe this.'

'What? What don't you believe?'

'You used to dream about making it out of here, out of Rutland. I admired you so much for that, for having that goal. The way you chased it was . . . awesome. Now you're giving all that up.'

'I'm giving nothing up. I've got what I want, Tim. I'm sorry you can't see that.'

It was his mother's tone – that was how she used to talk to him. The little boy who doesn't understand, no matter how slowly and patiently it's explained.

Annabelle's voice actually shocked him. The condescension behind it; she'd gained a touch of something. Confidence, he supposed, always the twin of contentment. She would now be able to hold her own among the Rutland non-working mothers' club with no trouble at all. He could never have stayed with a girl like this, he knew. Maybe you had to have dad's personality and experience to cope with her.

'If that's true, then I'm happy for you,' he said simply.

She studied him closely, as if suspecting some falsehood. 'Tim, I know this is hard for you most of all, but I really do love Jeff. All I want now is for him to be happy.'

'He will be. He's lucky to have you.'

'Sandrine was right.' She grinned impishly. 'You are so adorable.'

*

Tim found Jeff in the study, bent over the drawer containing the desktop synthesizer. Just for an instant, as he walked in, he saw a flash of guilt on his father's face. There was a giddy little moment when he recalled the last time he'd seen that expression on the same face.

Father and son stared mutely at each other.

The synthesizer pinged. Jeff picked some capsules out of the dispenser tray.

'What are you cooking?' Tim asked – anything to lighten the atmosphere.

Jeff ran a hand over his forehead, dabbing at the perspiration. 'Just some neurofen. I've got a headache, and it feels like a cold coming on. I think it's this damn air-conditioning. It's freezing in here.'

Tim, who'd never had a cold in his life, didn't feel much sympathy. He closed the door. It was uncomfortably hot in the study.

Jeff sat behind the desk. 'It's good to see you. Looks like the dye's almost gone.'

'Oh, that.' Tim's hand went automatically to his neck. 'Yeah. It comes out eventually.'

'How's Vanessa?'

'Okay. I'll probably go up and see her again next week.'

'Good. She's a nice girl.'

'How's Lucy Duke?'

Jeff let out an amused snort. 'Furious. But Downing Street has enough trouble right now trying to spin Lacey out of any blame for the riot. And even she had to concede that I went up in public estimation.'

'She must really hate that.'

'Oh, she does.'

Tim let out a long sigh, and checked the window.

Annabelle and Sandrine were back together on the terrace. The agency chaperone was blithely chattering away, waving her arms around as if she was at a rave. 'I remembered something on the way over here.'

'What did you remember?'

'Sophie. You took Sophie to bed after the summer ball, after Annabelle.'

'Ah.'

'Annabelle's so happy with you.' He was still looking out through the window. Annabelle was walking down the steps at the shallow end of the swimming pool. Sandrine had gone to lie on the side of the pool, propping her chin up on her hands to watch intently as Annabelle immersed herself. She shouted something as her legs waggled about, and Annabelle laughed. 'It would kill her to find out.'

'Tim,' Jeff said gently. 'She knows what I'm like.'

'Are you sleeping with Sandrine as well?'

'As it happens, not that it's anything to do with you, but no, I'm not. I can't stand the little brat, actually.'

'Poor Sandrine.'

'I remember telling you, Tim: never confuse love with sex.'

'I don't get it, dad, I don't understand what you are. She loves you. Doesn't that mean anything to you?'

'It means the world to me. The only person more important to me than Annabelle is you.'

'I don't get her, either, not any more. She just told me she's staying here, that she's taking Open-line University courses.'

'That's right.'

'She was going to go away to university. She used to have big plans for her life.'

'She still does.'

'She's not Annabelle, not the girl I . . . used to know.' He nearly said: loved.

'I'm sorry, Tim,' Jeff said. 'But she is exactly the same. And I haven't changed so much, either. Sure, this body means I can have a decent sex life again, but that's about the only difference. The rest of me's the same – the way I think, the way I behave. It's your perception of me that's shifted. You know me a lot better now than you ever did before.'

'Really? I sometimes wish I didn't.'

'Maybe I wish I wasn't what I am. But I did what I did, I fucked up, and I'm not going to try and gloss it over or justify it. All I can tell you is that if you ever need me, then I'll be here. That's the bottom line, Tim.'

'I guess I know that now,' Tim said sheepishly.

'I'd do that again. I'd do it every time for you.'

Tim cleared his throat, looked at his shoes. It wasn't anything he could answer.

'Do you want to move back here?' Jeff asked.

Tim flinched, his gaze went back to the window again. Sandrine was on her back now: she'd lifted her legs so they were pointing straight up into the sky, with her hands holding her knees. Presumably it was some sort of stretching exercise; Tim could only think of a tortoise on its back. 'Colin's parents have a bungalow in Norfolk; there's a few of us going down for a week or so. And I promised mum I'd visit the new house. Then I need to get ready for Oxford. But I was thinking, next holiday, when term's over, would it be okay to stay here for a while then?'

Jeff's smile was joyful. 'You'll be here for Christmas?'

'Guess so.' Tim sort of smiled back at Jeff; it was hard not to. Maybe happiness was infectious.

'I'd like that a lot,' Jeff said.

*

Lucy Duke arrived at the Manor forty minutes after Tim had left. She walked through the hall, nodding briskly to the Europol officer on duty. In the lounge, she frowned disapprovingly at the sight of the two naked girls sunning themselves on the terrace. Then she went into the study. Her flexscreen fell from shocked fingers, bouncing on the tough carpet. 'Shit! Jeff? Jeff, what is it?'

Jeff was on the floor behind the desk, curled up in a foetal position. His skin was pale and glistening with sweat. When she kneeled beside him she could feel his whole body trembling softly. He was conscious, dull eyes stared at her.

'Jesus Christ!' she gasped. His flesh was freezing under her fingers. 'Help! Someone help me. Get in here. Now!'

55. . . . IN THREES

It was one of those hospital rooms that could pass itself off as decent three-star hotel accommodation. The furnishings and décor were new, the colours carefully neutral; double-glazed windows provided a pleasing view out over the broad expanse of parkland which circled the Brussels University Medical Centre. Medical modules were all built into a tall wooden bedside cabinet, with a row of small high-resolution screens on top that monitored his body. There were sensor pads stuck on most parts of him, sprouting fibre-optic cables that snaked out from under the thin bedclothes to merge with the electronics. A single intravenous drip stood guard at the head of the bed.

Physically, Jeff was perfectly comfortable. He suspected part of that sensation was due to the sedatives. But his body temperature was constant and normal now. And there were no more headaches and chest pains and muscle tremors. It had taken the medical team the best part of a day to stabilize him after the EuroAir Defence Force emergency flight delivered him to Brussels. The symptoms he displayed were relatively easy to treat and contain with conventional drugs.

The cause of the problem ... that was something else altogether.

It had taken two days of tests before the delegation shuffled into his room, led by Dr Sperber. In his stuttering broken English the good Doctor had slowly explained what they'd found – and the implication. He'd looked fearfully at his patient who was also his creation as the news had sunk in.

All Jeff had done was smile faintly and thank them. After all, what else was there?

At his own request, they'd left him alone after that. Annabelle had stayed, of course; beautiful, terribly young and fragile Annabelle. She'd lain on the bed beside him, hardly moving for hours, just looking at him in that adoring way she had.

Love, he reflected, was such a strange emotion, so completely beyond any form of control. Half curse, half blessing; and always so desperately unfair in the pain it inflicted.

'I'm so sorry,' he whispered to her. 'I wish I could undo ever meeting you. You deserve so much more. I can't stand the idea of this hurting you. That's what I truly hate about this, the only regret.'

She squeezed his hand in hers, bringing the fingers up to touch her cheek, smiling dreamily at the feather-light contact, the reassurance it brought. 'I don't regret it. And I would never change a single moment.'

'I don't know what I did to deserve you. Nothing in this life, that's for sure.'

'A million things in this life.'

The next time Dr Sperber came in he was by himself. 'How do you feel?'

'It hurts when I laugh.'

Sperber frowned in concern. 'Where?'

'English sense of humour, Doc. Ever watched *Fawlty Towers*?'

'No. I'm afraid not.'

'I'm actually quite comfortable, thanks. I think the drugs are working.'

'That is good. We are putting together a treatment schedule for you.'

'Speaking of drugs, I've been taking a few non-prescription ones recently.'

'I know.' Dr Sperber's expression never changed. 'Our analysis uncovered traces of a desktop-synthesized Viagra in your blood. It was easy to find, the traces were quite large.'

'I was wondering . . . did that trigger this?'

'No. That is not possible.'

'Ah. Pity, really.'

That actually managed to shock the Doctor. 'A pity?'

'Yeah. Now that would have been true rock and roll.'

'I understand.'

'I really am feeling a lot better. I'd like to go home now, please.'

'Of course.'

56. SECONDARY ECONOMY

Grenada's one commercial airport had once caused a war simply by being built. The Pentagon deemed that its main use was not for tourist jets but to act as a base for Cuban fighter planes. As conflicts went, the world's most powerful superpower squaring up to a small Caribbean island was somewhat one-sided. The badass Commie puppet government was ousted, and the land made safe for democracy again, all inside of a week.

Coming in to land at that same airport over fifty years later, Jeff found it hard to believe that the whole event had ever taken place. That a single strip of crumbling concrete could be the cause of a military invasion now seemed ludicrous. In fact, he couldn't really be sure if the whole thing wasn't some perverse trick of his memory. Time's distance made such a thing so unlikely, more like a pre10 film rather than real life. He was sure Clint Eastwood had starred in it.

'Are you all right?' Annabelle asked. She was in the seat next to him in the first-class section of the late-model Boeing SC. They'd flown from Heathrow to Miami again, and caught the only scheduled flight out to Grenada. American International ran two a week, catering for wealthy visitors. Despite the collapse of Caribbean tourism, each of those flights was always full.

'Sure,' he said, looking out of the little window as they finished their approach circuit. 'I'm just not sure my memory is right about this place.'

'Do you want to check? The plane has an interface.'

He grinned at her. 'And I certainly don't care that much.'

After they landed they found their transfer car at the front of the ancient terminal building. A modern maroon-coloured Mercedes with a beefed-up suspension to cope with the island's roads. There were several similar vehicles lined up outside with the dilapidated local taxis. It was a twenty-minute drive in air-conditioned comfort to the clinic, which had taken over an old resort hotel. The main accommodation block and the beach bungalows had been refurbished for clients, while its medical work was conducted in a purpose-built facility apparently modelled on a Californian condo.

Jeff and Annabelle were shown to their room in the main block. Their balcony was directly above the pool, overlooking the small curving bay. When she opened the big sliding glass doors, a humid breeze ruffled her hair. 'This beach isn't as good as Barbuda,' she said.

Jeff came over to stand behind her, his arms going round her waist. 'Nothing could be. That whole time was perfection. And it was all thanks to you.' He felt her trembling again, and suspected tears.

'I'm sorry,' she said in a muffled voice. 'I want to be strong, especially now.'

'You are. You're the only thing keeping me going.'

'Don't say that.' She leant back into his embrace. 'What now?'

'Now we have a light snack for supper, then go to bed. I'm just about asleep now. I never get any rest on planes.'

'And in the morning?'

'In the morning, we go and see my old friend Dr Friland.'

*

It was almost twenty years since Jeff had seen Justin Friland. The last time he'd been at the clinic, Friland was the second deputy geneticist. Now he'd risen to the head of the genetics department, which gave him a big office on the top floor of the clinic's medical building. There were two long mirrorglass windows behind his wide expensive desk, providing a breathtaking view along the rugged coastline. He rose to greet Jeff with the kind of effusive near-greed that Jeff was growing accustomed to from anyone in the medical profession. But then, here of all places, he was likely to be regarded with extreme interest.

The doctor had aged well, Jeff thought: genoprotein treatments had maintained his thick chestnut hair and kept his skin firm and wrinkle-free. Only his slightly sluggish movements indicated that he was actually well into his sixties.

'A pleasure to see you again, Dr Baker,' he said as he gestured them to the long leather settee at the far end of the office. 'A true pleasure, especially for me. It's quite magnificent what my profession has achieved with your treatment.'

'Thank you.'

'And your son, how is he?'

'Tim's okay. He's off to Oxford University at the end of the week.'

'Good, good.' Dr Friland gave Annabelle an awkward little smile before looking back to Jeff. 'And the reason for your visit? It is to be similar to last time?'

'I hope so. Do you still have my sperm in storage?'

There was a minute change in the doctor's attitude. Still pleasant and eager, but Jeff could tell his curiosity had been roused.

'Yes, we do,' Dr Friland said. 'I reviewed your file when I was informed of your appointment. I believe the deposit was originally made as a safeguard in case of . . . problems.'

'Yes. I wasn't getting any younger, not in those days, anyway. My sperm count was falling. I think it was you who advised me to use storage. Standard procedure, you said. In case I wanted another child, or even a posthumous one. So, is it still viable?'

'Dr Baker, I have to tell you it is unusual to utilize such an old sample. Even cryogenic storage cannot hold back entropy for ever. I can't imagine you have a problem with your sperm count today.' He managed to avoid looking at Annabelle.

'It must be the old sample that's used for the procedure,' Jeff said levelly.

Dr Friland's smile was becoming forced. 'I see. Well, if that is what you require, then I'm confident we can facilitate that for you. We might not pioneer earth-shattering breakthroughs such as your rejuvenation, but I'm not exaggerating when I say that we are the leaders in our own quiet little field of endeavour. The range of improvements we can offer are considerably larger today than at the time of Timothy's conception.'

'I'm glad to hear it.'

'And Ms Goddard, you are to be the mother?'

'Yes,' Annabelle said softly. 'I'm to be the mother.'

*

Even through a good thick coating of factor sixty sunblock, the high, late-morning sun managed to make Jeff's skin tingle as they walked along the private beach together. He began to wish he'd put on something more than a T-shirt and trunks. It didn't seem to bother Annabelle, and all she was wearing was a bikini with a short sarong skirt. But then, something as simple as sunlight shouldn't affect her. That was the part of her which exerted the strongest attraction, the vitality which accompanied youth.

Other couples were strolling across the sands. They kept their distance here, just as they did in the clinic's restaurant and lounges. Even so, he'd glimpsed a couple of moderately famous faces.

'Everyone always used to say how Tim looked just like you,' Annabelle said. She squeezed Jeff's hand and turned to look at him. 'Is he a clone?'

'No. But neither is he a natural split between me and Sue; more like three-quarters me.'

'And enhanced.' Her free hand gestured at the main clinic building. There were institutes like it scattered all over the world, most of them sited in small impoverished countries that had no laws concerning human genetic modification. Outside the strictly regulated environments of Europe, North America, and the Pacific Rim nations, it was easy to buy what the tabloid news streams called designer babies. Wealthy couples went to the overseas clinics to have their *in vitro* child's health improved; and there was a growing trend for human clones, especially among people who had founded successful corporate enterprises and wanted to establish a new style of dynasty.

'Yes,' Jeff admitted. 'I had him modified.'

'Does he know?'

'Oh God, no. Although he's very smart – naturally smart, I'm proud to say. They hadn't mapped out the full neurological functions twenty years ago. He'll work it out eventually. There's no way he can't notice. He's got a much better immune system than me or Sue; he's highly resistant to cancer, his heart isn't susceptible to disease, his hair won't ever thin and recede, his bones are strong, his teeth won't decay. There was a hell of a lot they could offer to do for us, even back then. Now, of course . . .' Before they'd left his office, Dr Friland had given them a file containing all the possible modifications that the clinic could make to an embryo's DNA. It was a long, long list of traits that they were able to splice together. Everything that could give a child the best possible chance in life. Reading through it was the ultimate in temptation. As a prospective parent you just wanted to say yes to everything.

'How much do you want altering in our child?' she asked.

'I'm not sure. All the health stuff, I guess.' He gave her a questioning look, and she nodded. 'What about appearance? They claim they've got every feature mapped out.'

'No,' she said. 'Leave that alone. I want that part of her to be genuinely us, what we give her from ourselves. She should be able to look in the mirror and know where she came from and who she is.'

'Her?'

'Yes.' Annabelle smiled, and kissed the tip of his nose. 'Her.'

57. CITY OF STONE AND

MADRIGALS

Oxford came as an abrupt translocation shock after the quiet semi-reclusive life of a retirement estate in Rutland. Tim greeted university life with the same initial heart-flutter of reservation that all the millions of freshers before him had undergone. It passed soon enough as he struggled bravely through the wall to wall parties which characterized that first intense, chaotic week. His determination not to drink faltered on several occasions, though he never went back to the kind of destructive intake which had blighted his last few terms at Oakham. He could see that happening all too clearly among the other eighteen-year-olds who were experiencing their first true taste of away-from-home freedom, using it to reach maximum excess. So he merged into the mainstream with a minimal number of hiccups and gaffes.

The term played out against a backdrop of a classic autumn, with England's climate once again shifting dramatically over a mere two weeks. After arriving when the daytime warmth lingered long into the twilight, he soon found himself digging out thicker clothes to survive days of bitingly cold wind and rain, and others of bright, low, yet strangely heatless sunlight. Trees succumbed to the encroaching frosts, shedding their leaves across the city to form a water-slicked shawl, which made cycling and trike-riding a dangerous adventure before the council crews cleared the gutters.

Tim went to most of his lectures. He signed on for soccer and badminton. He steered well clear from the youth wings of the major – and minor – political parties. He tentatively started to make new friends. Everybody knew who he was, of course, which was some-what unnerving. But he learned quickly enough to dis-tinguish between who was interested purely in his mild celebrity status and those who were interested in him in his own right. He discovered which pubs and clubs to go to.

To his credit, he called his mother almost once a week, and sent her txts most days. Alison, too, was on the contact list. As was Vanessa, though that dropped away as term progressed – she was at Bristol university. The old crew from Oakham sent circular avtxts telling each other how they were getting on, though those were none too frequent. But he did stay in touch with Jeff. Nothing deeply significant, or emotionally meaningful – thank God. Tim found he got on best with his dad if they just swapped trivia: what he'd done today, what he'd eaten, lectures and essays. It was all perfectly normal, or at least as normal as it was ever going to get between the pair of them now. He was content with that. He even dutifully managed the occasional txt to Annabelle, whose modelling career seemed to have stalled.

And of course there was Jodie. Tim met her at the last

party of fresher week. She was taking computer sciences, and liked almost the same music as he did, though her taste in pre10 films was truly atrocious. Her hair was white-blonde, and came down below her shoulders. She was tall, and pretty, and came from a public school in Suffolk. Her family owned a lot of property in various European cities. All those little details locked together easily; with their similar backgrounds they could be very comfortable around each other. At first they were just friends, because he was still calling Vanessa on a daily basis. But then he decided that was stupid, he and Vanessa were never an item, not really – just a pleasant summer romance. It wasn't long after that realization that Jodie and he wound up in bed together.

*

Neither Tim nor Jodie heard the first tentative knock on his door. They were together on his room's elderly leather sofa, squirming round in a reasonable approximation of a wrestling lock. He'd already got her blouse open, while his own trousers were down round his knees.

The knock came again.

Tim's head came up, giving the door a worried look. For all that he'd settled confidently into university life, he was still scared of the bulldogs who ruled the college. Prowling through the cloisters and quads in their black suits and hats, ever alert for recidivist activity, they inspired the same level of fear in the current student body as they had for centuries past.

'Just a minute,' he called.

They hurriedly pulled their clothes back together. A last

428

quick check with Jodie, who was now sitting primly on the sofa, and Tim opened the heavy oak door, a neutral smile in place.

Annabelle stood outside.

All Tim could do was gape in shock. She was dressed in a black blouse and a vivid scarlet tartan skirt, both visible through the open front of a fawn-coloured camel-hair coat. Long looping gold necklaces completed the ensemble, making her appearance tremendously chic in comparison to the students her age. Tim very quickly damped down that thought.

'Hi, Tim,' she said, her voice quiet, almost shy.

'Hi. Er, come in. Please.'

Annabelle and Jodie looked at each other, then their gazes fell simultaneously to the bright pink fluffy sweater that was lying on the floor beside the sofa. Tim knew his face was red as he made the introductions.

'Sorry to interrupt,' Annabelle said. 'But I had to see you in person.'

'Why?' Tim asked. She was acting very strangely.

'You have to come home with me. I brought the car. I can take you now.'

'Home? Why?'

Annabelle bowed her head, as if she was no longer strong enough to hold herself upright. When she spoke he could barely hear her. 'Jeff's ill, Tim. Really ill.'

'He never said. I spoke to him a couple of days ago.' He was almost indignant with her: such a thing couldn't happen to his father.

'He hasn't said anything to you; he didn't want you to be upset. You know what he's like.'

429

'What's wrong with him?'

She simply shook her head. Tim was shocked to see a tear running down her cheek.

'What?' he demanded. Her reaction was making him nervous, which he tried to cover by sounding annoyed.

'Tim!' Jodie warned.

'Sorry. Look, Annabelle, what is all this?'

'You have to come home.'

He looked to Jodie, who nodded encouragingly.

'Okay,' he said, holding his hands up in surrender. 'I'll get my coat.'

'Thank you,' Annabelle said. She dabbed at her cheek with a tissue.

'What did the medical team say?'

'He won't let them in the house.'

'Jesus.' Tim was starting to get worried now. 'What is wrong with him?'

'He wants to tell you himself.'

58. THE WATCHERS

As with all avalanches, it started with the smallest breath of motion. Jeff had made the decision way back when he'd been lying in his bed at the Brussels University Medical Centre. It might have come from shock, or anger, though he preferred to think of it as rooted in youthful idealism. Jeff didn't blame Dr Sperber, but he'd been around long enough to know how the information would be used, twisted, sanitized, controlled, released in a way that left Brussels devoid of responsibility. That was the way of all government and politicians; it was never their fault.

*

THE OFFICIAL JEFF BAKER LIFE SITE/ NEWS
Turbosender destination: universal

There is something I wish to share with everyone. Please access me >hyperlink<.

*

People the globe over received the txt, and either frowned or sighed at the umpteenth piece of spam to sneak through their interface that day. Ninety-nine point nine per cent ordered their computer to delete it without even glancing at the message heading. Of the tiny number who did use the hyperlink, none cancelled it. Instead they started to txt their friends and family. The professional media caught up with the story a few minutes later.

*

The usual urbane calm of the anchorman behind the Thames News desk was visibly shaken as the breaking story was whispered into his earpiece. He smiled nervously at the camera, and said: 'We now take you to a live personal feed.'

*

It was the distributed-source network, which Jeff had helped to make possible through memory crystals, that allowed his broadcast to happen. The little camera in the Manor's study was sending its images into the datasphere, which immediately made it available to anyone with the correct hyperlink code, of which there were hundreds of millions. Simply by accessing it, they made themselves part of the source. It was impossible for anyone to switch off the interface of millions of people, especially if their identity and location were unknown.

The Brussels Commissioners, through Europol, might just have had the authority and technical ability to cut any physical landlines to the Baker Manor. But Jeff knew that. There were a dozen different live mobile connections linking him into the datasphere through various routes.

Whatever happened in his study would now be played out to the bitter end.

*

As the saying goes, nothing spreads faster than bad news. Ten minutes after Jeff began the broadcast, over eighty thousand people had accessed the feed. Five minutes later the number had jumped to three hundred thousand.

The Prime Minister, Rob Lacey, finally saw what was happening at the twenty-one-minute mark. He was brought out of a strategy meeting with his election team into an office with a big wall-mounted screen – it had been an intense session, the London Riot was acting like a millstone round the neck of his campaign. For a minute he simply stared at the scene, listening to Jeff's quiet voice talking calmly and rationally to his rising global audience. Every word was a needle-sharp accusation aimed right into the heart of Lacey's credibility.

'Get him off!' Rob Lacey shouted at an aide.

'But, sir . . .'

'Off! I want that motherfucker shut down!'

*

Alan and James sat on the plump settee in Alan's living room. Both of them stared at the giant screen on the wall opposite. The way it was set up, the angle of the study camera, made it seem as if Jeff was sitting in the room with them. Neither of them had spoken for the last fifteen minutes.

In the corner of the screen a small call-not-accepted icon flashed repeatedly.

*

In offices, workers tended to cluster round the cubicle of whoever had accessed the feed first. Silent crowds watched the unfolding event with a guilty fascination.

Out on the streets in cities and towns, people gathered outside any shop or pub that had a screen interfaced with the datasphere. Many pedestrians wearing PCglasses simply stood still in the middle of the pavement as the lens display played the images.

Jeff's study was just the primary scene; there were a number of other cameras in the Manor that were supplying images to the datasphere. Thirty minutes in, and five million people watched as Europol officers Krober and Cherbun approached the door to Jeff's study. Sue and Alison Baker stood outside, along with Graham Joyce.

'Please,' Krober appealed. 'Stand aside. We need to go in.'

'I'm too old to move,' Graham said. He brought his fists up in a boxer's stance. With his white hair and stooped shoulders he looked quite pitiful, standing in front of the two fit young officers. 'Come on, then. I don't suppose it'll take you long to bash an old fart like me out of the way. Did you bring your biggest truncheon, sonny? Do you like the sound it makes when it cracks bones in half?'

'Mr Joyce, this is not good,' Krober said.

'Come on.' Graham jabbed out with his right arm.

Krober barely had to move to dodge the attempted blow.

'Leave my house,' Sue said. 'Both of you. All of you. Get out.'

Krober and Cherbun looked at each other, neither knowing what to do next. Lucy Duke arrived, cursing her high heels as she ran. Her eyes searched round until she found the camera high up on the wall. She grimaced at it. 'Enough,' she snapped at the Europol officers. 'For God's sake.'

'We have our orders,' Krober insisted.

Lucy winced at the phrase. 'Don't make this any worse.' She appealed directly to Cherbun. 'Think!'

Cherbun nodded with slow reluctance. 'As you wish.'

*

The audience of eleven million now included Sophie. She sat cross-legged and alone in her new university digs, looking up at the small cheap screen that was perched on her desk. Tears flowed freely down her cheeks as she watched Jeff. 'I hate them,' she told his image. 'I hate all of them.'

*

One of the Manor's outside cameras picked up the Jag as it swept into the drive. Tim and Annabelle got out. Twenty-two million people watched them hurry inside.

59. DYING LIVE

Sue, Alison, and Annabelle walked into the study with Tim. Even though Tim thought he'd prepared himself for the moment, he was scared by the sight of his father.

Jeff was sitting at one end of the settee, wedged up into the corner. A thick rug was wrapped round him, as if it was holding back the cold of midwinter. The study heating was on maximum, turning the air to a sweltering fug. It didn't make any difference to Jeff who was shivering beneath the blanket.

He broke off from the monologue he was delivering to camera and smiled up at his son. 'Hello, Tim.'

'Hi, dad.' He so much wanted it to come out casually, as if he'd just got back from school to ask what was for supper. Instead, it seemed to get blocked in his throat, choking him. He gripped Jeff's hand with its icy, sickly-white skin. 'What's happened?'

'Poor Tim.' Jeff smiled gently, which showed up the dark circles round his eyes. Annabelle sat on the settee beside him and laid an arm on his shoulder, fussing with the blanket. She kissed his brow, like a priest bestowing a blessing.

'Something this big, it's too much for hints and allusion, isn't it?' Jeff said. 'We need to have it spelt out. That way someone else takes the blame, there's no guilt for guessing right.'

'Dad, please,' Tim pleaded.

'It doesn't work, son. As I've just been telling my viewing public.' He tipped his head to the camera. 'Rejuvenation Treatment is a load of crap.'

'But you're young!'

'I'm dying, Tim. There's some kind of flaw in the mitosis process. They can bring my body back down to twenty again, but after that something in the treatment disrupts natural cell division. They're not sure what, unfortunately, but no doubt they'll solve it in time.'

Tim started sobbing. 'That can't be right. They must be able to do something.'

'No escape, son. This is something that time doesn't forgive.'

'Why did they give it to you in the first place?' Tim cried. 'If it doesn't work, why did they tell you it did?'

'Because that's what Europe is, and this Treatment is Europe. It was started so that all of us would have hope that we could live for centuries. Once something so grand, so powerful has been set in motion, then it cannot be allowed to fail. I will just be a small, sad glitch along the route of progress to success. That's how Lacey and his kind would want to portray me. They've invested too much of themselves in this now; their association is total. My death will help the project to its final goal, so they would want to say with their solemn eulogies. Too bad that I'm the one who told people what actually happened, that I'm just a datapoint somewhere on their graph.'

'They lied!'

'Of course they lied. It's what they do.'

'But they've killed you.'

'Yes, Tim, but it wasn't a cheap death. Not for them, and not for me. Especially me. I was free at the end of my life. Free from age and all its horrors. Free to enjoy life the way only the young can. That was such a beautiful gift to own. You know what? If they'd told me straight, that it was a massive gamble which I might not survive, I'd still have gone for it. I'd still have wanted these last few months this way and no other. I have absolutely no regrets. Except for you, Tim. You're the only victim in this, and that's my fault.'

'No. You're dying! You can't die, dad, you can't. You're my dad.'

'You live on in the minds of people, those who love you, those who knew you.' Jeff chuckled, the old roguish predator briefly shining out through the decaying flesh. 'Which means I'm going to be the most alive corpse on the planet. Everybody knows me.'

'I don't. Not really.'

'You do, Tim, better than anyone after what I did to you. I still hope that some day you'll forgive me for that.'

'I do. Really, I do.'

'Annabelle is pregnant. She's having our daughter. Did you know that?'

'Yes, dad. I know.'

'You're going to have a sister, Tim. Look after her. The world is going to become very chaotic over the next few years, I suspect. She's going to need a lot of help growing up. But don't you give up university.'

'I won't, dad.'

'When my daughter asks about me, when she wants to

know what her father was like, what will you tell her, Timmy?'

And quarter of a billion people heard Tim say: 'I'll tell her that I loved you, dad.'

PETER F. HAMILTON

Fallen Dragon

PAN BOOKS   £6.99

From the best-selling author of the 'Night's Dawn' trilogy

Born in a colony world in 2310, Lawrence Newton hankered after the golden era of starships exploring the galaxy. But the age of human starflight was drawing to a close, so this hot-headed teenager ran away from home in search of adventure . . . Twenty years later, he's the sergeant of a washed-out platoon taking part in the bungled invasion of another world. The giant corporations call such campaigns 'asset realization', but in practice it's simple piracy.

While he's on the ground, being shot at and firebombed by resistance forces, Lawrence hears stories of the Temple of the Fallen Dragon – the holy place of a sect which worships a mythical creature supposed to have fallen from the sky millennia before the first humans arrived. Its priests are said to guard a hoard of treasure large enough to buy lifelong happiness – information which prompts him to mount a small private-enterprise operation of his own . . .

'A fine novel . . . successfully combines an action-packed storyline with convincing high-tech background detail'
The Times

OTHER PAN BOOKS

AVAILABLE FROM PAN MACMILLAN

PETER F. HAMILTON

MINDSTAR RISING	0 330 32376 8	£7.99
A QUANTUM MURDER	0 330 33045 4	£7.99
THE NANO FLOWER	0 330 33044 6	£7.99
THE REALITY DYSFUNCTION	0 330 34032 8	£8.99
THE NEUTRONIUM ALCHEMIST	0 330 35143 5	£8.99
THE NAKED GOD	0 330 35145 1	£8.99
A SECOND CHANCE AT EDEN	0 330 35182 6	£6.99
THE CONFEDERATION		
HANDBOOK	0 330 39614 5	£5.99
FALLEN DRAGON	0 330 48006 5	£6.99

All Pan Macmillan titles can be ordered from our website,
www.panmacmillan.com, or from your local bookshop
and are also available by post from:

Bookpost, PO Box 29, Douglas, Isle of Man IM99 1BQ
Credit cards accepted. For details:
Telephone: 01624 677237
Fax: 01624 670923
E-mail: bookshop@enterprise.net
www.bookpost.co.uk

Free postage and packing in the United Kingdom

Prices shown above were correct at the time of going to press.
Pan Macmillan reserve the right to show new retail prices on covers
which may differ from those previously advertised in the text
or elsewhere.